PRELUDE TO TERROR

Last night they had lain together on the cool grass beneath the silent smiling trees and she had run her fingers over his skin. He lay back on the grass, his eyes closed to the night and his tongue gently striking the sharp edges of his teeth as his flesh thrilled beneath her gentle touch. His mind seemed to sink deeper and deeper into a sea of visions, swirling forms and colors without definition or focus, until the vortex of his thoughts hummed with strange sound and lights, spinning beyond his control, driv in to an utter blackness and shriek of

He rememb

THE JADE UNICORN

JAY HALPERN

AVON
PUBLISHERS OF BARD, CAMELOT AND DISCUS BOOKS

AVON BOOKS
A division of
The Hearst Corporation
959 Eighth Avenue
New York, New York 10019

First Avon Printing, September, 1980

To Jackie
my lady of flowers
for all she has given
and all she has inspired
with her love

Acknowledgments

I wish to thank Steven Dansky, my friend, for his well-thought counsel and energies exerted on my behalf. I also wish to thank Joyce Jack, my editor, whose patience, good judgment, and hard work helped bring this book to completion.

1

CASPER Hauser never knew that his name derived from the child of German legend who had so captivated the imaginations of the Romantic poets: the child who appeared one day as if out of nowhere, ignorant of language and the most common household implements and practices, whose strange silence struck all who encountered him with a sense of eerie foreboding, as if they were in the presence of a supernatural spirit spilled disoriented and awkward upon the earth. Casper Hauser knew nothing of all that. He just sat in his raggedness in New York City's Central Park, greedily gulping down his wine and staring at the large, unusual star that was poised beneath the rotund rising moon.

His father, Gabe Hauser, had been of a mystical turn of mind. In his youth he thought he had a future with the university but despair and apathy had ruined that. The hypereducated man sank to the level of mankind's least common denominator. Drink ravaged his bowels, brain cells, and liver, and his wife took care of what was left. When Casper was born late in life, Gabe thought he was the victim of one of life's droll jokes; so he named the baby Casper after the mysterious child and, shortly after his wife regained the better portion of her strength and deserted him, Gabe calmed his heart and fingers long enough to scrawl the baby's name on a dingy shred of paper, pin it to the baby's wrappings, and then slink off into the night laughing to himself and shaking his head.

You could see his father in Casper's face as he sprawled on a knoll in Central Park, drunk, raising the bottom of a bottle of cheap wine to the rising summer moon. Like his father, he had oscillated from alcoholic stupor to sheer terror to belligerent cunning, over and over for the greater part of the last forty-nine years. Casper generally poured the burning fluid down his gullet with his eyes closed, savoring the pain and the swirling dizziness. But this night the chubby moon drew his eyes along the length of the bottle, over his trembling fingers and the surreal city lights to the heavens, where the strange star shimmered with frigid light.

Then he heard the sound—the strange cry.

It was around midnight and cool, gentle breezes soothed the bitter memories of the day's heat wave. The grass was soft and cool and the air was fragrant with summer smells of honeysuckle and pond water. The sound rose from a copse of trees, starting as an agitated murmur then rising slowly and steadily on the wings of the gentle wind into a crescendo of pain, terror, and . . . something else.

Casper had heard the cries of men whose brains had been jellied by alcohol as they thrashed themselves against the walls of their cells in the detoxification centers. He had heard the screams of young girls being raped just a few yards from him in the alleys he chose to sleep in. He had been roused from alcoholic stupors by the gaggling hysterics of mad men and women tormented by shades and visions in the wards at Bellevue. But no outcry had ever filled him with the intense terror that now jolted through him on that grassy knoll beneath the stars and the moon in Central Park.

For the first time in a long while, he was startled into a state that approximated sobriety. The sound was a horrifying mess of contradictions: high-pitched yet throaty; powerful yet tremulous; familiar and innate as the curves and bulges of one's own intestines yet alien as the ghostly moon.

2

The night sounds of the park, the lust of crickets and the rustle of leaves in the breezes, all ceased. The strange, terrifying scream rose horrible and naked into the night, a scream that was both an outpouring of unspeakable terror and physical agony and the ecstasy of illicit lust and orgasm.

Casper dropped his bottle in terror, staring at the nearby copse of trees. The scream kept rising into the night like a vapor, its final grace note cut off in midtremble like a popped bubble. Then all was silence.

Casper's sick heart raced and pounded in his weak chest. His brain, filled with unaccustomed blood, throbbed within his skull, torturing him and making his eyes swim. Then the silence was shattered by the violent cracking of tree limbs and the hasty shuffle and rasp of trampled leaves and torn earth. Casper's jaw slackened, anointing his ragged shirt with consumptive spittle, and his fat, pendulous lower lip quivered in dismay. Something emerged violently from the copse of woods and Casper strained his weak, watery eyes to see. The figure from the woods was a bit too far from him and, like a sleepwalker, Casper rose unsteadily to his feet, staring, constantly staring. He squeezed his eyes shut as hard as he could to clear them, shaking his head in hurried desperation.

He finally saw. The night silence enveloped him like a flowing velvet cape and his weak heart burst within his chest. He fell forward on the cool grass, his soul flying to the whispered summons of the great dark mother.

2

THE sudden, shrill command of the telephone's ring hurtled Abraham Ender, assistant DA, into startled wakefulness from a night of disquieting dreams. While his confused mind sought to orient itself, his hand instinctively grabbed for the receiver. His heart pounded painfully in his chest, more from his dreams than from the rude awakening.

It was John Brock from the mayor's office. He sounded sleepy, irritated, and in a great hurry to finish with Ender and get back to sleep.

"It's 4:37 in the morning, Abe. Don't bother grabbing for your clock. I've already fallen out of bed doing that. I just got a call from the watch command of the Central Park precinct telling me that there's been an 'incident' in the park and the officer in charge at the scene, Lt. Fedorson, feels that it's urgent that the DA's office be involved with the investigation from the start. Don't say a word: I already told the watch commander to fuck himself but it seems that Lt. Fedorson is adamant."

Ender struggled to clear his throat. "What kind of incident?"

"The watch commander had no details, just that it's, and I quote, 'kind of' a homicide."

"Kind of? What's a 'kind of' homicide?"

"That's what I'm telling you to find out. A blue and

white will be at your place in five minutes to pick you up. In the meantime I'm going to try to soothe a very beautiful but irate female lying here next to me so we can both get back to sleep and start the day like decent human beings."

"Thank you, John. You're very kind."

"I thought you'd appreciate my reliance on your considerable talents. Have fun."

In truth, Ender was glad to be awakened from his nightmares. He sat straight up in bed, inadvertently kicking a few books off his blanket and onto the floor, and stared straight ahead of him into the darkness, remembering his dream: Horrible, just horrible—that feeling of being pursued for no apparent reason, that terrifying sensation of flight where you run and lunge and claw at the air with desperate arms but you still can't get anywhere, and all the time they're getting closer, massive and ugly and malevolent.

He jiggled his head to dissipate the fog. Some of the details of the dream were yet quite sharp in his mind: the gaping serpent maws, the giant flicking tongues, the bat-winged demons that stared down at him from dizzying aerial heights beneath a macabre, blood-red moon. It all seemed so incredibly real, the kind of nightmare that only kids have, where sense and nerves are left naked and vulnerable to the assault of the bizarre.

Abe lurched out of bed, scattering more books, and hurriedly dressed. The adrenaline of terror combined with sudden awakening blasted his fatigue into energetic wakefulness, in spite of his lack of sleep. He had stayed up until past three studying archaeological decipherment. The study of ancient cultures and civilizations was an ardent hobby of Ender's and he liked nothing better, when the duties of the DA's office could be put aside, than to roam among the relics of ancient worlds. He had begun as a budding Egyptologist, but the more he delved into the intricacies of that culture the more he was sucked into the arcane and obscure societies that thrived on the periphery of the great Egyptian kingdoms. The mellifluous and liquid sounds of names of ancient gods and vanished cities called to him irresistibly, like Sirens, to fathom the mysteries of their origin and disappearance: Balphegor, Astarte, Kanu Kim. Perhaps this fascination was a rebellion against his mundane upbringing in Far Rockaway, Queens, and the emotional stranglehold of his mother, who "so very badly" had wanted him to become a lawyer. His older brother was a doctor; Ender had to be a lawyer. So he had submitted.

He looked the part of a momma's boy: short, pudgy, prematurely bald, with slender, delicate fingers and large, moist brown eyes. Puppy dog eyes, the girls teased him. And he had a slight speech impediment which he worked very hard throughout his youth to overcome, a kind of scraping of his words against his back teeth as he spoke. He hadn't wanted to be a lawyer. He knew the unimpressive figure he cut when he addressed a courtroom; there was nothing flamboyant or dynamic about him. He always felt that his brother should have been the lawyer, with his fiery, laughing eyes, his graceful charm and easy way with words. But their mother was willful, stubborn, and relentless, so Ender had become the lawyer.

But beneath that unimpressive exterior was a laser mind: brilliant, penetrating, incisive. Where some people sharpened their wits with chess, or the Sunday crossword puzzle in the *Times*, Ender tackled the mysteries of entire civilizations that had disappeared from history thousands of years ago. Indeed, it was only puzzles of such magnitude that could arouse his interest. His superiors, recognizing the powers of his mind, had sent him on more than a few occasions into the fight against crime almost in the capacity of a detective. The police resented this, of course, because Ender, with his puppy dog eyes, invariably made them look stupid. He would approach these cases with mild impatience, methodical yet always in a hurry to get back to his books on Xanadu and Heliopolis. His superiors still wanted to get him into the police force as a full-time detective but no, his mother wanted him to be a lawyer.

The hum of his electric razor counterpointed Ender's retrospective survey of his nightmare visions. As he stared into his own eyes in the bathroom mirror, he remembered one facet of the dream that had been extremely terrifying. Most of his dreams were primarily

7

visual with a bit of auditory content for texture, and he couldn't remember ever before having a dream with such potent olfactory sensations as this one. He had been striving against unknown assailants in an atmosphere that was thick, hot, and oppressive—as if he had been plunged into the atmosphere of an ancient earth, an earth surfaced with protozoa and amino acids in solution, an earth recently whelped from the gaseous cloud of the sun. He could feel himself strangle in the pungence of methane and ammonia, his mouth gulping like a fish for a last dollop of pure air. And his pursuers seemed to know it was only a matter of time . . .

There was a sudden buzz of his doorbell and Ender finished buttoning his shirt as he looked out of his window at the flashing red and yellow lights on the police car far below. Combing his fringe of hair, he flew out into the early gray of a New York summer morning.

3

THE heavy hand of Police Lt. Fedorson plumped down next to Ender's shoulder on the open window ledge of the patrol car as it lurched to a stop in Central Park. There were four other cars already on the scene, lights flashing, as well as the grimy box-like van from the city morgue.

"Well, if it isn't Mr. Ender," Fedorson said, smiling down into the front seat of the car. "I kind of hoped they'd send you."

"That's kind of you to say that," returned Ender, "even if you don't mean it."

"Now, now, that's not fair," answered Fedorson, feigning a wounded look. "I always say what I mean."

Ender climbed out of the car and stared at Fedorson's immensity. Fedorson was tall and well fed, with sharp little rat's eyes and Al Capp's face beneath a beat-up brown fedora. His voice was an unpleasant rasp and he incessantly talked out of one side of his mouth because the other side was always clamped down on a foul-smelling black stogie. Ender always thought of Fedorson as the Buck Mulligan of the NYPD because of his unshakable self-assurance and his endless sarcasm. But he was a good cop, an honest cop, a *damn* good cop. A little too theatrical, perhaps, with his brusque manners and

9

bold assertiveness, which was why he and everybody else in the department knew he would never make captain. But he liked his work and held no bitterness toward the diplomatic and conciliatory types who would, at intervals, pass him on the way up the ladder. And, in truth, no higher authority had ever interfered with Fedorson's own inimitable way of doing things.

"Have you had anything to eat yet, Mr. Ender?" asked Fedorson.

"Why, no I haven't."

"Good," said Fedorson, turning brusquely away and striding toward a nearby copse of trees. "It's better for you that you haven't."

Fedorson motioned to the morgue attendants to bring over the blanket-shrouded figure already strapped onto the stretcher.

"This is what first caught our eye," he commented, abruptly pulling the blanket down to the corpse's midriff. The attendants stood to one side, stone-faced, watching.

Ender bent over the body, scrutinizing, sniffing like a bloodhound, feeling the nap of its shabby clothes.

"One of the park winos," Ender concluded. "How was he murdered?"

Fedorson spit out a soppy black fragment of tobacco that had lodged on his tongue. "We don't know that he was murdered. There are no wounds on his body as far as we can tell here. We found him stretched out near that little rise of ground over there."

"Heart attack, degenerative disease, wood alcohol poisoning . . . So why the big deal?"

"No, counsellor," said Fedorson, bending closely over the body, "what intrigues me is this. Come close and look at his eyes."

He raised the dead eyelids with two fat thumbs. Ender bent down almost nose to nose with the corpse. The iris and pupil of each eye was totally obscured by a thick opaque greenish film. Ender realized the perplexity immediately.

"Have *you* ever run across a wino totally blind like that, counsellor?" queried Fedorson. "I haven't. I mean, there wasn't any cane near the body that we've come across yet, though we're still looking. How'd he get around? Those bums can go blind from the poison that they drink but then they usually end up in some hospital ward or welfare home. The good people of New York can accept their winos sleeping in the gutter, but not groping their way along the street. That's just too damn ugly. So what was he doing here, blind like that, with no cane and a half-filled bottle of red-eye on the ground next to him? Blind eyes like that don't happen overnight, I mean they just don't sneak up on somebody in the middle of a drink. Not usually, anyway. He looks to me like he must've been like that for years, but what the hell do I know? We'll just have to wait for the examiner's report."

Ender stroked his weak pink chin, his eyes narrow and intense. "Maybe somebody came along before you guys got here and stole his cane."

Fedorson spit again. "Maybe. It's still not kosher to me. And we can't forget the other possibilities."

"Such as?"

"Such as some poor blind schmuck was dumped here made up to look like a wino. The bottle, the smell of sour booze, it could all be some kind of setup."

Ender nodded. "Possibly. I suppose this is the cheapest way to dispose of a dead friend or relative: let the city do it. Gruesome thought."

Fedorson looked at Ender with a half-smile and wink. "A friend or relative, maybe. And maybe also a dead enemy."

Ender laughed. "Lieutenant, do you always have to look at everything in the worst light?"

Fedorson threw up his hands. "What do I know, counsellor? A suspicious nature comes with the turf. But now we're gonna look at something that can't be seen in any better light."

He turned on his heels, striding quickly toward some trees a few yards away, Ender trotting behind him. The attendants hastily re-covered the corpse and loaded it into the van.

The trees and the bushes before them were cordoned off by a multitude of police while the flashbulb of the police photographer shattered the pre-dawn dimness at

11

rapid intervals. Startled, Ender saw intimations of a holo-caust in the sick, tired eyes of the officers who had the ill fortune to be drawn into this case. They seemed to scrupulously avoid looking at the area in which the photographer and the detectives poked around, and they energetically kept a few early morning joggers far away from the scene. On certain portions of tree bark and bush leaves yards away from where the photographer worked Ender saw splashes of blood.

"We found this when we were looking for the blind man's cane." The officers stepped aside for Fedorson and Ender. Ender gritted his teeth: there on the grass, in the twisted posture of a rag doll negligently tossed away by some bored child, was the mutilated corpse of a young girl.

"O, my God," breathed Ender, his face gone ashen and his mouth twisted in disgust.

Thick, sticky jets of blood had coagulated on everything: the rocks, the foliage, all over the girl's skin. Her clothes had been ripped off her body and lay in shreds on the ground beside her, a few tatters of cloth still clinging to her shoulders. She was lying sprawled on her stomach, but her neck was mangled, evidently broken, for her head was twisted grotesquely over her shoulder, staring at the investigators. Strands of intestinal organs curled out along the ground from under her body. Numerous gaping wounds covered her back and sides, laying bare the striated muscle tissue and raw bone. From between her legs a fuming mass of glistening, bloody tissue spilled onto the dirt, already swarming with ants. Her left arm was completely severed from her body and dangled from some bushes about four and a half feet away. The unfortunate girl appeared to have just barely reached puberty; it was possible that she was no more than twelve or thirteen years old.

It was too much for Ender: thanks to the fact that his stomach was empty, he didn't vomit. But he threw himself up against a nearby tree with a gut-wrenching attack of the dry heaves. Fedorson left him his space, his eyes somber and sympathetic.

The photographer paused in his work, dabbing his brow with his handkerchief, and walked over to the lieutenant. He was tall and gaunt as a war refugee, dressed in a shabby brown suit with his heavy camera dangling from its strap around his neck. He had watery pale blue eyes and his skull with its sparse mousy hair seemed a couple of sizes too large for the skin that was stretched over it. His large adam's apple bobbed up and down as he spoke to the lieutenant:

"I can't blame the guy. I've just got to squint at it through a camera. With one eye. I'll tell you, lieutenant, I've seen murders, highway head-ons, even some wartime stuff in Asia. But I've never seen anything quite like this. And right here in Central Park, yet. It gives me the creeps."

Fedorson chewed on his stogie, deep in thought. Finally he turned to the photographer and said, "That's why I want all the pictures finished with before sunrise and all the markers laid out so we can police the area before word of this gets around."

A little fat man with a florid face, crew cut, and large moles on his ears finished chalking out the placement of the body: Detective Breen. He heard what the photographer said and walked up to them both.

"I saw something sort of like this once. I was up in Canada on a hunting trip with my brother-in-law. A crazy she-bear got to one of my dogs." He bent and fastidiously scraped some soil off his wing tips. "Blood and howling all over the place."

Fedorson clasped his hands behind him and dropped his chin to his chest. "Unfortunately, I don't think it was a bear that did this."

Breen and the photographer hung out somberly with Fedorson for a few more moments, then they went back to work. Fedorson strolled over to Ender who was leaning against his tree, wiping the cold sweat from his brow with the back of his pale hand.

"I apologize, lieutenant," said Ender.

"No need to. Can I have any of my boys get you something?"

Ender thought for a moment, catching his breath. "Yeah, lieutenant, have the photographer get me a close-up of a particular puddle of blood, the one right

13

near the girl's left knee. It's got a funny-shaped piece of slate right next to it so he can't miss it."

Fedorson raised one eyebrow in cynical surprise and respect. He thought Ender had just taken one look and gone off to barf. He had underestimated the power of Ender's big puppy dog eyes.

4

BECAUSE of the color of his eyes—an emerald green flecked with a minute archipelago of purple and blood —he called himself Jade. Just Jade. He passed into people's lives as Jade, and passed out again leaving only strange and wistful memories of Jade. He somehow felt defined by his eyes, as though they were silent mentors leading him through time and space toward an unknown destiny. They were not the mirrors of his soul; quite the contrary. His soul rested impassively behind the shield of his strange eyes and was impervious to the prying of others. What his eyes did, however, was lay bare the souls of those others to his silent scrutiny. All mankind lay naked and vulnerable before his strange eyes and Jade passed among the naked souls—poised, somber, biding his time.

Now he lounged against the parapet on the roof of Adrienne's building, savoring the caress of cool summer-night breezes on his naked chest and thighs. Adrienne was curled at his feet, clinging to his right knee, brazenly proclaiming her sin to the myriad silent eyes of the shimmering city. In her more rebellious moments she almost prayed that her husband would come upon them unexpectedly and discover how happy she could be in another man's arms.

She had met Jade at a bar where she had gone to drink herself into oblivion during one of her husband's frequent absences. He was just sitting in a dim corner, not drinking, impassive, surveying the gabbling crowd like a king surveys his dominions or a shepherd his flock. Their eyes met and he was transformed: he became an aged, weary hermit calling to a disciple from the dark recesses of his cave, and she was drawn inevitably into his quiet, cool, and holy darkness.

When Michelangelo set his chisel to the Carrara marble that was to blossom into the statue of David, he had portraitured the soul and essence of Jade. Jade exuded the physical energy and symmetry of youth together with the aura of ancient wisdom. A poet he said he was, and in the flickering light of the bar table's candle, with his rugged features chiseled in vibrant chiaroscuro and his fine blond hair and beard wild and passionate, Adrienne could envision him robed like a god on a stormy hilltop casting verses to the wind.

Jade stared out over the city at the strange summer moon; it appeared to be flushed with rage and was attended by a plump, silver cavalier planet. Selena, the Greek silver goddess of the moon, was his chosen daemon. She had urged him through reams of liquid verses, caressing his sensibilities with her wanton silver smile. But tonight he stared into a manifestation of her awesome power that he had never before experienced. She was a raging goddess, telling him that the time was drawing near when payment would be exacted from him for the blessing of her smile and her gift of sensibilities that had taken him beyond mortal realms. Jade remained impassive and serene. He acknowledged his debt and when the time came he would be ready.

"How beautiful it is tonight," sighed Adrienne as she brushed his leg with her cheek. "I look up into the sky and see that moon and that bright star and I feel so little and all my sorrows and aches become little with me and suddenly, as tiny as I am, I feel happy."

"Do you know why it's so beautiful tonight?" asked Jade. "Not just from the colors and the shapes and the shininess laid out like baubles to fascinate children. There's an energy in the universe tonight, an invisible shimmering fire passing from the moon to that star and enveloping the entire world. That's why it's so beautiful tonight. And the energy is growing like an electromagnetic foetus and will soon permeate all of creation."

Adrienne turned her beautiful face up to his, her shining eyes filled with doubt and longing.

"How can you see such things?" she asked.

Jade smiled. "I wish I could understand what it is I really do see. Remember that I'm a poet: I suppose we should both just chalk it all up to metaphor gone wild, a poetic juggernaut."

"Sometimes you're scary with your visions," she said. "But I wish I could spend all my nights with you, sharing the beauty you see all around you that is seen by no one else."

Jade looked down at her and the rich auburn cascade of her hair blended with the settling purple of the evening; her eyes became stars.

"I don't think your husband would care for that arrangement."

Her mouth curled in bitterness. "My husband can go to hell."

"Then why do you stay with him?"

"I stay with him because there's some part of me that cries out to be tortured!" She was startled by the vehemence of her own words and the alacrity of her thought.

"I've never been able to admit that to myself before tonight. O, when we first met he was charming enough with his continental manners and his delicate foreign accent and his dark mysterious eyes that every so often twinkled with suave mischief. I was poor with old sick parents depending on me, and I was tired of the hopeless, inane grind that being poor and responsible makes us endure. He seemed to seek me out and when I was most despondent he dazzled my eyes with glimpses of a world that I imagined could exist only in my dreams. I was right, you know. That world does only exist in my dreams."

"But doesn't he love you?"

"Who can say? I suppose he feels something for me: he made such a big deal out of getting me to marry him. He insulated me from the real world, took care of my parents, spun me traveling around the globe, took me to lavish parties brimming with dignitaries who treated me like a queen simply because I was there with him. I was swept up by the pampering and the glitter. I felt like some invisible hand of fate was bodily picking me up and carrying me to someplace I'd end up eventually anyway, so I might as well just lay back and enjoy it." She sneered angrily. "Like rape. Do you know, Jade, that he's never made love to me?"

Jade's eyebrows rose in amazement. "Never?"

"Never."

"Didn't that seem a little peculiar to you when you first went out with him?"

"Of course it did. He was doing so much for me and my family that I would have done anything for him. Giving your body to a man is such a little thing when you think about it. It was the least I could do even if I felt nothing physical for him myself.

"At first I waited for him to approach me. Then, when that never happened, I became the aggressor. But he rebuffed me. Gently, with soft words, with impeccable good taste, he told me to bug off. At first I thought it was because of his age and the whirlwind pace he was keeping, his interminable business trips, his courtship, his eagerness to please me. I thought perhaps it was his fear that he would fail with me and that I would be disgusted by him. I tried to tell him that such fears were groundless and he just seemed amused. In fact, the night we were married, he told me he was going to maintain our relationship as it was. He told me that someday I would be possessed by a man who could offer me, beyond my wildest hopes, all those things he did not feel it was appropriate for him to offer. He made it clear that all he asked from me was patience and complete faithfulness to our platonic life together."

She withdrew a joint from the pocket of her blouse. The flame from her lighter danced like an impish demon on the tip of the rolled paper and her face glowed fiery orange against the background of the night, all creased and seamed with shadows. For a fleeting instant Jade saw in her an ancient crone bending intently over her fuming pot of brew. She held the drag for a long time, passing the joint to Jade, then slowly exhaled quantities of smoke.

"Our platonic life together. How idyllic." She twined her fingers with Jade's. "I've never even seen him naked."

"You're joking."

"I don't joke about such things. Everything we have is separate: separate beds, separate bathrooms, separate thoughts. I don't think anyone can share his thoughts." She looked at Jade with an impish smile. "He's a bit like you that way."

Jade averted his eyes to the floor, saying nothing.

"You're such a quiet, private person. I never know what's going on in your head. Yet, the challenge of drawing you out is fascinating."

"I'm afraid that, once drawn out, my thoughts would stand naked in all their banal glory. You're far more puzzling than I am."

"In what way?"

"Well, I just simply can't understand how a woman as full of life as you are, a woman so warm and giving, can endure such a relationship. It sounds as though your husband keeps you like a pet ocelot, something he can trot out and show off and take with him to Europe for effect. You don't share a bed or your hearts with each other. It's so cold."

"I told you. There's a part of me that forces me to endure it. I can't understand it myself. But I've already broken half my promise: with you. I suppose the rest will fall apart soon enough."

Jade's face grew somber. Silhouetted against the burning moon and the city lights, he seemed to be the spirit of an ancient rogue Roman misplaced in time and space, awaiting that certain shrill ram's horn to call him to life.

"Yeah well, don't look to me for your salvation. You know what I am and what I do. I make love to lonely women for money. I deal coke and smoke. I go home to my tiny apartment and scribble verses in my tiny illegible handwriting, verses that no one will ever read. There's nothing for you in that."

"There's you in that. That's enough for me."

Jade chuckled cynically. "I don't even know myself where I am in all that. Sometimes when I'm bent over my notebook, lost in thought, I look out my window at the delicate leaves of a young sapling that's heaved itself up through the concrete and those leaves, so fragile and perfect in their symmetry and beauty, are a rebuke to me for wallowing in the sins of unthinking mankind. Still, I wallow."

There was a heavy yet tender silence between them. Then Adrienne carefully withdrew a tiny wad of tissue paper from the pocket of her shorts.

"I want you to have this. I stole it from Heinreich. He had taken it out of one of his locked curio cabinets the other day and was examining it. I just caught a glimpse of it and knew at once that I had to have it for you."

She placed in Jade's palm a tiny jade unicorn of exquisite workmanship. It was collared with a tiny band of gold which was in turn linked to a fine gold chain. It was not the docile unicorn of medieval ladies' prayerbooks, head bent down in the lap of the Virgin with sweet soft eyes: it was a satanic beast, full of rage and majesty, its eyes poised to cast flames.

"I had to pick the lock of his cabinet to get to it. I've never done anything like that before and it took me quite a while. But I'm very resourceful and persistent. He'll never know it's missing. I covered my tracks so well. And if he does find out, so what. He can go to hell."

Jade held the unicorn delicately in his palm. The light of the moon, grown frigid and sinister as a stained dagger, seemed to animate the eyes of the unicorn with smoldering internal fires. He suddenly felt very chilled and passionless, without hope and incredibly alone, burdened by innumerable nameless sins whispered into his brain by countless despondent voices.

"It seems carved out of your eyes," Adrienne said softly to him, smiling. She unclasped the chain, fastened it around his neck, and arranged the unicorn upon his bare chest.

Jade pulled her to him silently, cradling her beneath his arm, drawing from her love the warmth that had so suddenly fled him.

5

A S the morning progressed, turning into a typical hot,
humid, miserable August day, the mood of Ender's
co-workers in the DA's office changed from mild bewilderment to a frenzy of curiosity. Already vague rumors
had circulated about some "horrible" crime committed
the night before but Fedorson and Ender had established
such a tight news blackout on the case that nobody could
find out any further details for love or money. Ender,
himself, was unapproachable: he had stormed into the
office without a word, looking shaken and unwell, and
plunged into his private cubicle. A couple of colleagues
had, at intervals, timidly tried to draw information out
of him but he proved to be an impenetrable stone wall so
they gave up. Finally, about midday, John Brock showed
up from the mayor's office carrying a thick manila envelope under his arm. He exchanged merely the briefest
pleasantries with Ender's colleagues, waved away any
questions, and hastily secreted himself in Ender's cubicle.

"I picked this stuff up from the police lab and the
medical examiner's office on my way over here. I
thought you'd want their reports as soon as possible."
He dropped the packet on Ender's desk. Ender's head
was cradled in his arms flat out on the desk, his eyes

hidden, luxuriating in the tranquility of perfect darkness. He failed to even acknowledge Brock's presence.

"Are you awake?" Brock asked, a bit peeved. "What the hell's going on here?" John Brock was a political animal, not all that bright but eminently presentable. He was tall and good-looking, with the macho features of a cigarette ad model. When he left City Hall at the end of each day, he hastened gracefully down the stairs to the street, impeccably groomed, his suit jacket flapping rakishly in the breeze of his passage, his eyes intent and his nostrils slightly flared, just as if he were being filmed for the credit trailer of a TV series of which he was the star. He had a glib tongue, an ingratiating demeanor, highly cultivated boyish charm, and was sufficiently energetic so that his colleagues would consider him dependable but not so energetic that they would think him a "drudge" or "grind." Although he liked to think of himself as possessing the standard complement of ethical scruples, it was the reaction of the crowd clamoring around the center ring of the political arena that was always the bottom line for anything he said or did.

"John, John, John, John . . ." Ender said into his desk. Then, finally looking up at Brock, "We've got a particularly ugly murder on our hands. I mean really ugly: it was like some chain-saw massacre in a grade C movie."

It suddenly dawned on Brock how deeply affected Ender was by the morning's events. "Are you all right?" he asked.

"Yeah, yeah, I'm fine. Now. There should be pictures in that envelope: you'll see for yourself." Brock started pulling at the envelope's seal while Ender continued: "A little girl, John, a pretty little girl was ripped apart in Central Park and God knows what else they'll find happened to her."

Before he could finish opening the packet, Brock froze, staring wide-eyed at Ender. "A little girl? How little?"

"About eleven to thirteen. Somewhere around there."

The rugged muscles of Brock's face went slack. He replaced the packet on Ender's desk unopened and reached into his jacket pocket, withdrawing an envelope. He pulled a photograph out of the envelope and handed it to Ender.

"Is this the girl?"

Ender scrutinized the photograph carefully: a pretty little blond girl with big blue eyes, a pert child's nose, a charming smile, with her hair divided into two neat pigtails. She was wearing the uniform of a private school.

Ender nodded. "Probably. I wouldn't swear to it considering the condition in which I found her. But probably. Who is she?"

"Only the daughter of Anthony Welles, a top-level attaché with the British Embassy. That's all. He called in this morning to report his daughter missing. She went to bed as usual last night and, when the family woke up, she was gone. Because her old man's a diplomat, we got right on it with an APB. No forty-eight-hour wait."

Brock rubbed his brow nervously with his manicured right hand. "What do we do now? I'll have to notify the mayor and the commissioner and see how they want to handle this. I can see the publicity this thing'll bring: everybody involved is going to have his head on the chopping block. I can hear the media now, outraged and screaming at the top of their lungs, 'How can this happen to an embassy official's daughter? Is it linked to some terrorist group or some other kind of international political conspiracy? How soon can we expect an arrest?' O, it's gonna be terrible around here now, for a long, long while. And the family. Somebody's got to tell the family. Damn it, they'll make me do it. And it's got to be brutal yet. It couldn't be a simple shooting or kidnaping, something the public's grown indifferent to. No, it's got to be a chain-saw massacre in Central Park."

Brock's face grew wild with desperation and fright. "Listen, Ender, uh, Abe, listen, I've got to have quick results on this case. I'll talk to the commissioner myself and tell him that this murder has top priority. You're a good man, I've got every confidence that you both understand the delicate nature of the situation and will see to it that the case is wrapped up as soon as possible. Shit. We'll have the CIA and Scotland Yard sniffing all around us, making our lives miserable. If we don't get some answers right away, the city's police department and the DA's office are going to look like shit all around the world."

Brock had worked himself into a panic, pacing frantically back and forth in front of Ender's desk. "Calm down, John," Ender soothed. "Going crazy isn't going to help us solve this case. Now, I said it was probably the same girl but I could be wrong. But in any case you're lucky that a good man like Fedorson is in charge of the matter. He's already clamped down on the publicity: everything's tighter than a drum and you can count on nothing leaking out without our prior approval. If the girl turns out to be Welles's daughter, there'll be time enough later for us to inform the family. I'll do that myself; you won't have to worry about it. If she is the same girl, I'll want to talk to her father anyway." Ender's pacific words belied the smoldering contempt that began to glisten in his eyes. "Nobody asked for the crime to occur and it's just that more unfortunate that there have to be complications of a . . . political nature." The word *political* slithered out of Ender's mouth like a wad of phlegm aimed right at Brock's eye. As his agitation grew, Ender feared that his damned speech impediment would begin to manifest itself and make the content of his words seem laughable. "The only important thing, as far as I'm concerned, is that we catch the maniac that did this to her and make sure that he doesn't get the opportunity to . . . to do it again." He hurried to finish his sentence because he felt the infernal scraping begin at the back of his mouth.

Brock's eyes widened with rage. "That's the only important thing to you, is it? Well, that's because you're down here in the legal department where everything is cut and dried, cushioned by legal precedents and a thousand years of format and tradition. I'm up there in the zoo, in the wolf pack, with cameras spying over my shoulder every time I take a shit and reporters broadcasting to the world how bad it smells. I've got a hundred bosses as it is and now, if it is the Welles kid, I'm gonna have a thousand. And I've got to keep them all happy with fast answers. So don't tell me what's important to you: I'm telling you what *I* need, like a quick solution to this crime. I don't want to hear about mysterious lunatics or Jack the Rippers: that's all I need now, another two-year Son of Sam manhunt, I want the killer now, or, if

24

you can't give him to me, I want anybody who'll make a plausible, if not airtight, suspect."

Ender had had his fill of realpolitik in his years with the DA's office but Brock had just plumbed a new depth of degenerate expediency. "You're panicking, Brock, and it's not a pretty sight. I thought you had more spine. You don't even realize what you're saying."

"Goddamn it, Ender, I know fucking well what I'm saying! And if you know what's good for you, you're gonna damn well listen!"

"And what about the real killer?" Ender's speech started to jostle and slur. "While we're wasting time . . . making up lies that sound . . . good to you and your bosses . . . some maniac's still running around loose . . . in Manhattan."

"Ender, I want you to wake up to the fact that this is a dirty city. The animals in the South Bronx and Harlem carve each other up all the time and it's no damn big deal. Last night someone just happened to carve up the wrong person. Now it is a big deal and it has to be handled like a big deal. Once we've put the lid on this murder, then if something like it happens again, we'll just have to hope that the next victim won't be a diplomat's daughter. Then you can take your time, enjoy the press coverage, work yourself up into a national hero if you want. But right now we're doing it my way!"

Brock had stood up, drawing himself to his most impressive and domineering height, and glared into Ender's face. Ender swallowed a few times to compose his speech, then spoke up to him, without rising, in tones both measured and somber: "Brock, you are one of the reasons that this is a dirty city. Now get out of my office and let me do my job."

The impact of Ender's words struck Brock across the face like the fist of a prizefighter. He paled, his jaw dropped, his molars churned in rage. Then, unable to spit out another word, Brock flew out of the office, slamming the door behind him.

6

MORNING'S gray light filtered into the plush bathroom of the McConnelly apartment in the exclusive eastside Tudor City neighborhood in Manhattan. Adrian McConnelly was a self-made millionaire, having built an extensive brewery and distillery empire out of nothing with his own energetic hands. His son Marco, fifteen years old, knelt beside the cerulean porcelain bathtub, splashing cold water from the faucet over his face. He had tried to sneak quietly into the apartment some time before, but he hadn't anticipated the old man's premature homecoming. Suitcases, valises, and val-paks littered the main hallway, causing him to trip and fall into a French provincial telephone stand, nearly upsetting the whole thing and creating a great ruckus. He knew his parents and his brothers and sisters must have heard him but, since nobody emerged from a bedroom to investigate, Marco crawled quietly into the bathroom where he remained. He was sure to catch it this morning.

The clear cold water soothed his tired face, but it could do little for the tenacious fear that clung like a fungus to the hollows of his mind. What scared him most was that so much of last night was lost to his memory. He could still recall sneaking into Jenny's building through the freight entrance and meeting her by the basement entrance to the service elevator. They had left quickly for a long walk in the soft summer night, talking about solemn and secret things, a slim volume of Byron's poetry stuffed in the back pocket of his jeans. How she loved to listen to him read Byron! Her mind soared with his, far beyond their years, stirred by the elegant language into idylls of escape, conquest, and the affirmation of their unique identities. She especially liked when he read from "The Giaour," the passage that went:

> Why marvel ye, if they who lose
> This present joy, this future hope,
> No more with sorrow meekly cope;
> In phrensy then their fate accuse;
> In madness do those fearful deeds
> That seem to add but guilt to woe?

He could see her eyes brighten and drift into far-off, alien realms as the words spilled passionately from his lips:

> Alas! the beast that inly bleeds
> Hath nought to dread from outward blow:
> Who falls from all he knows of bliss,
> Cares little into what abyss.
> Fierce as the gloomy vulture's now
> To thee, old man, my deeds appear:
> I read abhorrence on thy brow,
> And this too was I born to bear!

Under the tutelage of Byron, they shared proud moments of youth together. They schemed and plotted how the two of them would defy the cumbersome and wretched edifice of the past, founded upon the blood and sorrow of wailing millions, and created for themselves the world anew. Somehow, in the midst of their talking and the twining of their fingers, they found themselves in the depths of Central Park, heedless of their parents' interminable, grave warnings. The cool breezes of the night had brushed away the last traces of the day's choking heat and the two children settled themselves among the shadows of some trees, beginning to talk of love.

Jenny had just begun to assume the aspect of a woman, as Marco was assuming the aspect of a man. The physical metamorphosis was as yet only partial: her nipples, still child-like, had begun to crinkle and swell and rested upon small mounds of soft fatty flesh; her pubis had begun thickening and sprouting strands of fine cornflax down; and her face and limbs had lost most of the fleshiness of her childhood, lending to her face in the filtered light of the moon the aspect of an ageless, ancient womanhood.

Marco knew all these intimate details about Jenny's body because, for almost a month now, the two had been lovers. Their minds were too potent to keep silent about the clawing urges that fluttered and splashed through their bodies. She had been the aggressor that first time, feasting her virgin wisdom on the countless mysteries of his body with her eyes, her tongue, her fingertips. They experienced with each other the mysteries of sex, comparing the bliss they trembled with to the tawdry and lurid descriptions they had garnered from books. How wonderful and sacred was the contrast.

Last night they had lain together on the cool grass beneath the silent smiling trees and she had run her light fingers over his skin. He lay back on the grass, his eyes closed to the night and his tongue gently stroking the sharp edges of his teeth as his flesh thrilled beneath her gentle touch. His mind seemed to sink deeper and deeper into a sea of visions, swirling forms and colors without definition or focus, until the vortex of his thoughts hummed with strange sounds and lights, spinning beyond his control, driving him to an utter blackness and shriek of nonbeing.

He remembered nothing beyond that until he stumbled against a metal awning post of a building not two blocks from his own. Incredible fatigue pressed down on his shoulders like a massive rock, warping him into the likeness of a tiny old man. He literally had to drag his feet into his building, trying to smile and wave off the doorman as if his coming home at that early hour of the morning was an offhand part of the regular order of things.

Marco stared at his dripping face in the bathroom. He

was a handsome boy with a thick head of long black hair, large blue eyes, and finely chiseled features that tapered into a strong jaw and clefted chin. His nose was somewhat too prominent, not really enough to detract from his handsomeness, although the other children had turned to that feature when they engaged in juvenile teasing. Jenny had considered his nose very thoughtfully one day and decided it was a fine nose bespeaking intensity of character and future greatness. But the eyes Marco stared into this morning were swollen and half-glazed, shining with a curious light. His cheeks appeared gaunt in the harsh light of the vanity, and his sensuous, bowed lips seemed made more for snarling than smiling.

Could it have been some exotic effect of the drugs with which they had been experimenting—smoke, ups, ludes? He had never heard of any such side effect happening and they had never overdone their experimentation. In fact, they had taken no drugs at all the night before. If they had at one time tried any of the hallucinogens, then that might have been the explanation: he could be coming down from some unexpected bizarre flash. But they hadn't as yet gotten their hands on anything like that. Marco couldn't understand for the life of him why he felt so ill and vaguely terrified, and why the events of the past evening had been so thoroughly erased from his mind. Further, his concern for Jenny weighed heavily upon him; he prayed that, even in his state of somnambulism, he had had the good sense and decency to make sure she got home safely.

The bathroom door opened behind Marco and his father's burly, florid form filled the doorway. He was impeccable even in nightclothes, his red silk pajamas and electric blue silk bathrobe neatly pressed and creased, the silk sash of his bathrobe carefully knotted and arranged so that the two ends dangled from his waist at a rakish angle.

Yet in spite of all his fine clothes and continental manners, his soft voice with the hint of brogue he was always trying to suppress, Adrian McConnelly had the look of a Dublin publican about him which could not be gotten rid of, especially in the eyes of his son. He had grown stout with prosperity, his portly form large and imposing, still bearing the broad back and massive arms of his youth that had gained him notoriety as a Dublin scrapper. His face was plump and rosy, sprinkled with light tan freckles. His hair, though silvering at the temples, was thick and bushy, the color of fresh butterscotch, but his sparse blond eyebrows were barely visible above his small, close-set, watery blue eyes. He stood glaring at his son, his little eyes narrow with rage. Whisking himself into the bathroom with a swish of silk, Adrian closed the door softly behind him. His thick though carefully modulated voice rumbled his rage:

"Where the hell have you been all night?"

Marco stared up into his father's face, his heart pounding with terror. "I've just been out for a walk, that's all. I was just enjoying the night reading a book out in the fresh air."

"Out for a walk, is it? Reading. Fresh air." His father grabbed Marco by his T-shirt with a tight, plump fist. "What kind of snot-nosed little ass have your mother and I been raising? Out all night carousing God knows where, scaring your mother half to death, sneaking out of your own home like a damn thief, then tearing the place apart trying to sneak back in, and then shutting yourself in the bathroom to soak your head. And he tells me he went out for a walk, reading." McConnelly pulled his son's face roughly up to his. "You little bastard! If you think I'm going to sit back and let you disgrace yourself and your family by loose living with your sottish smart-assed friends, then you're the biggest sot of the bunch. I give you a good home and a fine education and suddenly you think you're king of the world, free to do as you please and the rest of the world be damned. Well, bucko, it's stopping right here and now. I want you to tell me who you were with all night and what you were doing and you've got just five seconds to give me straight answers."

Marco's eyes were wide with fear of his father. He knew there was nothing he could say to his father that would pacify him, especially the truth. Already his father's mouth was churning with rage, his free hand clenching and spreading, repeatedly.

"Your time's up, bucko. Now, what do you say?"

"There's nothing I can say that will make you less angry. So I'll say nothing." Marco's face, though fearful, was firm and proud.

"Nothing!" his father shouted, his husky voice shattering into a whine. "Nothing! You godless insect! Then take this for your smart mouth and blasted stupid face!"

He pummelled Marco about the face and shoulders with the open paw of his hairy arm, hitting him roughly again and again, driving his son to the floor. A noise of rushing and pattering footsteps, and the hush of terrified whispering could be heard outside the bathroom door. Marco's eyes flooded with tears of pain and rage.

"That's it for you, old man!" he shouted up at his father from the floor, tears pouring down his cheeks. "That's it for you, you blasted bloody fool! It's your finish, you old blasted fool. Old, old, old, bloody fool!"

It was only the repeated frenzied tug of his wife on his arm that kept Adrian from beating his son further. McConnelly had wild murder in his eyes. Marco was crushed into a heap on the bathroom rug, sobbing, while the rest of the family struggled to pull the father out of the bathroom.

"Get out of here!" McConnelly shouted. "Get out of this house forever, you little bastard! I never want to see you again!" Just before the door closed in the father's face, he shouted, "You're not my son! You're no son of mine!"

7

"STRANGE clouds are gathering on the horizon, counsellor," said a raspy voice over the phone. "I'd suggest you get down here right away."

"Where are you?" asked Ender.

"At the morgue with Rothstein."

"I gather, then, that you've finished reading his report."

"About an hour ago. That's why I came down here to speak with him."

"Well, then, maybe you can explain to me what the hell this report means. It tells me everything I never wanted to know about this case and nothing of importance. I mean, what's this about 'suspected evidence of rape'? Was the girl raped or not? That's a simple enough question."

"Under ordinary circumstances, counsellor, I'd agree with you. But I've spoken at length with the doc and he's shown me certain unusual bits of physical evidence that complicate his findings."

"What kind of evidence?"

"I don't want to talk about it over the phone. I want you down here so you can speak with him personally and see for yourself exactly what's throwing this case all out of whack. Besides . . . if you saw this shit with me, I'd feel less like a raving lunatic."

A tremor of childish terror shivered Ender's guts to hear Fedorson, the tough cop, nonplussed by a corpse. "I'll be right down," he answered, hanging up the phone.

The report had been sketchy, to say the least: no confirmation of rape, no speculation as to the murder weapon, no mention of the old man's blind eyes. When he had seen that Rothstein himself had performed the autopsy and filed the report, Ender was astounded. A first-year academy student knew better than to file a report like that, with all those basic, unanswered questions. There must have been some unusual autopsy findings to stump the great Rothstein.

Ender greatly admired the good doctor, Danny Rothstein, chief medical examiner. He was a charming old man with a ruddy round face, small laughing eyes whose moistness gave them a glint of perennial mischief, and a thick brown walrus mustache the tips of which were always sprinkled with stray bits of pipe tobacco. He was a thorough and efficient forensic analyst, rumored to be the best the department ever had. Nothing ever seemed to shake his cool, professional analytical abilities: if a problem was particularly perplexing, he would methodically turn and re-turn the evidence over in his mind, attacking the problem from every conceivable angle until the evasive solution, fatigued and overpowered, surrendered itself to him.

Rothstein was the kind of doctor who refused to be shaken by the bizarre: he could be shown a bleeding stone by a religious zealot and he would study and probe the stone until at last he either discovered the source of the deception or healed the stone, all the while discussing *Hamlet* or the religious ecstasies of Jacob Boehme. Ender could remember the few, but most enjoyable, discussions he and Rothstein had had about ancient civilizations, the doctor expounding his theories as to the origin of the Easter Island statues in his odd, inelegant voice, an alternating series of throaty tones and sudden high-pitched cracks and tremors. Ender smiled to himself thinking how a conversation between Rothstein and Fedorson would be sure to draw every tomcat from Manhattan all the way to Westchester.

He surveyed the stack of photographs one last time

before sealing them in the envelope and bringing them with him down to the morgue. It was the Welles girl, all right, of that he was certain. Later that day he would have to call on the girl's father for final verification, a chore he did not look forward to. Brock, in his own screwed-up way, was right about the bureaucratic complications. But Ender could not permit that to influence the progress of his investigation. He would find the answers, one at a time, inevitably and with judicious caution: of that much he was confident.

He examined the photographs of the girl's body with his magnifying glass, noting on a piece of paper that he wanted a closer look at those marks on her neck. They seemed to be blood blisters or purple contusions with small lacerations spaced at what appeared to be regular intervals in the girl's flesh. And then he examined that photograph of the splash of blood next to the odd-shaped rock: there was definitely an imprint of some kind in the soil, and it appeared to have been made on top of the blood, that is, after the crime was committed. Could somebody have discovered the body before the police and not reported it, or could the killer himself have left an imprint in the blood? And what about the old man's eyes? Questions heaped upon questions: and this was just the beginning.

Cold and white and redolent of disinfectant, awash with the brilliant, painful glare of blue-white fluorescent tubes the shine of which caromed off the stainless steel fixtures and trim of the corpse racks, shattering into dancing points of light, like a thousand frigid suns: the morgue greeted their echoing footsteps with the blind, silent stasis of an oriental god. An attendant slid the girl's body, still hidden beneath its sheet, from its cubicle onto an examination table. Dr. Rothstein leaned on his knuckles on one side of the table, facing Fedorson and Ender as if they were grad students in forensic medicine. Fedorson had been previously briefed, so he watched for Ender's reactions out of the corner of his eye.

"As I explained to the lieutenant, Abe," said Dr. Rothstein, his bushy mustache dancing jovially as he spoke, "I deliberately left the preliminary medical report as incomplete and uninformative as it was simply because I don't believe in signing my name to anything other than verifiable fact. And, unlike that from most of the bodies we get down here for examination, the basic physical evidence obtainable from this one is very confusing and uncertain. Secondly, I didn't want to include any cautionary or speculative notations in the report because I don't know who is going to get his or her hands on it and I didn't want to create any more problems for you and the lieutenant than you already face."

Again, that thrill of excitement and terror raced up Ender's spine. He looked up at Fedorson. Fedorson grinned, chomping on his stogie, and said, "The doc's a good man. He's been around here a long time."

"In the matter of rape, for example," continued the doctor, "the question is usually cut and dried: a smear is taken from the vaginal walls and examined microscopically to see if it contains any trace of semen. In this case, however, the results of the examination were inconclusive. What I mean by that is that a seminal-type fluid was found to be copiously present throughout the girl's genital tissues, so copiously in fact that it far surpasses the quantity ever found in any previous case, to my knowledge, of extensive gang-rape. If any one man were accused of the crime in a court of law, I would be forced in my capacity as physician to assert the impossibility of his being responsible for the crime on his own. There's a semen sample being tested right now to determine if seminal proteins of other individuals can be detected, but, to be quite frank, I don't think we'll find anything." Rothstein looked down at the contours of the still corpse, stretched at length under the sheet.

Ender was intrigued. "If there was so much semen, then why do you rule out the possibility of multiple individuals?"

"Because, Abe, in both quantity and quality, the semen found in the girl's body just isn't human."

Ender recoiled from this revelation, his eyes wide and

questioning, his temples beginning to throb. "Danny, I hope you can explain what you just said to me."

"You see, counsellor," added Fedorson, "I wasn't joking when I said strange things were happening. I warned you."

"I wish wholeheartedly that I could explain what I mean any better," continued the doctor. "The semen we examined contained large amounts of some compound, possibly related to chlorophyll, giving the seminal deposit a distinct greenish color. As far as I know, this is completely unheard of in the entire animal kingdom. I've already called a friend of mine, a zoologist with the Museum of Natural History, to meet me here this afternoon and see what he has to say about what we're dealing with. But that's not all."

Ender rubbed his bald scalp with delicate, nervous fingers. "I can barely handle what you told me already. Any more might kill me."

"Now, Abe," smiled the doctor, "you'll just have to cope. You're a big boy now. As I was saying: not only is the protein structure of the semen totally unfamiliar to me, but so also are the individual sperm structures. Each sperm is about five and a half times as large as ordinary human sperm, and each sperm propels itself through the seminal fluid by means of the whipping action of three tails. Not one tail, mind you, which is normal for humans. But three. I have a photomicrograph in my office of the semen sample which displays the complete foreignness of which I'm speaking far better than my poor power with words."

Ender stared dumbfounded at the doctor who returned his gaze with a look of Hindu serenity, passive and unstirred by the unknowable mysteries of the universe. His small, jovial eyes seemed cognizant of the fact that the three of them in that room, chosen by some caprice of fortune, stood as one upon the brink of a yawning, black abyss that was ineluctably sucking them down into its dark, solemn, and irrevocable inner mysteries. Ender then turned to Fedorson. Fedorson just shrugged, his fedora pushed far to the back of his head, his hands jammed into his pockets, thumbs protruding, leaning against the wall of corpse vaults: a nervous grin pasted across his face showed that he, like Ender, was impotent and overwhelmed by the developments of this case.

"What's going on here?" demanded Ender. "Green come, three-tailed sperm? This is New York, isn't it? We're standing right in the middle of the city morgue with the body of a dead girl laid out in front of us . . . So why do I feel like I'm in a comic book waiting for Spiderman to crash through the wall and save the world?"

And then the solid forms of the three men and the corpse began to waiver and dissolve in Ender's mind, reduced to the constructions of an ancient hieroglyph, painstakingly wrought in pigment on timeless basalt walls by a slave grown withered and impotent in the service of his gods. The silence of death fell heavily upon Ender's shoulders, like a great fuming mass of volcanic ash.

"Tell him the rest, doc," said Fedorson, breaking the silence.

Rothstein again put on his best lecture hall face. "The wounds themselves"—and he drew the sheet off the girl's body—"are not knife wounds. They're not flat like a blade nor is the tissue sliced on either side of the point of entrance as occurs when a blade is shoved into a body and pulled with a motion perpendicular to the thrust." His thick fingers, coarse and stained with tobacco, moved deftly over the pale surface of the corpse outlining each gash and indicating with an extended index finger the angle of thrust. "It appears that each wound was caused by a pointed, cylindrical object, long enough to enter the torso from one side and emerge from the other. The penetration was directly forward, sort of like stabbing somebody with a rapier. But whatever made these wounds was much thicker than a rapier— at least an inch and a half thick, I would say."

Ender's eyelids drooped with chagrin. "That's just great. Now I can go to the mayor and the DA and tell them that a swordsman from Mars has landed in Central Park and is raping and killing little girls."

"Don't call the mayor yet, counsellor," said half of Fedorson's mouth as he relit his stogie. "There's more."

As if his words were a predetermined signal, Rothstein

stepped behind the head of the corpse and raised the dead eyelids with his middle fingers. "Take a look at her eyes," he directed.

Ender bent over the dead girl's face, peering intently. The iris and pupil of each eye were completely obscured by a greenish calcification: the same kind of mineralized tissue that blinded the eyes of the old man.

Ender stared into the girl's eyes and then turned to Rothstein. "Be straight with me, Dan. What's happening here?"

Rothstein smiled sardonically. "If I could answer that question, Abe, I'd have submitted a more thorough report. I have absolutely no idea what kind of thickening has occurred to obscure the eyes like this. Fedorson tells me that her eyes were clear this morning when she was found. Now the entire plexus of vision seems to be obscured by a thick green stone. Just like the other one." He tugged on an end of his mustache, silent, pensive. "I've never seen anything like this. No known degenerative calcification proceeds so rapidly. I just don't know."

"It doesn't seem to have happened as fast to her as it did to the wino," Fedorson contributed. "If that means anything."

"It might mean something," mused the doctor, "though I'll be damned if I know what. I'm afraid, gentlemen, that I'm out of my league in this matter. Nothing seems to conform to known physical phenomena, and I'm trained only in the rational and therapeutic manipulation of known and long-studied phenomena. I am as astounded by all this as you are."

Fedorson spit a curl of tobacco onto the floor. "We seem to have entered the twilight zone."

Ender bent over the little girl's eyes with the pocket magnifier he brought with him. The surface of the obstruction glistened like a jewel, highlighting the sea-green depths swirled with purple that lay beneath.

"Have the body of the old man brought out," ordered Ender. "I want to compare the two sets of eyes."

An attendant was called for and another examination table prepared. A shrouded corpse from a different cubicle was placed on the stainless steel slab.

"Would you mind holding his eyes open for me, lieutenant?"

"Uh, excuse me, counsellor, but seeing as how we are dealing with rather . . . uh, peculiar things that are happening, I hope you won't mind if I decline the offer to touch the damn things."

"Perfectly reasonable, lieutenant," said Rothstein as he stepped to the head of the corpse and raised the eyelids.

Ender peered closely into the old man's eyes with the magnifier. He stiffened, staring for a long time.

"Well, counsellor?" asked Fedorson, peering over the doctor's left shoulder. "Do you see anything?"

Ender's voice was somber and funereal. "God forgive me but I do. See for yourself."

Rothstein quickly switched places with Ender, bending closely over the body.

"What was it?" asked Fedorson.

"Right in the middle of that green mass is the tiny reflection of something's face, solidified in the stone. It looks kind of like a man's face, bearded, pale, with angry eyes. Yet it's elongated and distorted: like the face of . . . of a horse." He paused, searching for words. "Or a centaur."

"Horse? Centaur?" exclaimed the lieutenant. "What kind of shit is this?"

"And . . . it's got a long horn growing out of the center of its forehead," Ender concluded.

"A unicorn," said Rothstein, rising from the corpse, "sort of."

The three men stood around the old man's body, silent, amazed, lost in thought. A timorous attendant lurked in the far corner awaiting instructions.

"I'm afraid I'm out of my league in this, gentlemen," said the doctor, softly and sullenly. "I recommend you find yourself a witch doctor. Or a sorcerer. Yes, I'm certain that's what you're going to need."

8

SURROUNDED by deep shadows, a pale imp of flame nodded in somber quadrille from atop a heavy carved black candle that squatted on a broad mahogany desk. The thick vapors of burnt wax, must, and the pungence of old leather filled the air, and an old man sat immobile but for his hand in the circle of candlelight, tapping out the passage of time with a single finger, tapping slowly a stately, funereal cadence on the ornate green felt blotter of the desk.

The flickering candlelight gouged deep, thick crevices in the old man's face; patterns of burnished bronze and flesh tones danced over it. Fire illuminated his large, owlish eyes, half-shut in deepest revery, and cast black cones of thick shadow upon his forehead just above the stately arch of each eyebrow. The old man's face was dignified and timeless, an aristocratic and commanding visage that could be expected to emerge, worked by long-dead craftsmen in gold or granite, from the burial mounds of ancient kings in the silent black forests of northern Europe. His nose was thin and straight with arrogant flaring nostrils and his mouth resembled nothing more than the gash of a knifeblade, bloodless, unlipped. His firm, chiseled jaw and the strands of muscles in his gaunt cheeks were set like stone in an attitude of subtle, expectant ecstasy beneath his thick, meticulously groomed head of hair, which now appeared jostled by ancient arcane winds, whispering secrets.

The door to the room opened silently, revealing a broad, plodding man with head and hands too large. He entered and stood, a hulking, slow form, behind a thick leather chair placed squarely in front of the desk. The visitor waited in silence to be acknowledged, patient as if squatting lotus-legged before a serene and silent idol.

The old man remained immobile, taut, and enraptured.

"Master," the visitor finally whispered, his voice rising in hushed, deep resonance from the cavern of his bowels, "the transit has occurred. The moon and the planet have conjoined in the precise configuration you anticipated from the texts. It cannot be long now."

There was a long silence and then the lips of the old man finally quivered into life: "It has already happened, Bennett. I can feel the great power electrifying the air all around me. I can sniff it into my lungs and feel the atoms of power tingle and burn within me. Such joy it is, Bennett, such joy you can never know, to realize that the hour has come and that the child of the Great One has begun to throb with blood and life. And we are close to him, Bennett, very close, as I foresaw. The silent cries of his nativity blast my ears with holy sound. We will find him now, quickly, here in New York, and then we will take him with us and prepare him for the Great Work. Is all in readiness at the Chateau?"

"Yes, all is prepared, Master."

"And the woman?"

Bennett hesitated before answering, carefully weighing his words.

"There are problems with the woman, Master."

The old man's eyes flared like a solar prominence, piercing Bennett with his rage. This sharp Germanic accent staccatoed into the judicious probing of a grand inquisitor.

"What problems? Answer me fully, holding nothing back."

Bennett squirmed under his Master's gaze. "Karl and Stully have just returned from their work in Europe and are awaiting your further orders here in New York. In the process of making final arrangements they discovered that the woman has violated her celibacy while you have been in Europe."

The old man slammed his fist viciously down on the desk. "Damn the sow! How could she? I had her thoroughly diminished and controlled."

"Apparently something broke the control. Perhaps she broke out of it herself."

"That is impossible! She hadn't the aura or the power or the cunning."

"Well, Karl and Stully assure me that it's true. They'd been so taken up with preparations at the Chateau and so certain of your control that no surveillance had been maintained."

The old man's eyes glowered distant and pensive. "And I was too absorbed in listening for the Moment. Damn the putrid sow! Have they been able to determine when the control was first broken and how often she has been rutted?"

"They've been able to make discreet yet forceful inquiries among the personnel of the apartment building. She doesn't appear to have exerted much energy in keeping her liaison a secret. It seems the affair began about six months ago, during the Christmas holidays while we were at the Chateau. There's one man only, so far as they can determine, a man she picked up in a bar close to where you live."

"One man only? Are they sure?"

"As certain as they can be. She seems to have been quite smitten by the man. Statements by the doormen and the superintendent indicate that she called him to her bed every time you've left her since then."

The old man rose to his feet in a rage, pounding his fists on the desk, his thick gray hair falling in stray wisps about his forehead: "Damn the filthy slut! She can ruin everything! Everything I've worked for and dreamed of for so very many years." His words hissed bitterly through his teeth. "So very many years. And now that the Great Moment has arrived . . . the damned sow! I can't conceive how the control was broken. I studied her, probed her guilt and energy levels, I had my mind wrapped tighter around hers than a pregnant woman is wrapped around her foetus. It's impossible . . ."

Then the old man's face slackened with a sudden epiphany. His flaming eyes smoldered and his thin lips twisted with wry intensity.

"Of course. It wasn't the woman. I'd assured myself quite correctly of her weakness and docility. It can only be . . . I hadn't anticipated that: the texts on that score were silent." His lips curled into a sinister smile. "Tell me about the man."

Bennett stared down at the large polished black shoes that encased his splay feet.

"Speak to me, damn you, or you'll never speak again!" The sudden burst of the old man's voice made Bennett wince.

"He's a disreputable fellow, Master: a gigolo and a drug dealer and a pimp as well." Bennett turned his eyes again to his shoes. "I'm sorry, Master."

The old man's eyes had widened with this report but then, once he had assimilated its import, the strange sinister smile returned. He stepped slowly and softly around his desk and patted the hang-dog Bennett on his square cheek.

"Bennett, my love, my dear, dear servant and faithful friend, it's not your fault, it's not anybody's fault. I understand now, and I am with you as always. My spirit shall not forsake you. Such a person, you say. Who could have known? It seems that the mysteries of fate and the universe are never fully revealed in all their complexity to any man, regardless of the potency of his mind and his vision." The old man smiled broadly. "The ways of our Lord are circuitous and strange and the instruments of His Will are diverse and unpredictable. To say the least."

The old man stepped farther from the candlelight, pausing near the dark shadows of his bookshelves, his voice becoming a soft and disembodied presence that filled the room.

"We must make new preparations, Bennett, and quickly. We must gird ourselves for battle. O yes, the energy spills throughout my body, I can feel it, I tremble with it, like a thousand tongues licking the mortality from the flushed internal organs that chain me to the earth. He has come, Bennett, and He shall vanquish all enemies. Yes, I can feel it. I am confident."

Bennett cheered at the old man's unexpected revery, but then his brow clouded. "And the woman, Master?"

The old man responded with a short bitter laugh. "The woman? Need you ask?" He returned to the far side of the desk, beside the flickering flame, seating himself. "She will have to be replaced."

And then Heinreich Mercadante sent his servant Bennett far from him to do his bidding, out into the light.

9

MARCO McConnelly sat on the end of the Bank Street pier dangling his legs over the water. He wouldn't go home. Ever.

The murky waters surged and stank, lapping the old, crumbling stanchions with tongues of slime. The waters called to him with a hiss and sputter.

He picked at splinters of wood on the pier with nervous fingers. His lapse of memory about the night before still frightened him. Was he ill? Amnesia was nothing to be trifled with: a corrosion of sensitive brain tissues, the malignant specter of paralysis, of uncontrolled twitching and drooling, of imminent madness. Marco was terrified of the possibilities.

His face and shoulders ached from the morning's beating. His father's eyes: wet, staring, beady. Yes, he had angered and provoked him. But he couldn't have answered his questions any better had he wanted to. Not with that strange black globe floating in his consciousness, impervious to his frantic efforts to remember. And nothing could tear from him the truth about his love for Jenny.

It was forbidden, that love, and that was the end of it: by her parents, by his, by the whole fucking society. It was a taboo that was useless to question. No philosophical reasoning, no tears and pleading could dissolve the prehistoric bolus of the taboo: the frenzied defense of the elders against the youth and vigor of succeeding generations. The young must be possessed like chattel, to be confined, abused, terrified, raped, maimed, used for barter: only thus could ancient, frightened fathers with ridged eyebrows and sloping jaws preserve themselves from the iron fists and determined wills of their own sons. The taboo against the sexual independence of children hung like rigid wasp's nests in all their minds. Marco saw his father's raging face as he beat him floating upon the murky water: he and Jenny had listened too intently to secret voices of their souls and now the tribe was poised to avenge itself upon the transgression.

The August sun burned hot above, a thick and humid white haze. The backs of Marco's thighs stung from the heat of the wood and his fingers moved gingerly over the surface of the pier, pulling at shards of wood, twisting fine hempen strands of old rotten wood. How thin is the veneer of civilization: Marco hadn't been born when his father had tended bar in some seamy Dublin pub on the outskirts of Nighttown, but he could see him as he must have looked then, younger, broad of shoulder, the flesh of his face pulled tighter around his skull. Arabesques of thick tobacco smoke swirling over the patrons' heads, spewing from their nostrils and gaping mouths, the bursts of laughter, the guttural hacks and wads of phlegm sailing into the sawdust on the floor. He could see his father provoked into a rage by some foul-mouthed sot who secretly longed to be propelled from this life into some better by the fists of a nameless soul angered by his insults and abuse. The oaths, the fighting, the unholy use of the name of God.

Marco thought his father was no better than a beast in spite of his fine clothes and his affected tones of speech.

He closed his eyes in the oppressive heat. He tried to blot his father's face from his mind and think of Jenny. He strained to remember, strained hard until he panted with the effort by the edge of the water, and slowly, cell by cell, certain scents and forms and swirling colors from the previous night rose like pungent incense to his consciousness: Jenny's face staring up at the strange star, Byronic phrases dropping from his lips, her eyes sapphire and shining in the light of the moon, the gentle touch of his fingertips on her tiny naked breasts. But that was all. He couldn't remember how they had parted or what her words were that night or even if they had made love. But he would remember; he demanded that of himself.

They were both supposed to be in summer school right now. She was probably wondering why he didn't show up. Later that afternoon, when he was sure she had gotten home, he would call her and tell her that he was all right and ask her about last night.

The water lapped higher up the stanchions toward his dangling feet. Marco opened his eyes and stared at the police launch that silently glided by, a few officers gathered on deck to wave to the naked homosexuals who lounged on the adjacent pier to sunbathe. He was strangely amused by the haughty upthrust of the launch's bow and the numbers inscribed in white on a field of blue, like a talisman or incantation. The hot, oppressive sun, the throbbing boat with the strange numbers, the convocation of naked men, the tide-scarred rubble and rust of the piers: somehow these tableaus melted as one in Marco's mind and erased the fear and turmoil of his soul. The raging specter of his father shrank to the dimensions of a pathetic mouse futilely squeaking in protest against a descending heel. His decision to leave his family suddenly lost its corollary guilt and opened far-flung vistas to his imagination.

Marco filled his lungs with the hot, sticky air off the docks, feeling like a wild horse sniffing the coolness of prairie freedom.

"There's much that's still beautiful about that dirty river," came a voice from behind Marco, which he ignored.

The man who had spoken to open a conversation did not pursue it, afraid to offend. He stood to the left of Marco, his hands clasped behind his back, looking out over the water. Rocking back and forth on his heels, the man seemed lost in thought, though the way he twisted and braided his fingers betrayed an unspoken agitation.

Marco's sudden sense of inner peace mingled with exhilaration made him bold. An increasing flush of omnipotence flooded through Marco, causing him to study the tall silhouette that stood starkly black against the glaring heat haze, and inwardly mock the man's nervousness. The man feigned nonchalance for about a minute and then turned to face Marco, only to find the boy staring up into his face, his eyes glowing like polished silver disks. Startled, the man backed away a couple of feet, turning his head toward the river and rubbing his own eyes with the sweaty palm of his hand. When he turned again to face the boy, Marco was staring into the river, his eyes their wonted pale blue.

The man chalked up his hallucination to a trick of the summer sun. He was a tall and stylish black man with deep chocolate skin and a trimmed beard of tight black curls framing his face. He was dressed in tiny satin jogging shorts and a matching tank top that gleamed like burnished copper in the sun's glare. When he smiled at Marco, his large white teeth diverged from each other in the middle, leaving a broad, dark space.

"I'm not a cop, you know," he said to Marco, smiling, trying to win the boy over with the soft articulation of his voice and the sincerity of his eyes.

"I didn't think you were," answered Marco, an odd half-smile crossing his face as he stared out over the water.

The black man sat next to the boy, dangling his long, slender legs over the edge of the pier, carefully avoiding splinters.

"I don't recall ever seeing you here before," commented the black man. "I come here quite often, myself. Nearly every day, actually. To jog. I know almost everybody who hangs out around here. That's why I mentioned about not seeing you here before."

He let his eyes surreptitiously linger on Marco's body, studying his broad shoulders and the gentle sculpture of his lips. He carefully avoided the eyes.

"I'm usually in summer school at this time," Marco answered, staring out onto the water at a sea gull bobbing at rest upon the current. "And anyway I don't come here very often. Once in a while, maybe, when I want to look at something massive, like the river. It gives me peace of mind."

"Yes, that's true. The river does give you peace of mind. I mean, it's always affected me like that, too. That is, when the wind doesn't blow the smell of it onto the shore."

The black man followed Marco's eyes to the sea gull, his heart beginning to throb ponderously in his chest.

"My name's Kermitt," he said to him.

"I'm Marco."

"Marco? Italian, then. I thought there was something European about the way you look. You have such strikingly handsome features, so full of character. American faces are so drab. So uninteresting."

"Irish, actually," Marco corrected. "It's just that my father has continental pretensions."

"I daresay," said Kermitt, a faint limpness in his voice, trying to keep the conversation going. "How old are you, Marco?"

"Fifteen."

Kermitt grinned slightly, brushing a fly off his bare knee. "And what keeps you out of school today? Are you on holiday?"

"Not hardly. I just needed to come here to put my mind back together."

"Heavy problems, huh? I know the feeling. Man, do I know the feeling."

Marco turned to Kermitt, channeling all his innocence into his large pale eyes. "Do you? Really?"

Kermitt thrilled at the opportunity to show his compassion. "Sure I do, Marco. I remember what it was like being fifteen and wanting to make a place for myself in the world and having my parents and teachers and even the other kids my age hedge me in with their stupid rules and demands and restrictions. All their old-fashioned thinking, trying to convince me that I was just a foolish child and not a young man ready to face life on my own terms. And all the time I could see through their lies and see how they were the stupid ones, just plodding along with their dull lives, hating each other and themselves, envying the fact that my whole life lay ahead of me and that I had a chance not to make the same mistakes they did. That burns them, really: that you've got a chance to turn out happier than them and then you'll look down on them and see what fools they really are. That's the real reason they try to keep kids down."

Kermitt watched Marco's impassive face to see what effect his words were having on the boy, but Marco just stared out at the sea gull.

"That's why I ran away from home when I was your age," Kermitt lied, trying to make himself appear heroic in the eyes of the boy.

Marco sardonically smiled to himself but played the fool. "Really? How odd it is that I should meet you today of all days. I've just run away myself."

Kermitt grinned broadly. The boy seemed so pliable that all it would take would be a few more kind words, a few sincere glances.

"So, you've run away too. Trouble with your father or your mother?"

"My mother's a wimp, nothing more than a cringing pantry girl. She doesn't count."

"Your father, then?"

"An hour ago I would've said yes. He does make the most noise and the most demands. But now it's not even him. They're nothing to me. It's strange. I step over them like waterbugs near a sewer. They've served their purpose and now suddenly, very suddenly, I just feel that I've flown beyond them. I was angry earlier, angry and bitter and humiliated. I don't feel that way now."

Marco contemplated the brackish water which reflected the sun in the myriad of painful imps of light that danced like gay flames on the surface. Just beneath them, rising from unseen depths, vague outlines of squirming, ghostly forms began to coalesce. The river was different to his eyes from what it was to any other eyes. He realized this with a strange pulse of intuition that both dazzled and pleased him.

"Now what's your next step?" Kermitt asked.

Marco gazed intently at the forms beneath the river. "I'm not sure. Not yet."

Meeting this incredibly handsome boy who was lost and in turmoil was a godsend for Kermitt. He kept silent for some moments to ease the eagerness and lust from his voice.

"Do you smoke grass, Marco?" he asked.

"Yes. Of course."

"Well, you're in luck 'cause I've got some dynamite smoke on me right now, I think we could both use a little mellowing."

"It's a bit early in the day for me," Marco teased.

"O Marco, you know it's never too early for good smoke. And believe me, this is the best."

Marco feigned more reluctance, then acquiesced.

"But we really can't do it here, right out on the pier," Kermitt cautioned. "Come with me where we can smoke without being hassled."

"Where?"

"Right inside that old dock building over there on the next pier."

Marco surveyed the burned-out, crumbling ruin that Kermitt indicated. A few male forms glided slowly past a broken window inside on the second floor.

"That place looks like it's ready to collapse any second. Are you sure it's safe?"

"Of course it's safe. Everybody goes in there to smoke and hang out. Come on."

Marco stared one last time into the rippling seaflame. His eyes hardened and froze, as if emitting deadly radiation, and he could see beneath the tongues of glare ancient demonic forms crying out to him, supplicating him with palsied arms and scaly tentacles, burning into his brain with their insistent multitude of eyes. The hiss and sputter of their voices filled his brain as if mocking the death of innumerable votive candles extinguished by a black and malignant sky.

Marco rose abruptly, unsmiling, heedless of Kermitt's pampering eyes, his voice stern and aged: "Let's go."

He led the way briskly back along the pier, heedless of the crevices and the uneven footing. Kermitt trotted after him, bewildered by the boy's sudden haste and eager to catch up. Neither of them noticed the pretty blond girl who sat beside one of the line posts on the south side of the pier, lost in thought, and who suddenly blanched as the two hastening forms passed her on their right.

Unsmiling, somber men lounged at intervals in the dark shadows of the crumbling dock house which had been abandoned to fire and decay. They stared without emotion at Kermitt and Marco, and Kermitt half-smiled back at them, surreptitiously. The air inside was dense with the dry pungence of weathered wood and stale cement. A tall young man, lean and well muscled but whose face was covered with strawberry eruptions capped with pustules, stared lingeringly at Marco's young, lithe form. Across the concrete walls was a worning written in red paint:

BEWARE OF PICKPOCKETS

Kermitt had captured Marco's hand in his; Marco offered no resistance. Kermitt drew himself carefully up a flight of crumbling steps to a hidden recess behind a broad old pillar where some dirty old mattresses had been dumped. A huge waterbug poised on the pillar, agitating its antennae to apprise itself of the intruders, and then scurried off to the friendly solitude of fresh shadow. Kermitt plopped himself down on one of the mattresses and beckoned Marco to sit by his side. Marco acquiesced, still unsmiling and silent. The only source of light was a small window far above their heads, the filtered light of which left the two of them in shadow burnished with grayed silver. While Kermitt withdrew a large joint from his pocket, Marco kept his eyes averted to the rotten floor.

The joint flamed orange in the sullen shadow as Kermitt dragged on it, prodding it to life. He passed it to Marco, wordlessly, while holding the smoke deep within his lungs. Marco took it from him without raising his eyes from the floor. Perhaps the boy was just shy or nervous, Kermitt thought. But he certainly was beautiful. How the others down below had envied him.

Kermitt tentatively placed his broad palm with the languid, slender fingers on Marco's thigh. The boy just stared at the floor. Uncertain as to his next move, Kermitt tried to moderate the waves of lust that threatened to overwhelm him and cause him to frighten the boy away. But then, without raising his eyes from the floor, Marco reached his right arm around Kermitt's neck, slowly drawing his dark face nearer.

Marco turned his face to Kermitt with the stately, unhurried cadence of a virgin bride being led to the marriage bed, the concourse of all mystery. His eyes were closed but as Kermitt bent forward to join tongues with him, they flashed open, glowing like plums of liquid opal with their own terrifying fire. Kermitt gasped in fear and struggled to pull his head from the painful grip of the boy's hand. But although Kermitt was much larger than the boy, he couldn't shake off the grip. The boy's glowing eyes loomed relentlessly closer while his lips twisted in a malicious smile born of arrogance and limitless power.

Kermitt's desperate, struggling form appeared to Marco as if through the wrong end of a telescope, puny, mouse-like, of no consequence. Although Kermitt mouthed his terrified screams, no sound could emerge past Marco's vicious grip around his throat. A growing darkness settled upon the boy's consciousness but a darkness not nearly as thick and confounding as that of the night before. Marco's body surged with power, his blood electric, his chest cavernous and swollen with the sheer rasping relentlessness of his heaving lungs. The horrified man was enchained by Marco's strength, cracked like a fragile porcelain doll streaked with red, and ceased struggling.

The next time Marco's consciousness rose from the black pool of oblivion he found himself running east through the Village, laughing hysterically, his eyes wet with passionate tears.

10

ENDER'S passage through the British Embassy was
expedited by an eager young aide, his polished face
radiating deep concern and urgency, who led him from
the security station along a short corridor to a special
bank of elevators and from there up to Welles's inner
sanctum on the ninth floor. Ender and the aide stopped in
front of a broad, elegant door of polished wood, the rich
swirls of the grain warmly alive in the soft light of the
hallway. Ender stopped the aide before he could rap gently on the door.

All the way uptown in the cab he had tried to find the
right words to inform this man of his child's murder as
gently as possible while concealing the fact that the case
had gone from the mere brutal to the bizarre. There was
so little he could say to the flood of questions Welles
would put to him. And he didn't have an easy way with
words. The aide stood aside, patiently, bemused, waiting
for Ender to compose himself and signal for entry. Ender
wished he could have left this dirty business to Brock but
he felt that fool would cause the father more pain in the
long run by his glib answers and blatant lies of convenience. In consideration of the horror that Welles was going to have to learn to live with, Ender felt that he
deserved better.

He tried without hope to tighten the muscles of his tongue, then nodded. The aide knocked, then left Ender alone upon his entrance into the office.

Welles was standing in his secretary's outer office waiting for Ender. He was tall and distinguished-looking, with gray hair and a full but carefully trimmed mustache that accentuated the firm straight lines of his lower lip and jaw. Although he was dressed in an expensive suit of conservative elegance, there was an aura about him of vital rusticity, as if he would much prefer to leave his formal responsibilities here in New York for a full life in the English countryside with a small house, a brace of sleepy old hounds, a well-fondled meerschaum, and no clothes more formal than a bulky sweater and a tweed hunting jacket with leather elbow patches. He studied Ender's face for telltale signs of morbidity, but all he could see was shy nervousness.

"Mr. Ender," he said, his outstretched palm offered in greeting, "please come into my office."

Welles ushered Ender into a spacious room lined with bookshelves which were filled with large leatherbound volumes tooled richly in gold. His desk was massive yet neat and orderly, each article of daily service placed precisely in its proper place, the morning's paperwork completed and neatly disposed of in deference to Ender's coming. Welles offered Ender a thick leather chair in front of the desk and hurried to seat himself behind the desk.

"Do you have any news about my daughter?"

Ender clenched his back teeth and quickly swallowed a jet of saliva. "I'm afraid I do, Mr. Welles. She was found this . . . this morning, murdered in Central Park."

Welles stiffened perceptibly in his seat as if slowly raising a massive weight that had suddenly fallen on his shoulders. The muscles of his lean jaw swelled and knotted and his eyes grew tender with anguish. He rose abruptly from his seat and faced the window, staring at the silent forms below, his arms limp at his sides, his strong fingers chafing at the light fabric of his trousers.

"I can't tell you how sorry I am to have to bring you this news," said Ender, his large eyes moist with compassion for the crushed father. "There's no easy way to say that kind of thing. Just a lot of clichés." He then sat silently in the chair, staring at his hands in his lap. He felt cheap in comparison to his surroundings: the elegance, the solemn atmosphere of tradition, the weighty sorrow. He could feel Welles trying to hold back his tears and was consumed by an overwhelming need to represent the factotum of decent humanity and apologize for the fact that we all lived in an ugly, sordid world.

"How did it happen?" The voice floated softly, almost inaudibly, from the window and over the desk and fluttered like a dove on Ender's mind.

"She died of multiple stab wounds, sir, sometime shortly after midnight." Ender felt that any further details of the murder would be inappropriate and unproductive at this time.

"My God, Mr. Ender, that's a horrible way to die."

"When we're speaking of sudden death, violent death, particularly of one so young, there are only horrible ways to die."

Welles turned from the window, his eyes brimming, yet with a strange smile across his face.

"I'm afraid I'll have to correct you on that point," he said, his voice trembling, his eyes distant. "There was a young boy who served next to me at Normandy. We just happened to meet in the hysteria of the charge up the beaches. He was a conscript and I could see the terror in his eyes, but then the sounds of the battle and shouting of human voices all around us seemed to strengthen him and his eyes swapped terror for courage and pride. In those last seconds that boy became an idealist for some inexplicable reason and his whole being seemed to swell with the righteousness of his self-sacrifice in the face of unrelenting evil. You'll have to remember, Mr. Ender, that those were the days when war still had a meaning, a purpose. It was easy then to think that each of us was doing his small part to save the rest of humanity. And all of a sudden the sacrifice of our own lives was not too great a price to pay."

Welles dabbed his mustache with a bright white linen handkerchief. "I saw that boy change, Mr. Ender, right before my eyes. He grew old suddenly and his eyes sparkled with honor, and he charged up the beaches, shouting encouragements, putting all of us veterans to shame. His energy seemed to flow into all of us and we followed, shouting and cursing like Attila's Huns, heedless of the enemy fire." He sat down weakly behind his desk and gazed softly into the eyes of his daughter as she smiled up at him from a photograph on the desk. "A few moments later that boy was dead on the beach, flat out dead, yet still he bore the look of pride and honor in his dead eyes. That, Mr. Ender, to my way of thinking was a glorious death."

Ender bowed his head in silent affirmation. Welles started flourishing his arms over his desk, shaking his head in confusion.

"I'm afraid I'm not taking this well. You'll have to forgive me, Mr. Ender: I just simply don't know what to do. Up until this moment my life had been a broad, relatively sunny avenue leading to ever-greater things. I had my Jenny to care for, and my work which, to a greater or lesser extent, is of importance to the world. But right now the road has shattered, crumbled into useless lumps of concrete that cost me my footing. And there's no measured end to it anymore, no heading off in a straight line to the golden glow of a setting sun. Just a wasteland." There was a desperate look of apology in Welles's eyes as he looked across his desk at Ender. "Unlike those of you who work every day here in New York with the police department, I haven't experienced enough of death to be able to properly handle it. I never had any parents to lose, and my wife died of a painful, lingering bout with cancer where death was welcomed by us both as a deliverer, not a villain. I . . . I can't seem to absorb the fact that Jenny's been killed."

"You mistake me, Mr. Welles. I'm not around death all that much. I'm just a lawyer working for the district attorney. They call me in on special cases and I get involved in the police work and maybe then I'll be confronted by the horrors of death. But it never becomes easy. There's no etiquette around it, no tradition of proper bereavement. It just hurts. You and I both have to live with that truth: it just hurts."

"Special cases," Welles commented bitterly. "And what about the thousands of parents who aren't special cases and don't get the benefit of your special talents? Those who are forced to just sit at home and grieve for their children." The tears began to flow freely down Welles's cheeks.

Ender sat silently.

"I'm sorry, Mr. Ender. I don't mean to accuse you or your department of insensitivity. You're quite the opposite, really: you seem a caring and sensitive person. Please forgive my rudeness."

"There's nothing to forgive, Mr. Welles," soothed Ender.

"It's just that somehow I feel that if I weren't a special case, an official of a foreign government and all that, then Jenny would still be alive."

"If you keep on thinking like that, Mr. Welles, you'll push yourself to suicide. No evidence has turned up so far to give us any indication that your daughter's death was politically motivated. It's a possibility, but only one possibility among many. I understand and sympathize with your grief and anger, but we're going to need you in one piece, in one coherent whole, and in the fullness of your powers, to help us apprehend whoever it was who did this thing. There are a lot of roads rising out of grief, Mr. Welles, but most of them lead to dead ends. I won't have you going that route."

"But if it wasn't to get at me, then who could do such a thing? Why? What purpose does the murder of a little girl serve?"

"There are a lot of sick people in this city. Your daughter was found in the middle of a park that swarms with them. People have died in this city for smiling at the wrong time, or frowning at the wrong person, or for letting their dogs pee on the wrong guy's tire. It doesn't take very much."

Welles slammed his fist down hard onto the cushioned green felt blotter, upsetting a tray of paper clips.

"But why would they kill my Jenny?! Why?"

"I told you, sir, we have no idea as yet. She may have been killed by a random mugger or her death may be some sort of conspiracy. This is where we need your help. Can you think of any person or group of persons specifically who might want to get at you through the death of your daughter?"

Welles swung his head from side to side in despair. "God, Mr. Ender, I've been asking myself that question all day. When I woke up this morning and my housekeeper and I discovered her missing, the first thing we thought of was kidnaping. I'm a rather wealthy man so it might have been done purely for money. But I'm not a very important man in the political sense. You see, I'm an engineer, not a politician. My function here in this embassy is to coordinate British expertise with that of other governments and the various agencies of the UN for the purpose of designing and building many public works projects around the world: dams, roads, bridges. My work here is, to be quite truthful, one of the few facets of British government that is strictly humanitarian. Indeed, my intelligence clearance in other departments is really quite low."

"As an engineer, are you privy to classified information relating to any new devices or machines that might be valuable to another government or to an independent profiteer?"

"Not at all. The only innovations I'm ever informed of are those that the other side already knows about and just doesn't give a damn. But why would a kidnaper kill her and leave her in a park? Whoever did it has taken from me the last thing that I loved: they'd have no hold over me now."

"That's part of the reason we've pretty much discounted kidnaping: unless, of course, it was a kidnaping attempt that for some unknown reason had to be aborted. Left alive, your daughter would be a very dangerous witness. They'd then leave her in the park, make it look like something else, then disappear to hide out and try it all over again at another time, another place."

"What do you mean 'look like something else'?"

Ender had no intention of delving into the lurid details of the crime: and he couldn't speak of the rape. That would be too much for the already distraught father, an unnecessary source of pain.

"It's simply this, sir, some of the physical evidence is . . . uh, rather confusing and contradictory. That's why we need your help in piecing this case together. Tell me: assuming that your daughter was not carried to Central

Park against her will, what the hell was she doing there in the middle of the night?"

"I have no idea, Mr. Ender," moaned Welles, his voice desperate and imploring. "My housekeeper tucked her into bed last night about ten o'clock just like she always does, and I looked in on her when I got home around ten-thirty. She was sound asleep."

"Could she have gotten out of the apartment without your knowledge?"

Welles thought a moment. "I'm sure she could, Mr. Ender. I love my daughter but I'm not her jailer. To my knowledge she has never given me reason to mistrust her. I can't conceive of her even feeling that she had to sneak out of the house without my knowledge. We shared everything . . ."

"Yes?" prompted Ender, aware of the final hesitancy of his voice.

"There's this boy in her school, Marco something . . . We've had a few disagreements in the past couple of weeks about him. It was puppy love, I think that's what you Americans call it. He seemed a nice enough boy but I had only met him on a few occasions. Even though he was fifteen and Jenny was thirteen, ages at which children have generally very little in common, it seemed that the two of them were developing a very strong intellectual rapport. I was merely concerned that their relationship was beginning to step beyond the bounds of the intellectual. I made my feelings known to her and we quarreled. A subdued quarrel, I assure you, Mr. Ender. No tantrums, no dogmatic commandments, no threats. She seemed overwrought and defensive, perhaps a bit embarrassed. I'm afraid I might have struck a chord with my questioning." Suddenly Welles glowered at Ender, angry and frantic. "Do you think that boy could have something to do with this? Could it be possible . . ."

"No, no, Mr. Welles, from what little we are sure of, it's not very likely. But perhaps the boy can fill in some of the gaps about your daughter's evening. Can you remember his name?"

Welles pressed his hand against his forehead until the knuckles whitened. "Marco . . . Marco . . . O God, I can't think of his last name. Something incongruous with

63

the name 'Marco.' I remember being amused by it when I first heard it. His father's Irish, I think. Something to do with liquor. I might even have met him at a Commonwealth social of some sort. O God, Mr. Ender, I just can't think, I can't think, my head just swims, fighting against me . . ."

And the distraught father broke down, weeping heavily over his desk. Ender rose to leave, embracing the shuddering shoulders with a gentle arm.

"The worst is passed now, she's out of the ugliness of this world. You just let it all out of you: don't leave anything bottled up to form scars. I'm leaving a man with you to bring you downtown later whenever you feel up to it. Certain formalities, you understand."

And the father continued to weep as Ender passed silently out of the room.

A small crowd of office personnel had gathered in the outer office, drawn by the emotional cries that had been audible through the door during Ender's conversation with Welles. Ender drew the middle aged, rather nondescript woman with the flowered shirt who had welcomed him into the office to one side.

"Are you Mr. Welles's secretary?" he asked.

"I am, sir. Is there anything wrong with Mr. Welles?"

"I'm afraid there is. Now this must be kept just between you, me, and Mr. Welles. Do you understand? It's of the utmost importance."

"I understand, sir," she replied in a conspiratorial whisper.

"Mr. Welles's daughter has been found murdered—"

"O my God!" exclaimed the secretary, beginning to swoon.

"For Christ's sake, ma'm, there's no time for that. Mr. Welles needs you to help him right now, not decorate his carpet."

"I'm sorry, sir," she replied, pale, shocked. "O the poor, dear man."

"Contact a close friend of his here in the building, anyone who can help him out with moral support. And call a doctor. But remember, most of all, be discreet."

"I understand, sir. You can count on my help."

"I'm certain I can."

Ender turned to leave when the secretary called him back.

"Excuse me, sir, but an associate of yours called before. He just left this number for you to call; he said it was urgent but he wouldn't permit me to interrupt you while you were in with Mr. Welles. He said his name was Lt. Fedorson."

He dialed the number written on the piece of notepaper she handed to him, Fedorson was sent for, and finally the familiar rasping voice sprang out of the phone: "You better get down here to the Bank Street pier, counsellor. We've got another one."

11

AT twilight, Manhattan rises from its hot summerday ashes and becomes transfigured. The sky forsakes its white haze and regains its sultry blush with gleaming wisps of gold and orange and purple clouds that gather around the waning sun to bid it farewell as it plunges beyond the sea. Lights, like awakening eyes, sparkle by the millions from the massive buildings, aglow with the setting sun. As the twilight darkens into night, Manhattan rests like an enormous glowing jewel on a cushion of rich purple velvet. The stars emerge from the glare of the sun, shimmering, calling silently to their neon fellows, gay and mischievous. Cool winds swirl along the avenues as if by magic, dissipating the residue of the day's heat.

To Adrienne, twilight was a reward for enduring the pointlessness of the daylight.

She sat on her balcony, high above the pale copper glare of the vapor lamps and the rhythmic throb of traffic, gazing thoughtfully at the colors of the setting sun. She heard Heinreich arrive at the front door precisely on schedule but she did not rise from her soft chair. The usual ruckus ensued: doors opening and shutting, suitcases gathered and distributed throughout the apartment, Heinreich's clipped commands to his silent, strange cohorts, the drag and shuffle of boots as they passed over thick carpets and glistening linoleum. Finally, all was in its proper place and the servants dismissed, filling the apartment with heavy silence.

"You no longer come to greet me when I return from business?" His voice was quizzical, not severe, his irritation overlaid by a mellow liquidity of tone that seemed almost fatherly.

Adrienne dutifully rose to kiss him as he stood in the doorway of the balcony. "I'm sorry, Heinreich. I guess I was just lost in thought. I was barely aware of your coming home. Besides, I didn't think you needed me to help you."

"My dear child," soothed Heinreich, "my need for you is not restricted to household chores. A simple smile from you would do wonders for an old man's heart when he returns from a particularly grueling joust with the magnates of the financial world." He approached her with a charming tenderness in his eyes and she allowed herself to be cradled, though briefly, in his thin arms.

A twinge of mingled pity and fear coursed through her as she embraced this stranger who was her husband.

"I'll get you some food," she said, camouflaging her eagerness to get away from him. "You must be starving."

"No, no, my dear, no food. I've already eaten."

She stopped stock-still, her back to him, stymied.

"I think what I would like to do this evening," he said, unbuttoning his jacket, "is just sit and talk with you a while. It's been a long time since you and I have had the leisure to just sit and chat, to—O what is it you young people call it?—communicate. Yes, it's been much too long."

She stepped back onto the balcony and walked to the metal railing, leaning on her palms and looking out over the Hudson. Heinreich stepped behind her and hugged her shoulders, his thin lips hovering by her ear.

"Do you remember those talks we used to have on the jet, when we'd laugh a lot and tell each other silly stories and toast the sun setting over the Atlantic with champagne?"

Adrienne remembered very well. He had been so eager for her to love him then. Every gesture, every arch of his eyebrow, every soft syllable that spilled from his lips was a futile foray in his battle to win over her love. It wasn't his fault that she would never love him. Nor was it his fault that now only one man could satisfy the impertinent cravings that overwhelmed her and could reclaim her arid emptiness. Virulent waves of guilt washed over her as Heinreich ran his palms tenderly up and down her arms.

"Come, my love, into my study with me and there we can share some brandy and soft music."

"O Heinreich, couldn't we just talk out here? The twilight is so . . . so majestic, all the changing colors and the strange shapes of the clouds. Please, couldn't we talk out here?"

"I'm sorry, my love, but I'm really quite fatigued. I would like to indulge you in the poetry of your twilight, but the glare of the sky and the streetlamps is burning my eyes. And the height is a bit dizzying."

She turned to look into his face, concerned, and surprised a sinister glimmer in his eyes that changed instantaneously to an expression of tender fatherly devotion. "Are you feeling ill?" she asked, now somewhat nervously.

"No, no, my dear. Just tired. Come. Into the study with you."

She followed him into the large study and sank languidly into an overstuffed leather chair, watching him pour them each a snifter of brandy which he twirled and eyed with sophisticated expertise. The brandy was fruity-sweet on her tongue, and the pungent fumes rose luxuriously to coat her palate and fill her nose with the scent of blackberries. She did not notice that he had unobtrusively shut and locked the study door.

This was the room in which Heinreich kept all the artifacts he had collected on his travels throughout the world. He leaned against one of the ornately carved display cases, eyeing her from beneath half-closed eyelids. The case he leaned against was the one from which she had stolen the jade unicorn. It seemed to Adrienne that every place she turned to in the study cried out in mute reproach at her deception. She had to distract herself with a flow of trite words.

"Tell me, Heinreich, how your trip was. Did you have any adventures? Any bouts with international jewel thieves or radical Marxists?"

Heinreich laughed. "No, no, nothing like that. Although you shouldn't make such jokes. We live in terrible times. The great European cultural centers are infested with so-called proletarian heroes who would not think twice about slitting anybody's throat whom they found offensive to their churlish sensibilities. Indeed, my dear, it has now become a crime against 'the people' to earn an honest living and enjoy the fruits of one's labors. That is why I have always insisted on maintaining a low profile as far as the general public is concerned. Let the Rockefellers indulge in the politics of confrontation: I prefer to be left alone."

"I quite agree with you, Heinreich. You're not a political animal. And besides, I don't want you to get hurt."

"Getting hurt is not my fear. I have surrounded myself over the years with more than adequate protection. What I fear most is the loss of time, valuable time, that inevitably follows any accessions to the public. You must be seen at the right parties and smile politely for those damn paparazzi who hound you day and night. And of course you're pulled back and forth by those parasites who wish to glow in your limelight. You lose the freedom to be yourself and accomplish the tasks that you must in the short lifespan allotted you."

Adrienne saw something in his eyes that she had never seen before: a desperate man, fighting against the ravages of time and the encroaching disability of old age, whose immortal soul was young and vibrant and thus all the more agonized within the mounting shackles of an aging corpse. Again, the venomous bite of remorse confused her thoughts and made great torrents of pity for him swell within her.

"You don't mean to say that you feel such pressures yourself? Why, Heinreich, you've lived enough for ten men and have accomplished marvellous things. You've amassed a vast fortune, you've made yourself welcome, even needed, in the homes of the finest families in the whole world, and in your own unobtrusive way, you wield greater power than most of the world's political leaders. My God, what more can one ask out of life?"

Adrienne thought her words would comfort Heinreich, if indeed he needed comforting. But he answered with a bitter laugh, his eyes riveted on the dark pool of brandy tossing in his glass.

"You mistake me, my dear. I didn't mean to imply that I shared the average fear of the average old man when confronting death. As you have pointed out, I've accomplished more than enough to satisfy any mortal longings." He raised his eyes from his glass and stared sternly into her face. "It's the immortal longings that torment me."

"What do you mean by immortal longings?"

Heinreich waved off the question. "The details needn't concern you now. Suffice it to say that profound changes are about to transform the world. I have fought for a . . . a lifetime to catalyze that transformation against impossible odds."

"What kind of transformation? Economic or political?"

"Neither, really, although it will embrace both those realms, I'm sure. No, what I'm speaking of is a spiritual transformation."

"Spiritual? But I thought you had nothing but profound contempt for the metaphysicians of the world."

"O I do, I do, my dear." Heinreich began pacing slowly back and forth in front of his wife, watching the soft leather of his shoes sink step after step in the plush oriental carpet. "Metaphysicians and philosophers are the least spiritual people in the world. They are enslaved by a phantom called logic and reason which blinds them to the realities woven secretly into the fabric of the universe, realities which manifest themselves without warning, realities which suddenly shine forth and overwhelm. Sometimes they then vanish without a trace." He gazed curiously into one of his display cases at a brilliant crystal globe seated on the shoulders of a quartz Atlas. "Other times they stop the universe completely. And then everything is different."

Adrienne was frightened by this strange aspect of her husband. He had never spoken to her like this before with such intense passion in his eyes. Spiritual? She had always thought of him as a hard-nosed businessman, suave perhaps and articulate in many fields of knowledge. But this "secret reality" business seemed bizarre coming from his thin lips.

"Heinreich, I don't understand a word of what you're

71

saying. I feel like you're handing me a book with a few chapters cut out. You'll have to fill in the blanks if you want me to understand you."

"Of course, of course, my dear," Heinreich answered gently, a slight smile playing upon his lips. "I can't expect you to understand what I'm saying to you. After all, you really know so little about me, about my dreams, my ambitions. Odd, isn't it? A man of my age and achievement still prattling on about ambition. Most of my peers have settled themselves down to a long wait for a slow death, occupying themselves with transitory pleasures, smug and self-satisfied with their material success. I've always been . . . different. I can't define it, really, though God knows I've tried to for years. But it seems that ever since I can remember I've been strangely attuned to those secret realities that are in flux and movement all around us. They speak to me, caress me, soothe me in my tormented hours. They even speak to me of my own immortality. Can you imagine?"

Adrienne stared at him with raised eyebrows. "You're talking now like a mystic. Or a madman."

"Or a poet," he added slowly, with a deliberate sneer that shivered Adrienne's spine. He looked up from the crystal globe to flash her a humorless smile, his eyes smoldering. "I suppose we're all of the same ilk, deep down. Yet there is one vast difference between me and the rest of them. The poets and the mystics merely put words to their fantasies; when they die, the fantasies die with them, leaving only the skeletal remains: the words. But I, on the other hand, have very little imagination. A true businessman in that respect. My ambitions and fantasies are imposed on me from outside myself, from where I don't know, but I can call upon them, as to wayward friends, and have them sweep me up in their glorious arms and manifest themselves in the real world, with me cradled in their bosom. Poets merely distract men's thoughts; mystics merely attune themselves to ecstasy, then perish; whereas I shall bring those secret realities down like a thunderbolt upon the rest of the world."

Heinreich turned again to stare into the depths of the crystal globe and into the tormented eyes of straining Atlas. Adrienne began to think him mad.

"Heinreich, stop this talk now, you're frightening me. You sound like a lunatic. I'm not used to this from you."

Heinreich turned to Adrienne, his eyes flinty and mocking. "A lunatic? I suppose so. I can understand your feeling like that. I was simply trying to explain to you about the transformation. Much of my work in Europe for the past few years has been to prepare myself and a few trusted associates for the event that is to come. The others: you've never met them. But I've told them quite a lot about you. They were very happy that we met and married. The union seemed auspicious."

He crossed to the far side of the room and sank into another leather chair, his legs stretched out at length, his eyes intent upon Adrienne. His arms were crossed upon his chest, his chin resting in his hands.

"I've arranged a celebration in honor of the transformation. Such planning and arranging just to have everything perfect: you don't know. It's been exhausting."

"Too exhausting, it seems to me."

He smiled at her remark. "Perhaps. Did you know that I had planned for you to play one of the primary roles in this celebration? Of course you didn't. But now, most regrettably, I've had to change my plans."

Adrienne started to flush with anger. "Well, if the rest of your mysterious friends are as crazy as you, that's all right with me." She rose hastily from her seat, setting the brandy snifter on the broad mahogany desk and made for the door.

"Don't go yet, Adrienne. I haven't finished talking to you."

She stood paralyzed, staring at the door, waiting for his next words with a pounding heart. He didn't rise from his seat. His voice, suddenly frigid and stern, saw through her consciousness like a blunt knife.

"You've been a disappointment to me, Adrienne. You've unwittingly deprived me of one of my 'immortal longings.' "

She turned to him outraged. "I? I've deprived you of nothing!"

"An heir, my dear," Heinreich said calmly, though his eyes flashed like glinting steel.

"An heir? How dare you reproach me for that! I've offered myself countless times to you and each time you've turned me away. I always felt that at least if I couldn't love you I could give my body to you for your pleasure. I was more than willing to bear your children. But you've always treated me as if I were diseased. I've never even seen you naked! That hasn't been by my choice. It's been your sickness, not mine."

She stormed toward the door of the study and pulled the knob. The door wouldn't move.

"Not yet, my dear. I haven't explained myself fully to you yet."

"I don't listen to explanations when I'm imprisoned in a room with a madman. Open that door and perhaps we can continue with your 'explanations' at another time. But open that goddamn door!"

"You don't understand. I was saving you for another, someone far greater than myself. You, in your purity, were to be my gift to him. Now that can no longer be. You've betrayed me with another man."

Adrienne's jaw dropped. Suddenly his strange madness seemed to have some plausible origin. Her anger was being eroded by floods of guilt and humiliation at being caught like a child in a transgression. Her lower lip trembled as she tried to respond to his sudden thrust.

"You have the audacity to tell me that you were going to give me to somebody else, that you were saving me for a gift like a stuffed doll or cheap ring, and then in the same breath condemn me for being unfaithful? Unfaithful! To what? To this farce of a marriage? To an old man with ice water in his veins who leaves me alone for three quarters of the year, who obviously thinks of me as nothing better than a whore to be bartered among his perverted friends? Why should I be faithful? All the money in the world can't change the fact that you're nothing better than a dirty, stinking pimp!"

"Enough, slut!" Heinreich shouted, flying out of his chair, a leather riding crop appearing suddenly in his hand. He slashed her across the face with the crop repeatedly, tearing her cheeks, beating her frantic, weeping form to the floor. "I would have made you a queen, queen of the entire world! The son you were to bear would have been the Prince of the forces of darkness. But now I can't sully the honor of the Great One with your foul and repellent body."

He beat her repeatedly until her cries for mercy were silenced. She lay limp on the carpet, drops of her blood mingling with the oriental arabesques. She was not dead, though her breathing was very shallow. No, she was not dead, though it would be a long time before she would ever again be beautiful.

12

". . . out of the forests the light the great light woe unto the blessed and the stars that shine from his eyes the eyes of a cat the cat of the night the glow of the eyes and the bellowing of the wind out of the night and the crumbling of all the stars and planets they fall they fall they fall into his eyes his eyes sullen his eyes burning out of the forest comes the great light woe woe the great light seeks you out hunts you down no way to escape no way we must bow our heads down to the earth the earth of the great forest our foreheads smeared with slime and he smiles down on us out of the light we tremble and he smiles down on us and the millions cry out to him we cry out for mercy mercy from the great light and we cry out with all our might woe to the blessed and the stars fall all around us the desert catches fire and the pale sands froth the sands swirl and froth and his eyes loom large woe to the blessed his eyes transform the light his eyes pull the world to his side he reaches for us reaching for us with horrible demon hands the hands of the night reaching out to touch us to pull us to tear our flesh yes we who know so much yes we who know the night and the stars and the eyes of cats and he changes a horrible beast an unknown beast with glowing eyes that stalks the night we who know so much we who dare to presume grovelling in the slime the slime at the foot of the great forest the slime enfolding the night we huddle together yes must huddle together against his eyes and the great light woe to the blessed woe woe . . ."

Beverly Forbes opened the door of her West Village apartment, her arms laden with groceries, and found her roommate and lover, Elizabeth Wylie, crouched on the floor in a far corner of the living room, her hands pressed tightly against her ears, her face frantic with madness, keening strange and wild words to the silent room. Her body swayed in rhythm with her endless flow of words, back and forth, her blond curls dank with sweat, twining between her slender fingers. Beverly dropped the bags of groceries and flew to Elizabeth's side, falling to the floor beside her, sheltering her swaying form in her arms.

"Liz, Liz, what's the matter? Are you all right? What's happening to you, honey, oh, sweet, sweet Liz, what's happened to you?"

The flow of Elizabeth's strange words could not be staunched. At first Beverly tried to listen to what she was saying, hoping that she might at some point communicate the source of her sudden madness. But the words spilled on and on, rhythmic, senseless, terrifying.

Beverly was a tiny woman, her face impish like a pixie, her dark hair bobbed like a Greenwich Village Peter Pan. But her small size belied the tremendous energy that quivered throughout her body. When she quickly ascertained that Elizabeth could not be untranced or even moved from her spot in the corner of the living room, she ran to the phone to call the police emergency number. As she picked up the receiver, however, she realized what a stupid waste of time that would be, particularly under the circumstances, so she paused, frantic, to think of a wiser alternative.

Suddenly she dashed into their bedroom and dug their address book out from under a pile of old paperbacks. She thumbed through it quickly, found the number she wanted, and ran back to the phone.

"I must speak to Dr. Crile immediately! It's an emergency! No, I don't have the time to hold on until he finishes with a patient. He'll understand once I get to talk to him. Please, hurry!"

She waited in breathless silence for a few moments, staring at Elizabeth who still chanted her bizarre monologue, nodding and swaying, rivulets of sweat pouring off her face and soaking her T-shirt.

"Yes, yes, doctor," she snapped back into the phone, "I'm sorry to interrupt your work but there's an emergency here. I'm Beverly Forbes, Elizabeth Wylie's roommate, and there's something wrong with her, she's having some kind of fit or something, chanting all kinds of crazy words that don't make any sense and she's in a terrible cold sweat. I don't know what's happening to her and I can't snap her out of it. I thought you might be able to do something for her. You might know what's going on or how to handle this particular situation. O doctor, I'm so frightened, I've never seen her like this, first those damn dreams and now this! You've got to help her! . . . O thank God, I'll be right here with her waiting for you. That's right, 64 Jane Street, right, that's the place. Thank you so much."

Dr. Crile arrived at their door within half an hour which, considering midtown traffic, was remarkably good time. He was a short, stocky, pugnacious man who stormed into the apartment like a little bulldozer. His usually affable face was darkened by concern, his thick, dark eyebrows drawn tightly downward, shading his intent eyes. He fell to his knees at Elizabeth's side, carefully laying his black medical bag by his knees on the floor while his neat goatee jostled up and down in cadence with the soft words he was trying to pour into the entranced girl's ear. He listened for a moment to the content of her words and ascertained the continuity of their mad flow while working his quick, skilled hands down her arm to her wrist, studying her temperature and pulse, the girl's flesh like chilled ivory in his hand.

"You did the right thing calling me, Miss Forbes." His voice was deep and urgent, gentle at the moment but one knew from its timbre that it could be devastatingly brutal when he was angry. "She's in the midst of some form of psychic possession, some mediumistic state that's tearing at her mind and she doesn't seem to be able to fight it off. Ordinarily, people in such states simply flow with them, if you understand me, sort of submit to the forces that are

79

trying to communicate to others through them. When the seizure passes, everything both physiological and psychological returns to normal. That's not the case with Elizabeth here. Her mind has latched on to something that just won't give way." He reached into his medical bag and withdrew a small bottle of bronze liquid and a syringe. "I'm going to have to help her out of this with an injection before she goes into complete shock, which could kill her. Her pulse is already dangerously rapid and her body temperature has fallen much too low." Beverly held Elizabeth tightly while the doctor extended her arm and inserted the syringe. Slowly, the bronze liquid seeped into her vein.

Dr. Crile withdrew the empty syringe and waited. The flow of Elizabeth's chant and her odd swaying motions did not abate.

"I've never seen a seizure as strong as this," whispered the doctor in astonishment. "One more injection and that'll have to be it. Too much of this medication is deadly."

Beverly stared up at Crile with wide, quizzical eyes. He commanded her with a short gesture to help him extend the girl's other arm. The new needle plunged into the vein, the bronze liquid flowed and emptied, and the doctor kneeled back on his shins to watch. Slowly, ever so slightly, Elizabeth's speech began to slur and her voice grew fainter until at last the bizarre tirade was no more than faint puffs of empty breath. Then she fell into Beverly's arms unconscious.

Crile surveyed her with his sensitive fingers until he was certain that she had passed into a relatively normal state of drug-induced sleep, the color returning to her cheeks and her limbs warming with the flow of fresh blood. He helped Beverly carry her into the bedroom where she was placed between blankets and left to sleep.

Once the crisis had passed, Crile and Beverly had time to relax from their frenzied labors. Her offer of a large glass of ice tea was readily accepted by the doctor. They sat across from each other in the living room, sipping from the tall glasses upon which the afternoon's humidity was condensing.

"What the hell just happened to Elizabeth, doctor?"

Beverly paused, staring urgently into the doctor's eyes, demanding with her own the absolute truth.

"I can't say for certain, Miss Forbes," Dr. Crile replied. "As I said before, she appeared to be in an extraordinarily powerful mediumistic state that proved to be too much for her. I daresay it would've proved too much for anybody."

Beverly was not satisfied. "Doctor, I have to apologize in advance if anything I'm going to say gives you offense. Are you aware of how close Elizabeth and I are?"

Dr. Crile looked up at her impassively over his ice tea. "I am."

"Then you must also know how much I care for her and how strongly protective I am of her. I might be the little one in this household but it's Elizabeth who's fragile. Now, before she and I met, I never had much interest in psychic phenomena. I thought merely that for every legitimate, unexplained psychic mystery there were a hundred charlatans waiting in the wings to profit from it, to exploit the poor people involved, and to make a killing off a gullible public that's just starved for cheap thrills."

Dr. Crile smiled tenderly at her. "There are many people who would strongly agree with you, Miss Forbes, particularly my colleagues in the medical profession."

"Then I'm sure you can understand my concern. When I came home this afternoon and found her like that, I didn't see a woman in a 'mediumistic state': I saw a woman going through a babbling psychotic breakdown. The first image that came into my mind was that of the bag women who roam all over the city talking to themselves or to the pavement or whatever. Now, I'm well aware of your standing at the Parapsychology Research Institute and I'm also aware of the high regard in which you are held by a large segment of the medical profession, regardless of whether or not they believe in the reality of psychic phenomena. But my question is this: isn't it possible that by viewing Elizabeth's nightmares and now this . . . this seizure in strictly parapsychological terms, couldn't you be keeping her from receiving the real help she needs from doctors who are willing to call a psychosis a psychosis and not something else? Believe me, doctor, I'd much prefer to believe that what she's going through is really mystical and romantic and, in the end, harmless. I really would. But I'm just so worried about her, doctor, and I don't want to take any chances that might seriously damage her mental health."

Dr. Crile sipped his tea then settled back in his chair, stroking his beard. "Please believe me, Miss Forbes, I take no offense at anything you've just said. None whatsoever. In fact, I'm pleased at your concern for Elizabeth. I've worked in close association with her at the institute for over three years now and I, too, care for her a great deal. And please believe also that I'd sever my own jugular vein before knowingly causing any harm to that girl, regardless of my commitment to parapsychology or anything else."

"Well, doctor, I hope it won't come to that. But I do find what you say reassuring."

"Then please allow me to reassure you still further. You see, there are very major and distinct differences between what are commonly felt to be mental disorders and the kind of psychic abilities Elizabeth possesses. Most mental disorders are traceable to some form of emotional trauma experienced either over a long period of time, throughout childhood, let's say, or to some sudden and overwhelming tragedy. Nothing of the kind is applicable in Elizabeth's case. She just seems to have been born with a remarkable psychic acuity which has in no way, until very recently, caused her any anxiety or interfered with her processes of socialization.

"Secondly, mental disorders appear to exist as a continuum: they are always present in the sufferer, whether manifestly so or not, and the sufferer has absolutely no control over those manifestations. Again, with Elizabeth this isn't the case. She has always demonstrated to me a remarkable degree of control over her psychic experiences. Many of the psychics I've studied over the years have lacked this control. Extrasensory perceptions just seem to sweep down on them and overwhelm them. They're suddenly confronted with visions of the dead or imminent tragedies, a thousand varied horrors that average folks like you and I are quite fortunate not to be privy to. As you know, this hasn't been true of Elizabeth. When she's been asked to demonstrate her abilities for testing purposes, she goes through an elaborate meditative ritual, an intense channeling of psychic energies, and only when she is consciously aware of her readiness can her powers be called upon."

"Until now, that is."

Dr. Crile frowned. "That, Miss Forbes, is quite true. And you've just put your finger on the cause of my grave concern, at this moment, for Elizabeth's condition. I'm at a loss right now to explain this sudden onset of visionary nightmares and now this near-fatal trance. I'm hoping that Elizabeth, herself, will shed some light on this when she's recovered and is able to be questioned. But it seems that some powerful psychic energy is eroding her control of her special receptivity. That is what can push her over the edge, Miss Forbes, and precipitate mental illness." Crile sipped again from the misted glass. "Or nearly kill her, as we've seen today. But today's seizure was most extraordinary. I've never seen anything as nearly fatal as that in anybody before, be they psychics or psychotics. I doubt if an extensive research job would be able to come up with even one analogous case history. It's all most intriguing."

A tremor of impatience seeped into Beverly's voice. "But how do you know, doctor, that what happened today isn't the result of all her years of apparently controlled psychic abilities being tested and demonstrated and re-tested *ad infinitum?* How can you be sure that you and the rest of your psychic researchers haven't just driven her crazy?"

Dr. Crile paused for a good while before he responded. His face was thoughtful and grave.

"I can't be sure, Miss Forbes. None of us can. One could just as easily attribute this attack and those dreams to the pressures of the maverick life-style the two of you have chosen for yourselves. Don't misunderstand me: I don't mean to imply in any way that that is what I think. Quite the contrary. I honestly feel you're living in the healthiest way possible for you both. But if the continued use of her psychic abilities has brought on this mental crisis, then it would demonstrate a previously unknown and unanticipated mental fragility that may be a hidden factor underlying all psychic powers. That would be a very significant discovery, Miss Forbes, but one that I would not want to purchase at the cost of Elizabeth's well-being."

He stroked his beard thoughtfully, contemplating the shine and sparkle of the ice cubes as they floated in his glass.

"But all my experience," Crile continued, "and all my gut intuitions tell me that that is highly unlikely. Did you catch any part of what she was saying while she was entranced? The great light, cat eyes, the sheer terror in the presence of some mysterious malevolent force? All of these factors are significant and repeated elements of her nightmares. It's almost as if something occurred today which somehow dislodged her nightmares from the dream state and thrust them up into the light of day, overwhelming her consciousness. That is an extraordinary occurrence, don't you see? And I think that is the direction in which our researches to puzzle out this whole strange affair must be directed. I'm hoping that tomorrow, after she's awakened, she will be able to enlighten us both on this matter. But until then we can't do much more than bide our time."

He finished off his ice tea in one massive swallow and rose to leave.

"No, Miss Forbes, I'm almost positive that the solution to this mystery does not lie in any mental instability native to Elizabeth. There seem to be massive psychic energies coalescing at this point in time and space to which she is attuned. I can't for the life of me imagine what is causing them or from where they originate. But if her nightmares are any indication of what is in store for the world in the near future, then all I can say is God help us all."

13

THERE was no keeping the second murder under wraps. As soon as the calls went out over the police band stating that a homicide had occurred dockside in the Tenderloin district, every scandalmonger and yellow journalist flew to the site to capitalize on the public's fascination with sex-related crimes, particularly those involving "psychotic homosexuals." Fedorson did his best to keep the reporters at arm's length, but it was evident to Ender when he arrived at the scene of the murder that his patience was wearing thin.

Ender found the lieutenant on the dim second floor of the pier house berating a diminutive reporter who had somehow sneaked past the officers Fedorson had stationed to cordon off the area. The reporter's camera had flashed over the mutilated corpse even before the police photographer had had a chance to set up. Fedorson had him grabbed and none too gently hauled before him.

"Well, well, well," sneered Fedorson, though his tired eyes glowered down on the intruder, menacing and defiant. "You slimy cocksucker, I had hoped never to run into you again, Peale. And damn it, I'm not the only one. You've got quite a reputation among us cops. You're a real pain in the ass. You use that press card of yours to interfere with our investigations, and we don't like that.

Like those pictures you just took. Now, I'm sure that rag you work for won't think twice about running the goriest one right on the front page under some kind of screaming headline. And then you're gonna start to hound my boss, day and night, like a fucking rotten tooth. Now, my boss likes his beauty rest. And if you or one of the scumbags you work with badgers him too much, he gets on my back. He asks me for answers when I can't give them. And then I've got to put him off with some bullshit that never checks out and then the big brass come down on me. And in the meantime, your paper's caused a panic throughout all of lower Manhattan. And you just don't give a shit."

Quentin Peale dusted off the officer's hands from his slight shoulders with an arrogant flourish. "Your personal problems with your boss don't concern me in the least. You know where I stand, Fedorson: the public has a right to know."

Fedorson fumed, staring down into the reporter's beady eyes, the tip of his stogie glowing hotly in the semidarkness.

Ender thought Peale looked more like the cooking editor for a woman's monthly than an investigative reporter. He was a slight, rundown-looking man with pinched-in cheeks and a meticulously trimmed mustache which served to emphasize the arrogance of his facial gestures. He had one of those wrinkled and sagging faces with tiny dark eyes that made Ender think of an invigorated mummy rather than a man. Yet his wrappings were of the finest make and tailored to fit his frail form perfectly, the elegance of the whole set off by the polish of his tiny manicured nails and the glistening brightness of his rat's teeth.

"Why, you little sonofabitch," pursued Fedorson, about to lose control, "I'll take that press card of yours and shove it—"

"Now, Mr. Peale, I'm sure the mayor's office will do everything in its power to assist you very able men of the press in fulfilling your responsibilities to the public."

The lieutenant and the reporter turned in unison to stare at Ender who approached Peale with an outstretched, diplomatic hand.

"And who the hell are you?" demanded the reporter in his forthright, investigative manner.

"My name is Ender, Abe Ender," he responded, cordially shaking the little man's reluctant hand. "I'm with the district attorney's office and I've been assigned to assist in the investigation of this case. It's part of a new program of the mayor's to sort of mingle the efforts of the police and the justice department so that ultimately the citizens of New York will be benefited by swifter apprehension of felons and more certain criminal convictions."

Fedorson left Ender and the reporter to return to the mangled corpse, disgusted by the line of smooth words Ender was unreeling. He left them in close conversation and, a few short minutes later, Ender rejoined him. Peale had vanished.

"What happened to that little cocksucker?" asked Fedorson bitterly.

"He's gone, at least for now," Ender smiled. "You were about to lose your cool, my friend. That's the last thing we need right now. We can't let anyone see how edgy we're getting. Especially a guy like that. He might begin to suspect something."

Fedorson's broad mouth curled into a bitter pout, somewhat like an overgrown child. "Listen, counsellor, it's not my place to tell you your job but you've got to understand that that worm is just no damn good. He's made more trouble for me and the department over the years than I care to recollect."

"Precisely why I stepped in. I got rid of him by promising him exclusive access to certain relevant bits of information pertaining to this case through my office. I told him it was because I admired his ingenuity in being the first reporter on the scene. But first he'd have to leave and let us do our work without interference."

Fedorson looked down at Ender and pushed his fedora far back on his head. "And he fell for that?"

"I was perfectly sincere," Ender smiled. "With eyes like mine you can't get away with a lie. I learned that early in life: a man must recognize his limitations."

"You mean you're really going to give that creep exclusive details about this case? Real details?"

"Yes, I will. But before I explain why, I want you to

tell me what makes you think this killing is related to the little girl's."

The lieutenant shook his head and walked Ender over to the new corpse. Fresh blood glistened all over the rotten wooden crates that were scattered around the area and a very large, dark pool of blood surrounded the body, thickened and coagulated by the filth and stray motes of garbage over which the blood had flowed. The body was sprawled beside some crates in an odd, disjointed posture as if it had been tossed aside like a rag doll. Just like the little girl.

"It's the same as with the kid this morning. The same multiple wounds apparently made by the same weapon. The same posture of the body. That same greenish thickening beginning to form on the eyes. And the same kind of sexual assault. Almost."

Ender's eyes widened. "What do you mean?"

"The guy's been butt-fucked. Really brutal. His bowels were spilled all over the floor. Wait a minute and I'll get a flashlight—"

"No, thanks, that won't be necessary," Ender hastened to interrupt. "I'm sure the photos will be sufficiently graphic. One vision like that a day is enough, thank you."

"Yeah? Well, that's not all." Fedorson pointed to a far, darkened corner of the dock house. "We found his cock and balls over there. They were literally pulled out by the roots and just tossed. Whoever or whatever we're dealing with has a real sick fascination with sexual mutilation."

"Jesus Christ, what's happening around here?" Ender sighed, stricken by the brutal enormity of the sheer evil that was striking right in the heart of the nation's most important city. "How can anybody do this to somebody else, right here in broad daylight with people roaming all around the corridors, and disappear without a trace?"

"We have a couple of guys who were the first to stumble on to the body. But, apparently there weren't any screams. Nothing." Fedorson tipped his hat far back on his skull. "Whoever's killing these people is quick; too quick if you ask me. Wham, the guy's full of holes. Bam, his rectum's spread all over the floor. Thank you, ma'm, the cock's ripped and tossed and whoever did it is already out the door. No, counsellor, I can't figure it out myself.

It's just too fast. I mean, even Jack the Ripper couldn't dismember corpses and shoot his load within seconds." He chewed his cigar introspectively. "Hell, it takes me a lot longer than that just to get it up."

"Please, don't use old Jack's name too loudly. The walls have ears and they could start a panic." Ender looked nervously around at the officers who lounged nearby at their posts, speaking in whispers.

"Yeah? Well, don't think your friend Peale is going to miss the dramatic impact of the comparison."

"He's not my friend. I just intend to keep him glutted with information about this case so he'll be distracted from the other, should he get wind of it."

"O come on, counsellor! After this he's going to be looking for others, a whole series of them. He may be a pain in the ass but he's no fool. You just wait. He'll be hounding you night and day."

"Don't you think it's better that he hounds me than you? I intend to feed him just the right information to make him think that this murder is just what he expects. Nothing crazy like the other. I'll have Rothstein dummy up a report. That'll give Peale just what he wants to hear . . . and no more. A juicy psychotic homosexual rampage should keep him happy." Ender looked over at the body illuminated at intervals by the flashing bulbs of the forensic photographers. It lay twisted and wrenched on the filthy, splintery boards, torn, still sticky with blood, the dead mouth agape in a final gruesome testament to the unfortunate man's last horrible moments. Ender turned away from the corpse while the lieutenant, exhausted and sullen, chewed deliberately on his stogie. "I don't think any reporter can handle the reality of this situation. I'll just have to feed them all half-truths. I don't like it but I have no choice. I mean, really, what if the public found out about the semen samples and the . . . the unicorn's head staring out of those dead eyes?" He thoughtfully rubbed his balding scalp, then stared up pathetically at Fedorson. "Are we all going crazy, lieutenant?"

"I don't know, counsellor. Something's going crazy in this world. At this moment I don't think it's us, but ask me again in a couple of days." He leaned against a wooden crate and lit a match with a rapid flick of his wrist, relighting the dead stogie. "Look, counsellor, I appreciate what you're trying to do. I appreciate your willingness to keep Peale off my back. But do you think you can do it? You yourself said that with your eyes you can't be a convincing liar. I tend to agree with you. It's been less than twenty-four hours and there've been two bizarre murders already. How long do you think we can keep this all under wraps? And what are we going to do when the truth becomes known?"

In the presence of the tired lieutenant's concern, Ender relaxed his energetic facade and the hours of fatigue, horror, and overwhelming dilemma clawed traces of withering agedness in his pudgy face. His eyes were narrow and red, swollen with lost sleep. He leaned against the crate next to Fedorson, staring down at his small feet encased in tiny, brightly polished shoes.

"When my mother insisted I become a lawyer, she was thinking in terms of some soft, lucrative practice with a big corporation, handling their corporate shenanigans and getting fat and rich with a loving though eminently bourgeois wife who would always be both a prod and a reward for my daily efforts. And then there'd be the house and the kids and the two big cars in the circular driveway in Roslyn. And she'd start dragging my old man and me to shule again, just to show me off in my glittering respectability. Like she wanted to do with my brother, only now he's too busy to indulge her in her Jewish mother's whims. Besides, after he started interning at the Bellevue emergency ward, he became an atheist.

"So what do I do? I go to work for the city for shit pay and I'm up to my elbows in blood and guts. And now this. What a disappointment I am to her." He watched the lieutenant's men as they danced gingerly around the body, taking pictures, chalking the outline of the corpse, dusting for prints. A shudder of vague fears and discontentment shivered his body. "We've got to handle this right, you and I. We're the only ones who can right now, not because of any great abilities that we possess, though I'm sure we can hold our own against the competition, but because this damn thing's been dumped right in our laps. Neither of us asked for these murders: they happened, that's all. And now we've got to straighten out the mess.

I prefer to think of what's happening as an intricate plot to confuse us by some murderous psycho with an IQ somewhere in the six figures who wants us to run off like anxious children hunting for ghosts. If that's the case, then we'll get him, sooner or later. We'll play out his chess game, discover the weak link in his strategy, and nab the bastard." Ender looked one final time at the twisted, mutilated corpse and his ears filled with the noise of flies buzzing around the caking, extruded organs. "If that's not the case, then what can I say? We do what we can. Maybe we should take Rothstein's advice and get ourselves a sorcerer.

Fedorson stood silently watching swirls of acrid blue smoke from his stogie rise like divinatory incense toward the ceiling far above him.

Ender's voice trailed off: "A sorcerer that's on our side . . ."

Ender stayed with the lieutenant until late in the evening, searching the dockside for possible witnesses and listening in as Fedorson interrogated those few who came forward to tell what they heard or saw. Which wasn't very much. A few men saw the victim enter the dock house with a boy and they, not thinking too much of it, never noticed when or if the boy left the area. A thorough search was conducted for a possible second body, but none was found. A few other men thought they heard some scuffling but, not wanting to get involved, ignored it and knew nothing more. Just bits and pieces that only served to confuse the situation.

Fedorson knew just one thing: he wanted to find the boy. Was he another victim, as yet undiscovered? Was he abducted? Was he a witness to the crime who got away and was trembling somewhere in a dark alley or crash pad, half out of his mind with fear? Or did he know nothing? Had he and the victim finished with each other and parted before the murder had occurred? Fedorson thought that unlikely: the timing was just too close between the entry of the man and boy into the dock house and the discovery of the body. But who could tell? The search for witnesses dragged on.

When at last a possible eyewitness was found who thought he could describe the boy, the lieutenant sent him downtown to a police artist and headed uptown, himself, for some much needed sleep. Ender thought to do the same, but first headed downtown to the police stables on Varick Street. He identified himself as an assistant DA and asked to speak to the man most expert in the matter of horses. An officer indicated Patrolman Hemel who was just in the process of grooming a horse in one of the back stalls. "There are others who might have logged more time with horses while in the department," the officer said, "but, for my money, nobody here knows more about them than Hemel. He's a displaced farmboy, you see. Grew up with the animals."

Ender found Hemel in the stall with the horse, humming to himself, whispering confidences to the silent beast, currying its sleek hide.

"Excuse me," interrupted Ender, "I've been told that when it comes to horses you're the man to see around here."

Hemel looked up from his work with a surprised smile on his face. He was tall, lean, and boyish, his young face framed by longish sandy hair cut in the fashion known unofficially as cop-hip.

"I'm from the DA's office," continued Ender, "and I'm hoping you can help me out with a case I'm handling."

"Well, sure," smiled Hemel, his large eyes eager and cooperative. "I'd be glad to help you out if I can."

"I'd really appreciate it," said Ender, and he produced a blowup of the photograph of the smear of blood found beside the dead girl's body that he had been particularly curious about. "Take a look at this, and tell me if you can identify the rather oddly shaped indentation in the bloodstain."

Hemel put aside his currycombs and gazed sharply at the photograph.

"I'm just a city slicker," smiled Ender as the officer studied the picture, "and I don't know shit from Shinola about horses, except that I know not to bet on them, and I'm just working on a hunch, sort of whistling in the dark, you see, and I thought you might be able to help me out."

"Where was this picture taken?" Hemel finally asked.

"Central Park. Near the body of a murdered girl."

"Jesus. That's a shame. Well, if you were wondering if maybe that print was made by a horse, your hunch is correct."

Ender's face clouded at this knowledge. "My hunch may have been right but that doesn't make me any happier. But tell me, why is that print so different from the typical horseprint that you see in westerns? It's certainly not obvious to me at a glance that a horse of some sort stepped on that bloodstain."

"Well, Mr. Ender, that's because whatever horse made that print was unshod."

Ender's eyes widened. "Unshod? Damn, so that's it! I knew there was something strange about it."

"That's not all that's strange about it," cautioned Hemel. "In the first place, if this picture was taken in Central Park, well, there just aren't any unshod horses running around there. I mean the cops and the stables are the only ones who use the park and the riding paths, and there's just no way an unshod horse gets out into the park."

"What about private owners who board their horses in the city?"

"Listen, Mr. Ender, if you go to all the expense of buying and boarding a horse in Manhattan, you just don't take the chance of letting it get crippled by riding it around without shoes. When do you think the print was made, I mean, what time of day?"

"Last night, sometime after midnight and probably well before dawn."

"There, see what I mean? If you're crazy enough to ride your horse unshod in Central Park, well, you still don't do it in the dark. This is really strange."

Ender sighed. "You're telling me? Well, thanks so much for your help."

"There's another thing, Mr. Ender. This print was made by a horse, alright. I can tell that even though it's not the clearest imprint in the world and I really don't have any frame of reference in the photo to determine its size. But there's something strange about it, something I just can't put my finger on at the moment, you know what I mean? Like the width of the bony ridge doesn't correspond to the sharpness of the curve of the hoof in a way that's familiar to me from the various breeds with which I've had experience. It's got something of the mustang about it in curvature, you see, and yet the depth of the impression and the width of the ridge could only come from some kind of larger horse like an Andalusian or Arabian."

"That figures," commented Ender sardonically. "Nothing's coming out plain and simple for me today. But you're sure it's a horse?"

"Yes sir, damn sure," smiled the officer. "Of some kind."

While Ender was questioning Hemel on the west side of town, Adrian McConnelly's secretary was just filing away the last of a large batch of correspondence that she knew McConnelly was desperate to clear up before the office was closed for the night. The poor man was still locked in his office like a monk in his cell, analyzing reports from his distributors and trying to work out a shipment schedule before they were flooded by holiday orders.

Miss Riordan admired her boss. She had been his right hand for over nine years and was well aware of how hard he worked to earn the millions that he had accrued. Some people thought that being rich meant being either just plain lucky or just plain crooked. She knew better because Mr. McConnelly had shown her differently. He was such a hard worker, away from home all the time, keeping long hours at the office, making sure that every single facet of his distillery empire was personally guided by his own inimitable genius. He trusted his managers and advisors but only up to a point. He wanted no surprises in his business, no disguised losses that might indicate an embezzlement, no turns of fortune that he could avert with prior knowledge.

And if all that wasn't enough, Mr. McConnelly had had a row with his son that had caused him to storm into his office this morning in a most uncustomarily uncivil manner, cursing the burden of being a father. The poor, poor man. As if he hadn't enough problems, now he had to worry about his son turning against him. She was surprised at the boy. He had always seemed a most quiet and courteous lad, with a shy demeanor and a proper old-fashioned upbringing.

The last manila folder was laid carefully in its place. She looked at her watch and saw that it was well after nine. "Why do you do it?" her friend Dorothy would be asking her when she got home tonight. Somehow Dorothy couldn't understand that she didn't resent the long hours her employer required of her. Well past her prime of life, she knew there was nothing else waiting for her out there in the big lonely city. As she rubbed lotion into her hands, she looked out at the Manhattan skyline from her vantage point of the fifty-fourth floor. The night was clear and appeared unseasonably crisp, with all the millions of lights calling out to her, tempting her with obscure dreams of a hidden and inaccessible world of excitement and glamor. No, acknowledging the truth with a strange, tingling warmth in her heart, she knew that her purpose in life was to be ever diligent and hard-working by the side of her employer, without requiring gratitude, appreciation, or even the simplest of kind words. Dorothy teased her about her sense of responsibility to McConnelly, calling it love, or at the very least a dangerous and unhealthy infatuation, doomed to eternal frustration. Let her think that way. Let her criticize an aging friend's tenuous hold on life. Miss Riordan knew what was what with her life and would continue to act accordingly.

"Mr. McConnelly," she called into the intercom, "I've completed the paperwork and filing for the Dorset merger. Is there anything else I can do for you before I leave?"

"Miss Riordan," responded a rather distant, preoccupied, metallic voice. "I had no idea that you were still here. No, no, there's nothing more for you tonight. Go home, get some sleep, we both have a very busy day tomorrow. In fact, since I will be here for a while longer, let me have my car brought around and I'll have William escort you to your apartment."

Miss Riordan's eyes widened and her heart thrilled with

her employer's unlooked-for magnanimity. "O no, sir, I couldn't let you do that. I'll just take a cab—"

"Nonsense," retorted the voice in the intercom. "It's been a very trying day for both of us, I daresay. I insist that William take you home. I shan't be able to rest easy thinking that you are out alone at this hour of night."

"But, sir, I often leave this late and there's really no trouble about my getting home. I'll be perfectly safe."

"No more discussion, Miss Riordan. I'm calling William now and he'll be right up."

Imperiously, the intercom snapped into silence. A broad smile crossed Miss Riordan's face as she thought of the expensive limousine that was being summoned, just for her, to see her home in. What a fine man, what a fine and considerate employer, Mr. McConnelly was. Some people might mistake him for being cold and unfeeling but that was because they didn't know how to handle him. They didn't know how to earn his respect with hard work and devotion. As she arranged her purse and her hair, she started humming to herself. She hoped that Dorothy would happen, by chance, to pass the front door of her building as she was emerging from the back seat of the limo. Then maybe she'd understand and shut up.

Suddenly, the silence of the night was shattered by a resounding cracking of wood from Mr. McConnelly's office followed by a strange, horrifying sound, somewhat like a throaty whine or growl. Then McConnelly began to scream, bloodcurdling screams, calling for help, straining to force desperate words from his throat which sounded as if he were beginning to gasp and chortle from relentless strangulation.

"Mr. McConnelly! What's the matter? What's happening in there?"

She pounded on his office door, which was locked from within, and shouted to him at the top of her lungs. The only sounds emerging from within were those of a fierce struggle, the toppling of furniture, the growling, the tremulous groans of a man in dire agony, the smashing of glass. Then one final thunderous smash of glass and all was silent.

"O my God! O my God! Mr. McConnelly! Are you all right? Please, please answer me, let me in, I'll help you!"

She hastily put in an emergency call to the police department, but mere seconds after she hung up William arrived to escort her to the car. He found her weeping and hysterical.

"O William, hurry, hurry, he's in there! It sounded like someone broke into his office and was hurting him! Hurry! See if he's all right. He doesn't answer me. O God, I'm sure he's hurt, maybe dying!"

William was a strapping red-haired Irishman, fully six-foot four, who also served McConnelly in the capacity of bodyguard. He threw all his weight against the inner office door, smashing it inward, fracturing the lock and the doorframe.

He stood like a behemoth before a tableau of total chaos and rampant destruction. The room looked as if a wrecking ball had missed its mark and plunged headlong into McConnelly's private office. The heavy mahogany desk was overturned, the books torn from their shelves, papers scattered all over the floor, and a chill wind was coursing through the office from a huge hole which had been smashed through the thermopane picture window. There was fresh blood glistening on the walls and the floor. A door toward the rear of the office was lying in pieces on the floor. It was the door to a somewhat clandestine passageway which led out of the building and had been installed by McConnelly as an extra precaution against fire. It had been violently ripped from its hinges.

Both William and Miss Riordan stared at the destruction in shock and horror. Rapid nightwinds swirled the spilled papers and Miss Riordan's dress. McConnelly's body was nowhere to be seen.

14

Benedictus qui venit
in nomine Domini.
Hosanna in excelsis.

Strains of the holy music rose like embattled legions against the deafness of eternity. Waves of medieval polyphony billowed off the cool granite of the nave interior, urging the metaphor of God out upon the world through the pores of the stone like a sacred sweat.

Sanctus, sanctus, sanctus,
Dominus Deus Sabaoth.
Pleni sunt caeli et terra
gloria tua.
Hosanna in excelsis.

The limpid voices of the choir in rehearsal wove an invisible fabric of harmony that floated down like a silken net upon Jade and the empty pews. The choirmaster's delicate fingers made slow, rhythmic passes in the air while his sharp eyes followed the spangling of notes laid out before him, his brow furrowed with creative intensity.

It was not surprising to Jade that he should feel uncomfortable in the back row of the cathedral, bathed in the resonant strains of the Ambrosian chant. Devotional music always reminded him that, to his regret, he could not make that "leap of faith" necessary to partake of the joy which had inspired the musical poets to create such beautiful and mystical sounds. While he could, of course, enjoy the luxuriant chords of sound on a shallower level, it was the ecstasy provoking the creation of it that he craved and which eluded him. There was a poetry in the universe that he felt he had once grasped, perhaps in the distant years of his early youth, but which was now lost to him. He had followed the ineluctable course of human growth, had experienced the vacant senselessness of institutions, had come to know many people and seen their ugliness and cruelty, and had been broken on the wheel of many sorrows. So that nascent poetry grew fainter to him as he grew older, gradually becoming the wistful stuff of fairy tales rather than a commanding and irresistible presence.

What did surprise Jade was that suddenly this morning the music spoke to him differently than it ever had before. There seemed to be a silent voice speaking to his mind through the intricate fabric of the music saying, "For long enough have I been a reproach to you. You are aware of your emptiness and further reproach would be sterile and tedious. Now I shall leap to you, brimming with love, without prior commitment of your devotion. I shall teach you by my example how you must radiate your love to me. Be at ease and be joyful."

And suddenly the music descended upon him like a caress. He settled back in the pew smiling, amazed, eager to welcome this music that had so generously accepted him as a friend. Or was it as a lover, too? His heart quickened ever so slightly as the music throbbed and blended around him.

"You pick the damnedest places to meet," said a voice close to him on his left. It was Needham in his Stock Exchange togs. He slumped quickly into the pew, placing his attaché case between himself and Jade.

Needham was a small man, lean and hard, whose facial flesh was burnt-out and shrivelled from drugs and aristocratic hedonism. He had made a bundle in the straight world of high finance but his real wealth came from the cocaine traffic. Jade and he had first met on a Route 80 roadside in the middle of Pennsylvania farm country. Needham's Harley had spewed out some crankcase bolts and Jade had pulled his bike over to lend a hand. After a few hard hours of sweat, cut fingers, and a crankcase oil bath, the two had finally fixed the Harley and Needham, out of gratitude, treated Jade to a night at the nearest Holiday Inn. Jade learned of Needham's special interest in coke and Needham learned that Jade had close contacts with many very wealthy women who had many wealthy friends, all of them great partiers. A lucrative business relationship between the two seemed inevitable.

Jade's mind clung to the strains of music in spite of Needham's presence. He sat impassively in the pew absorbed in the rhythm and unison by which the mouths of the choir opened and shut, resembling to Jade a mythic hundred-headed beast paying homage to great Zeus.

Needham was annoyed at Jade's impassivity. "The least you could've done was pick a church that wasn't rehearsing for a funeral."

"That's not death music, Needham. That's praise for God."

"Yeah? Well, I can do without hearing that kind of praise more than once in a lifetime, thank you. It gives me the fucking creeps."

"You've got a guilty conscience. That's why the music scares you."

"O is that so? Thanks, doc. Don't forget to send your bill to my office. And don't hold your breath waiting for me to pay it."

Jade smiled. Without taking his eyes off the choir, he took a thick envelope out of his pocket and handed it over to Needham. Needham opened his attaché case, placed the envelope inside, and withdrew a small box wrapped in brown paper. He handed the box to Jade who promptly stuffed it in his knapsack. His attention, diverted only briefly, returned to the choir.

"Well, I can see you're not fit to bullshit with today," said Needham a bit testily. "I might as well head back downtown before this music makes me sick." He looked at Jade's profile, rigid against the backdrop of a distant, intricate stained-glass window. "Are you feeling okay?"

Jade looked at him curiously, an odd smile playing across his face. "You sound as if you're really concerned."

Needham sucked in his worn cheeks and widened his eyes in boyish surprise. "Hey, man, I got a vested interest in you. Don't you realize that? Besides, I'm old-fashioned in my own decadent way. I worry about my friends."

Jade was irritated by Needham's concern. "I don't need anyone to watch out for me. Just like you don't need anyone to tell you about your conscience."

"Well, if that's the way you want it, that's fine with me. It's just that you look like you've been doing too much snow. Or not enough."

"I'll watch myself in the future."

Needham snapped his attaché case shut and rose to his feet. "Yeah, Jade, you do that. 'Cause you'll be the only one."

Jade heard the clicking of his heels soften and disappear as he headed out of the church. Finally the chant ended and the choristers dispersed for coffee and mutual criticism. The spell of the music was broken, leaving Jade oddly buoyant. He looked at the icons in their flowing granite robes lining the nave interior. Their blind eyes stared out at nothing, yet, to Jade, they all seemed poised to turn to him and smile. Jade felt that their stone minds shared in the profundity of the music that had . affected him so deeply.

"Can you speak to me, stones?" Jade whispered, cautiously and self-consciously. "I know you want to say something. Speak to me like the music did."

One icon in particular drew Jade's eyes: St. George, armored, his hair falling resplendent to his shoulders in stone curls, leaning on a long spear that was thrust deeply into the spurting stone neck of a dragon. The blind eyes of the icon were intent upon the dragon's death throes. Not the music nor the glitter of the altar nor the robes of the ministers, nor even the postures of holy revery assumed by its fellow icons could distract the saint from the kill. The fact that it was only made of carved stone didn't seem to diminish the icon's intensity in fulfilling its mission. For a terrifying moment Jade was flooded with a great fear that the icon would tire and give over its spear thrust, and the dragon would rise from the wall with a serpentine slither and a horrendous growl and crawl out onto the street once more to roam the world. With a mighty effort he shook himself from his fear by wrenching his eyes away from the icon, looking down into the darkness of his lap.

And that was when Jade's eyes inadvertently met the fiery, outraged eyes of the jade unicorn that hung around his neck. The demonic horn was poised to thrust at his throat.

When it was obvious that the choir wasn't going to return, Jade draped his knapsack over his shoulders and walked solemnly out of the church. Had he turned around and looked behind him, he would have seen a silent figure rise from a front-row pew, gazing after him, that slowly followed his retreating form to the street outside the church. It was an old man, a very old man with a face scored and seamed with countless wrinkles. He was rather small, with a bushy snow white beard and long, flowing white hair that cascaded like fine platinum webbing around his shoulders. Although his face gave the appearance of great age, his pale blue eyes sparkled with humor and vitality and his body moved with sleek, impressive vigor. In his right hand he hefted a thick, very heavy and intricately carved walking stick made of glossy ebony. In spite of the weight of the stick, which would have given pause to the most brash and energetic twenty-year-old, the old man swung it negligently at his side as if it weighed nothing. The carved stick was a cornucopia of finely detailed heads and torsos, billowing and swirling out of the ebony core like things alive. Woven among the energetic postures of the carvings were strange symbols, like alien letters or some bizarre form of hieroglyphics.

The old man stared after Jade, a smile of somber joy playing across his face.

15

ENDER threw himself on his bed fully clothed. In spite of the warmth of the summer night, his hands and feet were chilled, a metallic chill that he couldn't shake. In the darkness he kicked off his shoes and rubbed his hands together vigorously. No luck.

There were no meetings now, no running around town from corpse to corpse, no glaring morgue lights, no politicians to argue with or weeping fathers to console. Just memories. He was alone in the darkness with those memories.

Some vague light filtered into his bedroom from the Manhattan neon glitter, turning his furniture into shadowy protean blobs of gray. Tonight Ender's tired and troubled mind distinguished among the accustomed gray and slate patterns a sinister electric trembling, as if something moved in the shadows every time he felt the approach of peace.

He closed his eyes and rubbed his palm down along his forehead, over his eyes, and across the bridge of his nose, massaging the tension from his head. His chilled fingers, however, startled the skin of his face and he was alarmed to think that his own touch was like that of an animated corpse. He gasped, pulling his hand off his face.

It was no good, this darkness and solitude. All he did was think of that long day's events, running them back and forth in his mind, struggling to acclimate his soul to the horror so that he could fight it and be of some use in getting to the bottom of the grotesque mystery. Welles's tears weighed heavily on his mind: that tall, elegant man reduced to bawling and shivering over the death of his daughter. And the reporter Peale's rat's eyes. Trouble there, lots of trouble. And the crumbled westside dock house, with the painted warnings and the sullen men with cunning eyes who had stood quietly in the background watching the police work.

And the corpses. He refused to permit his mind's eye to reassert the gory details in their entirety and his mental censors eagerly acquiesced in this decision. Still, images of the girl's fine blond hair and the smiling photo of her that Brock had shown him floated in his mind. And the elegant manicure of the black man's fingernails, glistening in contrast to the worm-eaten wooden planks on which the body lay sprawled. These pretty, refined images symbolized for him in some acceptable form the unspeakable horror that generated them.

Then the flies intruded themselves, like insolent demons. The flies that hovered and buzzed over the spilled guts of both corpses, preferring steaming, bloody tripes to skin or firmer meat.

To them the horror was a feast.

He squinted his eyes hard, straining to push further nightmares from him. But the terror of the vision of the flies lurched his bladder. He had to take a wicked piss. He hadn't taken a piss all day; there hadn't been time. Now, stretched out on the bed in the darkness he had to take a piss real bad. But to do so meant rising and walking through the terrors of the moving shadows in his bedroom. He was scared to move and the urgency in his bladder grew worse. He opened his eyes and stared at the shadows, the nighttime curves of his bureau and his mirror and the soft chair in which he did most of his reading. All familiar, all benign, all tempting him to his feet with their unspoken goodwill so that he could take a piss.

But it was almost worth it to Ender to piss in the bed all over himself and his clothes and the bedsheets so as not to have to walk to the bathroom.

What fucking childishness, he thought to himself. He

hadn't been this scared since that one Halloween night so many years ago when he and his brother were kids. They had lived in a house then, in the suburbs. Their father, for a lark, bought a ghost costume and went dancing and prancing for them in the driveway. Their mom brought them to the window to look out and they both stared in mute fascination and giddy terror. Then Ender finally tore himself away from the window and, without giving his mother a chance to stop him, ran downstairs to the dining room, thinking to alert his father to the presence of the ghost. What he didn't know was that his father had, in the meantime, reentered the house and was standing in the darkened dining room trying to take off his costume. The little boy flew into the room calling for his father and saw the ghost in the darkness, not ten feet from him, weirdly waving its arms and undulating its whiteness. The boy swallowed his voice, aghast at the figure, and stopped his forward momentum by throwing himself on the floor and crawling out of the room, clutching the carpet with his fingernails, his eyes streaming tears and his little heart pounding with terror.

Ender laughed to himself at that memory of his youth and shook himself free of his paralysis. None too soon. The golden stream of urine spilled into the toilet in a high arc.

When he returned to the bed, he felt more at ease with the night and the silence and the darkness and the shadowy shapes after that mental catharsis. His breathing eased, his limbs seemed to warm up, he was more in control of his thoughts. He began to confront the memories of the day's events as a professional, coolly, analytically.

He lay back down on the bed in the darkness and eased the tenseness out of his breathing. He followed the rise and fall of his lungs with careful attention, regulating its rhythm, easing the jerky, gasping stiffness from his diaphragm. Then his analytical mind focused on the most salient image of the day's events, what could be seen as the nexus of the mystery: the image in the eyes of the victims.

The images in the six eyes of the three victims were identical: a pupil-sized head—a centaur's face with a unicorn's horn yet—floating in the glossy green of the mysterious occlusion. The magnifying glass revealed the fine details of the image, the bony chiseling of the face, the wild curling of the hair, and the glistening spiral sharpness of the bone that protruded menacingly from the forehead to a distance which Ender judged in relative terms to have been about eighteen inches.

He suddenly remembered what Rothstein had said about the stab wounds in the girl's body, that they were cylindrical like the wound from a rapier and not slash wounds like those caused by the thin blade of an ordinary knife. The horn? A unicorn's horn?

Absurd.

And the hoofprint? Hemel couldn't identify the breed. Though how could one man know all the breeds of horses and be expected to recognize each one, especially with only a fragment visible in a photograph? It was probably some early morning rider in the park who first stumbled on the body and panicked when he saw it.

But then how to explain the eyes?

He could go on like this all night, back and forth, and never get any sleep. A few more hours of worsening fatigue and he'd be ready to believe anything. He could just see himself explaining to the mayor and the commissioner that a wild unicorn was on the loose in Manhattan, killing and mutilating everybody in its path. Sure, they'd mark that down in their day's calendar notation: "Saw Ender today. Tried to give us some story about a supernatural killer stalking the city in the form of a unicorn. Stabs people to death and pulls out their balls. This guy must be removed from the payroll. Quickly!" End of notation.

He stretched out in the darkness, rubbing his hands and feet into the softness of the bed and trying to ease the tension from his body by relaxing his muscles. What was that trick, now? Flex your toes tightly, hold it, then relax completely. Then the ankle. Then the calf. All the way up to your goddamn ears.

A philosophical problem: should concrete evidence, the external nature of which is indisputable and corroborated by impartial observers, be discounted out of hand simply because the analytical conclusion to which it leads seems utterly fantastic? His mind was trained to accept solutions to trains of inquiry even though they were painful or personally repugnant to him. But . . . supernatural?

Another explanation. Something natural. Some well-contrived plot deliberately laid out to mislead the police. A series of bizarre distractions perhaps to link one special crime with a random series of others.

Holmes's hound of the Baskervilles. The phosphorescent lights in the night.

Could it be the Welles girl? The daughter of a diplomat. A terrorist group, perhaps. Get at her father? If so, they played their hand a bit too strongly. They'd have no hold on him now. An error? And now they had to keep on to cover it up?

The old wino, maybe. More to him than meets the eye?

But that bastard wasn't even wounded. Some kind of trauma, a heart attack.

And why wasn't that girl asleep in her room? Why was she in the park that late at night? And apparently alone, except for her killer, or else the police would've heard something about the incident from whoever was with her and escaped. Another body maybe? Kidnaped, buried, burned? Not likely.

Of course nothing about this case was likely.

And the guy in the dock house. Cruises a young boy in front of witnesses, enters the area in which the murder occurs, and never comes out alive. And the kid disappears. Vanishes.

Damn. Just five minutes alone with that boy, ask him some questions.

Flex the thigh, hold, relax.

What's Fedorson doing right now to fall asleep?

A boy couldn't have committed the crime. No one could really. Pull a larger man's body apart like that. Yeah, of course anyone can stab anybody else. But pull their bodies apart?

More than one killer at a time? O sure. Great idea. They just grab on to different parts of the body and run in opposite directions. Can't even find traces of one killer, now try for two.

Her arm, tossed like that into the bushes. Like a piece of garbage, a Kleenex or a paper cup.

Then there's the sperm. Greenish semen, three-tailed

sperm. Figure that one out. How can that be faked? Rothstein would've detected any inorganic trickery. Some idea, though, if it is a con. Like to meet the man who came up with that one.

Pectorals next, never had much in the pectoral department. Flex . . . okay.

I don't think this relaxation shit works.

That face in the eyes. A centaur's face really, angry, brutal, shaggy like a satyr. With a horn. Horsey face too. Like a man, like a horse.

Equus.

Damn good play. Lots of primitive energy.

That's just great. Something's running around town shtupping people right and left, three in one day, and I'm playing theater critic.

That old superstition, what was it? Wait, wait—yeah, that a murderer's image lingers in the eyes of his victim. To condemn him. Bring him to justice.

Wish it were true. Then maybe people wouldn't be so quick to . . .

Could it be?

Nah. If something like that were running around town, we wouldn't have to wait for it to kill somebody to hear about it.

But something strange is running around. The sperm. The image in the eyes. The unshod hoofprint in the blood. The brute strength and ferocity evident in each attack.

Let's assume it is some creature, maybe one that even looks like the face found in the eyes. God forgive me for this assumption but let's play it out.

Flex neck, hold—hold—okay.

Whatever it is sneaks up on its victims, tears them apart, then disappears without a trace. How?

Okay, Abe, you made the first assumption, now flow with it. If it's supernatural, then anything's possible. Go with the current then. So it disappears.

Invisible? It creeps up on its victim then turns invisible and runs away.

Great. For that I went to law school. I mean, this is Manhattan, man. There's barely enough room for the people, no less an invisible unicorn walking around the streets. Somebody'd be sure to bump into it or drive into it or be trampled by an invisible presence fleeing from the noise of the traffic. Or something.

An invisible unicorn. I must be out of my mind.

But then so's Fedorson. And Rothstein.

Maybe it becomes invisible and insubstantial. Like Phantom Girl in the old Legion of Super Heroes. My comic book days.

Wait, wait . . . who else was it? Chameleon Boy. The boy who could change his shape into anything.

The muscles of Ender's neck involuntarily stiffened.

It comes as something ordinary, a man, a woman, then changes into whatever it is and kills, then changes back again. No trace. No complications.

And no luck of ever convincing anybody else of this ridiculous idea. Keep it to myself. Back to the terrorist conspiracy theory.

But there was that boy on the pier, the one that couldn't be found . . .

Forget it, man. It's crazy.

I bet that guy Peale'd like it, though. Maybe I'll phone him anonymously. Secret meeting. Make some extra money. Cash in plain brown wrapper.

Maybe that stretching is working. Can't hold on to my thoughts . . . dropping off . . . No.

Why, though? Why those victims? Nothing in common: a little girl, wino, gay guy. Nothing in common.

Sure?

Find the motive, all murders have a motive, even the crazy ones have a crazy motive. Why, then?

Nonsense, all this. Enough. Tomorrow . . .

Thick, gummy atmosphere. Choking.

Yes, yes, remember: that other dream, the night before. Terrifying.

Shadows in the vapors, moving, slowly moving but faster than me. Gestures, shades, like flutter of batwings. Hollow resonant growls. High-pitched shrieks. Get out of here.

Everything's a sickly yellow: the vapor, the soupy slush

clinging like mucus to my legs, even my skin, a jaundiced, sickly yellow.

Same dream, man. Not another night like that one. Please.

Screeching, howling shadows coming closer. Louder. Run, man, run, pull those fucking legs out of the muck, run you bastard, got to get away, those howls have teeth behind them, big fucking teeth. Rip me apart.

If you dream you die, you really die. Right in your bed. Heart attack. Got to run.

Fresh air, too. If the shadow monsters don't get me, I'll choke to death anyway. Holding my breath, can't hold much longer and run too.

Nowhere to run to. Everything's the same. No directions, no up, no down. Tired, legs and arms feel like lead, slowing me more. Dizzy.

Ready to give up.

O God, those sounds. O God. No! I don't want to die. Cruel dream.

Wait. Up ahead. Oblong shadow in the fog. A door?

Three shadow figures: men sort of, stooping, passing through the door, flanking it. Huge men, black robes, masks. No faces.

No faces, yet I see their mouths. Like caverns. Stinking. Waiting for me.

O God, shit, shit, shit. Got to slow down now, nothing for my feet to grab, hold on to the air, doesn't it figure, now I'm really flying.

They're waiting for me, masked yet grinning, waiting to kill me. Even the shadow monsters behind me fled from them.

O please let me stop, I'm screaming, too fast, slipping, tumbling, falling right into their damn hands . . .

Shit. Slid past them, right into the doorway.

Dark tunnel. Tunnel slopes down. Slippery. Gaining momentum. Too many things working against me.

Dim light flickers. The walls around me are slimy stone. Subtle shine in the dim light.

A cave. A tunnel beneath the earth. Running along a tunnel beneath the earth. Flecks of sparkle.

Mica? Quartz? Jewels?

At least I can breathe. The air of a tomb, though: there's death in the air.

Up ahead another door lit by phosphors in the stone. Two figures flank it.

Shit. They're waiting for me. I know it.

Got to stop running, slow down, check this out.

Can't.

The one on the right: kind of short, like me, big square head, too big, square jaw and mouth, lifeless eyes. Ugly sonofabitch. In a black monk's robe.

Face reminds me . . . Yeah. The Queen of Hearts in *Alice*. Tenniel's drawings.

And he's got a spiked collar around his neck. A dog collar. Heavy chain shines in the phosphor light, hangs down his back, long chain, coils on the ground, thick, serpentine coils, glistening, trailing along the ground.

Ending in the other figure's hand.

Veiny, bony hand.

The other: a man, tall, gaunt, black monk's robe.

Face under the hood: cavernous, bony, ancient. Intense, commanding presence. He's the bossman. Watch out for that guy. Watch out where his eyes turn. Don't want to be controlled like that dim bulb on the leash.

Just keep my distance.

Uh oh. He's turning to face me. Slowly. So slowly.

It seems like an eternity.

No time for the social graces. Look down at my feet. At the stone floor. At the door. Anywhere, but not right in his eyes.

Why the fuck not? Who the hell is he anyway?

Watch that. He's doing that to me, making me ballsy, tough. Playing with my pride. He wants me to look. Careful, now. The motherfucker is smart.

Staring at his mouth now, those ugly thin black lips. Wants to draw my eyes higher. Tough shit, buddy. That's as high as I go.

Shit. Those lips, curling, trembling with rage. Lower lip twitching.

Won't this dream ever end? I'll shit in the bed. I just know it.

The free hand, the one without the leash: it's rising,

the long thin pointer outstretched, curling toward me. Beckoning. Come here now.

You've got some case, buddy. I'll stay right where I am, thank you.

Why's he smiling? Pretty teeth, though. Ugly lips, ugly face, but pretty teeth.

Pretty teeth, maybe. But a horrible smile.

Why's he smiling? I'm not moving.

Behind me: a noise. A low roar.

Getting louder. Quickly.

Shit. Behind me a flood of water, filling the tunnel, rushing at me, going to push me right into his arms.

What can I do? Where can I go?

His laughter echoes behind me. It fills the tunnel.

Damn. Knocking the shit out of me: pain, everything inside me's broken, spots in my eyes, rushing water all around me, lifting me, tossing me like cork, bouncing me off the cave walls, O God the pain, the endless pain.

I'm going to drown. I'm going to drown and I'm falling right into his clutches.

Keep my eyes closed.

Wait. I'm past him.

Right through the doorway. Spinning, dizzy, right through the doorway.

Still hear his laughter, louder than ever.

Everything's black, drowning, sinking down and down, endless.

O God, O God, O God.

Slammed flat on my back. Pain, probably crippled for life. Everything's black. But the water's draining. Slowly draining, a sucking noise, obscene and disgusting, like a wet fart only backwards.

Maybe I won't drown. No. My time's not up yet.

What the fuck? My office? I'm in my office? Flat on the floor in my office? Goddamn dream.

Not crippled, anyway. On my feet, soaking.

What's that in my chair, behind my desk? Facing away from me out the window.

Big mother. Must be over seven feet tall, judging from the size of its back and shoulders. Built like a brick shithouse. Muscles, bulging muscles so taut it makes its skin look too tight. Hairy back: thick tufts of coarse hair all over its back. Long, coarse hair hanging from its head to its shoulders. Huge hairy arms.

Shit. The room stinks like shit.

Stable shit. Horsehair all over its body and the room stinks like stable shit.

O God. Could it be . . .

Its head's nodding, lolling imbecilically from side to side. Taking its time. Just taking its time.

Don't turn around. Please, in the name of all that's holy, don't let that thing turn around.

It's turning around.

Rising from the chair, huge, dwarfing the window and the room, facing out over the city, huge, long, so very long beast's legs, furred like a satyr, coarse brown fur, stains of shit crisp in its fur, its naked rump spilling pungent brown pellets, all over the floor, the desk, facing out over the city, a low, resonant, growly rumbling emerging almost tenderly from its hidden face.

Still turning. Stop it please, O God, stop it.

I can't move.

There: the horn. Dagger sharp, a foot and a half ivory spiral, the first thing I see as it turns around.

No. No more.

The face: the shaggy human-equine face in the dead eyes.

Huge, the creature's so huge with its shaggy legs, broad muscular chest tufted with coarse hair, thick black horsepaps pendant for at least two inches among the tufts of chest hair, an impossibly long horsecock swaying obscenely from between its legs, thick and leathery with a slimy pink tip dribbling smegma from the foreskin.

Vomit. Got to vomit. And the horse-like distorted face opens in its bizarre version of a grin, showing its broad, flat horseteeth, continuing to growl.

To mock me.

Big soft brown eyes. Horse eyes. Tender.

Its horsecock stiffens slowly. Rising like a gloved forearm. Still grinning, the creature stares into my face, pushing me to the floor with the power of its will. Can't move. Must run out of there, back to the men in robes or the shadow monsters or the giants. Anything but not this creature.

Can't move.

Clutching at the floorboards with my fingernails to pull myself out of there. Just like that time when I was a child. My screams aren't stopping it and no one's coming to help me. Still I scream, I scream. Relentless. Mechanical. A siren, screaming, hopelessly, just screaming, screaming. That's all I can do, all that's left to me. The screams pulse from my throat like heaves of puke, violent, wrenching, unstoppable.

A strange resonant gong fills the room as the creature grins, stalking closer, slowly, its cock stiff and huge in its hand, its unshod hoofs slow and rhythmic, clacking like wooden blocks on the floor, slowly coming for me, taking its time, reveling in my terror and my screams, sucking every last vestige of horror and agony out of my soul.

Its head bends toward me, leveling its horn at my chest, its hot, husky breath fuming and stinking all around me. Screams, more screams and the gong seems louder, more insistent.

The creature stoops low over me, its horn inches away, wavering, an eager whinny-whine chilling my screaming soul . . .

No! No! Goddamn it, NO!

And Abe Ender shot bolt upright in his bed, bathed in cold sweat, the alarm clock clattering madly on the table by the side of the bed.

The assistant principal took Ender to Jenny Welles's homeroom teacher. Ender waited out in the hall because the classes had already started and he didn't want to make too much of a disturbance.

He was running late. After that nightmare, no wonder. It had taken at least twenty minutes for his heart to stop pounding in his chest. He reproached himself for letting this case get the better of him. Another nightmare like that and he'd be ready for the funny farm.

The assistant principal, a short, portly man, tapped Ender on the shoulder. Ender jumped, startled, his arms flailing outward from his side. Startled in turn, the assistant principal jumped.

"Mr. Ender! Are you all right?"

Ender sighed, rubbing his forehead. "Yes, yes. I'm very sorry. Bad dreams last night. You know how edgy they can leave you."

"Of course I do," said the assistant principal dabbing at his cheeks with a handkerchief. "Your line of work complicates things, I'm sure. Being involved all the time with crimes and criminals. Give anybody bad dreams."

"Yes, sir. You've got the picture."

The assistant principal gave him a knowing wink. "Unless, of course, it's a guilty conscience that's got you in its clutches. We all know how *those* dreams are."

"Well, unfortunately, my job doesn't leave me much time to do anything that I should feel guilty about. Will this Mrs. Uh—"

"Miss. Miss Cranny."

"Yes. Will Miss Cranny be out soon?"

"As soon as she finishes taking attendance. Why don't I leave you here? She'll be out in a couple of minutes and I do have a lot of work to do. First-of-the-morning business that really can't wait."

"Fine. Thank you so much for your help."

"No problem. Let me know if I can do anything else for you. Or the girl's family."

"I will. Certainly."

"Terrible thing, that business. It really makes you wonder."

"Yes. Yes, it does."

"She was such a charming girl."

"I'm sure."

"So much to live for. She was one of our better students, you know."

"No, I didn't know."

"A lot of promise. And she came from such a fine family."

"Yes, that's true. I've spoken to her father." Ender wondered when the assistant principal would be getting back to his important early morning work.

"A fine man. Such a tragedy. A real tragedy."

An uneasy pause.

"Well. Better be going now. You will let me know if I can be of further assistance to you, won't you?"

"Of course I will. You can count on it."

Finally, with a nod and a flourish of his polished bald head and a quick smile, the assistant principal scurried down the hall. Ender leaned against the wall shaking his head, both amused by the little man and trying to shatter the hold on his consciousness that the memories of last night's dream had. So goddamn vivid. He feared they'd cling to him all day.

Finally, Miss Cranny emerged from the classroom. She was a small, unsmiling old woman, her face a sour web of wrinkles dusted with face powder that gave her the look of an old, neglected corpse left exposed to the elements in an ancient, cracked, and dreary mausoleum. Just the kind of face Ender needed to make his day.

"You're Mr. Ender, I presume? From the district attorney's office?"

"Yes, ma'm, I am. I'm sorry that I have to take you away from your duties but I promise you I'll try to be brief. Is there someplace we can talk?"

"Of course. Please follow me." She led him to a small room down the hall, the teacher's lounge. This early in the morning it was deserted.

She seated herself across from Ender at a small table. "I can't for the life of me imagine what it is that I can tell a man from the district attorney's office that would be of any interest to him."

"Well, ma'm, to be perfectly truthful, I'm not sure myself. It's about a student of yours, Jennifer Welles."

"Oh, I see. I noticed that Jennifer was absent yesterday and is absent again today. I hope there's nothing wrong with the child."

"I'm afraid there is, Miss Cranny. You see, she was murdered the night before last, sometime around midnight. Her body was found early the next morning by the police in Central Park."

Miss Cranny blanched. Her old head swayed as if kicked senseless by a mule and Ender feared that the news of the child's death might precipitate another casualty. He rushed to her side.

"Are you all right, Miss Cranny? Can I get you anything?"

There was a somber pause while the old teacher tried

to compose herself. "Some water, please," she finally said. "Over there."

Ender ran to the water fountain and brought back a brimming paper cup. Miss Cranny drank delicately, then placed the cup on the table in front of her.

"I knew that the news would be a shock to you," Ender said. "I'm afraid that there's never an easy way to tell somebody something like that."

"I understand, Mr. Ender. I certainly don't envy you your job if it includes being the bearer of such sad news often."

"To be truthful with you, Miss Cranny, it's really not a part of my job. Jenny's death is, in a way, a special case and the police have brought in all sorts of special operatives to handle it."

Miss Cranny's hands hung limply at her sides and her eyes wandered helplessly to her lap. "O dear, how horrible. How utterly horrible." She looked up at Ender, her old eyes brimming with tears. "Who could do such a thing? Who could commit such a horrible crime? Are there such monsters walking the streets and can it be that the skies don't open and rain fire on them to rectify Nature's error in permitting them to be born?" Her shoulders began to heave with sobs and Ender placed his arm around them to soothe and comfort her. "She was such a good child. Never any trouble. So well spoken and intelligent. In all my years as a teacher, Mr. Ender, I have made it a point not to single out any child for special praise or blame. To me they all possess unlimited potential, regardless of what I hear about them from other teachers or parents. It's not easy, you must understand, to resist the temptation to wax poetic about special children with special gifts that you recognize five minutes after they enter your classroom. But I do resist that temptation. And Jennifer was one of those children who stretched my powers of resistance to the limit." She withdrew a Kleenex from her handbag and pressed it against her eyes, gingerly. "Please, Mr. Ender, how can I help you?"

"There are some puzzling aspects to this case that you might be able to shed some light on, Miss Cranny. Her father assures us that she was safely tucked away in bed at her regular bedtime the night before last, sometime around ten o'clock. Yet, two hours later she was murdered in Central Park. Our experts are as certain as they can be that the park was, indeed, the scene of the murder. The body was not transported from elsewhere. So that leaves me with the question of what she was doing in Central Park that late at night.

"Now, I'd tend to think that either she was forcibly removed from her apartment or she sneaked out of the house without her father's knowledge. At this point in time it seems unlikely that the former possibility was the one that occurred, although we're still checking it out. After all, her father was there in the house with the serving staff. It is unlikely that she could have been kidnaped without someone being alerted. Possible, though unlikely. It's also possible that someone on the staff was involved in her killing. We're checking all that out. But I'd like to examine the other possibility for a moment. Let's suppose she did sneak out of her house. Now, I remember as a kid that when I sneaked out of the house it was always to meet somebody. A group of guys for a joyride or a smoke, or a girl rumored to be 'fast' among my parents and their friends. I'm sure you know what I mean."

"Indeed, Mr. Ender. I certainly do. And let me assure you from the outset that Jennifer was not the kind of child to go sneaking around the streets of New York. Her father's an extremely kind man and he doted on his daughter. Besides being a joy of a child, she was also the only link the poor man had to his dead wife. She would have had no reason to keep her activities from him. He's not the kind of man to go into rages and beat her. He couldn't harm a fly, much less his daughter. Poor Mr. Welles. He must be shattered by this. Absolutely shattered."

"Yes, Miss Cranny, he is taking it hard. But he's drawing on incredible reserves of strength to help us catch her killer. Now, can you tell me if she had any special group of friends, girls or boys, or some secret girls' club that might have prompted her to sneak out of her house?"

"Mr. Ender, I assure you that Jennifer . . ."

She paused as if struck by an unbelievable idea.

"Yes, Miss Cranny?"

"One minute please. A minute. I—I must think this out before I do anyone a grave injustice."

Cautious, careful lady, thought Ender to himself. Good. "Mr. Welles recalled a young boy she had been keeping company with for the last few months. He only saw him on occasion and couldn't recall his name. Could he be the one you're thinking of?"

A long pause. "Yes, Mr. Ender. He's the one I was thinking of. But I'm sure he had nothing to do with her death."

"You're probably right, Miss Cranny. But he might've seen something or heard something that can lead us to the killer. What's his name?"

"Marco McConnelly."

"And what can you tell me about him?"

"I had him as a pupil two years ago. He's a fine boy, very intelligent and extremely well-bred. He comes from a very wealthy family, as do most of the students in this school. His father is a self-made millionaire, the owner of an international distillery or something."

"And just what kind of relationship did he and the Welles girl have?"

"Please remember, Mr. Ender, that they're only children. We can't think of any relationship between them in the same terms in which we think of adult relationships. Over the last few months—dating, I think, from sometime last spring—the two of them began to develop a fondness for each other. I personally felt that perhaps their involvement with each other was becoming too intense for young people their age. You know fifteen-year-old boys, Mr. Ender. Their bodies and all the new hormones splashing around in their systems sometimes take away their good sense and render ineffective much of the cautionary guidance of their parents. Yes, I was concerned about all the time they spent together: after school, in the lunchroom, between classes. I was concerned for both of them, but mostly for Jennifer because girls of her age can be swept up into a situation that gets out of hand and then there's trouble. And it is something of a status symbol to a girl her age to be seeing an upperclassman." She paused, her eyes flowing freely again, her old mouth working into a tender, quick smile. "How absurd to be talking like this about the two of them, relationships and all that. Upperclassman. He's fifteen years old. A child."

She composed herself with a visible effort: a deep intake of breath and a stiffening of her shoulders. "But there was no way in which I could fault them for their feelings for one another. They're precocious children, quite mature for their ages really. They spent their time together, as far as I could tell, pursuing all sorts of aesthetic and intellectual interests. They'd often spend their lunch periods on the school terrace reading poetry to each other. Sometimes when I had lunch duty I'd eavesdrop, not so that they'd know it of course, and I'd be entertained as much as they were by the readings. A lot of Romantic poets: Keats, Shelley, and especially Byron. Great poetry. And they seemed to love it. It gave me such great pleasure to listen to them. You can imagine how rare it is for children that age to take such an interest in affairs of the mind and the spirit. And the boy, Marco, can certainly read such poetry with eloquence. I suppose it's because he was sharing it with someone he cared for. But when his soft, gentle voice carried with it all those powerful images and rhythms, well, he had the power to send all of us back to our youth."

She paused a moment in wistful revery, recalling their serious eyes and the intensity of their passionate voices. "And they didn't frequent the usual kids' hangouts. No, from what they happened to tell me on occasion, they spent a lot of time in museums and admiring the horticulture of our local parks. Jennifer particularly had a great interest in plants. Whenever she has a science project to do for me or for another teacher, she usually chooses one involving some aspect of botany . . . She has seedlings sprouted right now in class for some demonstration she's contrived to show the effects of auxins on plant development."

"Auxins? That's pretty advanced stuff."

"She is . . . was an advanced child."

"And do you think that Central Park might be a favorite meeting place for them? I mean, a place they'd go to talk and read."

"Mr. Ender, isn't Central Park like that for everybody who lives in Manhattan? I know they enjoyed the park and had no fears about it. Children don't think in the same jaded and cynical terms that old folks like me tend to be caught up in."

"Miss Cranny, you do yourself an injustice. I find nothing jaded or cynical about you."

"You're kind, Mr. Ender. But I feel the callousness of age growing within me. That's why I've devoted so much of my life to teaching these young children. They keep my thought processes and my attitudes flexible and well oiled, if you know what I mean. I try to guide them, instruct them, but even more importantly, learn from them. I try to see myself with their young eyes: am I getting crotchety and dogmatic? Can I still encourage the remarkable creativity that stems from naive innocence and the total disregard of the fact that there are certain standard and traditional ways of looking at the world?" She sighed, looking down into her lap. "Still, the years catch up to you. So many of your own dreams have been shattered that you begin to think that the children would be better off if you stripped them of their illusions so that the cruel world outside wouldn't be able to scar them as deeply when they grow up to confront it."

She twisted a Kleenex in the fingers of her spotted hands. "But when you see children like Jennifer and Marco enjoying themselves together in the ways that they did, you can't help feeling that maybe there is some hope that a new generation will rise to somehow clean all the accumulated societal filth that has gathered over the ages. I never felt there was any real harm in what the two of them were doing together and I saw there were many positive aspects of their relationship. So I said nothing to anybody and buried my small worries within myself. Perhaps I was wrong."

"No, Miss Cranny. Under the circumstances you did the right thing. Don't start trying to blame yourself for any part of this damned misfortune. I can assure you that the boy had nothing to do with her death. I just want to find him and talk to him because he might've seen something or might be able to put me on the track of the third party that intruded on this relationship."

Ender rose to leave.

"I hope you don't mind if I don't leave with you," said

Miss Cranny. "I—I'll be ready in a few minutes. I don't want my class upset. I suppose I should tell them. But I'm just not ready. Not quite."

"Of course, Miss Cranny. I understand perfectly. And thank you. You have been a lot of help."

She looked up at Ender with tired, aged eyes—an old woman.

"Have I? I wonder."

Ender learned two important facts from his visit to the Welles girl's school: Marco's address and the fact that he, too, was absent from school both that day and the day before. He put his wild suspicions and fantasies of the night before in the back of his mind. What most concerned him was the possibility of another murder victim.

He found the McConnelly apartment a scene of furious activity. Greeted at the door by a strapping Irish giant in a chauffeur's dark livery, he produced his ID and was ushered hastily into the apartment. In the center of the apartment, seated on a large elegant couch, a small woman was weeping. The other McConnelly children seemed to gather around her, weeping, needing comfort, trying to give her comfort. Other men and women fussed around the apartment, talking in hushed voices together, making apparently urgent calls on the telephone. He saw a couple of men with notebooks questioning the red-eyed maid.

Cops.

Ender waited until one of the questioners was finished and then he buttonholed him.

"Excuse me, but can you tell me what's going on here? I'm Abe Ender from the DA's office."

The man scrutinized his ID. "I'm Lieutenant Watkins, Manhattan South. What are you doing here from the DA's office if you don't know what happened?"

"I'm just checking out some leads for a case I'm working on. I was hoping to find their eldest son here and ask him a few questions."

Watkins was a large heavy-set man with swarthy skin and shiny black hair. He looked like an ex-fullback with one of those thick necks that seems to pull the head straight into the shoulders without intervening definition. He took Ender aside.

"The boy you're looking for ran away yesterday morning. That's what his mother told us. Had a big fight with his old man."

"A fight? I've just come from his school. Everybody there seems to think he was so cultured and refined. A great home life. And now he's a runaway? What happened?"

"As far as the mother can piece it together, the old man was pissed that the kid had stayed out all night the night before last. Found him in the bathroom the next morning, fully dressed and splashing water on his face. She says that he tried to get an explanation from the kid but the kid was stubborn. Wouldn't say anything. Not even a plausible lie. So the old man flew off the handle: started to belt the kid around. Then, after the old man went to work, the kid split."

"And when was all that?"

"Just yesterday morning. Very upsetting it all was. You gotta realize that the old man was a very refined, wealthy gentleman. Not the brawling sort, at least not as far as we can tell. There hadn't been any blowups like this before in the family."

"What do you mean, 'was'?" Ender looked around him at the kids and the activity and all the men somberly speaking in dark suits with badges on their lapels. "Are you guys from missing persons?"

"Hell, no, man. Homicide."

Ender slapped his forehead with his fist. "Holy shit," he breathed. "You better fill me in on all this. Slowly."

"Well, it seems that it's not bad enough that the poor woman over there has to see her husband belting the crap out of her son and then have the son run away. But then last night, just a little after nine o'clock, her husband takes a flyer out of his office window, fifty-four fucking stories. That's why we're here. Finishing up our questioning, keeping an eye on the place. You know. These are very wealthy people. Probably have a lot of enemies."

"You mean it wasn't suicide?"

"Not likely. The husband's secretary had been working

late with him and he had just arranged to send her home in his personal car, driver and all, when she heard all kinds of noises in his private office. It seems it was his habit to lock himself in the office so he wouldn't get disturbed and she couldn't get in to see what was happening. That big guy over there, the one that looks like the red-headed tree, is the driver. He's also the old man's bodyguard. He comes into the office and finds the secretary hysterical, so he busts down the door. The whole office is a wreck: I mean, it looked like a bomb hit the fucking place. I saw it earlier. And the old man's nowhere around. There's no one in the room. And then they see that the picture window is shattered. They called us right away and sure enough the guy's spread all over the street below. I mean a mess. It seems that someone or something got into his office and just tossed him out the window."

Ender shook his head in astonishment and dismay. "Jesus Christ. What the fuck's happening around me? Everywhere I go there's another body." He looked up into the lieutenant's dark eyes. "Tell me. What did you mean by someone or some*thing?*"

"Well, you gotta understand that the secretary was pretty hysterical when we got there. But she insists that she heard strange noises coming from the room, like growls or howling. Animal sounds. I know it sounds crazy but that's what she says and that's what's on the official report. So your guess is as good as mine as to what the hell really was in there. All I can tell you is that there was blood all over the fucking place and everything, books, papers, the desk, chairs, was ripped to shit. Forensic's still down there now, checking the place out."

"Damn!" Ender leaned against the wall, his forehead pressed against his fist. His mouth worked in a chewing motion as if he were working his thoughts with his jaw. Watkins stared at him curiously.

"What's the problem? You been running into a lot of bodies lately?"

"Lieutenant, you don't know the half of it. Tell me, have you got a picture of the kid? The oldest son?"

"Yeah, I do. We figured we'd take one to see if there might be some kind of connection . . ."

"Well, listen, give me a copy and have a copy sent immediately to Lt. Fedorson."

"Fedorson? What's he got to do with this?"

"I can't explain now, but it seems that he's working on the same case only from a different angle."

Watkins raised his eyebrows uncomprehendingly. "Huh?"

"Never mind. Just let me have that picture. I'm sure the mother has a lot more. I've got to get back downtown right away."

And Ender snatched the picture out of the detective's hand, heading for the hall.

16

ELIZABETH stretched luxuriantly under the warm bundle of blankets. Too warm, some would say, for this August heat. But the air conditioner hummed on low power and the windows were closed against the thick waves of moist heat that shimmered malignantly among the monoliths of Manhattan. Only the sunlight came through, streaming brightly, almost painfully, through the window.

A sigh of pleasure rose from Elizabeth as she stretched, slowly drifting into wakefulness. Beverly's naked, soft arms cradled her and she automatically nestled more closely into her lover's body. Then slowly, delicately, the real world began to swirl into Elizabeth's consciousness, parting soft gray mists that trailed faint odors of lilac and fragrant olive. That face, dissolving with the mists, the golden curls, the thick beard with the strawberry cast that had jostled with the silent words he had spoken to her, those haunting green eyes . . .

Suddenly the height and brightness of the sun jolted Elizabeth wide awake. She sat bolt upright in bed, shoving the covers from her, shaking her head in haste to dispel the last foggy vapors of sleep.

"Beverly, wake up! We've overslept! God, look how late it is. It must be afternoon already. O Christ, how come you forgot to set the alarm clock again? Bev, come on, wake up!"

Beverly grumbled and started to turn away from Elizabeth in her sleep, sinking more deeply beneath the blankets, when she too, suddenly sprang into wakefulness and grabbed at Elizabeth's shoulders to calm her down.

"Beth, are you all right? It's okay, it was just a dream. I'm right here beside you, don't worry, I'm not about to let anything happen to you."

She started to cuddle Elizabeth protectively in her arms but Elizabeth brusquely pushed her away.

"What's the matter with you, Bev? Wake up now. The day's half gone and we're both late for work. Now come on and let's get our asses in gear. Maybe I can still salvage some of the backlog that's going to be waiting for me at the office."

Beverly, now fully awake, stared strangely into Elizabeth's eyes, quizzical and analytical.

"Have you just had one of your nightmares?"

Elizabeth sprang out of the bed and dashed to the dressers to get some clothes.

"Nightmares? What nightmares? I'll be walking into a nightmare when I get to the office, I sure as hell know that. Now you better get dressed or you're going to be in a lot of trouble with me."

Beverly sprang out of bed and pulled on Elizabeth's arm.

"Wait, Beth. Hold on!"

Elizabeth looked at her with surprise and some agitation.

"Really, Bev, I don't have the time now to—"

"You've got the time, Beth. Neither of us is going into work today."

Elizabeth frowned at her, a pair of panties dangling from her fingers. "What do you mean? Is it some kind of holiday?"

"No, no, of course not. You were . . . sick yesterday. Dr. Crile was here and he said you weren't to go to work today. Maybe not for a few days."

Elizabeth stood rigid as a statue, frowning, staring into Beverly's eyes. "Sick? What do you mean I was sick? I feel fine." She closed her eyes and pressed the tips of her fingers against her forehead in a massaging motion. "I don't remember being sick. O damn it, Bev, I couldn't have been sick. You must've been dreaming. Now wake up and let's—"

Beverly whirled on her, grabbing her shoulders tightly, jostling her breasts as she shook her.

"Don't you remember? You were sick yesterday. Very, very sick. You almost died!"

"What? Died? Are you serious?" The panties fluttered to the floor at Elizabeth's feet. Her eyes flashed brilliantly at Beverly, moist with shock, disbelief, and terror. Tightly clutching Elizabeth's shoulders in silence, Beverly stared right back at her. The two women endured a long moment of silence, the atmosphere between them charged with a pulsating aura of fear, anxiety, and love. Then Beverly began to gently massage Elizabeth's shoulders.

"I didn't mean to blurt that out to you the way I did. I can see now that you just don't remember anything that happened yesterday. I'm sorry I yelled at you like that . . . I just had to stop you somehow."

Her knees suddenly shaky, Elizabeth sank down on the bed. "Tell me what happened yesterday."

"First you tell me what you remember."

Elizabeth frowned thoughtfully. Moments passed while her mouth twisted in agitation and a tiny vein near her temple began to swell beneath her skin. Then she shook her head hopelessly.

"It's so strange, Bev. When I woke up I wasn't even aware that a day had been wiped out of my mind. I was feeling really good. Really ready to run to the theater, make my apologies for my lateness, and get right to work. And all the while I've lost a whole day from my memory." She faced Beverly with wide, frightened eyes. "God, that's scary, Bev. You can't know how scary until it happens to you. I could've been in the middle of a phone conversation and suddenly it would've hit me, 'I can't remember yesterday. Here I am on the phone taking ticket reservations and I can't remember yesterday!' What's happening to me, Bev? What's happening to my mind?"

Tears began streaming down her cheeks although she fought against the desire to break down and sob. Beverly cuddled her closely, rocking her back and forth, whispering softly into her ear.

"We'll get to the bottom of all this, lover. You'll remember. You've been through a lot since yesterday: visions, trances, tranquilizers. It's no wonder your memory's a little foggy."

"It's not a little foggy! I can't remember anything! It's like last night and yesterday just didn't happen!"

Elizabeth turned on her stomach and pressed her face tightly into the pillow. Beverly's fingers on her neck and shoulders tried to knead the torment from her body. She turned her head to one side, speaking toward Beverly's naked thigh.

"I'm frightened. I've never felt like this before. The terrifying part is that I feel perfectly well! It's like something outside me has swooped down and scooped out a piece of my mind. I should be able to remember yesterday but I can't. And I don't have any good reason for why I can't."

"Listen, Beth, you've got to get a hold of yourself. If you panic, then there's a good chance you're going to flip out into the trance you were in yesterday and there's no guarantee that anybody's going to be able to bring you back a second time. So hold on to yourself. Let's be analytical about this. Slow, methodical, patient. Now, try and think back. Stay calm, don't rush yourself. Just try and think back gently about yesterday. Is there no part of yesterday that you can remember?"

Elizabeth concentrated on her breathing, calming herself with its reassuring rhythm. She smiled. "It's so odd. I seem to remember yesterday morning with no difficulty. When I start at the beginning: getting up, dressing, opening the theater, finishing Mabel's bookings chart, even tossing Burbage out of the office because he was climbing all over the files and snagging the folders with his claws. I can remember something, after all."

"Quite a bit, it seems to me. Keep going."

"Then there was the lunch break. I remember leaving the theater to walk in the sun. Not far, a few blocks. Wait, yes, Bank Street. The Bank Street pier! I sat on the Bank Street pier to get some sun and eat my lunch!"

Her enthusiasm instantly vanished, however, along with

132

her smile. She sat up on the bed, her fingers probing and braiding each other as if she were trying to calculate motes of lost memory on the abacus of her hands.

"When I thought of the pier, I suddenly felt really cold inside of me. Like ice. You know, like that feeling when you're afraid and your hands and feet start to sweat and your stomach rolls and churns inside of you. I remember going to the pier for lunch and that's the point where it all ends. Nothing after that. Just waking up here and rushing to dress. And a little bit of that dream."

Beverly's interest was piqued. "What dream? One of your nightmares?"

"See now, that's something else that's bothering me. You asked me before about my nightmares as if I should know what you're talking about. I don't know anything about any nightmares."

"Beth, now listen to me. For about the last three months you've been having recurring nightmares. You'll start tossing and talking in your sleep, then you pop awake just like you did this morning, but drenched in cold sweat, panting and sobbing. You've been seeing Dr. Crile about them. You can only remember bits and pieces about them: weird monsters with strange eyes, cat's eyes, and a pervading sense of evil. Something about the good people suffering and doomsday. Like Armageddon. That's all you've been clear about. O, and there's always been something about a boy in your nightmares. A young boy who terrified you."

Elizabeth trembled visibly when the boy was mentioned but didn't seem to remember anything about him.

"Did I say what he looked like?"

"No, you've never been clear about that. You told Dr. Crile that it's like you can see him clearly in your mind but are totally unable to describe him to anybody. Not even the color of his hair or his height or anything specific. Just a young boy. Handsome, you said once, though you couldn't explain what you meant by that."

Elizabeth closed her eyes, pressing her palms against her temples. "I can remember all those talks with Dr. Crile about the nightmares. How strange! I must've had them, they must've been a big concern to all of us for the past few months, and yet I can't remember ever having them or being concerned about them. Just talking about them to others. That's all I remember. And even that doesn't remind me of just what the nightmares were." She leaned her elbows on her knees and stared thoughtfully between her toes. "It's sort of like the nightmares happened a million years ago and all I can remember is talking about them to other people. Maybe they've been wiped out for good by whatever trance you say I was in yesterday."

Beverly comforted her by saying that that could very well be true.

"I'm sure that if I had had such a thought yesterday, I'd be elated," Elizabeth replied. "But today, not even remembering the nightmares, I'm really not moved by the possibility of their disappearance."

"Then tell me about last night's dream. The one you can remember."

Elizabeth smiled, leaning back against the pillows, pulling her knee toward her chest with clasped hands.

"It was very strange and very pleasant, really. There had to be more to it than I remember because, in the part I can recall, nothing really happens. Nothing that could account for the overwhelming feeling of well-being, of pure happiness that the dream caused me to feel. I just remember being in a park, Central Park it was, I can even remember the exact spot, not too far from Bethesda Fountain, near the jogging track. And there was this man, you see, a young guy somewhere in his mid-twenties, really good-looking, tall, with curly blond hair shining in the sun. And he seemed preoccupied with something, staring down at the ground although there wasn't anything on the ground. And he kind of turns me on, noticing me real nonchalantly, and then he smiles at me and, God! he has the strangest, most beautiful eyes I ever saw. They were a greenish purple and sparkled like lanterns in the sunlight. And he just smiles at me and all my anxieties are washed away." She turned to Beverly, whose eyes had narrowed during the recitation of the dream. Furrowing her brow to make a very serious point, Elizabeth said, "I feel as if seeing that man smiling at me in my dream somehow cleansed me. As if that's why all my memories of my nightmares are washed away. And you know something? I'll damn well bet I won't be having any more of them."

She stared at Beverly, waiting for her to say something encouraging but Beverly just stared back at her in silence.

"Well?" asked Elizabeth. "Aren't you happy for me?"

"Of course I'm happy for you if your nightmares are really gone for good. It's just that there's too much left unanswered. We must call Dr. Crile and speak to him. Maybe he can find some connection between this new dream and the others. I only hope that nightmares haven't been traded in for something far worse."

But the doctor didn't have to be called; he arrived on his own initiative a few minutes later. Beverly greeted him at the door with Elizabeth close behind. He saw the women in their robes and apologized for waking them, offering to leave and return later.

"Don't be silly, Dr. Crile," said Beverly. "We've been up for a while already talking. I was just going to call your office and see if you had the time to stop by."

"For my Elizabeth I make the time." He entered the apartment with a wide smile, though his darting eyes took in every aspect of Elizabeth's form and coloring. "You look quite well, my dear. How do you feel this morning?"

"She feels so well that she jumps out of bed and is ready to hustle us both out of here and off to work. At twelve-thirty. Can you imagine?"

Elizabeth laughed. "I do feel fine, doctor. I'm amazed that I do after what Bev tells me happened yesterday. But today I seem to be all right."

Beverly interrupted: "You see, doctor, she doesn't remember anything about her seizure yesterday."

Dr. Crile opened his medical bag and was placing some instruments on the living room table.

"I'm not terribly surprised," he said calmly. "The mind likes to protect itself from trauma. It doesn't like to dwell on that which it can't handle to protect us from our curious, conscious selves who would dredge such things up continuously in an effort to explain things rationally to ourselves."

He probed Elizabeth's eyes with a shining instrument, examining her pupillary reflexes to see if the effects of the drug he had given her had worn off. He sought her thin wrist with his white paws to ascertain her pulse.

"Yesterday isn't all she can't seem to remember. She remembers nothing of those nightmares."

Crile's eyebrows arched and he looked straight into Elizabeth's eyes. "Nothing? You don't remember having those nightmares for the last few months?"

"I know it sounds strange, doctor, but I don't. I can remember speaking to you about them, and I can remember how upset and concerned Bev was when they happened. But I remember nothing about having the dreams."

"You don't mean you just can't remember the content of the dreams? You were never much able to do that."

"No, no. I can't even remember the fact that I was having them. It's as if they were a very disturbing part of my life that's just been erased." She bared her arm for the doctor's blood pressure apparatus. "Just like a tape, with bits and pieces snipped out but everything else remaining the same."

There was a ponderous silence as Dr. Crile took his readings and then unwrapped Elizabeth's arm.

"This is all very unusual," he commented. "First something unknown precipitates a traumatic seizure and then something equally unknown erases all traumatic memories." He continued fussing with his equipment. "I'd like to think it was my excellent skills as a physician that so rapidly eliminated all that trauma in your life," he smiled at her, "but I doubt if anything I did yesterday could have had such a salutary effect."

"Elizabeth seems to have an idea about what erased those memories," Beverly interjected. "Tell him."

Elizabeth laughed. "It's just a feeling I have, doctor. Nothing at all substantial."

"My dear Elizabeth," said the doctor, "you've become known for the accuracy of your insubstantial feelings. Tell me what you think."

"Well, I was just telling Bev about the dream I had last night, the one I woke up to. There was this beautiful man, you see, with hair all gold from the sun standing in a specific part of Central Park, an area I know well and could recognize immediately in my dream. And he has these outrageous greenish purple eyes which, when he turned and looked at me and saw me staring at him, flashed with such a warm, pleasant light that I immediately felt warm and good all over. And he smiled at me in the dream and beckoned for me . . . and that was it. I woke up full of energy, feeling sort of . . . well, sort of cleansed. And it was then that I discovered, at second hand, what had happened to me yesterday. And about my nightmares."

"And you mean that even after Beverly told you about yesterday and about your nightmares . . ."

"That's right. I still remember nothing. That is, I remember that I spoke to you and her about them, and that I was looking for help, but I can't remember anything about having them, or anything about whatever it was that flipped me out yesterday. Nothing. Nada."

The three sat in silence for sluggish, irksome moments.

"Trying to discover what's happening in your mind, my dear," began Dr. Crile, "poses certain difficulties that I wouldn't face with any other patient. Your telepathic sensitivities indicate that your mind has channels and resources that are nonexistent or dormant in the average patient I'm called upon to treat. Together we are going to have to puzzle out whether these sensitivities are throwing us off base. Were your nightmares, and now that traumatic seizure of yours, generated spontaneously from some inner recesses of your mind? Or were they symptoms of something external to you that your sensitivities are picking up and communicating with in bizarre forms that are emotionally disturbing to you? If you were an ordinary woman, I probably wouldn't even consider the latter possibility unless evidence thrust itself upon me and made me take notice. But with you, my dear, I have to leave my mind open to all possibilities."

"You mean to say," Beverly queried, "that her nightmares and her seizure yesterday resulted from the telepathic part of her brain tuning in on something that she wasn't consciously aware of?"

"Precisely. It's quite common for telepaths to be assaulted by dreams and seizures that leave them shaken and bewildered. These are the times when those who possess psychic gifts like Elizabeth rue the day they were ever born abnormal. But those are usually cases in which the psychic involved has a history of precognition, the ability, to a greater or lesser extent, to see into the future. Elizabeth was never before like that. Her psychic abilities were always limited to unknown but co-temporal events: she could search for thoughts and information about the present and about the past as it exists in the unspoken memories of people, but she never felt the call of the future. And now, suddenly, for the past few months, she's besieged by these dreams and mediumistic trances. She seems to have become more the vehicle for some psychic vibrations than the commander and controller of her own abilities." Dr. Crile leaned with his elbow on his knee, stroking his beard. "Believe me, I've been puzzling over your condition since yesterday. And now this sudden loss of memory, this feeling of being cleansed. It's most confounding."

Beverly interrupted the heavy silence to go into the kitchen. She returned with ice tea for all. As she distributed the glasses, she asked, "Do you remember, doctor, what she said about the boy in her dream? The one who terrified her so badly but who she couldn't even begin to describe more than to call him a young boy?"

"Yes, I certainly do. I'm sure you don't remember this now, Elizabeth, but when I was working with you on your nightmares you spoke of this young boy who was responsible for viciously and sadistically tormenting a young woman who, during the course of the nightmares, inevitably became transposed with you. You would feel the pain and the terror and the brutality that she was subjected to. And there was always that ambivalence about whether you were just the psychic ally of the young woman or supposed to be the victim herself. I must say I find it doubly disturbing to think that the latter interpretation may be derived from a precognitive experience. I hope we are definitely not getting such a painful glimpse into the future."

"But isn't it odd," Beverly continued, "that even though Beth's seen that boy clearly in her mind, she is utterly unable to verbalize his appearance? And now, this morning, a new 'main character' enters her dreams, a person she can describe almost with a passion and the other dreams are wiped out of her mind entirely. Doesn't there seem to be some sort of transplant effect?"

"It does seem quite possible," answered Dr. Crile. "When she first told me about the boy in conjunction with the other monstrous and grotesque events of her nightmares, I simply concluded that her inability to describe him physically was due to her subconscious need to repress the visualization of such brutality and violence. I was puzzled by the fact that the acts of torture were not themselves obscured but rather painfully intact. Only the boy's appearance. Then one day she's found in a trance mumbling phrases and images that both you and I recognized derived, to a large extent, from her nightmares.

"I suppose one might look at yesterday's seizure as perhaps an overdose of nightmare—one that spilled from the subconscious to the conscious, controlling her mind and almost killing her with the ferocity of the attack. And yet today she's smiling and happy, she's forgotten all about her former mental anguish and can sit here with us talking about it and reminding her continuously of what she had previously gone through and still she can look on at us, curious but still unruffled by any dredged-up memories. A new dream character, one that she remembers and can describe, has supplanted all the pain in her system. It's most intriguing." He turned to Elizabeth with a cheerful smile. "You evidently owe a great debt to your golden-haired savior of this morning's dream. He's taken quite a burden off your shoulders."

"Well, then, could you say that now that this transplant has occurred, she'll not be bothered by her nightmares anymore? That yesterday's attack was a kind of kill-or-cure passage of her psychic disturbance?"

"Of course, that's very possible. If such is the case, one could assume that now the nightmares are gone forever and everything's back to normal. The worst is behind her and mercifully forgotten. I would be delighted to believe that such is the case. But there are too many loose ends attached to her experiences to permit me to feel satisfied with that solution. If such is the case, I want to know why. I want to know the genesis of each event that led to yesterday's trauma and today's euphoria. I want to know why she couldn't describe the evil boy in her dreams even though she could remember him and what he did. I want to know why, when that seizure passed, did all the traces of her nightmares vanish with it. And who is this new figure in her dreams? Is it a psychic visualization of her cure or does it spell more trouble for her on some new front?"

Crile took a healthy drink from his glass, licking with quick flicks of his tongue the droplets that clung to his mustache. "But most of all I want to know what the essential meaning of these mental events is for Elizabeth. Has she just passed through some bizarre series of mental events that, in some mysterious way, were generated as they would have been in you or me by emotional transitions within ourselves and not through any outside medium?" He turned and looked very somberly into Elizabeth's eyes.

"Or shall we look upon you as the very special case that you are and conclude that you are picking up within your mind some cryptic revelation of something that will occur or that might even have begun to occur? Something that we must learn to interpret so that we can protect you from some future harm that is bearing down on you." Dr. Crile took one of Elizabeth's hands in both of his. "Or must we recognize that you, my dear, may be warning the rest of us of the harm that's heading *our* way?"

Shortly after, the three sat in the bedroom with the blinds pulled for darkness. Elizabeth sat cross-legged on the bed and Dr. Crile sat on a chair at the foot of the bed facing her. Beverly sat with her legs curled under her on the floor, watching the proceedings with grave concern.

"I realize," Beverly had said, "why you'd want to trace the events of her day just prior to her seizure to see if anything external ticked it off. And if so, what it was. But she's forgotten everything that's happened to her since her going to the pier. Doesn't that mean something? Isn't her mind trying to lay it all to rest with this strange, selective amnesia? I want to know if anything significant happened on that pier as much as anyone, if not more. But if you force Elizabeth to recall it, won't it just precipitate a second seizure, possibly even more powerful than the first?"

Dr. Crile couldn't come up with a satisfactory reassurance to her objections. It was a calculated risk, he said. Either probe more closely or back off, hoping for the best. But that alternative didn't satisfy anybody.

"What I propose is hypnosis," said Dr. Crile. "An intensified form, to be sure, which I will be able to produce with Elizabeth's cooperation. You remember that when she first came to me about her nightmares we tried hypnosis and it was a dismal failure. The same psychic strengths that make her a powerful telepath effectively blocked my hypnotic efforts. But this time Elizabeth will assist me in her own hypnosis. She will enter into her telepathic state through her meditations but this time she will direct her mental probings within her while I will try to fine-tune and monitor those energies with hypnotism. In effect, I hope that the two of us, by our combined efforts, will enable Elizabeth to read her own mind and then tell us what we want to know. If at any time I feel that she's slipping back into one of those seizures, I'll try to call her back with my hypnotic control."

Try to. There's the rub, thought Beverly.

Dr. Crile sat like Michelangelo's *Moses* on the chair, his right foot pulled toward the back legs, his torso thrust forward, his eyes intent and flaming as he watched Elizabeth close her eyes and regulate her breathing in preparation for her telepathic efforts. Slowly, ever so slowly, her face assumed that expression of serene repose which he had come to recognize as the herald of her power.

"Elizabeth. Can you hear me?"

Her head nodded ever so slightly in affirmation.

"Good. I want you to maintain your concentration. My voice will not harm the flow of your energies. Your energies will simply bob on the surface of the waves of my voice like a cork bobs on water, self-contained, unaltered, unconcerned. You will channel and focus your energies just as I've taught you to do in the past, using the pineal region of your cortex, the ancient site of the third eye, like a lens. The third eye sharpens the beam of your mind. You are now radiating great power. You can control it. You will not let it get away from you. Your will is supreme."

There was such intense concentration between the doctor and Elizabeth that Beverly could almost hear the crackling hum of a high voltage wire passing overhead. The doctor's heavy eyebrows and stony, intense scowl lent him the aspect of a patriarch furious to acquaint his followers with the magnitude of their sins. And Elizabeth was lotus-legged on the bed, confident, powerful, yet troubled. Beverly could feel their combined fears rise, coalesce, and float around the room like a mottled bird.

Dr. Crile's voice grew huskier as the session progressed. "You will now probe that nexus of energy suspended within your mind, the seat of all psychic wisdom, the pineal process. Feel the thick, pulsating jet of energy flowing out from you to the world beyond. It sizzles, it crackles, it waits in all its great and awesome power for your command. You are focusing it, you have focused it, it awaits the touch of your mind. But today you will direct it differently. Concentrate on that point beneath your skull, the third eye. That is the seat. That is the root. Concentrate now. See the filaments of all that power gathered at that spot, swirling, twisting, braiding in and among each other. You will first gaze upon those filaments and stop their swirling motion. Concentrate now. Cool them, freeze them, they're growing sluggish and still, mighty and potent as they are you are bringing even them under your command. Feel their submission? Feel the chill and the stillness within you?"

Dr. Crile was as wild-eyed as a madman staring into Elizabeth's now pale face. Her expression was still serene, but beads of sweat gathered over her forehead with the effort of her concentration. Beverly's heart pounded in her chest as she watched the sweat gather and spill in tiny cascades along those pale cheeks. She was poised to rise and throw herself between the two to shatter the mystical alliance between them and break the spell that was being woven, the spell that might cost her lover her sanity.

"Now is the time, Elizabeth. Now you must gather those frozen strands of energy and pull them back within you, deep, deep into the center of your brain. Bring that energy within you, Elizabeth. Feel it grow, feel it stretch back into your mind, one immense tendril of force stretching outward to the end of the universe and inward to the ... the end of the universe."

Elizabeth lurched as she sat concentrating. Her head and neck trembled with the vibrations of her effort. Her mouth lost its serene poise and began pursing and pulling like that of a desert castaway searching for water. The sweat fell copiously from her brow.

"You are in command now, Elizabeth. You must remember that and then nothing can take that power away from you. Your psychic energies have embedded themselves deeply within the central core of your mind. They are yours to command. They are rigid and immovable. Nothing can release them until I tell you that it is time to release them. They are rigid. They are frozen. They are inflexible. Use them now, Elizabeth. Use them to probe your hidden memories. They lie locked behind a large gate of iron. There is no key. There are no windows. They would keep you out. But you won't let them. Prepare to thrust now and open that gate. Poise the energies now. They pulse and vibrate to do your bidding. Be swift now and sure. Now! Shatter that gate!"

Elizabeth's scream was piercing and painful, a mighty alien howl, a cry from the limbo between the realms of the dead and the living. Her body sprawled on its stomach, flat on the sheets, her hands clutching the air, her feet digging madly into the sheets, her eyes gaping wide, blind to the images of the outside world, filled with the terrors and secrets of her hidden soul. Beverly lurched out of her seat to grapple with her, but Dr. Crile, never taking his eyes off Elizabeth, pulled Beverly's wrist with an iron grip and forced her into her seat, roughly, without apology.

He was bent low to the bed now, almost face to face with the squirming, gaping-eyed girl. "You've done it, Elizabeth! You're through the gate. You've found the power to do it, and now it is control that is essential. You don't want to know all that is contained behind those iron doors. Just what I ask you. Still the fires of your powers, bridle them, soothe them beneath the mighty stroking of your will. Easy now, Elizabeth. You don't want to see all that lies there secretly in the profound darkness. You don't want to know. Be in command. Forget everything but the sound of my voice and the questions I will put to you. Forget all else. You don't want to know."

She stopped thrashing and just lay quietly on the bed sprawled on her stomach, her arms and legs outspread. Beverly chewed her lips in stifled terror at Elizabeth's ordeal, her whole arm hurting from the force of Dr. Crile's grip.

"You have been plagued by nightmares, Elizabeth. I don't want you to remember them. They are painful and frightening and might hurt you and we don't want anything to hurt you. But there is an image in those nightmares that I want to explore with you. There is a young boy, Elizabeth. You must look at him and draw him out from the nightmares. I only want to know what he looks like. Not what he's doing. Not what he's done to you in the past. Just the boy, Elizabeth. Tell me what he looks like."

"The boy . . ."

She squirmed violently on the bed, her back was arching, her head thrown up and backward, her spine crackling with her brutal movements.

"Easy, Elizabeth. Just the boy. Find me the boy and tell me what he looks like."

Her thrashing stopped and she was frozen in her arch on the bed with wide, unseeing eyes shining like mirrors in the dark room. Both Crile and Beverly gasped in terror, lurching backward.

"The boy . . . pretty boy, pretty pet . . . long, dark hair . . . blue eyes, blue like a southern sea, a sea swept by hot winds . . . a cleft in his chin, to catch and hold the shadows . . ."

And then she screamed again, throwing herself out flat on the bed, clutching the sheets in her hands, her knuckles showing white with strain.

"Elizabeth! You are in control! Remember that. And tell me what's happening. Tell me what you see!"

"Changing . . . the boy fades and smears like wet paints, all swirled together, fading, changing . . ."

"To what, Elizabeth? The handsome boy is changing into what? Tell me."

"Can't . . ."

"Tell me!"

"I can't! The monster will punish me . . ."

"Monster? What monster?"

"O, I see it all now, I see the changing, the message in the dreams, I see the changing and the horror! It will kill! It will kill me if it can get at me!"

Dr. Crile grabbed one of her hands and cradled it in his. "No one, nothing can hurt you Elizabeth. Only what both you and I wish to happen can happen. Your are in control. It is your mind that directs the piercing light of your vision. Be calm and look at the monster. It is only an image. It is harmless. Your will is invulnerable to it. It can't hurt you in any way so there's no reason to fear it. Now. Tell me about the monster."

Her eyes wide with oracular vision, her voice rose steadily from the depths of her trembling chest.

"Out of the darkness . . . it stares at me, waiting . . . staring . . . like a horse, a face with huge teeth, yellow flat teeth . . . cat's eyes, all around, they stare into the darkness, cat's eyes . . . the beast sits in the darkness, thick darkness, thick stench, the beast breathes, waiting . . . woe to the blessed, woe to the blessed, the darkness . . . wait, now the light, a great light, hot and flaming and unbearable . . . it rises now, a horn, sharp, pointed, sticking out of its forehead like the rays of the energy of my mind, like the rays of the energy of my mind . . ."

Her voice began to trail off into inaudible babbling. Crile cradled her head in his two hands and turned her vacant, gaping eyes to his. But before he could speak she began to shout, terrified.

"Elizabeth! What is the matter?"

"On the pier . . . I saw him! . . . I saw the boy! On the pier, with a black man, walking on the pier . . . That's why! That's why it happened! . . . I saw him, I saw him on the pier . . ."

And with a bloodcurdling shriek she arched again, her cheeks taut with her screams, her eyes bulging and the veins throbbing in her throat. Crile could see her losing control and being overpowered by her visions. He kept shouting at her stiff, straining form, calling her back from the depths of her psyche, urging her return before it was too late.

But it took the leap and lunge of Beverly's slight body right on top of Elizabeth's rigid, howling form to spill her to the floor and release her from her visions to the blissful darkness of unconsciousness.

17

MARCO sat on the Wooster Street curb bathed in strange tints of lime and lilac that filtered down from the early morning sky between the grimy factory buildings, lofts, and warehouses. He cradled his head in his hands, his elbows resting on his knees.

Time. That was it, like gum, slipping slowly from him, clinging to him thick and sticky and oppressive. And the rusty trucks vomiting smoke and shattering the morning stillness with the howl and rage of their mighty engines blasted through the cloying, invisible vapors that seemed to swirl around Marco and enfold him. It was as if all the rest of the world had slipped its moorings to reality and become no more than a flat procession of darting light and shadow, images unhampered by space or time, watery splashes of color and brief but piercing explosions of noise.

Marco squeezed his head between his hands, nodding slightly from side to side, his eyes tightly shut. He could no longer bear the flat, bright colors that made the world so unfamiliar and strangely menacing.

Jenny with her wide blue eyes, Jenny staring up at him as he read to her, following his lips with her eyes. He could hear her voice coming to him as if across eons and parsecs, all echoey and reverberant, lamenting the perplexity of Byron's Manfred: "How very sad to be so alone, Marco. To be looking out over the steep ravine and the rushing water and be filled with thoughts of death. To be so alone, with no one to understand you and no one to see how sensitive and wise you are. So alone. So sad."

A truck roared past Marco's knees, its cargo of heavy machinery jolting with squeals of outrage as the truck bounced and lurched over the potholes and shards of pavement. He neither flinched nor grimaced. He just sat on the curb with his head pressed between his hands and his eyes tightly shut, nodding slowly from side to side, listening to Jenny's voice speak to him in whispers.

And the flies.

He had wandered along the dark side streets of Manhattan all night. The crown of the Empire State Building had been floodlighted in bands of green, yellow, and red. He remembered staring at the huge, glowing monolith from a darkened corner of a deserted parking lot. He just sat and stared, his heart pounding in his chest, his lungs raw with running.

The flies had started gathering then, night flies. Or at least that was when he first noticed them. Buzzing around his knees and hands, alighting on his soft cheeks with their tiny, tickly legs, crawling up and down his neck and arms.

He didn't brush them away.

He remembered that last night in the park with Jenny when she had begun to touch his body with her light hands and he had lain back amidst the grass and the thick foliage of the bushes. There was a gap between the leafy branches overhead and he could see the crown of the Empire State Building then, too, glowing the same green, yellow, and red. Deep, glistening colors. His eyes had then been drawn by the moon with the strange star floating so near to it. And he remembered how Jenny's fine golden hair had become mottled silver in the shadow-scattered light of the full moon.

He remembered nothing more of that night.

He wanted to weep but the tears wouldn't come. They froze like icebergs, somewhere deep within him in the froth and foam of his thick, jellied blood.

The swarm of flies circled around Marco's head like planets around their sun. They buzzed near his ears, fading then louder. Over and over. Some alighted on the backs of his hands, passing gingerly from vein to vein. One alighted on his cheek and walked slowly along his lips. Marco just nodded his head from side to side, listening.

There were voices in the droning of the flies. Something like when he had looked into the depths of the Hudson from the pier and had seen the demon shadows and heard the whisper of their babble mingling with the lapping of the waves. Indistinct, maniacal, senseless. And now one voice was swelling, coalescing out of the cacophony of the flies.

Marco inclined his head, the better to hear. He was being summoned. Or hunted. He listened for the voice, searching his memory, both frightened and eager to confront the voice and link it to the visual image of a face.

Frightened and eager. Like a boy's first lust.

That man on the pier. How he had come apart like a doll made of moist tissue paper, shred by shred. He had seen the spurting fountain of his blood spewed out from his groin, but Marco couldn't hear the screams that appeared to lurch out of the struggling man's mouth. It all seemed so inconsequential: the man, the blood, the screams.

O God, he thought, what was happening to him? What was he becoming? What had he already become?

That line from *King Lear?* "We are to the gods as flies to wanton boys; they kill us for their sport."

Marco sat on the curb and began to laugh. He laughed like the genie tortured by a feather, painfully, spasmodically, without humor or respite. How strange his father looked last night, taken by surprise in the midst of his business affairs and the appurtenances of his money: the fine wooden desk, the papers with columns of numbers, the file folders, the embossed letterheads, the pen and pencil set of polished jade and gold, the calculators, the ticker tape, the exotic telephone with the rows of glowing buttons. And all those figures and affectations and utensils could do nothing to keep him from Marco's marauding grasp. It was so damn easy. The door leading to the emergency stairway just flew apart at his touch and his father flew backward on his rolling chair, slamming terrified into the shelves behind him, his eyes wide, his mouth gulping air, searching for his voice.

Marco held out the palm of his hand to the flies. A few alighter, crawling among the wrinkles of his palm, buzzing, mounting one another, preening their multiple eyes. He reached down to them with a forefinger and stroked their backs and crystal-veined wings. They didn't fly away. They just purred up at him contentedly with the drone of their wings.

A demonstration first, to show him the rage of an injured son or a jealous god. He had splintered the desk with his fist. He had pulled with one hand on the shelves and cracked them from the wall.

And then he grabbed the cringing man with the expensive suit and the manicured fingers and raised him high above his head, facing the broad expanse of window . . .

The drone of the flies filed his ears, as if the universe were melting into one massive cascade of raucous sound, throbbing, interminable, ever downward to some dark core of vacuum that waited silently like a plump black toad at the end of all things. He felt no remorse, no pangs of guilt, no voice of conscience. Perhaps an odd sort of pity, not for what they had suffered but for what they had been: insignificant wraiths leeching the essence of their puny lives off the universal forces that were now gathering within his veins.

What madness was this . . .

Marco dislodged a caked wad of refuse from the asphalt and sent it tumbling end over end with the toe of his sneaker. With a last trembling bounce it came to rest in the center of an asphalt crevice, lying atop an unearthed cobblestone. He stared at it intently as it danced across the street, so slowly to his eyes, end over end, shivering and tumbling, slowly in its dance like that Indian goddess Shiva, spinning and whirling with an unearthly grace unique unto itself.

That movie they had shown to his class, the one filmed in India with multitudes of brown-skinned people following a wooden wheel decorated with flowers and fireworks, borne upon the shoulders of robed priests: a strange name for that wheel, Miss Cranny told them. A symbol meaning many things, powerful things, like the hand of god or fate or time, something relentless and unswerving. The end of the world. To be seen shredding hugely through the sky and earth on the last day.

Juggernaut. That was it: the name of the damn thing, Juggernaut.

He rose from the curb and felt the blood rush from his head to his buttocks and legs. He had no idea how long he had been sitting there. Since late last night. Hours. Or maybe just minutes. Long enough to block an artery and stop the flow of blood to his legs. He couldn't remember very much after running from his father's office. Just headlights and vapor lamps and the distant sound of horns.

And the gathering flies.

He steadied himself against a No Parking sign. He felt dizzy and his spine tingled. And the flies swarmed all around him, buzzing, landing on his neck, crawling all over his skin. He looked down at his hands and saw thick patches of calloused flesh sprinkled from the backs of his fingers all the way up his forearm. They were grayish and brittle and looked as if they should be hurting terribly, but Marco felt nothing. The flies seemed to congregate upon those patches, brushing themselves up against the coarse hairs that had begun to sprout.

The drone of the flies grew louder to Marco's ears and he strained to listen for that one voice struggling to rise above the other sounds and whispers that were laced among the drone of the flies. Nothing.

He felt overfilled with blood, as if his blood were whipped into a frothy foam and moved so slowly within his body, like thickened paste. His skin seemed to him a stiff parchment stretched over a pillar of sand. A tiny kernel of consciousness flashed like a beacon through the dark granular fog—for an instant Marco's mind was almost able to survey the irreconcilable void that loomed between what he had been and what he was becoming. This portion of his mind trembled with a fear unknown even to madmen, aware as it was that it was being slowly crowded out by the darkness and the black

chill, and aware that soon nothing of it would remain.
And the rest of his body was hard, cold, and alien.

And mighty.

Marco walked very slowly up Wooster to Houston,
then headed west. Toward the river. Toward that pier.
The rhythm of Manfred's words undulated with Marco's
slow passage among the lofts and factories and machine
shops:

> My slumbers—if I slumber—are not sleep,
> But a continuance of enduring thought,
> Which then I can resist not: in my heart
> There is a vigil, and these eyes but close
> To look within;

Taxis flashed past him like golden chariots, briefly swirling the summer air around him. Laborers and factory
hands and sewing machine operators dragged themselves
glumly to their jobs, silent, thoughtful, tired. Obscenities
were scrawled upon the grimy walls of the buildings in
two languages.

> . . . and yet I live, and bear
> The aspect and the form of breathing men.

Because of the width of Houston Street, the sky seemed
suddenly to open and redeem Marco's quizzical eyes
from the chill shadows of the tall buildings. But why the
killing? How had he been so transformed that the horrible deaths of innocent people meant nothing to him?
He repeated to himself, very slowly, as he walked, "I
killed my father. I killed my father. I killed my father."
A few sea gulls from the piers circled overhead for insects while bloated gray pigeons puffed and swelled in
stately circles on the hot pavement, burdened by their
lust. There seemed to Marco an order to all things: the
flow of traffic, the flight of the sea gulls, the hum of machinery from the binderies and print shops that he passed.
An order and a time and a place for everything except
for him. Once he had been a part of that order, that "right-
ness" of thought and deed that kept the world functioning without cataclysmic ruptures that would disturb the

peace and security of that vast majority of people too subdued to shake their fists at fate and the glowering, thunderous skies. And he had lamented the ordered world into which he had been born, in which people strove to guide him with timeworn platitudes so that he could slip without friction or whimper into the trough of iron that was forged to receive him. Those nights with Jenny reading out loud to each other in the park, he had yearned to stand upon a majestic pinnacle and confront the yawning abyss and all the poetic phrases would come rushing to his head and his blood would quicken at the thought of surrendering himself to the dictates of his own genius, unafraid to risk death and scorn.

And now he was swept beyond all that. His will shrivelled like a moist gland left to scorch on cracked desert wastes. He walked on, an outlaw and outcast from the comfortable world of things and values in which he had been nurtured. The abyss he now confronted was bloody and senseless, reeking of power and immortality yet horrifying and bizarre. For at the bottom of his newfound omnipotence was the horror that he was losing control of his mind.

He couldn't dwell on the horror because there was always the drone of those flies, pulling him back to the abyss, demanding his surrender, urging him forward with subtle promises of omnipotence and secret wisdom.

But why the killing? And why couldn't he feel remorse?

At Bedford Street he turned north, laughing uncontrollably, gently rubbing the hardened patches of skin on his arms with delicate fingers.

At the next pay telephone he hurried to deposit a dime. The phone at the other end of the line rang for a long time but Marco let it ring, determined to speak to someone. At last a weak, shaky voice came on, the Welles's housekeeper: "Hel-hello. Welles residence."

In a sudden panic, Marco didn't know what to say. "Hello? May I help you?"

Marco set his lower jaw. "I must leave a message for Jenny."

Stunned silence at the other end, then: "Who is this? Who's calling?"

"It's . . . Marco. I must leave a message for Jenny when

153

she gets home from school." Her summer classes would be over soon and he wanted to see her before he disappeared from human sight. He wanted to ask her about that night to see if she noticed the change in him, the incipient power and madness that was overwhelming him. Perhaps she could mollify his unsettled spirit.

"Marco? Where are you? This is Mrs. Gates, the housekeeper. The police have been looking all over for you."

"The police?" He almost said "Already?" but caught himself. What could they want with him? They couldn't know.

Mrs. Gates's voice started to shake. "Your mother needs you now, Marco. The police told us that you ran away and that we should tell you to come right away if we should hear from you. You poor, dear boy. You've been away so you can't know."

"Know what?"

"I—I shouldn't tell you something like this over the phone. Go home and be with your family. Let them tell you."

"Mrs. Gates, please excuse my rudeness but I haven't time for riddles. My family problems are my own: I won't have you or anyone else try to trick me into going back home. I'm perfectly safe where I am—and I find the atmosphere much more congenial. Now, will you take a message for Jenny?"

He thought he knew what she was going to say to him and he had to play dumb, like a criminal.

"Marco, don't feel so harshly about your family. Such thoughts can make you sorrowful for the rest of your life. Especially when you find out."

"Find out what? Damn it, Mrs. Gates, I'm at a pay phone and I haven't the time to play these games. Just tell Jenny . . ."

"Mr. Marco, this is no game and I'm shocked at your tone of voice. You've never spoken to me like that and I certainly expect never to hear the like from you again. Your father is dead, Marco. You hear me? He was murdered last night. I'm sorry you had to hear it from me in this way, over the phone. But you forced me. You gave me no choice. Now get back home to your mother

154

and your brothers and sisters. You're the eldest and they are all going to depend on you for a lot now."

Marco was silent for a moment to let her think he was stunned at the news but an intent smile curled his lips.

"Mrs. Gates, I appreciate your concern for me but, as far as I'm concerned, the bastard only got what he deserved. I'm only sorry I wasn't around to see it."

He took perverse pleasure in the shock value of what he was saying. There was a frigid, stunned silence on the phone as if the electric impulses stimulated by his voice froze in stony horror at what he said.

"My God, Mr. Marco! How can you say what I've just heard you say? It's not human! It's monstrous!"

"It's also the truth, Mrs. Gates. Whether you like it or I like it or my family likes it, it's still the truth. Now please tell Jenny that—"

"She's dead too, you cruel, heartless little boy! And she's better off being rid of the likes of you! And to think how we both welcomed you into this house . . ."

Dead. Marco's face slackened and he stared at the telephone as if he had never used one before in his life. Mrs. Gates ranted and raved but the receiver dangled limply from the pay phone. So it happened just as he feared, only he couldn't remember it happening. He still couldn't. But the brutal, horrible deaths of the others— had he . . . ? The answer frightened him far more than the question, so he tried to block such speculation out of his mind.

That shrivelled, dying kernel of Marco's own mind saw his world collapsing: Jenny's death was like Orwell's Room 101—the Worst Thing. But still the tears wouldn't flow. He felt no rising, passionate grief within him, no pain, no sense of emptiness and irreplaceable loss. Nothing.

Just the drone of flies hovering around his head and ears, ever louder, stronger. Speaking secrets, making him smile.

Near Hudson and Christopher streets, Marco hesitated in front of St. Luke's Church. He had been too much in the sun and was overcome by a frantic desire for darkness and solitude. Jenny was dead, and he knew he had killed her. They didn't know. There was no one to accuse him. But now he knew and he could imagine the horror of her last moments.

If he let himself imagine it.

Almost like a thief, he rushed inside the church.

The chapel fixtures were mostly wood, redolent of fresh wax and stain. No lights were on: only dim sunlight filtered through the small stained-glass windows. Forward past the rows of glossy pews was a raised platform with a pulpit and some scattered music stands. Although an old and venerable church, St. Luke's was very progressive in its effort to reach out to the community at large with concerts and readings and theater groups. An old man, thin, bent, and wrinkled, dressed in a drab gray uniform with "St. Luke's Church" embroidered on it in red thread was busy folding the music stands and putting them away.

Marco sat in the last pew, huddling in the darkness, embracing it. If he could murder her, then how could he later expect tears? And there were none. He felt nothing but a cold solidity within him, a harsh strength that left no room for tender feelings.

And the drone of the flies had followed him into the chapel. He picked at the calloused eruptions of his flesh, pulling at the long coarse hairs that had sprouted, closing his eyes and bathing in the cool darkness to focus on that single strident voice emerging from the cacaphonous drone.

He was being summoned.

He opened his eyes and stared forward at the altar. There was a wooden crucifix, varnished though otherwise unadorned, quite appealing in its stately simplicity. It was very large and thick and heavy—almost a full five feet tall and at least half a foot in width. How many people over the years had sat where he sat now and looked reverently upon that cross and wished for a voice from that other world to float down upon them and heal their tired souls.

And now he heard a voice—he was being summoned.

And in the rear of that chapel, huddled in darkness, Marco began to tremble with fear.

"Are you all right, son?" An old man's voice came to Marco from his right. Now the sun was much further along in the sky, already preparing for its leisurely summer descent. He could tell by the angle at which the light filtered through the stained-glass windows.

"Do you feel okay?" It was the old caretaker, sitting down next to him.

"I feel fine, thanks."

"Well, kid, you might feel fine but you look like hell. Are you sick?"

Marco kept his eyes riveted to his lap. "No, sir, I feel fine."

The old man sat in silence for some moments, his toothless gums working in perplexity.

"You a runaway, boy?"

Marco didn't look up. "No. I'm not. I just came in here for some peace and quiet. It helps me think."

"You're a mite young to be needing peace and quiet to think. That's for old codgers like me. But I know what you mean. Sure do."

A kindly old man. Marco could hear the note of genuine concern in his shaky voice. A frigid pulse of terror sparked through him, scurrying up and down his spine. He feared for the old man.

"You been here for hours. You know that?"

"I wasn't aware of that. I guess I got lost in thought. Kind of carried away, you know."

"You been sitting here for hours kind of shivering and mumbling weird things to yourself. I think something's troubling you, like maybe you're sick or something and I'd like to help."

Marco turned his back to the old man, facing the aisle. "I appreciate your concern, mister, I really do. Please believe that. But I'm just fine. Listen, I think I better get the hell out of here now. I've been here much too long. Just like you said. Hours. Much too long. I think I'll just leave now. We'll both be better off if I go."

Marco rose to leave and the old man reached for him with trembling hands. "Now wait a minute, kid. I didn't mean to sound like I was chasing you out. This here's a church. We help people here. Damn, if you can't come to a church for help, well, where else can you go? That's my way of thinking. Now, look at those things on your arms. You can't tell me you ain't sick. Now why don't you wait here till the pastor gets back? I'm sure he'll prove to be a man you'll feel like talking to. He's such a good, kind man, he is. A young guy, too. Understands young people and their problems."

With his back to the old man, Marco's voice grew suddenly soft. "He sounds a lot like you." But then a timbre of metal put an edge to his words. "That's why I must leave now. Now, let go of me. Don't try to stop me. I— I've got to get out of here. Don't hold me back."

"But—but I just want to help. You look like a kid with problems. Please, wise up. Let me help you. Or let someone here help you."

Suddenly Marco froze rigid as he was about to step into the aisle. He heard a harsh alien voice rising from within him. The drone of the flies became unbearable, deafening. And that voice, insistent, calling out to him, summoning him.

"If that's your wish, then I will let you help me."

And Marco slowly turned around to face the old man. The old man's wrinkled face blanched in terror. And then the chapel shook with the boy's laughter.

Since the evening was still quite young, Grand Central Station swarmed with commuters hastening for their trains. Later on it would quiet down as the short runs became less frequent, leaving only the long-distance travelers, the noncommuters.

Marco stood in the center of the great hall near the information booth. He stared up at the map of the zodiac painted across the high ceiling. Yes, Scorpio. That was the one. That was his sign. The one with the stinger.

Jenny was dead. She was a Pisces. And now she was dead.

He remembered a beautiful lake from his childhood, recalled from a brief camping trip with his family to upstate New York. Chapel Pond. It wasn't really a pond;

it was large and deep and dark blue, like a liquid sapphire. And a great mountain had loomed beyond it, craggy and precipitous like a setting for Byron's tragic romances. As a child, he had sat on the edge of Chapel Pond staring into the deep waters, making faces at his reflection, throwing pebbles in with chubby fingers and laughing gleefully at the playful splashes.

He'd go there again. Now. To think. To be alone. To figure out what was happening to him. To flee the crowded city.

To listen for that voice of solitude.

He had stolen enough money from his parents before he left so he could leave right away. Studying a traveler's map he purchased at the magazine stand, he found the nearest train depot and bought a ticket.

Before descending into the train tunnel, he stared up again at the signs of the zodiac. He wished that Orion had been chosen one of the twelve instead of Scorpio. He felt that was more his constellation: the martyred hunter, made glorious for his pride, set in jewels upon the backdrop of inky heaven, solitary, alone, noble, and eternal. A Byronic hero, a Byronic memorial.

Once aboard the train, he settled himself comfortably in the soft seat. He switched on the overhead light and began to read his volume of poetry. Suddenly he heard the buzzing of a fly. He rested his book in his lap and held out his outstretched palm. Instantly a fly settled on his palm, crawling in tight circles, preening itself, flexing its wings. Marco stared at it for a few moments, then stroked it with the tip of his finger. The fly bowed to his touch, submitting. Then, with a sudden movement Marco popped the fly into his mouth.

As the train began to pull out of the station, Marco sat looking out the window, his book flat in his lap, smiling, chewing.

18

THE old parlor with the bulging ceiling and the cracked plaster from which the paint fell to the floor in chips and curls; the battered lampstand covered in cheap imitation lace so that the nicks and glued fragments wouldn't show; that gold clock under glass with the dancing Frenchmen who pirouetted when it struck the hour, their one piece of finery and ostentation that remained of their father's more prosperous youth and which Adrienne's mother cared for lovingly with polish and chamois cloth once a week, without fail; the parabolas of pale light that broke up the darkness of the walls at intervals around the room, emitted by the small lamps around which the kids had gathered to do their homework or read magazines or play with old bottles and cans on the shabby throw rug that was almost wall-to-wall in the small room.

It's amazing what one remembers when one hasn't thought of something for ten or fifteen years.

The old man in the easy chair with the padding spilling out. No matter how hard Adrienne's mother tried, she just couldn't keep up with the rips that kept appearing in the old, worn fabric, until in some spots there wasn't enough fabric left to stitch back together. Adrienne's father had sat in that chair, tall, thin-chested, his shoulders stooped and his head slumped forward just staring with pouched and tired eyes at his knees. He was an old man without humor or dignity. He just stared in silence, looking old beyond his fifty-eight years. And the kids scrambled around him, playing cops and robbers or cowboys or martians, muting their squeals and howls for his sake, careful not to trip against him or fall into him as if he were a part of the furniture.

It was his eyes and the flesh of his forehead and cheeks: a head like a shrivelled apricot seeded at the top with sprouts of gunmetal curls streaked with white, a face rarely caught smiling.

Mother must have been in the kitchen, scrubbing pots or whatever it was that seemed to keep her in there all night, emerging only when it was time to go to the bathroom or unfold the couch for sleeping. And father's chest could be seen to rise and fall ever so slightly with his breathing, keeping time with every seventh metallic click of the clock that danced. His mouth was twisted in a lax quizzicality as if life had suddenly swooped down on him by surprise and submerged him unawares.

He looked up, startled, and turned to her.

"Adrienne." His voice was tired, yet pained, with a trace of urgency to it.

"Yes, Father?"

"What has happened? I can't see you anymore. I know you're there, I know you're looking back at me, I can even see your eyes staring at me, watching me sit here, watching me think, wondering. But it's not you. Something's wrong. You shouldn't be like that. Has Mother been feeding you enough?"

Adrienne thought that an odd question. He knew she was fed the same as the others. Something was bothering him.

"She feeds me fine, Father."

"You're different somehow. Not healthy. Your eyes: there's a . . . a pain in them, an old sorrow like you've been carrying a burden around inside you for years. Centuries, even. That's not good, Adrienne. Something must be done about that. I don't want you being sick."

"Father, it must be your imagination. I'm fine, really. There's nothing wrong."

Father rose slowly from the chair, not taking his eyes off her.

"What's happened to you? I won't be put off with patronizing denials. You've done something and it's turning on you. Like that clock, turning and turning and you can never steady yourself it just keeps turning and those damned dancing fairies just smile and keep dancing, they can't see how sick you can get spinning along with them, they don't give a damn, just smile and dance and turn round and round." He started walking slowly toward her. She felt naked and vulnerable, as if he had come upon her wrapped only in a towel, waiting to dip her foot in the claw-footed old tub. "Something's wrong here and nobody's telling me. I won't have it kept from me!"

Father lurched forward, his eyes wide, his cheeks smeared with the blush of unnatural rage.

"What have you done? For me? For me, was it? Have I cost you so much? And he fell to the floor on his knees at her feet. Tears streamed down his waxen cheeks and the other kids stopped their play to watch the old man tightly squeeze his daughter's elbows. "Can't you take it back. Can't it be undone? I don't want another burden on my shoulders! Do you hear me? I can't bear any more guilt; I'm crushed by what I bear already."

His forehead dropped in penance to the dirty rug and he pounded it with his fists.

"I won't have it! I can't let you go on like that! You'll not kill yourself for me! Not for me! No, not for me!"

And the old man wept and pounded his fists. Adrienne was terrified and tried to pull him up to his feet, shouting at him, crying.

"It's not your fault, Father! Please, believe me, it's not your fault! Don't make it worse. Don't break like this in front of me and the others! Don't be like that, I love you! I love you!"

But the old man wouldn't stop and there were no footsteps coming out from the kitchen and he still wouldn't stop and the other kids looked at her with scowls as if she were responsible and she pleaded with him to stop, to stop now! to get up on his feet, and her eyes clouded with hot tears and the room with the pale parabolas and the smell of must and the old coarse rug began to spin all around, and still the others looked at her, scowling, pitiless, without hope . . .

With a piercing shriek, she awoke to total darkness.

Pain first, then sharp cold. Her stomach, burning and nauseous as if trampled by the thousand feet of an angry squad of soldiers. And her face, swollen, raw, her eyes puffed almost closed. Her tongue, stiff with contusions, painfully slid across the jagged edges of what had once been whole teeth. The darkness swirled about her and her eyes struggled vainly to latch on to some small point of light for orientation. Then, as her consciousness grew, she lurched to her knees as an electric jolt of all her body ills coursed through her. The floor beneath her was cold stone.

And she was naked.

Then she began to remember and terror drove her to her feet. She swayed, her knees wobbly and her head swimming, and suddenly doubled over with violent retching. It was an oily vomit by the feel of it, a vomit well mixed with blood the redness of which she couldn't see because of the darkness. But she could feel it. Then she fell back weakly on her haunches to the cold stone floor.

That bastard. That brutal, perverted bastard.

Violent chills overwhelmed her, compounding the agony of the rips and tears on her body. Chills from the cold floor which had pressed against her nakedness for God knows how long, chills of terror sparked by the evil man she had taken as her husband. She hugged herself seeking warmth as she squatted on the floor, waiting for her cramps and heaves to subside.

And she had felt guilty. All the time with Jade she had felt guilty. She rawly cursed her conscience with trembling, torn lips.

She remembered Heinreich's flaming eyes as he confronted her with her infidelity. But the terror and shame she had felt then vanished as she listened astounded to what had been all along his secret plans for her. A demon bride, a satanic lover. Madness, that was. And then that whistling, stinging leather crop that he raised so high above his head, his aged eyes wide and renewed with rage. She remembered screaming for him to stop, and the sharp, stinging thunderbolts of pain that wracked her body. Again and again that stick fell onto her, tearing her flesh with the force of the blows, cracking her face, filling her vision with blood and darkness.

She had been so dazzled by his wealth and prestige and by the substance of his cosmopolitan life. And beneath it all this maggot-strewn dung. This dark prison and her tortured nakedness.

Before she could try a second time to rise to her feet, the room in which she was imprisoned was flooded with blinding white light. Her eyelids slammed shut, points of color swimming before her blackened vision in unison with sharp pains flashing through her brain. She had no chance to see anything of the room in which she was imprisoned.

The sound of a door being unlocked from somewhere behind her sent her spinning on the naked pads of her feet, backing away from the sound, pressing at last into the cold metal of a far wall. She covered her breasts with one hand and squeezed her thighs together as she squatted against the wall, protecting her nakedness. With her other hand she shaded her eyes, trying to see who or what was coming into her cell.

The slow scraping of heavy shoes resonated off the metallic walls.

"Who's there? I can't see because of the light. Tell me who you are!" Her voice spilled like cottony gravel over her injured tongue and teeth. She was startled by the sound of herself, so throaty and alien and whistly, like one of the toothless bums she disdained to acknowledge as she walked down Broadway. She pulled her arms more tightly to herself for cover as she cowered against the wall.

"It is I, madam."

Bennett. Adrienne was ashamed of her nakedness, especially in front of him, and tried to hide herself even more with her arms and clasped thighs.

"Bennett, thank God! You've got to get me out of here. You've no idea what he's done to me. Please, get me something to wear and get me out of here! I'll see that no harm comes to you once we're out of here. He's mad. He's a raving lunatic. Please, Bennett, hurry!"

There was a long silence and a cold chill of terror began to seep throughout Adrienne's breast.

"I am in your husband's employ, madam. Not yours. I am also aware of what he has done to you. I watched the procedure, or at least the latter part of it, the stripping and imprisonment. Indeed, I, myself, played a rather major role in it, if I must say so. You are a lovely woman, madam, I give you at least that. Or you were, to be perfectly frank with you. At the moment you are rather . . . hideous, I should say. Swollen and discolored. And see here, see how you've messed this floor I take such pains to keep spotless. Ugh, horrible, madam, very inconsiderate of you, I must say. And it does smell. I'm sure you took no thought of me before spilling your guts all over the floor that I have to clean up."

Just as she feared: that slimy Bennett whom she had never liked was in league with Heinreich and they were both as mad as March hares. Why she should have thought otherwise was unclear to her: perhaps the clutching at straws to which condemned and hopeless prisoners are prone. She heard the tap of his big shoes as he walked before her in a wide circle, surveying her.

"And may I give you a bit of advice, madam? Before you promise protection to someone else, make sure first that you can at least protect yourself." He walked to the far side of the room and she heard the opening of drawer and the metallic rattle of chains and other sounds which she couldn't as yet identify.

Her eyes began to slowly adjust to the light and she could make out Bennett's vague shadow as it went about its business poking through drawers and pulling various shapes off hooks suspended on the wall. They had conspired against her and had backed her into a hopeless corner. Their mistake, she thought. She could do nothing now but rage and resist them. There was no middle ground, no game of give and take, no chance of her bending to her husband's will. Terrified as she was, with her body aching and agonized, certain strengths within her began to rise and swell to the fore.

They'd get nothing from her, no amusing shows, no contrite weeping and pleading, no defiant scenarios befitting their mockery: nothing that they didn't wring from her with their sweat and rage.

"I'm afraid, madam, that you will soon learn the terrible price that must be paid for disloyalty. Mr. Mercadante requested that I remind you how much he has given you and how shamelessly you cast it all away with some cheap fortune hunter who, we are sure, looked upon you as nothing more than an attractive meal ticket." He found what he was looking for and approached Adrienne with some ill-defined, ominous objects in his hand. Her eyes had just begun to adjust to the glaring white light and she backed herself more tightly against the wall, huddling in her nakedness. Bennett delivered his words to her like an arrogant actor who has suddenly found himself in a play that is beneath him. His words lacked all expression and emphasis while boredom competed with contempt for mastery of his facial lines.

"You're with him then," Adrienne suddenly snapped up to him. "I figured as much. The two of you are both madmen. You belong together."

"Don't call me mad!" screamed Bennett, his eyes blazing with sudden passion. With the half-hidden metallic objects, still in his hand, he drew his arm high over his head and sent the back of his hand smashing against the side of Adrienne's head. She yelped, sprawling along the floor.

Squat, square, and ugly, Bennett stood above her, panting.

"You won't speak to me like that, you slut." His humorless, expressionless face was taut with anger and his chest heaved as he tried to calm himself down. "I've been sent to prepare you and I shall. I won't have you making a monkey of me. I won't have you be the one to force me to transgress the bounds of my duty. You'll learn what it means to cross the Master. You've just gotten a taste so far. Just a taste. So if I were you I'd just keep my mouth shut right now. Just keep it shut."

And he stooped to where she lay, grabbing her wrist. Before she had recovered sufficiently from the blow to protest, he dragged her to her feet and quickly clamped something around it, a leather wrist clamp with a metal catch that snapped shut with a click and a teardrop eyelet of iron that dangled to one side. Then he reached for her other wrist but this time she lurched away from him and made for the opposite wall. With a brief curse and a sneer he caught her ankle with his heavy square shoes and sent her sprawling again to the floor. He flew on top of her, catching her wrist and manacling it like the other. Then he pulled her by her hair and wrist to the center of the room.

"You'd best not fight me, you bitch. Not me. There's enough in store for you as is." His wonted expression of servile idiocy was now replaced by increasing excitement and amusement at Adrienne's imminent punishment. He seemed to reach up into the glare of the light and brought back down two lengths of chain to which he attached the manacles. She struggled with him, pulling her arms away from him, twisting her body away, kicking at him with her legs. But he couldn't be stopped. With undaunted assurance in the iron strength of his arms, he calmly, methodically, bent her arms to his will and as she heard the snapping of two locks, torrents of tears fell from her swollen eyes. He left her struggling vainly to pull the manacles off her wrists while he strode to the far wall, the wall with the shelves and cabinets. He pressed a button with one thick finger and there was a muffled whirr of machinery coming from above, from within the glare of the light, and the chains rolled upward, winding up some invisible winch, drawing her arms high above her head.

She wept; that she couldn't control. But she was silent. She knew it was pointless to beg. And God only knew what other foul beasts she'd bring down on her if she screamed. Dignity. At least he'd not have that off her.

She was pulled upward until she could just barely rest on the balls of her feet. The sound of the winch ceased.

Bennett walked around her, surveying her helpless nakedness, keeping sufficiently far from her to thwart a potential kick from her legs. She was a beautiful woman if you could disregard the swelling and discoloration of her face and the blue-black blotches that were sprinkled up and down her flanks and abdomen. Beautiful breasts: well-shaped, round and firm and capped by large pink nipples, thrust saucily forward by her dangling posture. A full bush of dark, fine hair between her legs. Long, slim legs. A firm ass with well-defined dimples resting above each cheek. He circled her silently, breathing heavier with each step.

"It's a pity, it really is," he said to her slowly, letting the moist syllables slide from between his fat, square lips like beads of thick oil. "There was to be so much for you. So much glory. So many honors. So many worshippers who would have killed themselves or each other or anybody in the world if you should have so much as nodded your head in displeasure. You've thrown all that away. And the Master's respect. He chose you out of all the others. And there were many, many who volunteered, who wept grovelling at his feet, begging to be permitted to be the Great One's bride. But no, he told us that when the right one came along he would know it. And it just wasn't to be from within the fold. No amount of pleading could alter that twist of fate. Their kisses, their leering eyes, their obscene and lascivious eyes and tongues couldn't change his mind." Bennett swallowed drily, his narrow eyes coursing up and down Adrienne's body. "He's immune to all that. Nothing moves him but the words of the Great One, waiting for Him, searching Him out from among the swarms of others who crawl upon this planet. And to think you could have been His bride but for that hot gash between your legs that seems to rule you rather than serve you. Well, you've made your choice and now you've got to suffer the consequences."

Her resolve to be silent melted in her rage. "What choice? I've had no chance to choose. I've known nothing of this Great One and I've already been a bride, once too often. So what if I've been with another man? Your *Master* wanted no part of me." Her lips cracked and bled with her torrent of words, and her swollen tongue pained her as she spoke. "I offered myself for his pleasure a hundred times only to be coldly refused and humiliated. I respected him then, even if I couldn't love him. I tried to do for him whatever he wanted of me to repay him for his care and protection. And I also pitied him. Yes, I pitied him. I saw beyond his wealth and his friends and the many parties he took me to. I saw how alone he was. I thought he was a man isolated by his business affairs who never had the time in his life for love and real companionship. But I was wrong. I see now how wrong I was. He's not been isolated by his wealth or genius: he's isolated by his madness. Both of you belong together: you're both pathetically, horribly insane."

And once again Bennett smashed her across her swollen face with the back of his hand. The chains jangled and swayed above her with the force of the blow.

"You persist in thinking it's madness, do you?" shouted Bennett. "You still think that, even after confessing how little you know of him and the reasons behind his choosing to marry you! You still dare to tell others how crazy they are. You still dare to judge. You are a stubborn, ignorant woman who had a chance for greatness, if you only could've kept faithful to the man who had chosen you and cared for you. You think it's madness to know that the Great One, the Warlord of Heaven and Hell, has arrived among us. How pathetic you are, like all the rest of them with their slimy, sodden lives, unaware of the great changes that are about to fall upon the universe."

Bennett's face had purpled with his repressed fury and he turned from the suspended woman, hanging his head, nodding, mumbling to himself. His oily tongue wiped frothy spittle from off his lips. He looked back at her nakedness furtively as he plodded toward the door. Then he turned suddenly and disappeared behind her. With a sharp stab of pain coursing through her breasts, she looked down to see his square fingers pinching her nipples from behind, pulling them sharply out from her breasts, stretching them, twisting them.

"Stop that!" Adrienne squealed. Bennett dug his thumbnails slowly into the tender flesh of her nipples. Her lips and neck went taut as she winced with pain, the thin tendons of her neck stood out swollen and stretched.

"The lady wants to betray her husband," Bennett panted, his voice gone throaty and guttural. "The lady still commands, thinking others listen. The lady says we're insane. Sick. That's what the lady says. Trollop for scum . . ."

Bennett worked himself up into a fury, panting, slavering down the long sweep of her neck, twisting her breasts mercilessly with his stubby fingers, pressing himself up against her from behind, the bulge in his trousers becoming harder and more menacing. She squirmed to get away from him, twisting and arching beneath her bonds, trying to free her legs from the confining pressure of his so that she would be free to flail out at him with all her might. But the more she struggled, the more tightly Bennett clung to her, filling her nostrils with the sickly scent of his stale breath and torturing her ears with the obscene growling and lechery of his words.

Suddenly the lights went out. Both victim and tormentor were startled into sudden immobility. The thick silence of the darkness was broken only by the labored panting of Bennett. Then there was a slight whirr of machinery hidden somewhere behind the walls and the chamber became reverberant and echoey, ringing with the electric puffballs of its own silence.

Bennett thrust himself away from Adrienne, spinning to the far side of the room, terrified. Adrienne just stared wildly about her, searching for any random mote of light.

A thin shaft of light appeared and widened as the chamber door was slowly drawn open. The triangle of exterior light expanded as it swept the floor, first illuminating Bennett's form as he cowered in a far corner, shielding his ugly face with his forearm. Then Adrienne's naked feet, just barely touching the floor. The shadow of a cloaked man filled the doorway. His breathing, resonated by the echo chamber, was slow, firm, and steady. Bennett began to whimper, his moist inarticulation punctuated by clicks and pops of mucus suddenly gone dry in his throat. Adrienne's breathing, ever more rapid with her terror, seemed to fill the room. The door to the chamber slammed shut behind the entering figure, leaving the three of them once again in total darkness. Nothing could be discerned of the room's new occupant other than his slow, steady breathing until two faint, reddish glows began to shimmer and brighten in the darkness—his eyes.

A VOICE: [*that in the echo chamber sounded like the voice of Yahweh addressing his wayward flock from the peak of Sinai*] You would dare assault my prize?

BENNETT: [*amidst tears and whimpering*] I meant no harm, Master. She is nothing to me. She is yours. Only yours.

VOICE: You would intrude upon my vengeance?

BENNETT: I meant nothing by it, Master. I was bewitched by her. I was driven by her eyes . . .

VOICE: You were driven by your own weak lusts!

BENNETT: Don't hurt me, Master! I'm begging you. I'm on my knees to you!

VOICE: You belong on your knees with your tongue licking the filth off the floor. You belong bent and broken beneath the dome of night. Your every glance upward deserves to be a humble obeisance. Your every word deserves to be a whimper.

BENNETT: Please, Master. I've been faithful to you for all these years. I've tried in a thousand different ways to return the many gifts of your kindnesses to me . . .

VOICE: Your neck is too rigid. Your spine too stiff. That must be remedied.

Two pencil beams of ruby light flashed from the glowing eyes, bathing Bennett's cringing, kneeling form in a bloody glow. Slowly, inch by straining inch, Bennett was levitated upward within the glow and made to dangle like a stuffed monkey at a shooting gallery in the empty air.

Adrienne gasped.

VOICE: Though she defied me, do you think she is any less precious to me? She shall be established as an example for heretics among the new order. Her lust and ignorance shall live for eons in infamy. There is still much left for her to endure. There is much left for her to symbolize.

BENNETT: [*his voice shaken and choking, his arms reaching forward in supplication*] Master . . .

VOICE: You shall learn.

The glow intensified around Bennett and then his body was suddenly wrenched and twisted by invisible hands. There was a lingering, grinding sound as his spine was cracked forward into a hump. His neck was twisted far to the left until more bone and gristle were to be heard snapping and grinding beneath the invisible hands. A final blood-chilling groan filled the echoing chamber and Bennett's body went limp in space, floating, unconscious. Then it dropped to the floor with a ponderous thud, the beams of ruby light extinguished, leaving only the two eyes burning like hot coals in utter darkness.

VOICE: He will learn to serve me all the better in the future. His twisted body will be a constant reminder to him of my omniscience and my power.

There was a heavy silence broken only by Adrienne's terrified panting and the resonant clicking of shoes on the stone floor as the two glowing eyes encircled the pendant victim.

VOICE: There are lessons yet remaining for you as well, my dear. Many lessons. Slow, painful lessons. You will soon come to wish that his defiling hands were the worst of your torments. Perhaps I shall yet give you to him, as twisted as he is. He has been faithful to me for so many years. It would display my magnanimity to throw you to him like a bone to a dog. Now that he is a humpbacked cripple, he will appreciate you all the more.

ADRIENNE: Heinreich! What manner of beast are you? What monster have I married?

The eyes glowed into her own, shining like wet blood. His voice filled the room like a deity.

VOICE: You ask questions far too profound for your meager intelligence. I've come neither to bandy philosophies with you nor to explain the roots of my existence or the ultimate end of all my striving. Enough will become apparent to you in time. Rather, I've come with a question for you which it would behoove you to answer quickly and truthfully. I had in my possession a small jade unicorn. It is gone. What have you done with it?

ADRENNE: I don't know what you're talking about.

The glowing eyes brightened and Adrienne lurched and screamed. A large, odorous burn pustule erupted on her left breast. Her eyes flowed with tears of pain and rage.

VOICE: What have you done with the jade unicorn?

ADRIENNE: Damn you, you fiend! You hellish pig!

She lurched again, agonized, a new pustule erupting on her upper lip.

VOICE: I can endure my part of this scenario far longer than you can endure yours. Where is the jade unicorn?

ADRIENNE: I don't know anything about your damned unicorn! I'm not privy to your queer toys . . .

She lurched again with pain, a pustule rising painfully on the ball of her left foot, forcing her to stand on only one leg.

ADRIENNE: [*her voice cracked with pain*] I don't know anything of your unicorn. If I did, don't you think I'd tell you rather than endure all of this? Why can't you just leave me alone? Leave me alone!

VOICE: You are willing to endure all this pain and far more, I should guess, because you fancy yourself in love with an audacious pimp and gigolo. Whore that you are. Slut. The more you resist, the more completely you fulfill the facets of my destiny. The more you struggle against me, the more strength I possess. [*his voice became soft and cajoling*] Will you tell me now?

ADRIENNE: [*her voice filled with a tone of startled realization*] You know where it is! You've known all along where it is and you still torture me. For information you already know. Is it a game for you? Are you playing "let's pretend"? Do you want to see me beg for mercy or forgiveness for my sins? Well, I won't. Do what you want with your madness and your strange powers. How you reek of cruelty and evil! That jade unicorn has found itself a worthier home.

VOICE: [*bouts of resonant, billowing laughter, painful to Adrienne's ears; the eyes glow bright-dim, bright-dim, on and on, leaving trails of pustules all over Adrienne's howling body*] How damned willful we are. How noble. As you squirm and writhe at my mercy, in this pitch-dark chamber, I want you to be fully aware of the fact that, at this very moment, the jade unicorn is being returned to me, its rightful owner. Think deeply on that while you ache and burn and, if you still haven't gone senseless with agony, cast a last, lingering thought upon your lover. The lover for whom you are paying so very dearly.

19

A few hours before they had been total strangers. She
had come up to Jade in the bar after a few muted
words with the bartender; they talked; she smiled a lot
and turned her eyes up and down when she looked at
him, trying to be sincere, trying to be coy and appealing
with that little girl helplessness that everybody knows
all men love; and Jade let her wash over him like a wave
breaking against a rock: flinty, hard, his yellow hair
glinting like burnished metal in the flickering light of the
candle that rested in the middle of the table. Jade turned
his words carefully over his tongue, softening them, mellowing his voice, letting her know without exactly saying
it that he would be gentle and that he cared. For the
duration, at least. It was what they all wanted to hear.
Or, better yet, to feel. That wordless assurance.

She called herself Rosie.

Actually, she had broken into one of Jade's reveries.
Yes, he was in the bar to make money. Yes, his poetry
should have been cut off from his thoughts in order for
him to most expeditiously bring home the bacon. And
those troubling thoughts, too, that had been at the back
of his mind ever since the last time he and Adrienne slept
together—those thoughts should have been cut loose by
now, or, at the very least, left in his back room by the

window that looked out on the spindly sapling that struggled to rise from the concrete alleyshade up into the sunlight.

He supposed that was what had made Adrienne special for him. She had provoked him to melancholy. She had moved him somehow, not tritely like an infatuation or any of the common excitements, but somehow darkly and mysteriously, provoking him to feel an emptiness and a tension and an eerie sense of mission just waiting around the next bend in the road, waiting to be discovered. It was nothing she had said, exactly. Maybe it was her voice trembling with sorrow and loneliness, maybe it was her bizarre narration about her life with her husband . . . but no, he had heard all that in the same tones and pathetic inflections a thousand times before. Women who had never known love or who surged with a grand unreleased passion, tumbling them to ecstasy. Women trapped in marriages of convenience who suddenly one day awoke to the fact that their youth was gone and had been wasted catering to the parched indifference of feeble husbands and now the growing creases around their eyes and lips became, for them, a reproach, a symbol of their kinship with the sterile desert, cracked like the wasted, scorched sands.

No, it couldn't have been anything Adrienne had said.

"My friend Evelyn Parker told me where I could find you," Rosie continued, wading once again into the stream of his thoughts. "I'm an old friend of hers from Pennsylvania. We grew up together. I am visiting her for a week or so and I don't know anybody in this town . . ." Her voice trailed off suggestively while her fingers strayed to the stem of her wineglass.

With an effort, Jade shook himself free of his perplexity about Adrienne and charmed Rosie with an attentive smile. He raised his glass to her and said, "Well, then, here's to Evelyn's friend who has just made another friend in this big, bad city."

She blushed and nodded, laughing. Jade surveyed her with a coy lasciviousness that was designed to politely tell her "Aha! At last I've found a client who really turns me on!" And she wasn't bad-looking: petite, slim, not quite forty, with a pretty face framed by dark hair cut stylishly short, marred only by an excess of makeup. They always did that. Ruined what they had with paint and clay. They always feel so ugly and undesirable that they've got to do something. Smear themselves with something, as if hiding behind a gooey film. Unloved, afraid of growing old, needing their desirability reconfirmed: it was all quite sad, really.

Now don't get into that, Jade thought to himself. If they weren't sad, they wouldn't come to me. Think of all I'd miss out on then. How'd that poem he wrote a long time ago start out?

> A parasite sucking fluid from sorrow
> Swelling with poison
> Waiting for that other cry
> From the darkness

Written in one of his more self-deprecating moments. He reached over the table to light the cigarette she fumbled with.

"Come on now, Rosie. You really shouldn't be smoking. At least not cigarettes. It's not good for you."

Not preaching. He could care less about her health. Just an opening for conversation. Put her at her ease. She was new at this.

The flame of the match splashed gold onto her face. "That's just one of many bad habits I've learned to live with over the years," she answered. Her eyes flared in the flamelight as she dragged deeply. Ordinary eyes, really, betraying ordinary regret and average sorrow. A poor schmuck blaming herself for her emptiness, which *was* probably her fault. An attractive woman who got lazy and frightened, afraid no one would have her after a certain age and she had snapped up the best offer around. Now she was paying.

Not like Adrienne's eyes that last night in the darkened bedroom. Something . . . unnatural . . . extraordinary about her sorrow. Her eyes were the moist, sorrowful, and bewildered eyes of a . . . that was it! a sacrificial victim, a victim against whom the entire universe was conspiring.

Why hadn't he heard from her since then?

Rosie had gotten around to hinting that Evelyn Parker

had told her something about Jade's sexual prowess and was waiting for him to ask what she had said. She was looking for an opportunity to flatter him, sort of attempt to win him to her for reasons other than money. Jade obliged, reading her eyes. She blushed.

"Well, she's too well bred to have given me each and every delicious detail. But she did let me know that you gave her quite a workout."

Jade smiled. "I can only give what I'm given in return. It takes two to enjoy sex. I'm no magician or superman." He shrugged his shoulders, holding out his open palms. "I do what I can. I look for laughs and a good heavy humping. No expectations, no disappointments. If you're not satisfied with the results, then a night with me costs you nothing."

A lousy businessman. Then how'd he make all that goddamn money?

Rosie looked back at him, embarrassed by his frank talk as he knew she would be, and began stroking her wineglass with a sculpted fingernail.

"You'll have to bear with me. I'm new to all this. A small-town girl in the big city for the first time . . . It's just that . . . I mean, I'd like to think that you'll enjoy yourself being with me . . ."

"I've never made love to you before, either. It's my first time with you as well."

"O but you know what I mean . . ."

"I only know that we're both together as first-time lovers and that's that. Track records count for nothing when you're loving a woman. I can only promise to try and make tonight a pleasant evening for you."

Adrienne's eyes as she watched his face when she handed him the jade unicorn. Waiting for a word from him. A special word. Had he said it? He couldn't remember. He couldn't be sure.

His fingers twitched to touch the tiny carving which hung from around his neck but he stilled them.

"I appreciate what you're saying to me," Rosie smiled nervously at him. "It's just that . . . well, it's been so long . . . I'm not sure I know everything that I knew a few years ago. About lovemaking. Doing it right, you see.

My husband's not very . . . energetic, you see. Laziness can be contagious. I can't make any promises . . ."

Jade laughed tenderly and then took the cigarette out of her hand, crushing it in the ashtray. He held her fingers in his, caressing the smooth skin with his own slender finger. She squeezed his hand warmly.

"I don't make promises, either. And I'm a professional. But I really don't think you've got anything to worry about. I can see fires in your eyes that maybe you can't even see yourself. Professionally speaking, I think we're going to give each other a fine time."

His smile warmed her and Rosie gave his hand an ardent squeeze. But then she leaned toward him confidentially:

"But, I mean this is my first time with a . . . a . . ."

"A hustler? A gigolo?" Jade laughed again. "Yeah, I can say those words. There's no offense in words. I prefer 'hustler' because I like nouns that are made out of verbs and 'to hustle' makes more sense to me than 'to gig.' A mere matter of linguistic preference."

Rosie broke down in giggles.

"I can't say either of them. They sound so silly."

"Isn't that the truth?"

When Jade had first got involved with Adrienne, he had quoted to her in passing a line from one of his poems. He was a little high and didn't even realize he had done it. But she had picked up on it. And then she followed it up with the typical question: why did a man with his sensibilities do the things he did? And something about the way she asked it, as if his answer could mean something important to her life, made him give her a real answer, something he took time to think about, something like, "I do what I do precisely because my sensibilities are what they are. I'm not offended by what I do. My poetry, my women, my drugs . . . it's all part of me until something better comes along. Perhaps my sensibilities don't jibe with the accepted norm. Then fuck the norm, whatever that is."

How different he'd felt with her that night on the roof as he had stared up at the moon and the beautiful star! He had felt different to himself, like in the church.

Perhaps the change was coming. His sensibilities . . .

"But," Rosie whispered, "how do I . . . you know, *take care* of you?"

"You mean pay me?"

That first time with Adrienne, she had been bombed. One black russian after another at the bar and Jerry, the bartender, all the time giving Jade the eye. He came up to her at the bar and sat next to her, trying to involve her in a conversation. But she got sick and Jade had to take her home. Even then, as drunk and dopey as she was, he felt something emanate from her, a tired, silent howl for compassion that belied the decadent glaze in her eyes. That was why he bothered at all. He hated drunks. Drunken women disgusted him. But he helped her home and settled her comfortably on her bed after wresting the housekeys from her spastic hands. He pressed cool washclothes to her forehead and cheeks and watched over her until he thought she was asleep. But then, as he rose to leave, he heard one word rise from her ever so softly: "Please."

"I'm kind of a maverick, Rosie. A bad businessman, maybe, but I manage. You don't pay me until the evening's over. I'm different that way. You let me know if you've had a good time and then you pay me. If I don't live up to what you want, then I'll just slip quietly out the door. Nothing more than that. Did Evelyn discuss my fee with you?"

She nodded.

"Well, you pay what she paid and what all my clients pay. It's all the same. I'm very democratic that way."

Not with Adrienne, as the relationship got on. She didn't have to pay him anymore as they got to see more and more of each other. And she didn't have to meet him at the bar. But she still insisted. Every morning after he slept with her he found the money tucked somewhere secretly inside the pockets or cuffs of his jeans. But after that first time when she looked up at him with eyes as bright as the morning and pressed the folded bills into the palm of his hand . . .

Jade suddenly stood up and Rosie followed his long, lean form with her quizzical eyes. "C'mon, Rosie, let me take you to a dynamite after-hours club that's really wild. Throbbing disco, private romantic nooks and corners, thick pillows all over the floor, crazy lights." Jade tempted her jovially with arching eyebrows and fingers that danced expressively along with his words. "And there are strange people wandering around all over the place, doing themselves harm with drugs. You'll love it."

Rosie was so excited she could have peed. She jumped to her feet and pressed herself closely into Jade as he helped her on with the thin shawl she had brought with her. He stroked her shoulders and bent gently to flick the lobe of her ear with his tongue. Suddenly she turned and looked up at him saying, "Are you really as great as Evelyn says you are? In bed, I mean."

Adrienne, her legs wrapped tightly around his back, pulling him into her harshly, moaning, crying out to the pantheon of nighttime deities, straining to squeeze all of him into her, biting his flesh as she came, heaving and thrusting herself at him like a naked witch in a Sabbath frenzy . . .

"Now, Rosie, you know that nobody ever lives up to expectations. Most of the time people fall short; sometimes they surprise you and zap you to the stars. It can go either way. Let's you and me just give it a chance. Okay?"

The memories of Adrienne were getting to him. He had to leave that bar and submerge himself in distractions: spinning colored lights, hard dancing, the swell and rumble of spaced-out people laughing and joking together, doing drugs, making love. He strode quickly to a rack behind the bar and produced a metalflake purple motorcycle helmet which he held out to Rosie. She stared at it, troubled.

"What's that for?"

"It's for riding with me on the back of my motorcycle."

"But I can't do that; I've never ridden on a motorcycle before."

"So? That'll be a second first for this evening."

Rosie laughed, shaking her head from side to side. "O, I couldn't possibly . . ."

"Listen. I've got a big, beautiful bike, runs smooth and gentle as a lamb, and I'm the safest driver you'll ever want to meet. Now, we can go by cab if you prefer. No problem. But why don't you live up your long night in the big city to the hilt? Let yourself go. Have fun. Do things tonight that you never thought you'd ever do. Have one big blast of a night. What do you say?"

Adrienne had clung to his shoulders, her knuckles white, yet she had laughed and shrieked in amazed joy as they sped along the Manhattan avenues, dodging potholes, the bike awash with the reflected shimmer of the city lights. Some of her long dark hair had slipped from beneath her helmet and whipped around in the air like a beckoning finger.

Rosie, absolutely thrilled by the idea, still hesitated.

"Well?" Jade asked, smiling down at her.

"Well . . ." She looked up at him brightly like an eager child just barely poised to commit her first conscious sin. "What the fuck!" She blushed and giggled at her daring language.

"What the fuck is right! Now, let's get going!"

He grabbed the other helmet and started to hasten out the door with Rosie when she suddenly stopped him and turned him to face her, resting her hands lightly on his forearms. Her face was flushed with joy and eagerness and her eyes told him that she had something to say or else she'd burst.

"Jade . . . you—you've got the most goddamn beautiful eyes!"

He looked down on her tenderly and brushed her cheek with the backs of his fingers. "I'm glad you like my eyes. My mother always said they'd get me into nothing but trouble."

And then he swept her like a high school kid out with him into the night. Jerry, the bartender, smiled at them as they left and then made another stroke with the chalk on the slate he kept behind the bar.

The next night it rained. The headlights of hurrying cars reflected off the slick streets in wavy, irregular spumes of light, two by two, like cadres of gleaming spirits floating along streets of silver and gold. Laughing couples squeezed close to each other so that they could fit beneath the umbrella, bending against the rising breezes and the fine spray of summer rain, and raced for their cars or buses or taxis, anything to carry them somewhere dry and snug. The bar began to fill with patrons coming from Lincoln Center who wished to prolong an idyllic evening of art with a few lingering hours of midweek conversation and flirtation. There was always that vital electricity in the air at the bar among the midweek revellers, as if everybody felt slightly guilty that they weren't at home in bed resting for that next day's labor. They just laughed amongst themselves, clinking glasses and leering at each other's bodies, contending, after a few drinks, that anybody who said anything to them at the office tomorrow about looking hungover could just go to hell.

Jade sat at his accustomed table in the back of the lounge with sincere eyes trained on a new woman who chattered endlessly to him about how "hip" she really was.

With a flourish of whirlwind the door of the bar opened inward and a man dressed in a long black raincoat entered. The man's body and face were bent and twisted, but the raincoat and a dark hat slouched far forward on the man's head aided him in concealing his deformities to the extent that no notice was aroused among the busily conversing patrons. He sidled quickly to the end of the bar and gestured to catch Jerry's attention.

Keeping his face averted, he said, "I've been told that a man named Jade comes here frequently. Where can I find him?"

Jerry looked at the man in the raincoat with a wary eye. "He comes in here—sometimes. I'm really not sure if he's here right now. What do you want him for?"

"I want him for nothing. I was sent to bring him a message from the woman I work for. I'd appreciate it if you'd look for him and tell him that Adrienne Mercadante must speak with him or else point him out to me and I'll tell him myself."

Jerry looked the man over curiously. He observed the bent and twisted body and noticed how the man avoided exposing his face to the soft light from behind the bar.

"I'll look and see if he's here. You wait where you are. What's the lady's name again?"

"Adrienne Mercadante, although I think Adrienne'll do. And tell him it's urgent." The bent man then turned his back on Jerry and leaned against the bar, his thick, square fingers strumming lightly on its brass edge.

Jerry passed under the bar and made his way through the crowd to Jade's table.

"Could you excuse me a moment, Jade? I've got to talk to you."

The woman speaking to Jade was silenced and, after glaring at the intruder, she busied herself with the contents of her purse.

"What's the story, Jerry?" Jade laughed. Jerry leaned over his shoulder to whisper in his ear.

"There's a guy up front, see him over there? The hunchback in the raincoat. He says he's got a message for you from some lady named Adrienne Murk-something . . . a weird name . . ."

Jade's eyes flashed. "Mercadante?"

"Yeah, that's it. He says it's urgent."

"Well, send him right over . . ." Jade caught himself and glanced at the woman seated across from him. "No, better yet, I'll go over to him at the bar." He turned to the woman with a charming smile. "Please, Ann, you'll have to excuse me, just for a moment. Some business has come up and I must speak to somebody. I'll be right back. Don't you go away."

His long, lean form unfolded from the chair and he followed close behind Jerry as they threaded through the crowd.

"I don't know about this guy, Jade. Something's really weird about him. Besides his hunchback. Heavy vibrations."

"Thanks for the warning. You haven't been wrong yet. I'll keep my eyes open."

Jerry went behind the bar and Jade walked up to the strange, squat figure.

"I'm Jade," he said. "The bartender said you have an important message for me."

The hunchback slowly turned his face up toward Jade, bringing it out from the cover of the slouched hat as if it were worth whatever embarrassment it might cost him just to look with his own eyes upon the man he was sent to fetch. When he saw the face, Jade drew in a quick breath: it seemed to be what was once an incredibly ugly square face with an oblong nose and thick lips molded in haste by a sculptor in clay and then wrenched awry in a fit of the sculptor's passion at his failure. The chin was slung to the right while the nose was bent and twisted to the left. The left eye was nearly closed by the inhuman drooping of the bony ridge beneath the eyebrow. Jade turned his eyes from the man's face in fear that he should be offended by his staring.

"The message is from my mistress, Mrs. Mercadante. She sent me to bring you to her right away. It is most urgent that she see you immediately."

Jade's blood chilled. "Is she all right? Has she been hurt?"

"Her welfare depends to a great extent upon how quickly you come with me. I'm not at liberty to explain any more than that. The rest you'll learn from her own lips."

Jade knew something was wrong. He had had ominous and vague forebodings since he had left her that night when she gave him the jade unicorn. He hadn't seen or heard from her since then, and such a peculiar silence puzzled him. But why would she confide in a servant of hers about their secret relationship? She must either be in desperate trouble or . . .

Or else it was a setup.

Could her husband have found out? The last Jade knew, he was still in Europe on one of his prolonged business trips. But that could have changed suddenly. That would explain her silence for the last week.

Occupational hazard.

So either she was in some kind of trouble and really did send this messenger to him, or her old man found out about them. In which case she was still in a lot of trouble. He remembered the bizarre curios he had seen in the cabinets of Mercadante's study: carved deities and demons, strange amulets wrought in gold and silver and fine enamel, decorative goblets and curved daggers in sheaths of precious metal encrusted with gems, and rings with signets engraved in ancient and long-dead tongues. And that photo of him on the bookshelf in the gold frame:

a man with dark, sinister eyes set in a gaunt skull that fairly quivered with intensity right out of the picture frame. It was not an easy picture to look at and, struck by its sinister overtones but with far better things on his mind, Jade had taken no further special notice of it. But for all he knew, her husband might be crazy. Many of the super-rich developed along eccentric lines, which Jade knew well from conversing with their wives. On occasion.

Jade rubbed his forehead with his left hand, perplexed. The hunchback had again retreated beneath the slouch of his hat, waiting silently for his answer. Jade looked at Jerry, who eyed him with a troubled glance as he rinsed a few glasses.

If it had been any other woman, Jade would have dodged the encounter entirely. Marital problems weren't his affair. Besides, he was already booked for the night. He turned and glimpsed Ann's back as she sat quietly in the back, nursing her drink.

But it was Adrienne. Whether the messenger was legitimate or not, she needed him. And he hadn't been able to shake her from his mind all week. Not hearing from her had become disconcerting, even painful.

It frustrated Jade that he had become "involved."

"I'll get my jacket," he said to the hunchback.

He headed for the far side of the bar where his motorcycle jacket hung on a peg. Jerry followed along the other side of the bar and when Jade reached for his jacket they talked in quick whispers.

"A friend's in trouble," Jade said. "I don't know if Quasimodo over there is really from her or her old man. Either way, I've got to find out if she's okay."

"But if she's just a trick, why take the chance of getting in hot water?"

"That's what I'm saying to myself right now. I don't know, man. Maybe I've got too big a dose of the swashbuckler in me. Besides, Ann over there seemed like she'd make it a real dull night for me. Tell her I've been unavoidably called away."

Then, as Jade put on his jacket, he leaned closer to Jerry whispering, "Slip me the gun."

"Right," said Jerry, and with a fleeting movement,

whipped the revolver from behind the bar and passed it to Jade, who tucked it inside his belt.

"I'll get it back to you as soon as I can," Jade said. "Thanks."

"No problem. Just you take care of yourself."

Jade walked up to the hunchback who was looking out the glass door at the rain and tapped him on the shoulder. He spun around, wincing with pain. Jade pulled back his hand.

"Sorry, I didn't mean to hurt you. Just wanted to let you know I'm ready."

The hunchback averted his eyes. "It's nothing. I am just sore from . . . a recent fall. Follow me."

And they both passed out into the rain.

The hunchback walked with a slow, loping stride due to the difference in length between his legs. His clothes were ill suited for his misshapen body. As he walked, the trouser cuff of his short right leg dragged along in the puddles. It looked to Jade as if this misbegotten body had tried to clothe itself right off the rack in some department store.

What could such a creature have to do with Adrienne? Or her suave and elegant husband?

Jade fiddled with the zipper of his jacket, right next to the revolver.

There was a broad alley leading between the bar and a Chinese restaurant beyond which was a taxi stand. But instead of taxis, the stand was occupied by a single large black Cadillac limo. On either side of the alley were huge piles of refuse bagged in plastic and stacked together in large corrugated cartons.

A perfect place for a setup. Jade looked down the alley and saw the waiting limo. The windows were darkened so he couldn't see if anybody was in it. Besides, it was too far away and the lighting was none too good. Jade stopped at the entrance of the alley.

"Why have you stopped?" said the hunchback huskily, turning to him.

"I'm allergic to alleys."

The hunchback eyed Jade cunningly. "I don't see why

a man with my physical disproportions should be able to walk through unafraid while a man with your obvious attributes should hesitate."

"Yeah, well, that may puzzle *you*. But I don't know you from Adam and I've learned in my young but full life not to walk into any dark alleys with anybody but my friends. So have the car brought around here."

"You realize how costly any delay might be . . ."

"Delay, my ass. Bring the car around here or I'm not going anywhere."

The hunchback looked him over slowly one final time, his ratty eyes as hard and cold as flint.

"Very well." And the hunchback lurched his way slowly through the alley while Jade watched him pass the piles of refuse. Finally, the misshapen form reached the limo and slipped quickly into the back seat. There was evidently a chauffeur in the car because, once the hunchback was in the car, it sped off around the block.

Until the limo lurched to a stop right in front of him, Jade listened closely for any untoward, stray sounds from the alley. There were none. He wondered if he were being merely overly cautious or superparanoid. And then the door of the limo flew open.

A man squeezed himself out of the car, if one could call such a living mountain a man. Built like an immense Sumo wrestler, he was close to seven feet tall and weighed easily six hundred pounds. The suspension of the heavy limo rocked like a boat in rough seas as the man emerged. He had close-cropped hair and beady eyes buried in creases of fat. He smiled mockingly at Jade, as if he were glaring at a roast turkey or loin of beef. Jade was so startled at the man's size that he froze in awe, heedless of the gun stuffed in his belt. With a guttural snort, the man-mountain lumbered straight at Jade, shoving him with one giant paw head over heels into the depths of the alley.

Jade got to his knees on the wet concrete, shaking his head to clear it of the fog from the sudden, powerful blow. The way he had been thrown so effortlessly, the way his toes barely scraped the ground as he flew through the air: he had never conceived such strength to be possible in one human being. And now the man was lurching down upon him at a run, the mocking sneer still plastered on his face.

His eyes filled with the vision of that hurtling monster and with the patapat of hastening footsteps that would instantly be upon him ringing in his ears, Jade pulled the revolver out of his belt. But then, just behind him, he heard a wild commotion of spilling garbage cans and ripping cardboard.

An entire wall of garbage rose into the air, poised to bury him.

"Shit!" Jade muttered, rolling quickly to the alley wall to avoid both the careening giant and the deluge of garbage. But the charging giant stopped himself short and watched as the wall of garbage splattered throughout the alley, cans crashing against the walls and concrete floor, splitting, spewing stinking refuse and dangerous shards of rusty metal all up and down the alley.

Jade groaned with agony as a heavy metal can bounced off a wall and rolled over his legs. He stared wide-eyed back where the garbage had risen from and it all became clear to him.

A second giant, an even larger mountain of a man, was standing where the garbage had been piled. The boxes and cans of garbage had provided him careful concealment for the ambush. And when the behemoth rose, the ton of garbage rose with him, becoming a deadly ton of payload in his mighty hands.

The resounding crash in the alley was certain to attract attention. The hunchback bounded out of the limo shouting encouragement and the urgent necessity for haste. Then the two huge fiends closed in on Jade.

Jade's finger quivered on the trigger of the gun, steadying itself to shoot the first assailant right in the middle of his sneer. But the second one hoisted a garbage can lid from the ground and spun it at Jade's wrist like a Frisbee. Inflicting a tremor of blinding pain, the lid connected with Jade's wrist and the gun went sliding along the wet pavement.

"Profaning my master's household!" shouted the hunchback as he raved at the entrance to the alley. "Dallying with his wife like the common slut she is! You'll learn! You'll learn! Hurry, both of you! Get what we came for, then kill him!"

Before Jade could even get to his feet, the first assailant was upon him, gripping the front of his jacket with a hairy paw and raising him bodily up against the brick alley wall, his feet dangling a good three feet off the pavement. The pressure of the man's fist against his chest, pressing him ever more tightly into the wall, began to choke him. Jade strained with his bent legs kicking wildly at the man's chest and his arms thrusting out from the wall against the massive arm to try, if but for an instant, to push the monster from him. But the huge form merely smiled and remained immobile. Glowing spots began to dance before Jade's straining eyes.

"Where . . . is . . . it?"

It sounded at first like the murmur of an impending earthquake. Then Jade realized it was a voice, the giant's voice.

"Where . . . is . . . unicorn!"

Before Jade's throat was free to utter a sound, the man pulled him from against the wall and, gripping the leather jacket at its collar, ripped the jacket apart, closed zipper and all. It ripped with a slow, lingering "z-z-z" as the tiny metal teeth of the zipper flew apart, bit by bit.

"We . . . find . . . it . . . wherever!"

And then, as Jade's shirt ripped along with the jacket, the carved jade unicorn popped out from beneath the folds of fabric and sparkled angrily and menacingly in the subdued light of the alley. For a long moment the two assailants held Jade aloft and stared at the glistening object of their search. Then the giant who was holding Jade grinned even more broadly and triumphantly and reached for the slender gold chain. What must have been reddish impurities around the eyes of the figurine caught the stray light from the slick concrete and glowed like living coals, angry and deadly.

Just like at the church: poised to gore his throat with that tiny, menacing horn. And the red-washed eyes.

Give them the damn thing, he thought. It doesn't like me any better than they do.

But with a quick snapping of his arm, Jade brought the heel of his hand smack into the giant's nose, crushing it flat against his face. A combat trick from Nam,. from those dark years of which Jade never spoke. Blood sprayed in torrents all over the giant's ugly, fat face. With a howl, the man-mountain loosened his grip on Jade's shoulders and Jade fell to the ground.

Elbow punches, side-hand chops, death-dealing legs that flashed like lightning: Jade used every trick in the book. The assailants hadn't expected him to be trained in combat techniques so they were thrown off their guard. But just briefly. Every move Jade made to flee from the alley was blocked by some part or other of gigantic torso, hand or leg or great bloated gut, and he was grabbed and hurled against the walls mercilessly, blood streaming from his head and face, his vision stained red with his wounds, his ears deafened with the fierceness of his own painful cries. The giant with the crushed nose bellowed with rage and stumbled to catch Jade squirming amidst the garbage on the ground and hurl him against the wall to his death. But Jade was quick and resilient. Neither giant could quite hold on to him and they both cursed and spat at him in their rage.

Then Jade inadvertently stabbed his knee on a shard of broken bottle. His evasive rolls and twists came to an excruciating halt. And the two giants closed in.

The behemoth Jade had injured lifted him up from the ground by his face, palming it like a basketball. Jade swung wildly at him with his arms but his blows had poor leverage and little force. The great hand crushing his face closed ever more tightly and, with the increasing pressure, two fingers slipped ever closer to the orbits of his eyes. Cataracts of pain swirled in the darkness of agony that Jade endured. Bursts of residual vision, splashes of color behind closed eyes, horrifying snaps and creaks from the gristle of his cheeks: Jade began to welcome the imminent loss of consciousness that was prepared for him.

Until the grip of the giant hand on his face went slack and the eyes of the bloody giant went wide with shock and pain.

Jade fell to the rubbled ground. He fell at the feet of a powerful and vigorous old man with wild, streaming white hair and beard. In the old man's hand was a heavy staff covered with intricate and mysterious carvings. The center of the staff was splashed with blood from where it had landed on the back of the first giant's head.

From far away the urgent "woop-woop" of a police siren shattered the sudden stillness left by the first giant's crashing to the ground. Wordlessly, the old man flung himself at the larger remaining assailant, slashing at the startled form with his staff. The old man was all over him, lunging, smashing, swinging the mighty staff high over his head and sending it crashing down on the man-mountain's limbs and shoulders. The hunchback, having kept a safe distance from the fray, fairly hopped and pranced with rage.

"You fools have lost him now! The police will be here any second! We can't be found here. Get away! Get away!"

The second giant was too busy dodging the old man's blows to acknowledge the order. But he suddenly lunged past the swinging staff and roughly shoved the old man to the ground. He kept running for the alley entrance and the waiting limo but not without turning back for one last look of hatred and vengeance at both Jade and the old man.

He was evidently not someone used to defeat.

As the man-mountain passed his comrade, he stopped and raised the groggy giant to shaky feet. Then, arm in arm, the two titans lumbered out of the alley and down the street to a waiting van. The hunchback flew into the limo and the ponderous car peeled off from the curb and disappeared into the rainy night.

Jade was flat out on the wet concrete. His breathing came in labored pants and the old man sat near him on the edge of a box, panting also. Now that the danger was past, Jade luxuriated in the sudden silence and the freedom to recline at his ease on the ground. He pressed his face with his hands.

"I think they broke my face," he said aloud, with a touch of humor in his voice. "I never heard of such a thing. Broken noses, broken teeth, even broken cheeks. But not a broken face."

"We'd better get you home so you can fix yourself up," said the old man. His voice was soft and kind and tinged with urgency. "You're lucky that all they broke was your face."

"I'm not so sure that's all they did break," answered Jade as he looked up from the ground with puffed eyes. "And as for being lucky, you can forget about that too. I owe my life to you, not luck. There's nothing lucky about the way you swing that stick."

The old man smiled. "We'll talk about all that later. First, we've got to put you back together."

"It won't happen. No way. I think I'll just stretch out here and wait for death with a serene countenance."

The old man bent down and grabbed Jade's shoulders, laughing. "Come on now, up you go."

With the old man's assistance, Jade struggled to his wobbly feet. "Shit!" he cursed. "Shit! Fuck! PISS!" Jade steadied himself in an upright position, rubbing his head with his hands. "I knew I was looking for trouble going outside with that little hunchback. Christ, I'm in such pain right now, you wouldn't believe it."

"O I'd believe it," smiled the old man. "You just need to feel half as bad as you look and I'll believe anything."

Jade looked at the old man and started to smile. "O shit, don't make me smile. It hurts like hell. Say something sad, quick!"

"Come, come now," said the old man. He let Jade lean on him while he cursorily surveyed the young man's wounds. "You may hurt pretty badly for a while, and you certainly don't look too good, I must say. But, all in all your injuries seem basically superficial."

"O yeah? You wouldn't say that if you saw me at the beginning of this fracas. Did you get a good look at those guys? I never saw any human beings that large in all my life. They picked me up and were throwing me against the walls like an empty beer can. I think they broke every bone in my body."

"Not in the least. You've got a strong frame. You take good care of yourself. From what I saw, you were going pretty good."

"O sure, another few minutes and I would've broken his finger with my eyeball."

A crowd started to gather at the entrance to the alley. The police drew closer, only a few blocks away.

"I think we'd both better get out of here before the police come," the old man said. "Or else we're trapped for their infernal questioning."

"Yeah, you're right. Let's split." Jade then noticed the shreds of his jacket hanging around his shoulders. "Look what that asshole did to my leather jacket. It was my bike jacket, my one and only. Shit!"

"Worry about it later. Let's get out of here."

"Right, right." As Jade and the old man started to go out the back way toward the taxi stand, Jade remembered the gun. "I've got to go get something I left over there. It belongs to a friend and I don't want him to get into any hassles." He limped over to a dark shadow in which piles of garbage were strewn. Scowling, he finally spied the gun buried in some greasy trash. He looked at it as he walked back to the old man. "Yep, you sure did me a lot of good," he said, addressing the gun. "It's a lucky thing that that motherfucker knocked you away from me or else he might've eaten you."

"Those . . . things rarely do anybody any good," said the old man.

"That's easy for you to say. Anybody who can handle a piece of carved wood the way you do doesn't need a gun. But as for the rest of us poor mortals . . ."

"Now, now, conversation later. Right now we'd best make ourselves scarce."

"Yeah, well, I'm counting on that conversation. I mean, who the hell are you? Here you've just saved my life and I don't even know your name so that I can thank you properly. And you're old enough to be my father (no offense, of course) and yet you danced rings around the two biggest dudes I ever saw in my life." Jade stared at the old man's wise and humorous eyes. "Something strange is going on here."

The old man looked back at Jade with great seriousness in his eyes and voice. "You're right, you know," he said. "Something strange is going on. And furthermore, Jade, I promise to answer all your questions later. But now's not the time nor the place."

With that, the old man hastened around the corner

while Jade struggled to follow, wondering all the while how he knew his name. Then, on a sudden impulse, Jade stopped and reached among the shreds of fabric that were his shirt for the jade unicorn. It was still there around his neck, hanging from its thin gold chain. In the full light of the open street, the tiny figure seemed to have lost its malevolence: just a jade figurine, no more, no less. The flaming luster of the malignant eyes had paled into the waxy sheen of cold stone. Jade stood stock-still on the sidewalk, turning the unicorn over and over in his hand, beset by vague and nameless terrors. The unicorn seemed too passive, too restrained; and in that passivity and restraint Jade smelled treachery.

The old man had retraced his steps back to Jade. "Come along now, my son," he said softly. "There is much that we must talk about."

20

THE Rev. James Tully of St. Luke's Church made it abundantly clear to the investigating officer how outraged he was over the act of vandalism. He had returned to the chapel at about 7:30 that evening to prepare it for a brass quintet that was scheduled to play at nine. It was then that he discovered that the cross was missing.

"It's beyond me why anybody would want to steal it," complained Father Tully. "It was only wood, of no intrinsic value. No gold. No silver. No jewels." He clasped and unclasped his hands behind his back as the police officer jotted notes down in a small black pad. "It wasn't even a work of artistic value. O, it was attractive enough for its purpose: streamlined and simple and it held a good polish. But nothing out of the ordinary."

"About how big was it, father?" asked Dectective Foley.

"O, let me see now . . ." And the rector gestured with his hands at various elevations around his body, trying to quantify the image of the cross in his memory by relating it to his own height. "It had to be about like this . . . yes, and then this wide . . . maybe that's a bit too much, take off about half a foot . . . yes, it was something like five feet high with about a three-foot crosspiece. Something like that."

Foley raised his eyebrows. "Phew, father, that's a pretty big cross for somebody to just walk out with. I mean, I don't think it'd fit under anybody's coat."

"That's just what's been troubling me," said the rector. "I can't imagine how anyone could have taken it out of the chapel without someone noticing it. We have a full-time staff consisting of a groundskeeper and a sexton, as well as a secretary whose office is off the outer hallway. Both the groundskeeper and the secretary saw nothing."

"And the sexton?"

Father Tully looked vaguely around while his spread fingertips tapped together in agitation. "I haven't been able to ask him. He's nowhere around."

"Nowhere around?" Foley perked up. "Is he supposed to be around here this late in the evening?"

"Well, actually, officer, he's not supposed to be anywhere. The sexton's job at this church is basically a twenty-four-hour-a-day job. He lives in a suite of rooms right here on the church grounds. And he's expected to handle any sudden structural emergencies immediately, no matter at what time they occur. In consequence, we're rather fluid as to his scheduling of his days. There are many jobs that must be performed daily on a regular basis but, once they are finished, the man's time is his own. I can only assume that he went out somewhere this afternoon and simply hasn't yet returned."

Foley nodded and pursed his lips noncommitally as he made further jottings in his pad.

"If you think that our sexton might have something to do with the theft of the cross," laughed the rector, "you can forget it. Old Henry has been with the church for years. Ever since he was a young man. He's no wandering handyman who just happened to breeze in here on his way to San Francisco. And Henry's a man of impeccable habits: no drinking, no smoking, certainly no drugs, and he doesn't consort with unsavory characters." The rector looked toward the altar where the missing cross once rested and stroked his clean-shaven chin with a soft hand. "In fact, I don't think Henry consorts with anybody, savory or not. He keeps around here most of the time. He's got no family. Except us, that is. We like to think of ourselves as one big family here." The rector looked up at Foley with a smile, waiting to see if the news of this successful experiment in brotherhood-in-action would elicit any response from a cynical New York cop. But Foley only kept on scribbling.

"I didn't mean to imply, father," Foley said at last, "that your sexton was in any way under suspicion. I'm simply trying to find out if there were possible witnesses."

"Well, you can be assured that if Henry saw anything suspicious going on, he wouldn't wait for us to come to him asking questions. He'd notify the church office immediately."

"You're quite right, I'm sure," continued Foley. "Like you said before, this is probably a prank pulled off by some local kids. A club stunt or something like that."

"I certainly hope it's no more than that. I've been with this church for over seven years now, and I can't recall any similar incident. Yet I know that these are terrible times. One way-out cult after another springing up all over the country. All over the world, even. And, as I'm sure you know better than I, the Village is a mecca for crazies and weirdos. Not that most of the permanent residents aren't fine, upstanding citizens: it's the transients that stop off here for few months or a year that get themselves involved with weirdness. Yes, I certainly hope that this is nothing more than a kid's prank. I'd hate to think that our cross was being used as a backdrop for unspeakable or criminal activities. Devil worship and that sort of thing, you know."

Foley laughed. "You're right about those cults, father. You wouldn't believe what goes on in some of the quietest apartments here in the Village. Voodoo, animal sacrifice, religious orgies." Foley's voice grew wistful. "One day when I retire I'm gonna write a book . . ."

It was then that Patrolman Frank Feldman, who had been searching in and among the pews and supply closets, happened to glance up at the organ pipes hidden behind an intricate brass filigree some fifteen feet above and behind the altar. A six-inch oblong of wood protruded from among the pipes. Feldman hastened to Foley.

"Excuse me, sir, but take a look up there," he said, pointing upward to the protruding piece of wood.

Foley and the rector looked up, following the line of Feldman's finger.

"Is that thing sticking out up there a part of the pipes?" Foley asked the rector.

"No, I'm sure it's not. I've never seen it before."

Foley and the rector walked beneath the pipes for a closer look.

"That's it!" exclaimed the rector. "That's the tip of the crosspiece of the cross! Now, how in the world did it get up there?"

Foley smiled and closed his pad. "Well, at least you can rest easy now knowing that it's not in the hands of some cult."

"This is most disturbing," said the rector, puzzled. "Who would have put the cross up there? And how?"

"A ladder, I guess," offered Foley. "Somebody climbed up a ladder and stuffed it in back of the pipes."

"That's not as easy as you make it sound. You can't do that with a stepladder, you know. That's over fifteen feet in the air. You'd need a big ladder, something like the one the church has for changing light bulbs and exterior paint jobs. You couldn't bring a ladder like that in here and set it up without causing considerable commotion," said the rector. "It's most extraordinary!"

"What about when the pipes need to be repaired? Isn't there another entrance up there with a platform for workmen to stand on while they work on pipes?"

"In some churches, yes. We, unfortunately, aren't that well endowed. Any organ repair requires an elaborate scaffold to be set up for the workmen, and it would rest directly on the floor here behind the altar."

Reverend Tully paced nervously back and forth beneath the pipes, staring up at the protruding wood. "Why would somebody do such a thing? And how are we supposed to get it back down now?"

"Well," said Foley, nodding, "as for your first question, I think we'd best write it off as a prank. And if I were you, father, I'd keep my eyes on any of the kids who might be hanging out around here on a regular basis. As for your second question," and here Foley nodded to the rector with an ingratiating smile, "I think my men and I can find a few spare minutes to lend your church a helping hand. We like to let the public know that we're not all just a bunch of ogres."

"I can't tell you how much I appreciate your offer," said the rector gratefully, though his voice was tinged with a note of bewilderment. "It's most embarrassing to have you come all the way over here only to find the missing cross on the premises."

"Think nothing of it, father," beamed the detective. "I'm just glad that everything can be settled this easily. Now, let's see about getting it down from there."

Foley's "men" was Patrolman Feldman. After he helped the rector and Foley bring the church's ladder into the chapel from the storehouse and set it up against the pipes, he started a slow and careful climb. Feldman was always hesitant about these "do-gooder" jobs. A guy can last twenty years on the force with a history of busts and brawls and gunfights and then retire without a mark. But let him climb a tree to rescue a cat and he falls and breaks his neck.

Foley and the rector watched from below as Feldman reached the piece of wood and carefully grabbed onto one of the pipes.

"Are these pipes fastened up here sturdily?" he called down.

"Quite sturdily, I can assure you," answered the rector.

"I can hold on to one without pulling it off the wall?"

"Yeah, Feldman," barked the detective, "now quit stalling and get that cross the hell out of there." Foley paused for a moment. "Excuse my language, father." Reverend Tully waved off the apology, staring up at Feldman, nodding pleasantly.

"Quit stalling, quit stalling," muttered Feldman under his breath as he clung to the trembling ladder. "Sonofabitch." Then he grasped the pipes between which the cross protruded and pulled himself up for a look behind the pipes to see just how the cross was wedged in and what the options were for getting it out. He clung there for long lingering seconds, muttering something indistinctly, seemingly riveted to the pipes.

"What's that, Feldman? What'd you say?" Foley called up to him. "Come on, man, hurry up! What's happening?"

"Holy shit!" Feldman exclaimed with growing ardor. "Holy shit! HOLY SHIT!" He started to rush back down the ladder, missed a rung and slid a few feet before he could regrasp the ladder, smacked his ankles and shins against the wooden rungs, and finally stumbled to his feet on the floor.

"What the hell's the matter with you?" shouted Foley.

"Listen, listen," gasped Feldman, "you're not gonna believe this!"

"Believe what?"

"There's . . . there's a . . . body up there!"

Foley and Tully: "A body!"

"Yeah, an old man's body." Feldman started trembling and had to seat himself in a pew. "My good God, I never saw anything so horrible!"

Foley and the rector looked at each other. "What is it?" Foley asked. "What's so horrible?"

Feldman swallowed, panting, before he could compose himself to speak. "That cross . . . all five feet of it . . . thick as it is . . . somebody shoved that whole fuckin' cross down the old man's throat!"

Much to Ender's surprise and profound relief, John Brock left him alone about the Welles murder investigation. Of course, Ender had already interposed himself between Brock and most of his responsibilities in the matter. British Embassy officials, at Ender's request and with Anthony Welles's cooperation, came directly to Ender with their inquiries and left the mayor's office out of the business altogether. Ender cultivated a rapport between himself and Welles that effectively let Brock off the hook. But rather than appreciating Ender's assumption of unwarranted responsibilities, Brock avoided him whenever their paths chanced to cross and assumed an expression of righteous indignation, as if having endured an irremediable offense at Ender's hands. Ender resigned himself to the situation with equanimity because, in the first place, he had learned what a worthless person Brock really was and, secondly, he understood that the quickest way to make a deadly enemy out of someone was to be a witness to that person's weakness and insecurity.

But Welles had understandably become restive about the slow progress of the investigation. It had been over a week since his daughter's murder and the body had still not been released for burial. Although it was a painful choice for him to make, Ender still resolved not to reveal to the grieving father all the bizarre details of his daughter's death. Not until he was able to wrap up all the loose ends in the case in some sort of speculative package that made sense. To do that, the girl's body had to be retained for continued forensic study. Besides, Rothstein had called him just the night before to announce some startling new development that he refused to discuss over the phone. He arranged a meeting with Ender and Fedorson for that afternoon and Ender noted with concern the degree of agitation in the doctor's normally serene, if raspy, voice. Thus, Ender had absolutely no idea when, or even if, the girl's body could be released by the coroner's office. Each time Welles broached the subject of his daughter's burial, the sheer pathos of his voice struggling to retain its formal dignity combined with his agonized desire to put all the grievous details and memories of his daughter's passing to rest tore at Ender's heart. He had to weigh against these emotions, however, the ardent desire on the part of all involved to see to it that the killer, whoever or whatever it might be, was apprehended and permitted to kill no more. For this the police needed the girl's body.

But then Welles politely requested that Inspector Washburn, an investigative liaison between the British Foreign Office and the CID, be permitted to be briefed by Ender on the status of the investigation—a delicate way of obtaining a second opinion. He assured Ender that Washburn would be acting purely as a consultant with no official status and Ender, though admittedly reluctant, agreed. But when, at last, Washburn was ushered into Ender's cubicle of an office, Ender took an instant liking to the man. He was a tall, vigorous Britisher with charmingly archaic muttonchops and a florid, robust face. He had small eyes that darted excitedly around the office and sparkled. He shook Ender's hand warmly as he seated himself in a chair facing Ender from across the desk. For some lengthy moments, neither would indulge in the pointless repartee of custom. They both just sat and stared at one another, warmly, assessing each other, trying to find words worthy of the situation.

Finally, Washburn announced, "My God, Mr. Ender, you look exhausted."

Ender blushed, half-smiling. "It shows then, does it?"

"Afraid so."

"Well, to be perfectly honest with you, a select few members of this department, myself included, have suddenly found ourselves living in extraordinary times."

"I daresay." Washburn had the most expressive eyebrows Ender had ever encountered. They were dark, thick, and stood far out from his forehead in fibrous wisps. When he pursued a thought for analysis, they knitted harshly into an intense frown. When he was gay and jocular, as he seemed to be most of the time, they fluttered and danced like bamboo arches set to span a windy river. And when something puzzled him or raised a question in his mind, they rose into steady twin domes that didn't descend until the question had been formulated and put. Then they knitted while the forthcoming answer was judged.

Yes, Ender liked the man.

"I do hope, Mr. Ender," continued Washburn, "that my presence here doesn't contribute to your problems."

"O not at all, I'm sure . . ."

"You see, Mr. Ender, I am a law enforcement professional like yourself. I take my job most seriously and I work hard to live up to my repsonsibilities both to my employers and to my own personal passion for justice. At times (far fewer than a cynic would maintain yet more often than I would wish), these interests come into conflict. I pride myself on the fact that on such occasions I've always embraced the side of justice, regardless of the consequences to myself. I don't say this, Mr. Ender, in order to 'blow my own horn,' as you Americans would say. I say this merely to acquaint you with my personal standards. And because I take my job so seriously, I tend to become highly resentful of anyone looking over my shoulder while I work. Now I find myself with the unwelcome task of doing just that with you." He paused while he withdrew an elaborately carved meerschaum from his jacket pocket, a snarling tiger. "Do you mind if I indulge?" he asked, indicating the pipe.

"Please, inspector, go right ahead."

"Many thanks." He lit the bowl and puffed luxuriantly on the stem, releasing jets of gray cloud from his mouth to the open air. "Perhaps I'm an idealist. Perhaps I'm just naive. But I tend to impute to all of my ranking fellow professionals the same lofty standards that I myself try to maintain. At least until I'm shown otherwise. And that's what I feel about you, Mr. Ender."

"Well, thank you. I hope you're not disappointed before you head back to Britain."

Washburn laughed. "I don't think I will be. You see, I'm a bit of a physiognomist. The nature of my work and all that. And I see that the fatigue in your face and eyes is the fatigue of a man laboring over a very thorny problem whose solution is, quite literally, a life and death matter. It isn't the fatigue that grows out of a guilty conscience and the attendant sleepless nights," he said with a rakish wink. "So please let me assure you that I will do the utmost in my power to facilitate your investigation of the Welles girl's murder and not hamper it. In fact, the only reason I've been called in on this case at all is to investigate the delay in the release of the girl's body to her father for burial. Neither your competence nor that of any of your co-workers has at all been called into question. Indeed, Mr. Welles, himself, seems quite taken by you."

"Well, please assure him from me that the feeling is mutual."

"I shall, certainly. Now, I've looked over the official report on the case and, on the strength of that report alone, I can see no other cause of death than a senseless and brutal knifing. Surely such a murder wouldn't warrant all this excessive time for a forensic investigation. But your office has adamantly refused to permit anyone to view the corpse, including the victim's father. I appreciate your concern for his emotional well-being, but it is still obvious that such a tight prohibition as has been implemented is unusually excessive." He took another deep drag on his pipe. Ender simply sat with his arms folded on his desk patiently waiting for Washburn to finish. "It doesn't take a very experienced investigative nose to smell something between the lines in this case. What I want to learn from you is just what it is that you aren't revealing. O, please rest assured that if what you are concealing is done out of kindness to the father in order to save him from excessive mental anguish, your secrets shall remain safe with me. I've been instructed merely to determine if I feel that your department is conducting a competent investigation and that further delay in the release of the body is, indeed, warranted. I've not been asked to embellish on the details."

"And, if once you found out and were then asked, would you?"

Washburn blew a single, solemn smoke ring up into the air, his muttonchops swelling with the effort. "If I felt that you were competently handling the investigation, I wouldn't consider it my place to countermand any aspect of your game plan. Any secrets would remain secret until you saw fit to reveal them yourself."

Ender rested his chin on his hand, his eyes intent upon the inspector's face. "You give me your word for that? As a fellow professional?"

Washburn smiled. "As a fellow professional, I do."

Ender placed his hands palm down on the desk and heaved a sigh of relief. "Consider yourself, inspector, a member of the team."

"Good. And believe me, I can do quite a bit on your behalf to make certain that no other outside investigators interfere with your work."

"I wish I could believe that. Not that I doubt your word, mind you. It's just that I wonder if you'll feel the same way when once you know the whole truth."

"My goodness! It appears that I've stumbled on some delicious mystery." Washburn's eyes fairly sparkled with excitement. "Tell me more."

"Well, first of all, inspector, I want you to know right off that keeping secrets isn't my thing. I've only done so because my judgment keeps telling me that, at this point in time and under what you will learn to be highly unusual circumstances, secrecy is the only way to go. If this whole mess is somehow unravelled, then all will be told, fully and completely. Within the parameters of decency in respect to Mr. Welles, that is."

"I quite agree."

"Good. Now I can also admit to you that the official medical examiner's report has been falsified."

"Aha!" The inspector's eyebrows lifted.

"Not that anything stated there is false. No, it's all true as far as it goes. It's just that it doesn't begin to enumerate all the ramifications of the physical evidence. Not by a long shot."

"I see."

Ender rose from behind the desk and began to pace in front of his window. "No, I'm afraid you don't see. Not yet. But you will. In just about forty-five minutes, as a matter of fact. I'm due to meet our chief medical examiner, Dr. Rothstein, down at the morgue for a conference pertaining to the Welles case. And others."

"Others?"

"Yes. You see, the secrecy we've maintained around this case has only been partly due to concern for the father's emotional stability. Certain aspects of the physical evidence of the girl's corpse link her death to several others that have occurred during the last week."

"Ah, yes. It's beginning to make sense now."

"O, it'll make sense all right. Up to a point. Then all hell breaks loose. In case you might feel that I harbor a resentment against you for your presence in this case, you're all wrong. Believe me, I welcome the opportunity to bring in an outsider and show him everything my colleagues and I have been turning up. That way we can count on you to tell us if we're hallucinating or not."

"That bizarre, eh?" Another circle of smoke flew to the ceiling. "Maybe it's the New York water."

Ender laughed. "God, how I wish it were!"

Suddenly Ender's telephone rang. It was Fedorson.

"Hey, counsellor, were you going down to the morgue later to meet with the doc?"

"Yeah, lieutenant. Of course. Why?"

"Well, I'm down there now and I think you should get down here right away."

Ender paled. "What happened?"

"Another one just hit the slabs. You won't believe it till you see it."

Ender paused, steadying himself. "I . . . I'll be down there right . . . right away. O . . . I'm bringing an Inspector Wash—Washburn from the British Foreign Office. I've already spoken with him. He's okay."

There was a pause on the other end of the line. "Suit yourself, counsellor. If we're gonna look like stoned-out idiots, we might as well let the whole world know about it. Just get down here as soon as you can."

Ender hung up the phone looking stern and despondent. And a trifle terrified. "Come on, inspector. I know you'll find this interesting."

"Yeah, this is Fedorson."

The voice at the other end of the line was oily and sneering. "Well now, lieutenant, it seems you must have some enemies down at the commissioner's office."

"Who the hell is this?"

"Or else why would they be keeping you so overworked?"

"Listen, I can't waste my time with anonymous phone callers who're concerned for my beauty sleep . . ."

"Don't hang up, lieutenant. I'm surprised you didn't recognize my voice. You recognized my face fast enough."

Intrigued, Fedorson paused, scowling, and strained to fit the voice to a face.

"Well? You know yet?"

"Goddamn it, I don't have time to play games. Who the fuck are you?"

"Temper, temper! It won't do for one of New York's finest to blow his cool. Leaves a bad impression on the public. I'm Quentin Peale."

"O right! I should've known. It's not often I pick up a phone and the receiver smells like shit. How'd you find me down here at the morgue?"

"I've got my sources. The same sources that keep telling me how busy you are."

"And what's that supposed to mean?"

"It means I was down at St. Luke's this evening. I saw the whole thing, took pictures, got a score of interviews, the whole bit. It's going to bust wide open with the next edition."

Fedorson's voice was frigid with suppressed rage. "Congratulations."

"Thanks. And you know what else? You weren't on the scene at all, yet as soon as they shipped the victim's body downtown, cross and all, it's suddenly your case. Odd, isn't it? First the fag in the boathouse and now this. And they're both killed in the Village, which isn't your turf at all. Doesn't that strike you as peculiar?"

"Nah. When I first joined the force, they told me I'd get to see the world."

"Is that so? Well, I thought it was peculiar so I did some checking. This week alone they've got you down on the rolls for not only both Village murders but the McConnelly window dive and, catch this, folks, the murder of Anthony Welles's daughter in Central Park. A murder of public interest that nobody even knew about. Now don't you think that that's a bit much for any one man?"

There was a heavy pause while Fedorson tried to control his outraged tongue. Finally he said, "So what's it to you, motherfucker?"

"It's a scoop for me, lieutenant. That's what. And maybe a damn big one. See, the way I figure it is that all these murders have some common denominator that nobody's releasing to the general public. I'm going to find out what that common denominator is. I'd appreciate your help in this matter, Fedorson. But with it or without it, I'm going to find out what I want to know."

"I thought you already had an arrangement with Ender."

"Come on, now, lieutenant. You don't think I really fell for that crock of shit, do you? That boy Ender's a real loser. A big zip. Tells me everything *he* wants me to know. Now I'm insulted. I thought you'd give me credit for being smarter than that."

"Peale, I wouldn't give you credit for a pay toilet."

"Suit yourself, lieutenant. If you helped me out, there could've been a crock of gold at the end of the rainbow. For both of us. I don't forget the people who help me.

But with you or without you, I'm going to find out what's really at the bottom of all this."

"You know something, Peale? In all honesty, you're the one person I really hope runs into whatever is at the bottom of all this. Now listen to me and listen good. You've caused enough trouble as it is. If I find you interfering with my job again, in any way, shape, or form, I'm gonna arrange a nice, quiet mugging for you. And for your 'sources.' You get me, you worm?"

Fedorson slammed the receiver down on the cradle and strode out into the hallway and down the corridor to Rothstein's office. He fumed. The sharp tattoo of his heavy footsteps reverberated off the shiny white walls, making the man sound like a retreating giant.

At the end of the same corridor, Quentin Peale emerged from a phone booth wearing a white lab coat. He smiled to himself as the footsteps of the retreating giant faded into the distance.

Rothstein had chosen the late hour for the meeting so that the conclave would be undisturbed. But now with the new corpse from St. Luke's, reporters thronged the upper offices and corridors. They jostled one another waving notebooks and press cards and shouted out names of obscure individuals with the department who they purported to be special and sympathetic friends. Remote video crews lugged their lights and equipment back and forth along the reception corridor, hoping to catch the eye of some wandering and bewildered dignitary who might be persuaded to call off the security force and give them access to the bizarre corpse. But Rothstein's instructions that the morgue was off limits to the press were explicit, adamant, and enforced by a handpicked squad of Fedorson's own men. Fedorson, himself, had to meet Ender and Washburn at curbside so that he could personally lead them through the seething throng and past the security force.

The voracious crowd terrified Ender. Both Washburn and Fedorson, much larger men, flanked him as they forcibly cleared a path to reach the security blockade. Ender's eyes were wide with nervous scrutinizing and a waxy pallor was cast across his face. When a few of the reporters noticed the little man being hustled past the guards, they started to close in around him, pulling at his sleeves for attention and shouting questions. Then Ender recognized John Brock, who at a distance was frantically trying to address the unruly crowd of reporters and pacify them with some line of official jargon. But no one listened to Brock; more and more they rushed to try and corner Ender. Brock's eyes met Ender's and Ender could read in them Brock's anger that he hadn't been relieved of this responsibility as well. Then, following a few colorful epithets hurled at the crowd by Fedorson, the three men lurched through the line of security guards which promptly closed up behind them.

Down in the basement where the bodies were stored and the autopsies conducted, Peale had hidden himself in a darkened laboratory, from which he could see through a glass partition into the main autopsy room across the hall. He could just make out Rothstein's head and shoulders as the doctor stood examining a shrouded figure stretched out on a slab. Bending, probing, squinting through an assortment of optical magnifiers, Rothstein circled the slab, over and over, examining whatever it was that lay stretched before him from every conceivable angle. The doctor's face was seamed with fleshy puffs and wrinkles from lack of sleep and a dark shadow of beard could be seen beginning to rival the supremacy of his walrus mustache. He was in shirt sleeves and his gray-streaked hair fell in unruly curls upon his forehead.

From his back pocket, Peale withdrew an oblong object about the size of a transistor radio. He examined it in the dim light reflected into the laboratory from the corridor and adjusted some knobs and buttons. Then he took from his pocket an earphone which he connected to the object in his hand and then promptly screwed into his ear. A cunning smile crossed his face: the transmitter he had hidden in the autopsy room was working perfectly. He could hear with astounding clarity the labored sighs and muted ejaculations of the exhausted and bewildered doctor.

Suddenly multiple sets of footsteps could be heard clattering down the corridor. Peale backed off further into the laboratory, sinking deeper into the shadows.

As the footsteps approached nearer to the autopsy room, Fedorson could be heard complaining, his raspy voice tinged with disgust. ". . . and now the whole goddamn smokescreen's been blown. This last murder did it: it just couldn't be helped. There were too many witnesses when the body was discovered and, by the time I found out about it, it was too late to put a lid on it. The church was swarming with media people when I got there. Every yellow rag and cult journal had someone there, as well as the regulars. It'll be all over town tomorrow."

"And our friend Peale?" asked Ender.

"That cocksucker was probably the first to get there. He was gone by the time I arrived. He's already filed the story complete with pictures and interviews."

"Damn!" exclaimed Ender. "Well, at least the press has no way of linking this murder with the others. We can still keep the Welles case under wraps."

"No way," Fedorson countered. "Once those photos hit the streets, the panic's gonna start. Slowly at first, if we're lucky, but then it's gonna skyrocket. And there goes our main reason for the secrecy in the first place. Secondly, Peale found out about all the murders that have been assigned to me just this week. He put two and two together and smelled a cover-up. You can be sure he's gonna drag everything out into the open, counsellor."

Ender stopped dead in his tracks. "How'd he find all that out?"

"Who the hell knows? Maybe he paid somebody off in the Xerox room. Or some stupid clerk in the department. Grease the right palms, counsellor, and you can find out anything. And Peale's an expert at greasing palms."

"Shit!" Ender cursed, running his fingers through his sparse hair. "You see, inspector, how the complexities of this case just seem to escalate without end. And yet you still don't know one fraction of the tragic reality."

Fedorson spit a clammy morsel of his stogie onto the floor. "Yeah, well, the inspector's gonna have his eyes opened once we get past that door. You too, counsellor. Better get yourself ready."

Washburn and Ender looked quickly at each other. Ender's insides began to churn.

As the three men passed the autopsy room window, they paused to look inside. Rothstein heard the sudden cessation of footsteps and looked up from his work. Ender noticed that for the first time in all his personal experience with the doctor, Rothstein seemed pathetically shaken and overwhelmed. There was a look in his eyes that combined both resignation to an insoluble mystery and sheer terror. And then Ender looked down at the figure on the slab.

"For the love of God . . ." breathed Washburn, and he pulled a handkerchief from his pocket so as to swab his face. "I've never seen anything like that before in my life!"

"Wait," said Fedorson. "Just you wait."

And with that he tossed the stub of his stogie onto the corridor floor and the three of them entered the autopsy room.

Rothstein's voice was weak and faltering and his tired face, all but his eyes, seemed numb and expressionless. It took a powerful conscious effort on his part to keep his recitation formal, clear, and precise.

". . . You can see how the lower jaw has been forcibly separated from the main portion of the skull, somewhat like what happens with a snake when it devours a large rodent whole. See here how the skin of the cheek is stretched taut, almost to the point of ripping. Naturally, there's just no way that the internal cavity of the body can accommodate an object of this size without almost total destruction of all the internal organs. Look at the size of the cross, gentlemen. It's like fitting a railroad tie down your throat. Once this man's jaw was broken off and the cavern of the mouth stretched to capacity, the cross was then forcibly shoved straight downward, tearing through all the internal organs, until it finally emerged for about half a foot through the base of the pelvic girdle. You can see for yourselves how the pelvis is splintered and shattered and how, consequently, the hips and thighs have been jarred grossly out of alignment."

The grisly sight of the old man's thin, aged body swelled by the intruding cross and sprinkled with fragments of bone and splashes of blood was almost ludicrous in its savagery.

"What in God's name could have done such a thing?" asked Washburn, aghast.

"The same thing that killed the others I'm going to show you," Rothstein responded. "I wish I could be more explicit but that's all we know right now."

"And the eyes?" asked Ender.

"See for yourself," the doctor answered, handing him a magnifying glass. "The same opacity as the others. The image hasn't begun forming yet, however. It's too soon after death."

"Image?" queried Washburn. "I'll be damned but this is all beyond me. What are you talking about?"

Ender offered him the magnifier. "See that greenish opacity covering the iris and pupil? It's been the same for all the other victims. It seems to grow progressively denser as time passes until about twelve hours after death when it becomes and stays as hard as stone."

Ender looked at the doctor and the lieutenant and added, "And other changes occur as well."

Washburn bent closely over the corpse's face with the magnifier. "Incredible! And you mean to say these eyes were clear before the murder?"

"Presumably," answered Rothstein. "The others were."

"This is extraordinary!" continued the inspector. "Have you analyzed it yet, chemically?"

"Yes, we have," the doctor responded. "It's a calcium magnesium silicate with significant traces of iron. Similar to a mineral called actinolite but . . . different. There's no known natural correspondent. And as for how the tissue of the iris and cornea begin to undergo that transformation, and how such a transformation is restricted to just those tissues in every case . . . well, that's completely beyond me."

Washburn stood up from the corpse with a heavy sigh. "And you say there are others?"

"Show him the guy from the pier next," directed Ender.

Rothstein walked to the wall of corpse cells, the others following. He went to one of them and pulled it out by its chrome handle. It slid out almost silently on well-oiled rollers, revealing a corpse beneath a white sheet. Rothstein pulled down the sheet.

"God in heaven!" groaned Washburn, holding his handkerchief to his mouth.

"This one was found in the same general vicinity as the old man. As you can see, one arm was completely severed from the trunk. Ripped out, I should say. No blade of any sort was used. The genitals, too, were ripped out and discovered some yards away from the body. And the body's been sexually assaulted most brutally: prolapsed rectum, fractured perineum, acute lacerations of the gluteal tissue."

For what seemed a very long time, Washburn silently surveyed the battered corpse, walking slowly along its perimeter. At intervals he would stoop and examine one of the many puncture wounds that dotted the body.

"These wounds, doctor," he began. "Have you determined what caused them? They weren't on that other body."

"That's true. But they are present on three of the victims, including the Welles girl."

Washburn's eyebrows rose in startled arches. "Three of them? How many are we dealing with?"

"Five altogether," the doctor answered. "And all murdered within the last week. As for the nature of the wounds, . . ." Rothstein shook his head despondently, ". . . all I can offer is pure speculation. The size and shape of the wounds rule out any sort of blade-like, slitting object. A sharpened spear of some sort, perhaps, or a javelin."

Washburn shook his head. "I've seen similar wounds while I was serving in Africa."

"Caused by what?" asked Ender.

"Animal horns," came the reply. "Like the gazelle or impala."

Ender wasn't surprised.

"I'm not saying that an animal had to cause these

wounds," Washburn continued. "I've seen some pretty nasty-looking weapons made out of such horns."

"Yeah, me too," commented Ender, recalling his dream with a shudder. "I think we should show the inspector the image in the eyes now."

Washburn and the doctor walked to the head of the corpse. With heavy thumbs, Rothstein drew back the eyelids.

"Take a close look," he said to Washburn. "Use your magnifier."

Washburn bent close to the face of the corpse. He was silent for what seemed to the others an eternity and then straightened up. His face was ashen.

"I know that I've just seen it with my own eyes," he said softly, his mouth dry. "But I can't accept it." He looked into the faces of the other three men, studying their eyes and the lineaments of fatigue and unspoken terror that disfigured each of them. "I can see now why you each have the stunned and weary look of Moses about you. I feel like I've just walked into Hell."

"Welcome to the club," Fedorson commented drily.

"What you've just seen is apparent in the eyes of each of the victims," Rothstein explained, "including the Welles girl. First there's the formation of the mineralized opacity and then the coalescence of the image. You'll see. Within a few hours it will appear within the eyes of the last victim, the old man from the church."

"Show him the McConnelly corpse next," said Ender. Rothstein began sliding another slab from the wall. "You'll find this one particularly interesting, inspector. You may even have known the man. I guess you'd call him a distillery magnate. Irish whiskey or something."

The inspector's eyebrows flared. "McConnelly? Of course. I just read about his death in the papers. It was reported as a suicide."

"A bit of Mr. Ender's sleight-of-hand," explained Fedorson. "No, it was no suicide. You should've seen the guy's office: ripped to shreds, blood all over the place. The police logged it as murder pending the completion of our investigation. But the counsellor leaked the suicide angle to the press and to the man's business associates. A much better way to explain flying out of an office window than ghosts and monsters."

"And the family?" queried Washburn.

"A situation similar to the Welles case," Ender explained. "They know it was murder and are cooperating with us in the deception. I explained that it would help us catch the killer. But the time is beginning to drag and his wife is getting restless about the funeral. I suggested she have the funeral anyway, with a closed casket, empty. Due to the condition of the body, the casket would have to be closed anyway, even if he were in it."

With that, Rothstein unveiled the corpse. Washburn gasped and looked away. "Not much good for evidence, is it?" he asked.

"No," Rothstein answered, "I'm afraid you're right. We can't distinguish with any degree of certainty which injuries he received prior to his fall and which resulted from the fall. But you'll find that the eyes have been mineralized and contain the same image as the others. I'll have to pry them out to show you . . ."

"No! No, please," said Washburn, quickly. "That won't be necessary."

Rothstein covered the corpse up again and slid the slab back into the cubicle.

"So you mean to say that both Welles and McConnelly have been victims of the same killer, do you?" Washburn wiped his forehead with a cold, sweaty palm. "There seems to be no end to the intricacies of this case. The killer is cutting a swathe through all levels of society."

"So it seems," said Ender. "But it is interesting that there seems to be a link between McConnelly and the Welles girl."

"And the Welles girl? She was only thirteen. I think it unlikely . . ."

"Not that kind of link," continued Ender. "The Welles girl's boyfriend was McConnelly's son Marco. We also have reason to believe that this boy was the last person to see her alive, except for the killer."

"An intriguing notion," Washburn commented, stroking his chin thoughtfully. "And what has the boy told you?"

"Nothing. We haven't found him yet. It seems the kid

had a rather vicious fight with his father the morning after the girl's death. He'd been out all night, we think possibly with the girl, and he wouldn't explain his whereabouts to his father's satisfaction. Then he ran away from home. That night, McConnelly was killed. We have an APB out for the boy now but there's been no luck so far."

"Isn't that rather suspicious?" questioned Washburn pointedly.

"Yes, I'd say it is," Ender agreed. "Except for the fact that how in the hell can a fifteen-year-old boy do all of this? And where do the other murders fit in? The link between McConnelly and the girl is tenuous at best. Considering the . . . uh, *bizarre* physical evidence, and the other bodies, it fades appreciably."

Washburn stroked his chin while his brows knitted reflectively. "Still . . ."

"Yeah," said Ender. "I know. Somehow I think that kid can tell us an awful lot about what's going on. Doc, bring out the old wino next."

Rothstein proceeded to slide out another slab.

"This corpse was found not twenty yards from the body of the Welles girl," explained the doctor. "The time of death is the same for each, although there is no sign of external injury on this body. The old man died of a heart attack, a massive myocardial infarction. Yet his eyes manifest the same symptoms as the others. See for yourself."

Washburn bent over the dead man's head, peering into the lusterless eyes with his magnifier.

"When we first found his body," explained the doctor, "we thought the opacity might be due to a prior condition. Then, when the image of the unicorn face manifested itself and these other bodies turned up, we knew that wasn't the case."

Washburn looked up from the corpse. "A heart attack, you say? From fright, perhaps?"

Rothstein laughed weakly. "Two weeks ago I would've attributed his death to the ravages of chronic alcoholism. Now I know what killed him, yet I don't know, if you know what I mean. I've never witnessed an actual case of death from fright. Something like that tends to be more mythical than real. An emotional shock can aggravate a preexisting condition, however, and the man was in pathetic physical condition due to alcoholism. So perhaps he saw whatever it was that killed the girl and did die of fright. I can't really say. Maybe whatever killed the girl can just do that to people: explode their hearts. Who knows? All we have linking the two deaths is proximity in place and time and the eyes."

"But if the same . . . thing were responsible for both deaths at approximately the same time," queried Ender, "why was there a difference of hours between the appearance of the opacity in the old man's eyes and the eyes of the Welles girl?"

"I've puzzled over the same point," Rothstein said, returning the body to its cubicle. "All I can come up with is the theory that different people respond at different rates to whatever it is that has been causing these opaque eyes. The Welles girl had young and healthy eye tissue and the old man didn't. His eyes were affected much more rapidly. The girl was obviously closer to whatever it was that struck and was treated far more brutally. Yet her eyes remained clear longer. This leads me to believe that whatever it is that is precipitating these changes in the eye tissue is independent of physical contact. That's as much of a theory as I've got. For whatever it's worth."

The three men were lost for some moments in speculative silence. "I don't know, doc," Fedorson announced. "It doesn't help me out a whole hell of a lot."

"Me neither," added Ender. "Let's get to the last one: the Welles girl."

"You're in for a surprise with this one, Abe," said Rothstein. "There's been a new development." He pulled out the slab and drew off the sheet. Washburn buckled with the sight and turned away to lean against the wall of the morgue, his head resting on his forearm.

"Christ! Christ!" he moaned. "Won't this horror end?"

Ender's eyes opened wide with astonishment and his jaw dropped. The girl's body was in the same mangled condition as he had remembered, which was horrible enough. But now her abdomen was swollen like a taut, large melon.

"Danny!" he breathed. "That swelling! Is it caused by some sort of bacterial gas?"

"No, Abe," said the doctor. "That I could deal with. It's something else, far more incomprehensible. There's a living, growing foetus inside that girl."

"What!" Ender exclaimed. "Inside a corpse? The girl's been dead for a week!"

Washburn rushed over from the wall to see for himself.

"I told you, counsellor," said Fedorson. "I told you this'd grab you."

They stared down at the waxpale corpse, eyeing the mound of dead flesh that glistened in the brilliant white light that bathed the room. They stared in profound silence, showing the anguished stupor upon their faces of men who were witnessing Armageddon.

Washburn shoved his handkerchief to his lips and raced out into the corridor. Gasps and heaves and the splash of vomit echoed throughout the emptiness. Ender looked at Rothstein and nodded. The meeting would reconvene shortly in the doctor's office at the end of the hall.

"I'm surprised he lasted that long," commented Ender distantly, like a man whispering in a dream. "He's a better man than I am."

Rothstein wordlessly covered the corpse with the sheet and returned it to its cubicle.

"Are you . . . are you just going to . . . to leave it there?" asked Ender, his tongue grown impossibly heavy.

"What else can I do with it? Send it to a zoo? Or maybe send it to a hospital so first-year med students can take notes? Abe, we don't know what we're dealing with here. I just discovered it this afternoon when I was preparing for this meeting." Rothstein's eyes began to wander through empty space like the searching eyes of a man poised at the brink of madness. "I heard something inside like a rapid, powerful heartbeat. I felt it move." He turned to Ender with wild, pleading eyes. "I felt it move, Abe! With the fingers of this right hand I felt something writhe and squirm inside that corpse! You can see how quickly it's grown." Rothstein began pacing back and forth in front of the wall of corpse cubicles, his face flushed with awe and chagrin. "Do you realize how incomprehensible all this is? She had no reproductive organs left after her attack. Nothing that wasn't pummelled and ~

shredded beyond recognition. And still some demon sperm took root! And the damn thing lives!" Rothstein halted abruptly, pressing his palms against his temples, his eyes shut tightly. "I haven't dared to move it from this room, even for x-rays. Do I dare cut it out and try to destroy it, whatever it is? Or would I just be unleashing it upon a world that won't be able to control or confine it? I don't know what do do, Abe. I just don't know what to do."

Ender moved close to the doctor and, with gentle fingers, coaxed his hands from his temples. "You're doing all that you can, Danny. We're out of our depth in this. All our training, all our experience . . . it's just meaningless. We've just got to keep trying to figure it out. We've got no other choice. I've got a sickening feeling that there's far more at stake here than the solution to a few murders. You know that feeling you get when you read something or see a work of art and suddenly realize you've been grabbed by the balls and catapulted into a whole different world of values and colors and textures? And the old world you left suddenly speaks to you in a different voice? That's what's happened to us, all of us who are involved in this. We've been shoved out of what we knew and have got to make our way as best we can under the new rules. That's all we can do. And we're all in this together."

Rothstein nodded, sighing deeply. Then he and Fedorson and Ender left together, shutting the door softly behind them.

Pealc crouched in the darkened laboratory, unable to move. His heart raced within his chest and the rhythmic throb of blood flushing through his temples was unbearable. He crouched in the darkness chewing on a calloused knuckle, his rat's eyes darting nervously around him, without aim, without respite. He had to still the grotesque images that swirled through his mind so as to rise from his place of concealment and take action.

The things he had heard . . . the devastating things he heard . . .

A yellow journalist's dream, really. What a sensation, with the tape recording and pictures . . .

Pictures? The idea of photographing such corpses sickened him. Besides, he didn't know in which bins the bodies were kept. Later for the pictures. Once he had blown the whistle to the world, he would force them to show him the bodies. Public pressure would be on his side.

But first he had to recover the transmitter and tape recorder from the other room: not a pleasant thought. He'd have to force himself, fortify his spine and just plunge right into the room . . .

This was big. Really big. He knew it was his once-in-a-lifetime opportunity: the events of the world had shed all pretense to rationality and descended to the level of his kind of journalism. These murders weren't part of the sophisticated world of affairs trod by Reasoner or Cronkite. Yet they were nonetheless real and he could prove it. And the implications of these events . . . Who could predict how deeply the entire planet might be sucked into such a vortex?

In spite of his agitation, a shallow smile crossed Peale's lips. He might even cop a Pulitzer if he played it right. No longer would his name be linked with UFO hunters and astrologers. And then a book . . .

He slowly rose to his feet, his knees wobbly. He reached for the doorknob and was startled by how violently his hand trembled.

He passed furtively from the laboratory to the morgue. Pausing at the door, he withdrew a slender metal rod from his pocket and inserted it into the lock. A couple of quick twists of his nimble fingers and the door opened inward. Peale passed inside.

He fell to his knees beside the water cooler in the far corner of the room. He tried to work quickly, in spite of the fact that his eyes were not as yet accustomed to the brilliant glare of the fluorescent fixtures amplified by the gleaming white porcelain and chrome of which the entire interior of the room was composed. His sense of touch was unimpaired, however, and he reached into the narrow gap between the cooler and the wall, his fingers searching for the equipment he had planted. But his hand shook ever more intensely and uncontrollably as he slid it up and down, groping, and Peale cursed its unruliness under his breath. He was desperate to grab the devices and get the hell out of there as quickly as possible. The more he hastened, however, the more defiant his trembling hand became.

Suddenly the door to the morgue, which Peale had left slightly ajar, clicked shut. Peale gasped, fearing discovery. His head darted upward from its crouched position, craning toward the far side of the room, his eyes squinting in the bright light.

There was nobody else inside with him.

He felt the veins in his neck throb and swell with fear. Muttering a hasty, mute imprecation that was almost a whimper, he redoubled the effort of his hand and finally grabbed the small box-like object he had wedged behind the water cooler. But before he could pull it out, a loud metallic clank shattered the silence of the morgue. Peale bolted upright.

The noise came from the wall of corpse cubicles.

He stared wildly at the wall of square doors with chrome edging, his eyes wide with fright. With a trembling yank of his hand, the transmitter-recorder came loose but Peale lost his grip and it fell behind the cooler to the floor with a clatter.

"Damn!" he cursed, his eyes starting to brim with tears of frustration and fear. His heart pounded in his chest. As he bent closer to the floor, another metallic clank reverberated throughout the room. Peale jumped to his feet.

There, on one of the cubicle doors, were two large bulges of metal, pointing outward.

"O my God!" gasped Peale, immobile with terror.

Suddenly the cubicle door burst open with a sharp popping of metal and swung loosely on its hinges. A slab with a shrouded corpse rolled out to the limit of its iron fastenings. And then the corpse sat bolt upright, throwing its white sheet to the floor. Peale whimpered incoherently, stumbling to all fours on the tiled floor.

It was the mutilated corpse of the Welles girl. It sat up, its one remaining arm limp at its side, staring forward with horrible, gleaming emerald eyes.

Peale tried to claw himself forward along the slippery floor with his fingers. From his lips strange gurgles articulated his terror. His eyes were fixed on the glowing eyes of the corpse and, like in a nightmare, he couldn't seem to move himself nearer the door.

Slowly, deliberately, the corpse inched itself to the foot of the slab, its one arm slapping like a rotten log against the gleaming metal. Then, with a final lurch, it slid to its dead feet on the floor.

Its belly had swollen to twice its previous size in the brief minutes since Ender and the others had left. The corpse wavered for an instant on unsteady limbs of dead flesh, trailing shredded, dead organs from between its legs.

Its glowing eyes locked on the figure of Peale that cowered, insane with terror, on the cold floor. There was the echoey sound of slitting vellum, the sound of a sharp blade slitting the taut membrane of a drum. A black seam appeared running downward along the length of the corpse's swollen belly, releasing horrible, nauseating fumes that spread throughout the room.

Peale began to choke from the stench. He tried desperately to scream but his voice was mute within his throat.

A thing emerged from the belly of the corpse—a slimy, glistening thing with bulbous emerald eyes and a dark parrotbeak. It looked about for an instant, squeaking, clicking, filling the room with its hellish stench. Then it leaped for the reporter's throat.

Just the flash of an instant. Just a darting shadow and the quick caress of cold oily flesh on Peale's cheek. Then the beak plunged into the man's neck, spraying the anti-septic tile with thick gobs of blood.

In that final instant of terror before death, Peale found his voice. He raised a single piercing wail that rever-berated throughout the morgue like the howl of a hell-hound. The thing at his throat lapped and sucked.

Ender and the others in Rothstein's office were jolted from their charts and diagrams. In a body they leaped to their feet and plunged headlong down the corridor to the morgue. Before they reached the doorway, however, the grisly sight greeted them through the large glass partition that opened out onto the corridor: the risen corpse, its swollen belly now two flaps of dead, dangling corpseflesh, and the thing at its feed on Peale's neck.

"My God, my God," groaned Rothstein.

The bloody, feeding thing rolled its huge eyes and stared back through the glass at the men who were staring at it. It didn't stop sucking.

Fedorson and Washburn had their guns out and let fly with a hail of bullets, shattering the glass partition and blasting the creature off the limp reporter's body with the impact of the lead. The thing squealed horribly, spewing blood from its beak as it leaped and squirmed in rage. They emptied their chambers into the vile thing, tearing it to pieces, and then watched in mute horror and astonishment as the limbs and shreds of the beast dried and cracked and disintegrated to fine dust.

The eyes of the risen corpse dimmed and it fell stiffly to the floor.

21

FOREST rangers Allen and Crosby sat in their car parked on a mountain lookout point that overlooked Keene Valley in upstate New York. The lovers who regularly frequented the lookout on warm summer nights had started their engines and roared away within seconds of the rangers' arrival. Crosby laughed.

"Look at 'em take off," he said to Allen, prodding him with his elbow. "You'd think we was some kind of spooks."

"Yeah," said Allen. " 'Course I don't remember you hangin' around here screwin' when the rangers came by when we was younger either."

"That's for damn sure! Remember when the rangers found Luke Watkins with his bare ass pumpin' up and down right over there in the bushes that time he was plowin' that good-lookin' piece, what was her name? . . ."

"Mary Ellen Buford," answered Allen.

"That's it: Mary Ellen Buford. Christ, I would've loved to've dug into her a piece myself. That Luke always had a way with the ladies. But he was too much of a god-damned smart-ass. Thought he could fool somebody by gettin' out of the car and fuckin' in the bushes. Thought no one'd ever find him, I guess. Dumb-ass move. Those rangers just stood around watchin' the two of 'em go at it, all moanin' and pantin' and bangin' away like hogs in heat. And then just when they was about to shoot their loads, that old Sam Brown took one of them firecrackers he had confiscated from some kids down by Chapter Pond and he lit it up and tossed it a couple of yards to the side of the two of 'em and bang! there they goes flyin' outta the bushes draggin' their clothes after 'em, so fuckin' scared they dribbled shit all the way to their car and probably all the way back to the main road as well." Crosby roared with laughter. "Luke had blue balls for a week after that. What a sight he was tryin' to make it up and down those high school stairs."

Allen laughed with his colleague, shaking his head. "That must've been somethin' to see. Though it was damned cruel on Sam's part for doin' it. I mean, what the hell! A little fuckin' never hurt anybody. If they don't do it up here on the lookout, they're gonna do it somewhere else. It ain't our job to stop it. It's life. And if the girl gets herself in trouble, well, that's life, too. It's all part of the chances you take when you're young. They shoulda just let those kids alone and let 'em enjoy the stars and the sound o' the wind in the trees . . . and each other."

The two rangers sat in their car in silence, recalling wistfully their not so distant youth. Then Crosby turned to Allen and said, "Then how come we parked here and scared 'em off ourselves?"

"Shit," sneered Allen. "We're here workin'. We got a job to do. It ain't my fault if they all just assumed we was out to roust 'em."

"You didn't mention nothin' about no job. What kind of job we gotta do out here?"

"Listen for . . . spooks!"

"What?"

"Ghosts. Monsters. We got a report that there's a weird monster roamin' around Chapel Pond and vicinity makin' all sorts of weird noises and scarin' everybody half to death." The sarcasm in Allen's voice was ill-disguised. "At least that's what those new people who bought the old Taylor cabin reported to headquarters last night. Said they heard somethin' real big walkin' through the trees makin' a lotta racket. Bustin' branches, howlin'. You know the story. The state troopers don't wanna bother with it, so we got sent out. So we'll just sit here a couple of hours with the windows open and listen for anything strange."

"Shit," Crosby sneered, settling back in the seat and putting his boots up on the dashboard. "Monsters. It's probably just some city folk who moved out here 'cause they thought they was pioneers or somethin' and now the first night they hear two raccoons fuckin' they think it's monsters runnin' through the woods."

Allen laughed. "You're probably right. I don't know what they heard or thought they heard but the captain said they was pretty upset about the whole thing. So we'll just sit here and listen for a while. Can't hurt none and it sure as hell beats drivin' around lookin' for somethin' to do. Besides, a little Bigfoot rumor won't do the Keene Valley economy any harm, either."

"Shit," Crosby muttered after a long silence. "Monsters. Can I listen to the radio?"

"Just keep it soft."

Ranger Allen watched while the starry belt of the Milky Way began to fade as the moon, just past full, began rising over the mountains. Down below them the tiny hamlet of Keene Valley emerged from the darkness, cast in burnished silver. He could make out the church steeple and the squares of hayfields and the silos of several small farms scattered throughout the valley . . .

Then they heard the howl.

"What the fuck was that?" asked Allen, sitting bolt upright.

"Huh? You hear somethin'?"

"Listen . . . Turn off that goddamn radio!"

The two rangers waited in tense silence. The sound rose again on the night winds, a long, lingering wail, as if the very mountains themselves were groaning in agony.

"That's no raccoon," said Allen. "I can see why those folks was scared."

"No wolf or hound dog, neither," added Crosby. "What in blue blazes was it?"

"Let's get a closer look."

With a flurry of stones and gravel, the rangers sped out of the overlook and along the winding mountain road in the general direction of the strange sound. Crosby hung his head and shoulders out the window like a coon hunter, listening. A third time the sound rose from the mountains and the car ground to a halt in a fine spray of dust.

"It sounds like it's coming from the interior," said Crosby. "Somewhere by that pine coverlet just south of Chapel Pond."

"C'mon then. We better head in by foot."

They pulled the car off the narrow road and took flashlights from the trunk. Then the rangers plunged through the heavy underbrush and made for the pines just to the northeast of their position.

Mountain forests at night don't make for easy travelling, no matter how bright the moon. Although the rangers knew the terrain with exceptional accuracy, having both been raised in the surrounding area, they proceeded over the boulders and along vague footpaths with extreme caution. One slip on a stray fern frond and a man could be laid up for weeks with a bad sprain, if he had the good fortune not to break his neck entirely. They picked their way carefully through the underbrush, pausing at intervals to listen for any further sounds, until they could make out the shadows of the pines in the moonlight, about a mile from them.

"Let's wait here for a while," said Allen. "It'll be better if we keep our eyes on the pines from a distance. That way we can see if anything comes out of there or goes in."

So the two rangers stood together on the perimeter of a rock-strewn clearing that sloped gently down to the cluster of pines. They waited in silence with wide eyes, listening, watching. The moon, approaching its last quarter and having risen above a neighboring peak, made the landscape as unreal with its silverwash as a scene cast in pewter.

A horrible sound broke the silence of the forest night. It wasn't loud but it floated great distances on the night winds. It seemed to gain texture and momentum as it caromed off the peaks and crags of the mountains. Allen and Crosby looked at each other with astonished, frightened eyes.

Neither could say for certain if what they heard was a

burst of hysterical laughter or the sound of grievous moaning from some long-forgotten tomb.

"Shit," whispered Crosby, "I don't like the sound of that at all. What the hell could it be?"

"Not like anything I ever heard before," Allen responded. "But it's sure as hell comin' from down there. Somewhere . . ."

"Look!" Crosby interrupted, pointing. "Did you see it? Did you see it come out of the woods for a second?"

"I didn't see shit. What was it?"

"I'm not sure. I just caught a glimpse of it as it passed to the right of the tree. Just kinda saw a movin' shadow."

Allen looked sceptical. "Maybe that's all it was. Just a shadow."

Crosby was silent for a long moment. "Maybe," he said when he saw no further movement. "I sure as hell hope so. It looked awful damn big."

"How big?"

"O hell, I can't say for sure. I only got a quick look at it. But it looked big as a bear from here."

"A bear?" Allen paused, then smiled. "Maybe that's what it is. Just a bear."

"Hell, you know what a bear sounds like just as much as me. Those weren't no bear sounds."

"A trick of the wind, maybe. You just let it get to you. Talk about monsters in front of you and in ten minutes you start seein' 'em. C'mon. Let's go down and take a closer look."

"I dunno, man. I guess it might've been a bear, it bein' in the shadows and all. But somehow it just didn't move like a bear."

"Ah, nuts!" said Allen, and the two rangers picked their way carefully down the slope to the first pine saplings.

An eerie silence reigned among the pines. The wonted cries of owls and whippoorwills and the throbbing cacophony of crickets and other night hoppers were not to be heard. Only the soft breath of the wind rustling the pine needles.

"You're sure this is where you saw it?" asked Allen.

"Just about. It might've gone deeper into the cover."

233

Allen looked around at the gently swaying branches. "Well, let's head in after it. We're still downwind."

They worked their way among the pines, their flashlights' glare shielded from all but the forest floor in front of them. They had gone past the zone of forest pathways and now had to pick their way carefully among the underbrush and the random tree trunks that grew ever more crowded together. The ground they walked still sloped downward, bringing them ever nearer to the valley floor. Lush, star-shaped mosses began to pad their footsteps and every dead branch or rotten tree trunk they passed was covered with surreal turds of fungus. The further downward they progressed, the darker the forest became. The rangers were now shut off from all but stray wisps of moonlight; they lost the stars entirely.

"How much further we goin' down?" whispered Crosby. "We can't prowl around these woods all night."

"Not much further," Allen answered. "I just want to see if a she-bear's set up a new lair for herself down by the grottoes. For our records."

"Shit. Can't we come back in the daylight?"

"We're here now, ain't we? If it is a she-bear, they can get pretty ornery. Might even make the sound we heard if her cubs are threatened. If we do turn up her lair, at least we can set our minds at rest about what's roamin' around here, howlin'. What's the matter? You scared of your monsters?"

"No, dammit," Crosby muttered, irritated. "I ain't scared o' no monsters. But I ain't particularly fond of the idea of gettin' chewed up by no she-bear neither, dark as it is."

"Well, just humor me for a little while longer. We'll get back to the car soon enough."

Suddenly, a branch snapped loudly behind them.

"What was that?" whispered Crosby, tensing.

"Ssh."

A few more moments and then a loud shuffle of dead leaves, coming closer. The rangers unhitched their pistols. Suddenly, a sharp cracking of branches shattered the tomb-like silence right behind them, not three yards away, followed by an unearthly "woo-woo-woo." The terrified Crosby spun around and lost his footing, falling flat on his face in the ground moss, his pistol flying into the thick darkness of the underbrush. Allen's pistol was at the ready, aimed straight into a patch of blackness.

"Don't shoot! Don't shoot!" came a laughing voice out of the woods. A lanky old man emerged from behind a tree, peeking to see if the coast was clear, cutting through the night's silence with his tremulous laughter. His long beard and hair were matted with burrs and his laughing eyes were mischievous and wild.

"Don't shoot old Charley! He won't harm ye. Not unless ye've been bad little boys. Hee-hee-hee. Woo-woo!"

"Goddamn!" cursed Allen, lowering his pistol. "If that don't beat all! Crazy Charley Watkins! You ain't been heard of in years. Scared me half to fuckin' death."

Crosby peeped up from the ground like a turtle. When he saw who it was, he began to swear like a trucker. Allen broke up with laughter as he helped his partner to his feet.

"Nice move," he mocked. "Fallin' on your face and throwin' your gun away. Wish I thought of that."

Crosby rose to his feet and dusted himself off. He burned with humiliation. Allen turned to Charley.

"What the hell you doin' roamin' around in the dark, old man? You wanna get yourself hurt?"

Charley sniffed indignantly. "I be huntin'!"

"Huntin' what?"

"Can't rightly say."

"O. A secret." Allen winked at Crosby.

"Nope. No secret. Jes' can't rightly say, that's all."

"Well, stick with us for a while, Charley, while we finish doin' our job. I don't trust you in the woods behind me." Allen looked at Crosby with sarcasm smeared all over his face. "Huntin'."

"Crazy old fool," Crosby muttered in return. "Honest people can die from fools like him. Now how'm I gonna find my gun?"

"We'll come back for it in the daylight," said Allen. "If you're real lucky it won't have to come outta your paycheck. Tho' I wouldn't bet on it."

The three men started down toward the valley floor again, with crazy Charley muttering to himself and craning his skinny neck with the bobbing Adam's apple, staring into the forest blackness with his one good eye. Crosby complained to Allen, "Of all the places for that crazy old fool to turn up again, it's gotta be behind me!" Allen just laughed.

They walked a few minutes in silence, then Charley suddenly announced: "It be's powerful big!"

"What's big, fool?" snarled Crosby.

"What we be's huntin'. Powerful big."

"No, no," explained Crosby, "get this straight. You're the only fool around here that 'be's' huntin'. Not us. We're just sort of lookin' around."

They continued a way further through the pine forest and then Charley announced, "It's got a horn."

"What now, old man?" sighed Crosby, exasperated. "What's got a horn?"

"It. A big 'un. Sticks straight out like this," and Charley wiggled his hand about two feet out from his forehead.

"You got a horn, fool," sneered Crosby, wiggling his hand obscenely in front of his crotch. "Only you haven't used it in a hundred years." Crosby turned to Allen: "Probably why he's crazy."

Allen nodded silent agreement and ducked beneath a low pine branch. Another two yards pushing aside heavy scrub and then Allen stopped short, breathless.

"Sweet screamin' Jesus!" he exclaimed. Crosby and Crazy Charley hurried to look over his shoulders.

Their eyes ached with the sudden glare. Millions upon millions of fireflies floated and shimmied beneath the interlocked branches of a large pine grotto. It seemed as if every firefly in the adjoining four counties had assembled at this one spot to frolic. Their cold, gold glimmers danced and blinked in ecstatic profusion, turning the forest grotto into a dazzling fairyland.

"I've never seen nothin' like this!" gasped Allen. "This ain't normal."

They stood there stunned and overwhelmed by the profusion of dancing lights.

"Look!" Crosby called out. "Down there in the midst of 'em. What the hell is it?"

As Allen's eyes adjusted to the glare, he could make out the slender form of a young boy seated on the starry moss of the grotto. He was completely naked and his skin was blotched with thick calloused patches of skin which bristled with coarse hair. The boy's forehead and nose were foreshortened, his jaw and upper lip bony and protruding, his cheeks thick ridges of bone. To Allen the boy's face seemed half that of a horse.

Amidst the dancing multitudes of fireflies, the boyish figure looked like a sprite from fairyland.

"I can't believe what I'm seein'," Allen breathed. "I was taught that leprechauns ain't real."

"And I ain't even been drinkin'," Crosby added.

Crazy Charley was silent, his face bright with glee.

Around the boy on the soft moss was a circle of dead game birds, their necks wrung. The boy sat eating one of the birds raw, pulling feathers out from between his teeth, his equine lips smeared with fresh blood.

"I'm scared, man," moaned Crosby, trembling. "I'm shakin' like a leaf. I can't control it."

"I'm scared too," soothed Allen. "You're not alone. I don't know what the fuck's goin' on around here."

Then, without making a sound, the boy sniffed the air and turned to face the three men.

Robed like a wizard in folds of flowing black velvet, Mercadante sat in a room illuminated only by the somber flame of a single, squat black candle. In the light of the flame, his gaunt face slashed with stark shadows, Mercadante seemed the incarnation of Death. He bore upon his breast a heavy amulet of silver, intricately carved, depicting the Seal of Solomon, and upon the middle finger of his left hand he bore a heavy signet ring, also of silver, upon which were engraved the hieroglyphs of his astral genius. The candle rested upon a circular table of carved wood in the center of which a silver bowl of water was inset. The tips of his slender fingers rested on the edge of the table, amidst carved arcane symbols, and his eyes slowly, imperceptibly, became glazed with intense concentration. His lips moved slowly, his voice a passionate whisper, and the ancient syllables spilled upon the ornate table, evoking dark and forgotten powers.

As the cadence of the profane prayers and invocations

quickened, the clear, still water in the silver basin began to vaguely shimmer with opalescence. Mercadante's nostrils flared with his intensity; his whole upper torso began to move backward and forward in counterpoint to the rhythm of incantations which he half-mumbled, half-whispered. The knuckles of his hands grew white with their increasing pressure on the table. The colors in the water grew more intense, more striking, a collage of fluid gems swirling and blending, brought into existence by the sheer rapture of Mercadante's mind. His body began to writhe and twist and beads of sweat broke out upon his face and forehead and upon the hidden palms of his hands. Soon the radiance of the candle was dwarfed by the shine of fluid colors which filled the room with wild, dancing shadows. Mercadante's head rolled upon his neck, weaving, nodding, as he became absorbed into the final ecstasy of incantation. The swirling colors in the basin became too painfully bright to be endured, and their dance was maddening. At last, he spat the final mystic syllable from his lips and fell forward, close to the bright, burning water and stared with aching, wide eyes into the center of the dizzy swirl and flux. For long, lingering moments he was frozen in that posture, reading the secrets of the dark powers. Then his knuckles relaxed upon the table, his heavy panting stilled, and the burning colors began to dim and fade.

Mercadante leaned back against his seat, his eyes shut tightly, his hands gripping the armrests. Sweat poured off his forehead and cheeks, and his palms left their moist imprints upon the bare wood of the chair. The basin's luster faded entirely. His thin, pale lips curled in a satisfied smile.

When he had briefly rested and composed himself, he pressed an ebony button that was set among the filigree of the table. Seconds later the misshapen Bennett slunk into the room. He waited timorously for his master to speak.

"I admire the audacity that has seen fit to bring you back here to me after the dismal failure of your mission." Mercadante's voice was cold, sinister, and unrelenting. Bennett visibly cringed.

"I am not one to excuse failure," Bennett responded. "You know that much of me, at least. But you also know that Pimm and Brud couldn't simply pounce on the man and kill him outright; we wanted the unicorn and a dead man couldn't tell us where to find it. By the time we discovered it upon his person, this man appeared possessed of great and magnificent powers. He was upon us all in a moment, thrashing the brothers almost to the point of death. Who could have foreseen such power springing up against us? Surely not I!" Mercadante scowled at this pointed remark. "We were lucky to escape when we did, assuring you protection from the local authorities."

Mercadante stared coldly down upon his trembling servant. Then his eyes softened and relented. "I understand many things more clearly now. I understand and can, at least in part, excuse your failure." Bennett's face brightened at this unexpected beneficence from his master. "I've had dealings with that man before."

"Before?" exclaimed Bennett. "You know who he is?"

"I know." Mercadante pressed his fingertips together in front of him, squeezing his palms in and out. "I thought he was dead. I thought I was through with the man who sought to rival my powers and my cunning." His lower jaw tensed; the muscles bulged in thick, taut bands. "I, too, can be in error. But now I see that merely being cognizant of the Great One's manifestation is not enough. My mettle is to be tried in bitter combat. There are forces gathering against me which I hadn't foreseen. I don't know why. I see now that there are dark recesses in the realm of the Fates that are impenetrable even to my eyes. But I also see now the magnitude of the wheels that grind against me, and I'm prepared. We shall win out in the end, without the unicorn and in spite of the interference of that intruder. Tell me now: is the woman on her way to the Chateau?"

"She is. Stully's travelling with her to make sure she gets there."

"Good. I want the two brothers to follow in one of my other private planes. They are to remain at the Chateau until I arrive there myself."

"I understand."

"Good. Now, I want the third brother, Porfex, brought to me immediately."

Bennett was aghast. "Porfex? But isn't that dangerous? Isn't he—"

"He's too intractable for any but myself to control," Mercadante answered. "That's very true. But I shall be at his side continuously until we've arrived at the Chateau with the Great One."

Bennett's warped face brightened. "Then we're to retrieve Him soon, Master? You've located Him?"

"I almost lost Him. I didn't find Him quickly enough while He was in this city. Now He's fled. But I've relocated Him and now I shall take Porfex with me to retrieve Him. I won't have the failed hands of the other two near His presence." Bennett's face fell sorrowfully at this news. Mercadante smiled at his chagrin. "Don't worry, Bennett. You don't deserve it but I shall bring you with me. Perhaps at my side you will prove useful."

Bennett's twisted features tried to squirm into a smile. "O Master, thank you! I can't begin—"

"Then don't. Have Karl prepare the helicopter immediately."

"But it's already late at night—"

"We'll find Him more easily in the dark. There shall be a sign to guide us. I'll give Karl the coordinates of our destination when I reach the helicopter. Make it clear to him that he must maintain maximum altitude throughout the trip. I don't want that infernal noise arousing suspicion. Besides, there'll be mountains beneath us. I want no accidents. Porfex is to be stowed in the rear of the craft. I'll deal with him when I get there. Are there any questions?"

"No, Master." He turned to leave.

"Just think, Bennett," said Mercadante, his voice wistful, "soon we'll return to our beloved Chateau. And He will be with us. I will guide Him up to the High Altar and there He will accept the symbols of His dignity from my hands. My disciples shall be the phalanx of His warriors and, with His might at our front, we shall rule the earth as His ministers." His fingers strayed to the engraved hieroglyphs of his signet ring, twisting the heavy silver around and around. "I've dreamed of that moment for too long to delay it now by waxing sentimental. Hurry and get everything in readiness. I shall join you at the heliport in half an hour."

The helicopter banked against a brisk buffeting of winds that caromed off the high Adirondack peaks. Although the stars above glittered in bejeweled profusion, the treacherous land masses below were shrouded in thick darkness.

"Can't you get us up any higher?" stormed Mercadante angrily. "You'll smash us into a cliff!"

Karl, a small, fine-boned man with pointed features and moist, dark eyes, looked down at his instruments. "I'm doing what I can, sir. With that . . . that . . . boulder sitting amidships, we're lucky to be as high as we are."

The "boulder" to which Karl referred was Porfex, the eldest of the three giant brothers. And the largest—larger even than Pimm and Brud. Whenever Mercadante had occasion to travel with Porfex, he had to be smuggled into the various vehicles, either in a crate or beneath a vast tarpaulin. This was done so that no passing observer would be provoked to gawk or call out to others about the huge size of the human spectacle. Seated in repose, Porfex looked like nothing more than the fat, bronze Buddha of a major Eastern temple, an attraction for millions of worshippers. He even had the same blank, inward-looking eyes and the humorless half-smile so emblematic of meditation masters. But in Porfex's case, as well as in his brothers', this meditational gaze was the result of severely retarded intelligence.

A sudden downdraft sucked the helicopter into a dangerous yaw as they neared a mountain. The occupants of the craft were jostled wildly in the cockpit and an angry gnashing of teeth emerged from amidships.

"Blast it!" snarled Mercadante. "Can't you keep this craft on an even keel? You'll kill us yet."

Karl, an excellent pilot, cursed under his breath. His skilled hands flew about the controls, nudging the delicate joystick and adjusting levers. "I'll take care of the downdrafts, sir," he answered somewhat harshly, "if you can keep that thing back there from eating his way out through the fuselage."

Thanks to Karl's aviation skills, the large helicopter was righted and the tall peak looming blackly in front of them was gingerly skirted. It seemed smooth sailing all the way to the final coordinates.

"We should be there very shortly," Karl announced, pleased.

"Yes, I know," Mercadante responded, settling his heavy coat about his shoulders against the cold. "I can feel His presence all around me." He leaned toward the plastic bubble-window, his eyes pressed closely against its surface. Below, there was nothing but inky, impenetrable blackness.

Karl's voice was suddenly uncertain. "I still don't understand how you'll be able to know exactly . . . I mean, in all that darkness . . ."

"I'll know, Karl, I'll know. There will be a sign."

In his eagerness, Mercadante pressed his face against the frigid plastic bubble too long, burning his cheek. He pulled back reluctantly, breathless with excitement. "We're so near, my dear, dear comrades. I'm breathing the air of His majesty right now. Another few moments . . ."

The helicopter passed over a peak fringed with tall pines and there was a narrow valley which sloped steeply on either side. Suddenly, Mercadante pulled at Karl's shoulder.

"Over there! See? I told you there'd be a sign."

Far below, a single smear of gold light emerged from beneath the canopy of trees. The glow was shimmering and nebulous, as if in constant agitation. His curiosity piqued, Karl switched on the infrared scanner.

"I can't pick it up on the scanner," Karl said, amazed. "Any electrical device large enough to make that glow would've shown up. Or a fire. Or something. It's fantastic."

"Karl, you fool," sneered Mercadante, elated. "Do you think you can register His presence with your toys? Do you think He's standing down there waving a lantern? He's guiding us to Him in His own way. Can you take us down nearby? Quickly, find a spot for us to disembark."

Karl switched on the external floods and searched the vicinity. A clear grassy patch was revealed near the rim. The helicopter banked sharply.

"You will drop us off and then rise again to maximum altitude," Mercadante instructed Karl. "It's only a short hike through the woods to His beacon. We'll summon you by flare when we've got Him with us and we're ready to load. But be careful," Mercadante cautioned, his eyes narrow and his voice conspiratorial. "Watch both the skies and the land for anything out of the ordinary. I've been running into too many fortuitous setbacks. A foe from my past has turned up and I know he'll try to thwart me. He has great powers and I can't predict if, when, or where he might make some spectacular entrance. Just keep your eyes open. I can't say for what, just keep them open. If you see anything that might mean trouble, give a blast on the air horn."

"I understand, sir," responded Karl crisply. Then they all lurched with the queasiness of rapid descent until the helicopter hovered just above the grassy terrain. Mercadante and Bennett spilled from the hovering craft and ran to unlatch the large side door. Then, in the frigid silver of the moonglow, a large head appeared beyond the open hatch. Porfex stood for a moment at the edge of the opening, dwarfing it with his bulk. Then he leaped ponderously to his feet upon the soft grass.

The helicopter lurched with Porfex's descent and Karl had his hands full keeping the blades from spinning into the ground. While he steadied the craft, Porfex kept his hands tightly clasped over his ears, his face grimacing with pain. He stared at the helicopter in mute wonder, and made a sudden move as though he had recognized a giant new toy with which to play.

"No, Porfex!" Mercadante cried out, pulling on the man's arm. The giant's face turned from joy to bewilderment as he saw his angry master tugging at him. Then the three turned and headed toward the eerie glow.

(Man-things. Think to hide. Stare at me. Let them.)

The boy cracked a hollow bird bone between his teeth. Crazy Charley bolted from the cover of the bushes and capered ecstatically among the hordes of fireflies.

(Strange man, dancing. Not afraid. See if he comes near.)

Charley highkicked, whirled, fireflies clinging to his hermit rags and skin. Allen and Crosby looked at each other in amazement. The fairy-lad didn't seem to mind Charley's intrusion.

(Others come. Slowly. Frightened.)

"Do you think whatever it is is magic?" Crosby whispered to his partner. "Do you think it's hiding a pot of gold? Or maybe it'll grant us some wishes."

"Or maybe it'll eat us like those birds," Allen cautioned. "I'll believe anything now." He slipped his pistol carefully from its holster.

(Gun. Do they think . . .)

Charley crawled over to the boy on all fours, stopping just outside the circle of dead birds. He stared curiously at the boy with wild, ancient eyes, as if through a glass dome. He was grinning fit to burst.

(Old man. Harmless. Friendly.)

The boy tossed Charley a dead bird. Charley kneaded the fresh, soft corpse in his hands, staring down at it. Then he placed it on the grass and reached out to touch the boy. The boy pulled himself away, still chewing.

(No touch. Soiled. Hurt. No.)

Crosby and Allen, seeing that Charley was unharmed, crawled slowly toward the boy in imitation. Allen's finger was looped around the trigger of his gun.

(Behind them. Out of the shadows. Others. Strange others.)

"Look!" whispered Mercadante to Bennett in amazement. "Fireflies! Look how they dance around Him! What glorious beauty! This puts that manger and star nonsense to shame. This is truly the stuff of legend!"

Hot tears streamed down Mercadante's cheeks.

"How beautiful He is! A fledgling yet, half-formed, yet so delicate and supple! Quickly now, we must keep Him from those others."

He tugged on Porfex's arm to distract his grinning face

from the glittering spectacle. The giant turned and bent down his head. Mercadante whispered in his ear.

Before Allen could turn and look behind him to see what it was that crashed through the woods, he felt immense pressure gripping his neck and ankles. Suddenly his body was wrenched painfully off the ground and he found himself stretched out taut facing the dark canopy of leaves overhead. He tried to scream for Crosby but his voice was choked off. He had no idea what it was that was holding him and Porfex allowed him no time to find out. The giant placed the small of the man's back on the crown of his skull and arched his body, bow-like, above him. Then he gave a quick pull with both giant arms and a loud crack shattered the muffled stillness of the grotto. Crosby, voiceless with terror, tried to push himself out of the range of the giant's arms, his heels digging into the soft sward beneath him. Porfex tossed the limp corpse lightly to the edge of the clearing and then bent down for Crosby. The ranger's terror at last found a voice and he let fly with a shrill, blood-chilling scream. Porfex grasped the struggling man by his neck and, raising him high in the air with one hand, began to whirl him around. A deft twist of his wrist and a second sharp snap shattered the peace of the valley.

Crosby's scream broke the rapture with which Charley stared at the fairyboy. He turned and stared up into the glowering eyes of the giant. Crazy as he was, Charley had sense enough to bolt from the grotto. Porfex started to follow but Mercadante called him back.

"Let him go. The man is mad and within his madness shall be locked a testament to the glory of His manifestation." He approached the seated boy slowly, tenderly, his heart flooded with passion. The boy stared at him curiously in return, idly munching on his dead bird. Mercadante reached the circle of dead birds and stopped, his eyes streaming tears. Then he fell to his knees in front of the boy.

"My Lord! My dearest Lord! So many years have I yearned for You. So many hardships have I endured throughout the world to prepare for Your coming. Sweet Satan, at last You have arrived to redeem this world for Your worshippers! My poor mortal lips cannot speak sufficient words to compass my overwhelming joy!" He dropped his forehead to the ground and grovelled at the boy's feet, leaving the spongy moss wet and salty with his tears. Bennett, in the background, fell to his knees as well. Even Porfex, seeing the others, lowered himself heavily to his knees, grinning.

The boy stared quizzically at the three strange men. The old man's voice rose up to him faintly, as if from some distant, incensed altar of sacrifice. Then he slowly reached out over the circle of dead birds and touched Mercadante's silver hair. A pulse of energy flowed through his fingers into the man's ancient skull, shivering him with orgasmic delight. The boy's eyes glowed like twin silver beacons, diminishing the spectacle of the fireflies with their brightness.

(This is to be worshipped. Thrive on the sacrifice of others. Their bodies. Souls. A glory unconceived before.)

His eyes dimmed and he withdrew his hand from Mercadante's head. The old man rose delighted and weeping, yearning to embrace the boy yet not daring to presume too much.

"Come, my Lord," he said gently, his voice weak and cracking. "Come with me so that I may regale You according to Your holy grandeur. Come with me so that Your worshippers may honor You and bow before You. Come with me so that I may nurture You unto the fullness of Your vast power."

The boy stared into the eyes of the old man. He read something within them that human wisdom cannot begin to comprehend. Then he rose lightly to his feet and let Mercadante take his hand, leading him off into the darkness.

22

THE old man had azure eyes, pale as Caribbean waters, fluid with the gleam of uncanny vision. He knows me, thought Jade. He knows my depths and my shallows. He sees right through me as if I were crystal. He sits amidst my books and papers, idly thumbing through all that is an expression of myself, as if he had known them for centuries. I should be terrified by his strangeness but his eyes and his smile and his gentle voice soothe me. He saved my life, though I don't understand how. An old man who calls himself Daniel, with the eyes of a prophet. The ancient words passed in sedate review before Jade's memory:

YOU HAVE BEEN JUDGED BY THE LORD
AND HAVE BEEN FOUND WANTING

Jade searched among the shelves in his bathroom for a tube of ointment. Staring at his swollen face in the bathroom mirror, he delicately touched the puffed bruises of greenish purple that remained as traces of the giant's heavy hand. Although there were fortunately not any broken bones, every muscle in Jade's body seemed torn and aching. Icy water from the tap soothed his cheeks and cleared the violent fog that rose and surged at intervals within his brain, a fog born more of the strangeness of his battle than of any wounds.

He looked at the jade unicorn in the mirror. It hung from its chain cold and lifeless, no longer an angry power but rather, once again, a bit of carved stone. Jade touched its chill smoothness with cautious fingers. So Mercadante knew about Adrienne and him. Jade's stomach churned uneasily. If those three "characters" were part of Mercadante's coterie of servants, then Adrienne was in desperate trouble. He twirled the jade unicorn at the end of its chain, watching as the bathroom light reflected brightly off its spinning curves. Suddenly, he was smitten by a moment of desperate panic: he wanted to rip the unicorn off his neck and toss it far away from him with a howl. His hand closed itself around the figure tightly and, as he was poised to pull, he was startled by what he saw in the mirror: deep within the dark pupils of his own eyes he saw a fidget of movement, a tiny equine face bearing a sharp horn in its forehead which laughed at and mocked him silently. Jade's heart stopped and his jaw slackened as he bent more closely to the mirror to assure himself of the hallucination, his hand still tightly gripping the jade figure. The two pupillary images showed more clearly, moving in exact unison, laughing, sneering, fluttering a reptilian tongue in menacing challenge. Jade gasped, releasing the figure from his grasp, and lurched backward from the washbasin, stumbling against the wall of the bathroom.

Daniel stood beside him, gripping his shoulders.

"Are you all right?" the old man asked, staring quizzically into his eyes.

"My . . . my eyes . . ." Jade squeezed his eyes tightly shut, shaking his head quickly from side to side. He pushed past Daniel to return to the mirror and gazed sharply at his reflection. The mocking image was gone.

Jade backed away from the mirror, panting with released tension. "I must've been hit harder on the head than I thought." He smiled feebly but Daniel's eyes were filled with concern.

"Here, drink this," the old man said, handing Jade a steaming cup of liquid. "I brewed it while you were here fixing yourself up."

Jade looked down at the honey-colored liquid and sniffed. "Tea?"

"Not quite. My own concoction. Don't be afraid. Drink it."

Jade hesitated then suddenly laughed out loud at his own suspicions. He boldly drank the brew down with one long toss of his head. It tasted of jasmine and honey. "Delicious," he commented. "I hope that whatever you laced it with is good and strong. I can use a little relaxing right now."

Daniel smiled. "I think you'll be pleased by its effects. It'll help restore you while it soothes your nerves." Daniel lightly clasped Jade's elbow, leading him out of the bathroom and into the living room where the two men sat cross-legged facing each other on the floor.

Jade's tiny apartment was spartan in its furnishings: a throw rug, some large pillows scattered about the floor, a mattress shoved against a wall not far from the radiator, and walls covered with bookshelves. The bookshelves brimmed: literature, philosophy, religion, the sciences, the occult. Daniel sat with his hands resting on his knees and surveyed the rows of books that lined the walls.

"I was admiring your library," he told Jade. "Something here for everybody, I should think. Your interests are wide-ranging to say the least."

Jade settled into a comfortable half-lotus, feeling a strange, exhilarating warmth flush through his blood vessels. He half closed his eyes. "Renaissance interests, I'd call it," Jade responded. "That's been the bane of my existence: plenty of interests and few achievements." His body began to drift with mellow languor, as with prime hashish, yet his mind didn't drift with it. His mental acuity seemed to become honed and sharpened, eager to be tried with questions, puzzles, and new knowledge. "This is some drink you made me, Daniel. My body feels high and my mind feels intelligent. Usually a contradiction in terms. O, I don't mean to demean myself; I suppose I'm bright enough. But, in my line of work, you see, the opportunities for intellectual stimulation are severely limited." He massaged his scalp and fine blond hair luxuriantly. "I haven't felt as sharp as this in . . .

in years. Maybe never before. Damn, that was some drink!"

Daniel smiled. "It's good you feel that way. You're meant to. There's much I have to tell you and there isn't much time. I can't have your mind distracted by your aches from this evening."

"You're right," Jade nodded. "There's a lot that we both have to do. I, for one, have to go to the cops. A chore I don't relish, believe me. But a lady friend of mine is in one shitload of trouble, I think, and . . ."

"I know all about Mrs. Mercadante," Daniel interrupted. "And her husband. They're part of what we must talk about."

Stunned, Jade stared into the old man's face with disbelief. The soft light from a single lamp encircled Daniel's long, white hair in a soft corona and accentuated the contours of his thin, jovial face. For the first time Jade noticed that Daniel had almost no eyebrows, that the sparse hairs above his eyes were so thin and silvery as almost to disappear, making his moist aquamarine eyes even brighter and more lively.

"The way you popped up out of nowhere," Jade murmured, "the way you beat the crap out of Bluto and his brother back there, old as you are and with only a stick, the way you know my name and know all about Adrienne . . . okay, Daniel, you win. I'm impressed. Very impressed. Now, before I begin to think we're both out of our minds, could you elaborate?"

Daniel relaxed with a deep, controlled breath, composing his words. "First, my son, let me caution you that what I have to say may seem incredible. And tonight is all the time allotted us for discussion. I don't have the liberty to present you with elaborate proofs. Perhaps there are sympathetic vibrations between us that'll make it easier for you to believe what I'm going to say. Perhaps some of the things you've seen me do tonight and some of the things I know will also help persuade you that I'm speaking the truth. I hope so. I haven't the ability, nor the desire, to compel you to believe me. Yet it is of the utmost importance to you, to me, to the rest of the people of the world, and indeed, to the rest of the inhabitants of the universe that you trust what I say."

Jade's eye narrowed cynically. "Are you going to tell me you're from another planet and you've come here as an emissary to save the world?"

Daniel laughed, shaking his head. "No, I won't be telling you that. I'm very much of this world. However, what I have to say may make you equally sceptical. That's why I want you to listen to me with as open a mind as you can muster. You're a man of wide-ranging interests. It'll be easier for you to hear me out impartially than for most others. But I do respect the scepticism of your intelligence. If anything I say doesn't make sense to you or if it's unclearly presented or if you have any question at any time while I tell you all that I must, please stop me and ask what you will. As I said before, we haven't much time. Tonight's the night for decisions and I'm afraid that most of the burden of our future actions will rest upon you. I want you to understand completely what I'm going to ask of you so that you can give me a fair and well-reasoned response." He made a cautionary gesture with his finger. "I must warn you, though, that much of what is happening is completely out of both our hands. Your involvement in this at all is a sheer caprice of fate. At least of fate as we understand it. The powers lurking beyond fate . . . well, even I can't fathom such mysteries."

Jade's voice grew somber. "What is it I'm supposed to do?"

"Later for that, Jade. First I'll tell you a little about Heinreich Mercadante that I'm certain you'll find very interesting. Mercadante is a self-avowed satanist."

"What?" came Jade's startled reply.

"A satanist. You must understand that he's a man of very medieval temperament. As are most of us Westerners, actually. He believes in the literal existence of mutually exclusive powers that vie for control of the universe . . . a power of light and a power of darkness, if you will." Daniel shook his head. "I hate those superstitious metaphors. They're so primitive and they lock us into preconceptions that inhibit our understanding of the true mechanism of the universe. As if darkness is somehow evil and light, good. As if good and evil can be personified in the guise of anthropomorphic deities like

Satan and God. But that is how Mercadante thinks and I have to represent him thus to you so that you can understand what he plans to do.

"You see, Mercadante is, much like myself, a freak of nature. We both happen to have been born with an intracellular makeup that puts us in a synchronous relationship with an untold number of vibrations and radiations that permeate the universe. I don't understand the total mechanism myself, though I've spent a lifetime trying to puzzle it out. The net result of this, however, is that we can perceive things and act upon things in a multitude of ways that are far beyond the scope of ordinary men. A weak analogy would be the bees, who are able to perceive with their eyes ultraviolet radiation, or the deep-sea life-forms that produce their own bioluminescence. Because of their environmental needs these creatures have, through the long process of evolution, developed necessary senses and abilities, which, to life-forms like ourselves that have evolved along different lines, seem uncanny. Well, Mercadante and I are human mutations with powers that would seem uncanny to anyone who doesn't also share them. You know how sometimes we run across people who seem incredibly ape-like and stupid and we refer to them as evolutionary "throwbacks" reminiscent of our remote ancestors? I believe that Mercadante and I are just the opposite. We are examples of what lies in store for humankind in the millennia ahead, if our race is given the opportunity to continue its evolutionary growth."

Daniel paused, studying the questioning look in Jade's eyes. "Go on. Ask the question."

Jade's eyes widened. "What sort of powers, specifically?" he asked.

Daniel smiled. "I know that most people will begin thinking in terms like those of popular comic book heroes. No, I don't run into phone booths and change into some sleek, fancy costume, cape and all, and fly out to battle bank robbers and such. But both Mercadante and I possess highly developed telepathic abilities. We can, to a greater or lesser extent, read minds. We can implant thoughts and suggestions over vast spaces. We have psychokinetic abilities—the power to move things, to bend atomic structures with our minds. We have such highly developed powers of psychic control that we can even free our consciousness from the corporeal limitations of our bodies and roam at will among the stars—astral projection, the researchers call it."

Daniel's eyes began to sparkle and his words warm with eloquence. "O, such marvels I've seen, Jade! There's so much beauty and magnificence all around us that mankind is just not highly evolved enough to witness. We, as a race, have a tough enough time comprehending our own emotional states. Can you imagine the consummate joy it would be to literally share another person's sense of happiness or triumph? And to have caused that other person's joy? Well, the glorious sense within us would be ten times greater. Can you see what I'm driving at, Jade? If mankind is allowed to run its full evolutionary course, then all of us will share these abilities. The more evolved we become, the more powerful and self-sufficient we will become as well, making such primitive emotions as envy, hatred, and anger obsolete. Unthinkable, even. O, sure, in a world of grasping cutthroats such as exists now, such emotions are protective devices that help us survive as individuals and continue to reproduce. And slowly but surely, more and more individuals are being born who manifest the primal seeds of these special abilities and intellectual capacities. I can see which way we're tending, given the thousands of generations necessary for the change to occur."

Daniel pressed his fingertips together gently, his eyes drifting off into space. "It's such a warm, glorious vision, my son. And don't you see that when these abilities begin to manifest themselves among ever-greater numbers of people, they will be consciously used to amplify their own potency? The germ of such powers will draw upon itself to magnify itself, so that the evolutionary proliferation of such powers will eventually snowball and consume everybody in one vast complex of thought, feeling, and power. To use what is at least a pleasant metaphor, we shall become as gods. Not the angry, squabbling kind found in primitive mythologies. But gods in the true, archetypal sense of the word."

Daniel was silent, allowing his words to simmer in Jade's mind. Jade watched the lines of the old man's face pass in and out of the soft shadows cast by the lamp. Words came hard to him amidst the pleasant vistas of his thoughts.

"That's a beautiful picture you paint of mankind's possibilities," Jade commented at last. "Quite different from what I'm used to hearing. Can you see into the future as well?"

"No, not really," Daniel answered. "But both Mercadante and I can sense ripples in time."

"Ripples in time? You've lost me."

Daniel laughed. "I should think so! You see, any action or change of state of matter or energy must occur in both space and time."

"Einstein's theory, right?"

"Somewhat. But consider what would happen if an object suddenly appeared in the middle of space. It would manifest itself in a great number of spatial ways. It would displace whatever had previously occupied the space. It could be seen, if something were nearby to see it. It could be felt, if something could reach out and touch it. Well, it's the same with an object or process that occupies time as well as space." Daniel pressed his hand against his forehead, wrinkling the pink flesh of his brow. "How can I describe the feeling? It's as if things or events set up gentle ripples in time, reaching out both backward and forward in time from the present. Ripples, mind you, not a pounding surf. To those of us who are attuned to such ripples, like Mercadante and myself, as well as others scattered throughout the world, they are perceived as intuitions or hunches. I don't know, Jade: those are such poor words to describe the feeling. Suffice it to say that the more strongly you're attuned to 'see' or 'feel' these ripples, the more distant in time are the events that you become aware of."

"Wait!" Jade interrupted. "You mean that the process can work both ways? You can 'feel' into the past as well as into the future?"

"Of course. Most people find the concept of seeing into the future far more glamorous and exciting than looking backward to the past. They leave that for journalists and historians. But the past leaves its traces to be read by the eye that is suited to read them. What do you think ghosts are? Those, of course, that aren't the pure figments of an overwrought imagination."

"I had no idea . . . !"

"And speak to anyone who has visited the sites of the Nazi death camps. You don't need special receptivity to feel the horror that still quivers upward from the very soil upon which so many thousands were starved, tortured, and murdered. But to those of us who are specially attuned . . ." Daniel turned his eyes away from Jade and looked down at his lap.

A heavy silence rose between the two men, Jade dumb with wonder and Daniel silent with grief over the visions which he had just recalled. Then Daniel shook his head energetically and slapped his knees harshly, crying out, "Enough! I'm getting carried away from the point of all this and we've only got tonight. I'm not here to catalogue my powers nor those of Mercadante. I simply want you to understand how I know so much about you and Adrienne and her husband and about the colossal events that are fast being thrust upon us."

"Wait! Before you go any further," said the awestruck Jade, "you spoke before of 'others scattered throughout the world' just like you and Mercadante." He regarded Daniel with a suspicious eye. "Just how many of you are out there?"

"There are no other drastic mutations like Mercadante and myself that I know of. But there are thousands upon thousands of what you would consider average people who possess similar sensitivities, only drastically scaled down."

"You mean the ESP freaks who are constantly doing things like bending keys and talking to spirits and imprinting photo negatives with their mental images?"

"That's right. Of course, only some of them are legitimate. But, speaking in evolutionary terms, they are no more than tadpoles in comparison to Mercadante and myself."

Jade heaved a long, heavy sigh, nodding his head critically all the while. Then he broke out in helpless laughter. "I'm sorry, Daniel," he apologized. "I don't want to seem rude. I just can't help myself. All that you're saying to me . . . all that you want me to believe . . . I mean, I can't even believe that I'm here sitting on the floor in my own apartment listening to all this . . ."

Daniel reached over and caressed Jade's bearded cheek with a gentle hand. Jade's laughter suddenly stopped. The old man's eyes looked deeply into Jade's. "I understand, my son. I understand and I sympathize with your difficulty. But there's much more that I must say to you that'll sound even more insane and I beg you to hear me out with an open mind. O, if I only had the time to show you all that I could so that you could see the truth of my words demonstrated right before your eyes. But the net is closing in on the world and I must make you understand the part you must play to stop it."

"A net closing in on the world?" Jade returned the old man's somber gaze. "Please go on and explain what you mean."

Daniel looked up from the floor to some books on an upper shelf. He pointed upward with a slender finger. "I see you have quite a number of astronomy books. Can I then assume a serious interest on your part in the theoretical origins of the universe?"

"Yes, you can."

"Then perhaps you'll be interested in the results of my own researches. Keep in mind that I've been able to call upon my unusual abilities in the course of my studies. I've seen things no scientist in a laboratory with even the most sophisticated equipment has ever seen. I've been able to use the sun, itself, as the crucible for some of my experiments. The darkest vacuum of space has been the site of countless others. Don't bother yourself about the logistics; we haven't the time. Suffice it to say that throughout my many years of life, I've pushed the bounds of human scientific knowledge far beyond those of the research centers and laboratories. There are blind alleys and impenetrable walls that thwart my researches still, but even so, I've developed a rather comprehensive picture of how the universe began. And it's in those very processes of origin that the root of the impending catastrophe lies.

"Consider the beginning of all things as Chaos: but

not the Chaos of the ancients which could be represented by a cauldron filled with bits of earth, water, and hot coals, swirled with a spoon to comingle the mixture with air. Think instead of all that we know to be matter—earth, the stars, living flesh—then reduce all those things to their least common denominator. I know you're thinking now of atoms. But even these have been shown by physicists to break down further into even more basic particles. Now, I realize how difficult this is, Jade, but I want you to try and imagine all the cohesive bonds between subatomic particles to be shattered. Everything freed from the little bundles of atomic knots. There are no atoms; there are no components of atoms; no matter; no energy. Nothing that could be perceived by any senses, even if something with senses existed at that time by some miracle to try and perceive it. Your imagination cannot even begin to visualize such a state of affairs. It's not like the dark emptiness of sleep or death, because there would be neither darkness nor light, since they are states that exist only relative to each other and couldn't exist in the primordial Chaos of which I speak. There is nothing, yet there is everything: a peculiar state of existence which I call *potential*. If you could stand in deep space, far from any planet or star, and cup your hands in the ether, you would be holding that which we ordinarily think of as nothing. A stray molecule or two of gas or dust, perhaps, but essentially nothing. Do you follow me so far?"

"I think so," Jade replied, his brows knitted sharply with his efforts to visualize the images that Daniel paraded before him.

"Good. Now, if you could somehow be made to float around in the same way in the midst of the pre-universe Chaos and then cupped your hands, you would be holding enclosed within them the seeds of entire galaxies. That is the difference between nothing and the state of potential. It's an abstract, yet important, difference: the state of potential being those vibrations, distributed evenly throughout the immensity of infinity, which under the proper stimulation can begin to coalesce into wavelengths of energy and then into subatomic particles, and then into nuclei, and then atoms, and then molecules, and on and on until the entire matter-energy complex of the universe as we know it today is formed. Do you still follow me?"

Jade hesitated. "I think I do understand your distinction between that state of potential and pure nothing."

Daniel smiled. "Well, that's enough of a start. Cosmologists today have a relatively clear notion of how the galaxies came to be born: a supercompressed mass of simple atoms coagulating at one central point and then collapsing under its own weight until it heats up, explodes, and then all the material that is flung out in all directions eventually gathers in flying clumps to become galaxies, which in turn coagulate into multitudes of suns, which in turn, on occasion, develop associated planetary systems."

"The 'big bang' theory, right?"

"That's right. The big question then is how did the initial, static state of potential become that immense ball of condensing atoms which in turn exploded to become the stuff of the universe as you and I know it."

"That is a rather big question, for sure."

"And it requires a big answer, to which you'll have to listen very carefully. There are two basic, yet mutually exclusive, laws regulating the physics of the universe, as I've learned in my researches. The first law is that all matter and all energy seek the simplest state of existence. The state of potential which I've spoken about is the quintessence of such simplicity: things exist, yet they have absolutely no properties; no form, no movement, no loss or gain of energy. Nothing, yet everything. Do you follow me?"

"Yeah, I think I see what you mean."

"Good. Now, according to my theory, there is no reason for that state of potential to ever change into anything else. It should exist as such forever, or, to put it better, it should exist without change of any sort; without time, without space, without motion. Yet, we know that something did precipitate a crucial change, or else you and I would never have existed to discuss all this. This brings us to the second fundamental law, polarity.

"Just as all states of matter and energy tend toward maximum simplicity, they also seem compelled to divide equally into entities of equal and opposite orientation. Let me give you some examples of what I mean: you have the opposite poles of a magnet, north and south; you have the negative and positive poles of electrical devices, like a battery or an electric current; scientists have long known of right- and left-handed molecules which have made possible such things as polarized light filters; you have left- and right-hand orbital spins of electrons within atoms; and scientists are just beginning to study the differences between what they call matter and antimatter. You can see then how pervasive this polarity is throughout all matter and energy. It even has a necessary expression in the intellectual and moral spheres. The whole functioning of our logic depends upon the strict rule that things either are or they are not: never both. That a proposition is rational or it is irrational. That there is good and there is evil. That there is yin and there is yang. Do you understand how basic to our way of thinking such polarity is? Why, without such a basis of absolute and mutually contradictory division, neither you nor I would have a damn thought in our heads."

Daniel paused to allow Jade to absorb the import of his words. Jade stared silently down at his lap, his head slowly shaking from side to side. "That's an incredible concept, Daniel," he finally commented. "I'd never thought of things in quite that way. So what you're saying then is that at the root of all physics is a basic and irreconcilable conflict between the tendency toward absolute simplicity and the necessity for this complete and absolute division, this polarity."

"Exactly!" Daniel exclaimed, his eyes bright with enthusiasm.

"So now let me take it one step further: you're saying that somehow, when everything was in that state of potential, as you call it, suddenly this polarity arises which fucks everything up. Suddenly, this state of potential can't just sit there anymore. Things start to line up, pluses grabbing minuses, positives pulling on negatives, antis attracting pros. And like forces are simultaneously repelling each other. Therefore, where you had nothing but potential before, you suddenly have motion. That pre-universe state which was static, suddenly is active."

"Perfect!" Daniel thrilled. "You understand what I'm driving at perfectly."

"But I don't understand what all this has to do with you and me and Heinreich Mercadante!"

"O be patient, Jade. You've come so far, don't let yourself get thrown now. The rest is all downhill. I haven't yet discovered precisely why such polarity suddenly occurs. Maybe I never will. Maybe it's an axiom of the universe that is just beyond understanding. I don't think so, but as of right now, it's a puzzle greater than my powers are able to handle, as great as my powers are. But what I have been able to determine is that each opposing polarity began with a unified central core. It was the swirling conflict between these cores that created the first motion, that created time, that produced the first wavelengths of energy which produced the first offshoots of matter. And on and on until suddenly you have the great ball of matter and energy which collapses upon itself and leads to the 'big bang'—the creation of the universe as we know it.

"It's been about eighteen billion years since then. The substance thrown off by the explosion has since coalesced at an untold number of points, becoming galaxies and all that they contain. The galaxies, now solid to a large extent and now possessing their own internal motions and direction, have slowed considerably from their initial impetus at the first moment of the explosion. This, of course, is all well and good. This slowing down has permitted the formation of planets and the evolution of life. And the whole process would continue unabated if the status quo were left alone. But among the positive aspects of this slowing process is a certain sinister corollary: as the expanding universe slows down, the two kernels of polarity which had been dissipated at the very beginning of creation after they had begun the whole affair, have begun to slow down and coalesce as well. Who can say what state they existed in during the process of universal evolution? Vaporized, drifting, without properties, yet, just like the universe in the state of potential, far different from mere nothingness. And, as these vaporous polarities shrink and subtly solidify, who can predict what properties they may suddenly possess? A form of consciousness, perhaps, beyond anything you or I can conceive? Perhaps some form of ultraphysical presences that absolutely must meet once again and link in whirling combat as before, in order to precipitate a second catastrophe which will, by absolute physical law, tear apart all that has formerly come into existence so that the universe will be reduced once again, in a flash, to the pre-creation state of potential. I believe, Jade, that you and I are living on the brink of such a catastrophe right now."

Daniel paused, permitting his words to sink in. Jade stroked his beard, his lips pursed in concentration. "Let me get this straight now," he finally commented. "You mean to say that these opposite, polar forces or whatever they are are somehow shrinking down and heading for each other once again?"

"That's right."

"But what if they don't find each other. I mean, it might sound silly but the universe is a big place . . ."

Daniel's voice was rock hard: "Don't be deceived on that point. They'll find each other. It's not like two human beings hunting for each other. Those two forces are inextricably linked, like two halves of the same coin. Their fate, if you will, is immutably shared."

"And when they do link up . . . it's all over?"

"A chain reaction will begin at their point of contact the like of which has yet to be conceived by human mind, outside of this room, that is. The bonding forces within the cores of atoms will simply dissolve. And everything, with astounding rapidity, will just vaporize."

Jade slapped his knees with a smile and a shake of his head. "Daniel, excuse me 'cause I need some dope." He reached for his pipe which rested on the floor by his mattress and sprinkled a pinch of herb into it. Then he lit up, dragging deeply. The smoke swelled his lungs for a long time, then he blew out swirling curls of gray. "Christ," he continued, "I think that should carry me through the rest of this conversation. You've got to admit that you're laying down some pretty heavy words."

"I know."

"I mean, I appreciate the care with which you've chosen your words in order to make all those scientific complexities clear to me. And I think I've gotten the gist of what you're saying. Sort of. But really . . . the end of the universe?" Jade chuckled. "I mean, most prophets of doom are content to stop at the end of the world. Aren't you a bit extreme?".

Daniel's voice went frigid. His eyes stared into Jade's with a frightening intensity. "I'm truly sorry you feel that I'm making all this up for your amusement. I didn't ask for things to be as they are and I didn't ask for the cursed power to know about it. Nor have I chosen you, of all people, with whom to share this knowledge out of whimsy. I was compelled to seek you out just as I am compelled to finish telling you all that I know. Once you've heard me out completely, you can tell me to go to hell and I'll leave quietly. I'm afraid all the final decisions rest with you. My powers have reached their limits."

Jade was taken aback by the somberness of Daniel's tone. He hadn't meant to offend him. After all, the old man had saved his life and there certainly was a lot that was strange about him. Magical things. And everything he said, if you listened closely enough, made sense in a bewildering sort of way. But really . . . it was a bit much.

"Well, you still haven't explained what all this stuff has to do with me. If you can't stop it from happening, what the hell can I do?"

"I'll be as brief as possible," Daniel said coldly. "There's no way of knowing how many times this process has occurred in the past. The universe may have been created and destroyed countless times prior to the existence of the universe we inhabit. There may have been no way to stop the destruction. No prior warning. I don't know. But this time something . . . freakish has occurred. Those opposing polar forces, in some mysterious way and whether by chance or by design I can't say, have incorporated themselves within the life-forms of two separate living creatures."

"What! You mean to say that . . . that forces of such magnitude have been reduced to such manageable proportions?"

"It's not a matter of magnitude or reduction. These entities are as large as the universe and smaller than atoms. They are shouts and they are whispers. They are everything . . . and they are nothing."

"You mean sort of like . . . God?"

"If that metaphor has meaning for you, so be it. Only keep it plural."

Jade paused to take another toke, shaking his head. "So you're saying that these . . . things are inside two living creatures. What does that do to the poor shmucks who suddenly find themselves . . . well, *occupied?*"

"It depends, I suppose, on the individual host life-form. The effect could be drastic or extremely subtle. Indeed, I know for a fact that one of the life-forms isn't even aware that it's been entered and that the force has already commenced the process of inextricably embedding itself beneath that creature's consciousness. And I also know that the other life-form has undergone some mind-boggling transformations, uncontrollable and exceedingly violent. But the linkages aren't complete as yet. At this point, any serious change of state in the life-forms, such as severe injury or death, will cause the force within to withdraw and either seek another host or unite with its counterpart at some other point in space-time. Some place I may not be able to reach. If that happens, then it could be as it might have been countless times in the past: the end of everything will proceed apace and not a damn thing can be done about it."

"So somehow in your effort to stop this . . . Armageddon, you've come to me. Why?"

Daniel paused to release a deep sigh, his slender fingers straying upon the intricate carvings of his stick, which lay at his side. "Because," he began, "one of those entities has lodged itself within you."

"What!" Jade exclaimed, almost hopping to his feet. "You've gotta be nuts! In me? I don't feel anything inside me! There's nothing different about me, nothing that's not been there all my life . . ." Then Jade began to laugh. "Listen, I don't mean to be rude and I don't want you to think that I don't appreciate your saving my life, but you must be mistaken. I admit you've got uncanny powers and all that but I can assure you that if such a . . . an entity has inhabited a life-form, it sure as hell isn't mine!"

"O Jade, Jade, Jade!" sighed Daniel. "If only you could see yourself with my eyes! If only I could make you see how the power shimmers all around you, rainbow clouds of energy that make you shine like a beacon for eyes that are trained to see. It's inside you, all right. It entered more softly than the footfall of an ant and it's slowly probing and growing within you, tentative, fluid, ever poised to flee. Don't you see that's why it's so important that I seek you out and make you aware of what's happening? It's only through you that the process of destruction can be stopped."

Jade cocked his head with a half-smile, staring into Daniel's moist, azure eyes. "You're serious, aren't you?"

"Deadly serious."

Jade sat in silence, his hands unconsciously straying along the surface of his clothing as if feeling for a change in himself. "You know, Daniel," he finally said, "that brew you gave me before wasn't bad. Not bad at all. It made me feel kind of high, a little floaty, yet really sharp in the brain. And the couple of hits of smoke I just had weren't bad either. All in all, I should be sailing to the stars by now. But what you just told me has made me sober—straighter than an arrow." He shook his head chuckling to himself, rubbing his palms into his cheeks and along his temples in thoughtless response to his bewilderment. "You really know how to toss a bombshell, don't you? Suppose, for argument's sake, I'm crazy enough to go along with what you say. What does that mean for me, exactly? And what does any of this have to do with Adrienne and her husband?"

"I can't give you an exact answer to your first question," Daniel responded. "For the first time, perhaps a conscious creature has been host to such an entity. Maybe your mind can be trained to enforce a linkage with that power and then direct its incredible energies against the eventual union that will bring upon us the end of all life and the universe as we know it. Maybe somehow we can, together, prevent the end of that great experiment called life which is just about to be cut short."

Here Daniel rose to his feet and began to pace the floor, Jade following him with his eyes.

"Can't you understand what it is that has driven me across this planet to find you? I know what I am and what extraordinary powers I possess. And through me I know what all of mankind could eventually become if evolution is allowed to make its slow and tedious transitions. Mankind here on earth is just beginning to evolve in directions independent of the dictates of the environment. We're just beginning to evolve out of the animalistic 'survival of the fittest' stage and to manipulate our own progress toward becoming a better race, more suited to expanding outward among the stars. And we're not alone, my son. Not by any means. There are civilizations out there that make us seem like forest pygmies. They, too, are poised on the brink of discoveries and potentialities that could make of every life-form that crawls, walks, or creeps a god.

"If it were earth alone that were threatened by this holocaust, I'd say let it burn and take my business elsewhere. I have that power too, you know. Better and more promising civilizations than ours have done themselves in with their arrogance and stupidity. That, too, is one of the chances we take by encouraging the proliferation of life and the process of evolution. But it's a chance we all must be willing to take. Civilizations are born and then they perish; but each leaves some sort of seed behind it that spirals the conglomeration of life upward toward the great master destiny that awaits us far away in time and space. If I had no foreknowledge of these events, then the sudden destruction of everything would proceed almost imperceptibly, and without abatement. But I do see and I can act, and I have no other choice but to believe that some other higher destiny than tortured emptiness has granted me this knowledge and foresight and demands that I act as I must to preserve all life in the universe."

"But what if you're wrong?" Jade retorted sharply. "What if that sense of a higher destiny is just an idle fantasy of yours? What if the ultimate end of all life is nothingness? That illusion of some future ideal state for all living things is no more than a contemptible primitive dream, akin to a witch doctor's rattle or the stinking entrails of some poor sacrificial beast?" Jade rose to his feet and grasped Daniel by the shoulders.

"Take a close look at me, Daniel. Do you know what I am? Do you really know me at all? I'm a hustler, Daniel. Women give me their husbands' money so I can get their rocks off. A lot of idealism in that way of life, isn't there? And I deal drugs, too, Daniel. Smoke and coke, whatever you need, whatever you want. Don't you think that every once in a while I, too, am smitten with the fancy that I'm better than I am? I play with poetry, thinking that by scrawling out rhythmic words I'm somehow going to leave this fucking world better than it was before I entered it. Isn't that a laugh? And I'm not alone in this. There are millions of fools like me kidding themselves with their dreams and fantasies, living their entire lives waiting for that mantle of greatness and fulfillment to fall upon their shoulders. And how do they end up? Dead, certainly. Forgotten, mostly. Never being what they wanted, never having accomplished that great deed, never having been swept up in that great love. And that's it, Daniel. The curtain falls, the footlights go out and the audience files out to go to that other show down the block."

Jade turned his back on Daniel and bent for his pipe, sucking volumes of the acrid smoke into his lungs. "If you really want to know my opinion, Daniel," he concluded, jets of smoke pouring from his mouth and nostrils, "I think it's a pretty good idea that the whole business goes straight to hell every once in a while so that there can be a fresh start. Maybe someday, if we're ever worth the reprieve, things will hold together and start working. Obviously, we haven't reached that point yet. Until we do, I question the wisdom of interfering with what seems to be the rhythm of the universe." Jade turned a cynical, cunning eye toward Daniel, whose face was an impassive mask brimming with dignity. "That is, of course, assuming that everything you've told me tonight isn't just a lot of horseshit."

A profound silence filled the room. Jade turned his face away from the old man, seeking a retreat within himself. Even he was startled by his own cynicism.

Something within him had always clung to his dream of being a poet, of using the sheer force of his will and creativity to rise above the shallowness of his life and his actions and his world. But suddenly, in the presence of Daniel and when confronted by the specter of his greatest challenge, that kernel of defiance and heroism within him seemed to crumble. And as that foetal dream dissolved and drained from him, so too did that shell of cunning and street wisdom that had accrued to him over the years. He turned and leaned against the wall, his head bent forward, weak and frightened as a child, wanting to weep as if for something lovely that had died.

Then he turned away from the wall and saw Daniel gazing down at the knobby head of his staff. The old man's eyes and the slack lineaments of his face personified profound sorrow.

"I'm sorry if I've disappointed you," Jade said to him, a trace of softness creeping back into his voice. "You've got to admit that the story you've handed me is a tough nut to swallow in the first place. Besides, I've disappointed myself so often, why should you expect to be immune?" He retrieved his jacket from the back of the chair where he had negligently dumped it earlier that evening and started for the door.

"Where are you going?" Daniel asked.

"I don't like it but I've got to go to the cops," Jade answered. "You're welcome to crash here for the night. Consider the place yours."

"But it's useless to go to the police," Daniel said, grasping Jade by the elbow.

"Look, Daniel," Jade responded testily. "You've given me a whole line about Mercadante being a satanist. Okay, I can buy that. There are a lot of nuts in the world who can call themselves anything they want. Besides, I was introduced to three of his stooges earlier tonight. Any man who'd have those three working for him has got to be off the wall. And that means that he knows about . . . about Adrienne and me. If he was willing to have me killed tonight, then I can imagine what he has in store for her. So I've got to go to the cops and try and help her. The sooner the better." Jade

267

gently lifted Daniel's hand off his elbow. His voice grew soft and he half-smiled: "I may not be much of a savior for the universe, but I can do my bit for a person I care about."

"You're wrong, Jade," Daniel said grimly. "You can't possibly imagine what Mercadante has in store for her. And going to the police won't do you any good. He's already had her shipped to his chateau in Germany."

"What?" Jade queried, stunned.

"She's not even in the country anymore. She's been taken to this restored castle he owns in Germany."

"How do you know that?"

"I just know. There's very little about Mercadante that I don't know and that's why I'm telling you that going to the police tonight is a waste of time."

Jade paused at the door staring sternly into Daniel's face. Then he took off his jacket and dropped it back onto the chair. "You promised to tell me about Mercadante and Adrienne," he reminded Daniel. "You've yet to get to it. I think it's time."

Both men sat across from each other on the floor, lotus-legged.

"I've told you that Mercadante is a man much like myself," Daniel began. "A mutation. A freak of nature. Yet, I've also said that his mind has a medieval slant to it. Where I turn to science and natural researches for the explanation of what I am and what tasks I must fulfill in my life, well aware of my intellectual link to the Renaissance, Mercadante prefers the world of myth and metaphor for his reasoning and his justifications. He doesn't see himself as a mutation. He sees himself as a man to whom Satan, the Lord of darkness, has dispensed special powers. Consequently, he has used his abilities to amass a great fortune which he, in turn, has used to further the cause of diabolism. He has gathered wealthy and influential cohorts to his satanic banner from around the world. He has even purchased and restored an old castle hidden darkly among the foothills of the Brocken Mountain, the notorious peak which has known countless satanic frenzies and sabbath rites. He has outfitted the castle itself as a foul den of orgiastic lust and sadistic torture. The stone walls of the place reek with the blood of the victims that have been offered as sacrifices to Satan, past and present."

"You mean Adrienne . . ." Jade interrupted, wide-eyed.

"Let me finish and you'll know everything. Some years ago when I had the first psychic inkling of the tremendous power that was going to plummet to earth, Mercadante must've picked up similar vibrations. I have given you a detailed account of my interpretation of what is happening. To Mercadante the event isn't nearly so complex. To him it is the soul of Satan that is falling upon the earth in order to possess the body and soul of some innocent and then rule the world in corporeal form.

"Just like myself, Mercadante has telepathically followed the progress of the falling spirit, searching continually for years throughout the world to be assured that when Satan's soul does, at last, descend and become incarnate, he and his cohorts will be ready to whisk the creature off to his chateau and train it to assume the full potency of its powers. Much the same as I would've done for you had you believed me. In return, Mercadante expects to rule the world as Satan's minister. The only reason he married Adrienne was to preserve her, *virgo intacta*, to be the sacrificial bride of Satan."

"I see now!" Jade marveled. "That's why when I first met her she was a . . . holy shit! And that's what was behind the fact that Adrienne never even saw him naked." He turned to Daniel with fiery eyes. "I've got to hand it to you, Daniel. This part of your story makes all too much sense."

Daniel ignored the compliment. "It happened by chance," he continued, "that Mercadante's primary psychic link was with the counterpart of the entity that now resides in you. I don't know if he even suspected that there was a second force, since he was only looking for one. I hypothesized two of them, and therefore I've been telepathically tracing the progress of both. Maybe this gives me a strategic edge on Mercadante, but it's a slim one at best. His link with the other was too strong for me to interfere with, so I concentrated on reaching you."

"You mean he doesn't know that there's a counter-force in me?"

"At first, I'm sure he didn't. But I think he suspects now. You see, I'm sure that, in order to prevent Adrienne from indulging in extramarital flings, into which he knew his age, her enforced celibacy, and his frequent absences would eventually force her, he must've controlled her mind with a potent telepathic lock. Yet she fell in love with you on the spot and . . . indulged. Thus, she lost her value to Mercadante as a sacrifice and incurred his undying wrath."

"And I suppose that puts me on his shit list as well."

"At the very top. In a way it's quite funny, really," Daniel commented with a smile. "The one man against whom Mercadante's telepathic commands have no effect is also the man destined to be the carrier of the counterforce to his supposed 'Satan.' He probably thinks you're some kind of angel incarnate."

"Me? An angel? O Jesus!"

"Mercadante must appreciate the irony of that as well. But regardless, tonight's attack on you was kind of a test. He wanted to learn just what forces are gathered around you for your protection. Since you had no knowledge of the powers lying dormant within you and hadn't yet learned to control them, you would've been killed had I not shown up. That would've left Mercadante more confused about you than ever. You don't realize what an enigma you are: a man in possession of the greatest power in the universe, yet who doesn't know it and behaves like he doesn't know it, and still seduces the master satanist's sacrificial offering and survives an attack by his killer-servants. Yes, Mercadante has no inkling of what you are but still must puzzle over your charmed life."

"A charmed life?" Jade thought for a moment, straining to permit hazy thoughts to coalesce. "A charmed life . . . Wait a minute! That's it! That's why that big gorilla made sure I was wearing it before he finished me off. Take a look at this, Daniel." Jade held the jade unicorn out from his neck for Daniel's inspection. "They weren't sent just to kill me. They were also supposed to retrieve this for their master." Daniel turned the delicate figure over and over between his fingers, peering sharply at the intricate delicacy of its lines, his face grim. "Adrienne stole it from him to give it to me. He must think that it's somehow responsible for my 'charmed life.' "

"When did she give this to you?"

"A little over a week ago. Why?"

Daniel looked up at Jade curiously. "That's just when the power I spoke of entered you." The old man stroked his beard thoughtfully. "An odd coincidence."

"You don't think this unicorn has something to do with all this, do you? I mean, you're the man of the Renaissance, the man of science, the master of the rational explanation. I don't take you for a believer in talismans."

Daniel paused for a long time without responding, gazing all the while at the unicorn. Finally he said, "You're quite right. I'm not one for charms and talismans. That's Mercadante's forte. Yet, there's something about that unicorn . . . I can't quite read its emanations. It's most perplexing. But what I can tell you is that you must wear it at all times. I don't know why, to be honest with you. But I know you must wear it." He cupped the tiny jade figurine in his hands, rolling it gently along the surface of his palms. "There's a strong link between you and it, for good or ill I can't say. But you must wear it."

"I don't know, Daniel. Adrienne gave it to me because she said it matched my eyes. No more profound reason than that. Yet, ever since I started wearing it, I've gotten nothing but negative vibes from it. Sometimes I think it has a life of its own and that it hates me. That it wants to gouge my throat with that horn it's got. I don't know. I can't see that wearing this thing can ever do me any good."

Daniel turned cautionary eyes upon Jade. "I didn't say it would do you any good. I don't know how it's intertwined with your fate. I only said that you must continue to wear it."

Jade sank back against the wall, his eyes closed, his hands pressing against his temples. "Daniel, Daniel, Daniel," he sighed, "you're a bewildering person. First you give me an elaborate scientific explanation for the most oddball phenomena I've ever heard of. Then you tell me that another mutant like yourself believes in this Satan-God, good-evil bullshit. And now you're telling me to keep wearing this unicorn like you're some high priest of a coven. I can't figure out what's going on around here and yet somehow I'm stuck in the middle of it all." He looked up at Daniel with piercing eyes. "Are you positive that your scientific interpretation of all this is the right one? Are you sure that Mercadante isn't the one who understands what's going on and not you?"

Daniel thought for long moments, his face seamed with puzzlement. Then he smiled quickly to himself. "I've never represented my ideas as any more than a theory in which I happen to wholeheartedly believe. I still do believe in it, but no, I'm not wholeheartedly positive that Mercadante is entirely wrong. There's an interlocking of fate surrounding this whole affair, a sort of destiny that can't be simply explained by the sudden presence of these incredible powers here on earth. Your meeting Adrienne and her involvement with you long before the power entered you: that's a major mystery. And that piece of carved stone: it should be no more than that, yet it cries out to my mind that you and it are one. I really can't understand it. I suppose that behind all our probing rationality, there's a camouflaged destiny, something that no amount of power can discern in its entirety. Or even begin to control." He hefted his staff delicately in his hands, regarding the strange carvings, the mingling of heads and torsos and bizarre grimaces. "I've endowed this staff with great powers, as you've seen tonight. Yet without the power of my mind to focus the energies that I command, it is no more than an oddly beautiful stick of wood. I somehow feel that I'm the one that's the real tool. That you and Mercadante and that poor boy, as well, are caught up with me in a web of destiny that none of us will ever truly understand. That is, assuming we're all still around to care one way or another."

"Listen, if you think that last pointed remark is going to make me change my mind and follow your lead, forget it. Even you've begun to have doubts about what you said. So I'll just keep thinking for myself, thank you. But what did you mean by 'that poor boy'? What poor boy?"

"The one who's become the host of the other force."

"You mean the force that Mercadante thinks is Satan?"

"Yes. As I told you before, I've followed its progress as well. When the force entered you, it sort of slid itself inside of you, secretly, silently, without outward manifestation. That's because you're a mature man, a man relatively at peace with his emotions, a stable person possessing your own kind of discipline and steadfastness. Your mind, and most significantly your subconscious, never lost its adult control of itself. But the other power . . . well, it's a different story entirely: It lodged itself within a fifteen-year-old boy, a boy plagued as all boys that age by the hormonal and emotional turmoil of puberty. Under conditions of sexual stimulation, anger, and so on, the force within the boy was brought into bizarre activity. It acted upon those fleeting, hidden, even archetypal desires that lie at the deepest depths of the mind, an area of emotion that a man of your age and sensibility has learned to firmly sublimate. But that poor boy . . . you'll soon learn the gruesome effects of that power's presence within him." Daniel's face suddenly brightened. "Maybe that's how I can convince you!"

Daniel grasped Jade's shoulders with passion. "Listen to me, my son. Listen very carefully. Keep your doubts and misgivings. I understand them and should expect no better. But keep an open mind until tomorrow. Tomorrow I'll be able to show you what kind of force, what kind of sheer power, has possessed Mercadante's 'Satan.' And I'll also take you to a place where you'll be able to get a taste of the immense power that resides dormant within you. If you still have doubts, I'll step out of your life completely. Then you can go to the police and tell them what you will." Then Daniel's eyes narrowed cryptically, his mouth arched in a cunning smile. "In fact, if you go with me tomorrow, you won't even have to go to the police. The police don't know it yet, but they'll be coming to you."

23

THE mousy little man with the dandruff sprinkled liberally throughout his dark, dirty hair and across the shoulders of his threadbare jacket sat in front of Lt. Fedorson's desk and proceeded to explain how he'd done it.

"It's like I don't know what comes over me, ya see. One minute I'm just walkin' the streets mindin' my own business and then whammo! I got my fingers around these people's throats. And I'm squeezin' and squeezin' until their eyes just sorta bug out and their faces turn all kinds o' purple. I mean. I got this strength, ya see, that nobody even figures I got in me. I mean, to look at me ya wouldn't think I could hurt a fly." The little man laughed a noisy laugh that was half belch, half snort. "But I fool people. Lotsa people get fooled that way. They don't believe I got it in me. But I do. I really do. I'm too dangerous to even be let walk the streets."

Fedorson stared down at the little man and then leaned back in his chair. "O you got it in you, all right."

The little man's face lost its argumentative intensity and brightened into a triumphant smile. But then Fedorson cleared the police report forms from the top of his desk and stacked them neatly on top of the pile of forms inside the large side drawer. "The only problem with what you say, mister," Fedorson replied, "is that none of the victims were strangled. Lots of other things, but not strangled."

The little man flinched at this information, making guilty cow's eyes into his lap. "But . . . but I was comin' to that. I do lotsa other things too." He leaned forward conspiratorially, glancing quickly from side to side. "Dirty things, too. Real dirty things. I can't help myself. I mean, when I think o' what I done to them poor people . . . well, it just makes me sick. Ya want me to tell you what I done?"

Fedorson shoved his stogie to the corner of his mouth with his tongue, his eyes beginning to glower. "Listen, you little creep," he began, "don't you know it's a crime to waste a cop's time during the progress of an investigation? I could lock you up right now for interfering with my job, but I sure as hell ain't gonna lock you up for those murders. Now get the hell outta here before I get you put into Bellevue!"

"Bellevue? But don't you see, that's where I belong!" The little man rose to his feet, his voice pleading. "I'm a dangerous guy! If you throw me outta here, you'll be sorry. The blood o' my next victim's gonna be on your head!"

"Yeah? Well, I'll make sure I wear a hat. Now get the fuck outta here before me and my boys take you into the back room for some real questioning."

The little man made as if to answer, then turned on his heels indignantly and stormed out of the squad room. Fedorson leaned back in his chair, shoving his hat far back on his head, and stared around the noisy room that brimmed with a bizarre assortment of derelicts and weirdos all claiming to be the phantom killer. Peale's article hadn't been on the streets for a half hour before the phones started ringing and the crazies started lining up outside the squad room door, waiting for their opportunity to confess.

Dr. Rothstein picked his way slowly through the crowded squad room, staring to his right and left at the harried and disgruntled officers who were vociferously trying to reduce the wild tales they were hearing from the vagabond hordes into something resembling reason and plausibility. The doctor could tell from their frustrated, angry faces that they weren't having much luck. Finally, he reached Fedorson's desk and simply stared down at him with quizzical eyes.

"That's right, doc," Fedorson smiled bitterly. "All this thanks to Peale's article. And these are just the ones who could fit in the room to fill out reports. There's a line outside the door that stretches all the way down the hall. Fuckin' New Yorkers: sometimes I think we're all nuts. And you know what's the worst?"

"What?" queried Rothstein, staring around the room somewhat bewildered.

"No sooner do I get rid of a lunatic than I think to myself, 'Shit, that sonofabitch was just crazy enough to be telling the truth.' I mean, each story I hear is crazier than the next, but none of them match the complete insanity of the truth. And I end up sitting here like a jackass wondering if I haven't just watched some homicidal lunatic's backside wiggle out of here scot-free."

"I wouldn't worry too much about that," Rothstein said philosophically. "I don't think there's much of a chance that whatever it is we're looking for is going to walk in here and confess. But I may have a lead for you, if you've got some time to speak with a friend of mine."

"Doc, right now I've got nothing but time. And I'm tired of wasting it listening to all these psychos."

"Well, don't get your hopes up too much," Rothstein cautioned. "What my friend has to say may sound a little . . . unorthodox. You might even begin to think of him as a lunatic as well. But I can assure you, he's a most respected physician and a man of impeccable good sense. His interests may be a bit arcane, but then again this whole case . . ."

"Enough, enough! Don't remind me. Bring him right into my office in the back."

"He's already with Abe Ender in a room down the hall. And he's brought two friends with him. He assures me that one of them has some information that is vital to the case."

"Okay, doc, lead the way," the lieutenant replied tersely as he unfolded from behind the desk, drawing himself up to full height. "I've had it with the crazies. A little vital information is just what I need."

Rothstein led Fedorson to an interrogation room in which he found Ender, a heavy-set man with a goatee, and two very attractive women. One woman was tall, blond, and slender, and the other was attractively petite with dark, close-cropped hair.

"I'm glad Danny found you with some free time on your hands, lieutenant," Ender greeted them smiling. "I'll let him make the introductions."

Fedorson seated himself next to the man with the goatee whom the doctor introduced as his colleague, Dr. Crile. "Besides being a noted neurologist and psychoanalyst," Rothstein continued, "he's also head of the Parapsychology Research Institute here in Manhattan. I should add that that institute is one of the few in the entire world that is engaged in the scientific and methodical study of extrasensory perception and other so-called psychic phenomena."

Dr. Crile smiled warmly at the lieutenant. "Mr. Ender has been telling me what a hard-nosed detective you are. I hope your cynical realism won't prejudice you in advance against what my friends and I have come here to say."

"I wouldn't worry about that, doc," Fedorson answered, chewing on his stogie. "The events of recent days have softened my nose quite a bit."

"Good," continued Crile. "Then let me introduce my friend and associate at the institute, Miss Elizabeth Wylie, and her roommate, Miss Beverly Forbes."

Fedorson nodded cordially to both women and asked, "Is Miss Wylie a doctor at the institute as well?"

"No, she's not a doctor," Crile answered. "What she contributes to the institute can't be learned in any medical school that I know of. She's one of the few bona fide psychics that I've had the pleasure to work with. In fact, we've had a close working relationship for over three years. During that time she has afforded the institute ample opportunity to quantitatively measure her psychic abilities and, let me assure you, the powers of second sight that she possesses are truly remarkable. It's on account of her powers that we've come here today."

Fedorson looked the young woman over and she shyly, subtly retreated from his sceptical gaze. "You mean she can tell us who the killer is?" the lieutenant asked Dr. Crile.

"Perhaps," Ender interjected. "Or at least she can put us on his trail, if she's all that Dr. Crile says she is. Why don't you tell the lieutenant what you've told me?"

"As I said before," Crile began, "Elizabeth's worked with us at the institute for years. She's been subjected to every battery of tests ever devised to measure an individual's paranormal abilities and each time the tests have yielded astounding results. What I'm trying to say, lieutenant, is that her credentials as a 'psychic' or a 'sensitive' are irrefutable."

"I'll be happy to go along with you there, doc," commented Fedorson, "if you can clear up in my own mind just what a 'psychic' is. I'm not up on that kind of research."

"Of course, lieutenant. What we mean professionally by a psychic is an individual who is abnormally sensitive to events that occur beyond the boundaries of the average human senses. She has demonstrated her ability on countless occasions to read other people's minds and she has, less frequently, been the recipient of mental images that warn of impending disasters, disasters which, thanks to her, have been diminished in intensity."

"You mean she can foretell the future?" asked Fedorson, one eyebrow raised.

Crile smiled. "Don't make it sound so much like a gypsy tearoom bunko racket. What Elizabeth can do is receive mental images, sometimes when they are consciously sought for, sometimes without her conscious control or searching, that reveal to her a series of events or people, which turn out after a period of time to reoccur or reappear in objective reality. No one, as yet, understands why or how she's come to possess these psychic powers. But the fact that she does possess them is beyond question.

"For some months now, Elizabeth has been plagued by recurring nightmares. At first we thought nothing of them, thinking they were comparable to the recurring dreams that each of us suffers through at various points in our lives. But three days ago, Elizabeth was stricken by an unusual psychic seizure. The effects of this seizure were so traumatic and profound that it almost cost the poor woman her life. Fortunately, we were able to bring her out of it and when we did so we discovered that the seizure was triggered by something she saw on the Bank Street pier."

Fedorson's eyebrows arched high in surprise. "The Bank Street pier, eh?" he repeated.

"Yes," Crile rejoined. "I think you see what I'm getting at. It seems that the central figure of her nightmare, when stripped of its dream-state distortions, turned out to be a young boy. In her dreams the boy radiates overpowering amounts of demonic energies. Well, that afternoon on the pier she saw the boy from her nightmares pass by her in the company of a tall black man. It was the sight of that boy in real life and her close proximity to his real psychic energies that precipitated the seizure."

Fedorson and Ender exchanged meaningful glances. Ender reached into his jacket pocket and withdrew two packets of photographs bound separately in rubber bands. Crile continued his explanation.

"Once we'd been made aware of the reality of the boy in her nightmares, we realized that her dreams were manifestations of her psychic powers and not simply nightmares. In other words, we could now classify her dreams as prophetic. But we had as yet been unable to figure out what exactly she was prophesying. In the past, her prophetic dreams were recognizable; she could awaken and tell us what was going to happen to whom and where the events were to take place. But her nightmares had been a series of bizarre, disjointed fragments which still defy concrete analysis. This can be interpreted in two ways: either her psychic powers are beginning to manifest themselves in a confused and fragmented form, which, in effect, renders them useless as instruments of precognition; or"—and here Crile paused to allow the full weight of his words to sink in upon his listeners—"she has seen in her dreams events that will occur, or have the potential to occur, and yet which are in themselves so bizarre as to be unlike anything we consider to be common human experience."

Ender recalled his own dream with a shudder. Then . . . then it was possible. Here was an eminent doctor, a friend of Rothstein, speaking quite seriously about precognition and prophetic dreams. What if . . . no, too horrible to imagine.

"Of those two interpretations," asked Rothstein, "which to you seems most likely?"

"Speaking as a scientist, I can't give you a quantitative reason for accepting one over the other. However, I've tested Elizabeth for the past two days at the institute and her psychic powers seem to be just as they've always been: accurate and thoroughly lucid. This would lead me to believe that the grotesque horror of her dreams is due not to an aberration of her powers but to the grotesqueness of the events foreseen."

"Then tell me, doc," asked Fedorson, "what finally brought you to tell this to Dr. Rothstein?"

"The article in this morning's newspaper, of course. The one linking the horrible murder on the Bank Street pier to a number of others throughout Manhattan. The murder of the black man on the pier occurred shortly after Elizabeth saw the boy walking with a black man on the same pier. And certainly the powerful, overwhelming vibrations she received from the boy would lead me to suspect that there's more to him than he appears. Don't ask me what that means exactly; I can't say. But a person who emanates such incredible energies and psychic vibrations would also be capable of performing the most, uh, astounding and unexpected feats, including the series of murders and mutilations that were written about in the papers."

Fedorson thought for a moment, then perked up. "You mean to say that you think it's possible that a young kid could've done all those things to those bodies? I mean the physical things like tearing them apart and tossing grown men around like rag dolls?"

"What I mean to say, lieutenant, is that any entity that gives off psychic emanations such as those received by Elizabeth is an entity of almost absolute power. I don't care if it appears to be a young boy, an infant, or a dog. Appearances, as I'm sure you well know, are quite often deceiving."

"In which case it would surely fill the bill for our killer," Ender commented. Then he spread one packet of photographs on the desk in front of Elizabeth. "Miss Wylie, can you identify any of these men as the black man you saw with the young boy on the pier? You'll have to be very careful, I'm afraid, because these are all head shots from the morgue and are certain to appear somewhat different from the individuals when they were alive."

Elizabeth leaned over the photos and stared down, finally breaking her silence with the soft words, "Mr. Ender, I'm always careful in matters like this." She paused, running her fingertips gingerly above the surfaces of the photos. Beverly leaned over her shoulder to look at them as well, muttering, "God, how disgusting."

"Why are you waving your hands over the pictures?" asked Fedorson.

"Because I was mostly distracted by the boy. I didn't get as careful a look at the face of the black man, so I've got to prod my memory by trying to pick up vibrations from the pictures."

"Vibrations, vibrations, vibrations!" moaned Fedorson. "I don't understand a damn thing about any of this. It's just not in my vocabulary. But if it can help catch this killer, I'm all for it."

Elizabeth made a few more passes over the pictures with her hands, her eyes half-closed in concentration. Then she chose a picture from the group. "This is the man I saw the boy with," she said conclusively.

"You're positve?" asked Ender.

"Absolutely."

Ender took the photo and passed it to Fedorson and Rothstein. "It's the man we found murdered at the pier," he announced.

Fedorson let fly with a long, low whistle.

Ender took the rubber band off the second packet of pictures. "Now, can you identify the boy you saw with this man from any of these pictures?"

Elizabeth didn't hesitate an instant. "That's him! That's the boy!" she exclaimed, her voice resonant with shock and terror. Her index finger fell upon the photo of Marco McConnelly.

"Incredible!" Rothstein breathed. "Absolutely incredible!"

"No more incredible than anything else we've run across in this case," Ender advised. "In its own weird way it makes perfect sense. The boy's always been an odd link among some of the murder victims. Now, at last, we've got some eyewitness confirmation."

Fedorson threw up his hands in chagrin. "Come on," he sneered. "You mean to say that you really think the McConnelly kid did all those things? You'll have a damn hard time trying to convince a judge and jury of that when the time comes, counsellor."

"If the time comes," Ender corrected. "We've always suspected the kid was at the very least a witness. Now look how it all fits together: the kid's girl friend, his father, and now we can link him with the man on the pier. I'll bet ten to one we can find a witness who can place him at or around St. Luke's sometime around when the sexton was murdered. Think about it: the close relationship to two of the victims, the kid's fight with his father, his sudden disappearance. If it weren't for the supernatural aspects of this and the other random murders that we couldn't link him to, we would've been hunting the boy down for murder already."

"Shit" Fedorson snarled, "we can't even find him for a witness."

"Excuse me, gentlemen," Crile interrupted. "I'm afraid you've lost me. You know this boy?"

"We've been looking for him since this case began," explained Ender. "He was the boyfriend of the first murder victim. Then his father was killed a day later. He seems to have disappeared from sight. We've had an all-points bulletin out for him for about a week now and it's turned up absolutely nothing. What puzzles me is how come nobody I've spoken to about the boy mentioned anything strange about him. Surely a kid capable of doing all this would've attracted some sort of attention."

"Well, counsellor," said Fedorson, "we didn't actually ask his mother if she thought her son could tear people to pieces with his bare hands. Most families want to keep things like that to themselves."

"And there's still no accounting for most of the physical evidence," Rothstein added. He looked hastily at Ender for approval before continuing. Ender thought for a moment, then nodded. "The image in the eyes, the rapier-like stab wounds, the sperm samples. Not to mention the prodigious strength that was brought to bear in these murders. Don't misunderstand. I agree with Abe that our most likely suspect is the boy. What I want to know is how we can fill in the gap between a well-thought-of boy with no apparent abnormal abilities or tendencies other than the fact that he was rather bright as kids go and the marauding creature that's left us such an extensive trail of bizarre evidence."

"Bridging that gap might not be as difficult as you might think," Crile offered. "Have you considered some form of possession?"

"Possession?" asked Fedorson. "You mean like in those movies where the devil takes over a person's body?"

Crile nodded, half-smiling. "Something like that only not quite so Hollywood. I've personally observed cases in which powerful energies have in some mysterious way literally crept into the central core of a person's being and have transformed that person into someone or something totally unfamiliar to that person's closest relatives and friends. It's basically a personality change somewhat akin to schizophrenia, but there are the added factors of suddenness and totality that can be completely overwhelming to the individual involved."

While Crile recounted in scholarly fashion the bizarre documentation of instances of demonic possession throughout the world, Ender's thoughts locked on to the nightmare he had had some days past, just after the murders had begun. Rather than growing nebulous and ill-defined with the passage of time, the various images in the dream had become more distinct and even more terrifying each time he permitted his memory to recount and chronicle the details. And here was a woman sitting across the desk from him to whom premonitory dreams were a way of life. He had never been inclined to believe in such things, although his private scholarly researches in the histories of ancient cultures had made him familiar with the pervasive faith in the power of dreams that permeated antiquity. Scholar that he was, Ender believed that modern thinking had explained all that away. And yet—the intimate link between state of mind and state of body, the astounding effects of psychosomatic energies on physical reality, the growing contemporary awareness of the biophysical nature of thought, itself: try as he might, he couldn't fit his own dream experience, coupled with the realities he was encountering every day for the past week, within the parameters of these modern theories and assertions.

Ender's eyes grew heavy-lidded with meditative concentration as the dream repeated itself brusquely before his mind's eye. The terror, the sense of impending doom, the unswerving pursuit, the sheer horror when confronting the monster, itself: no, it had been distinctly unlike any other dream he had ever had, a whole different order of magnitude from any psychic event he had experienced. And there was also that hoofprint he had found at the scene of the first murder. Could events be in progress of such enormity that his close proximity to their occurrence had been sufficient to awaken in his otherwise uninspired mind abilities similar to those of that young girl? Ender's face grew deathly pale and the palms of his hands grew clammy. He looked up suddenly from contemplating his fingertips and found Elizabeth staring into his face with wild, startled eyes. Their eyes locked for moments that swelled into eternities and then Ender hurriedly turned his face away.

After Crile finished his recitation on the history of possession, Rothstein responded impatiently: "What you say is all well and good, but I don't think you can equate the effects of extreme psychological states with the concrete evidence we've had pushed right under our noses. I haven't had the opportunity as yet to fill you in completely on all that has occurred involving this case. But just let me assure you that there are no gray areas which may be rationalized away by talk of psychosomia or hysteria. We have, in essence, found ourselves transported from the age of twentieth-century rationalism to

an age of primitive astonishment at the uncanny work-
ings of the gods."

"But that's precisely why I've encouraged Elizabeth
to come forward and assist you in this case. It's obvious
that something's going on that's inexplicable to all our
contemporary minds. Elizabeth, on the other hand, can
bring her powers to bear in this case and perhaps find
some sort of explanation for what's been happening."

"And just how can she do that?" asked Fedorson.

Crile leaned forward conspiratorially in his seat.
"Take her to the scenes of the various murders. Let her
use her mental powers to pick up the traces of psychic
energy that are still lingering at each site and perhaps
she can piece together a trail of clues that will lead
you to the whereabouts of the killer, whether or not he's
in the form of a boy or some other manisfestation."

Ender looked again at Elizabeth but she averted her
eyes. Fedorson was sceptical. "You mean she can act
like some kind of mental bloodhound?" he asked.

"A novel way of putting it, yes."

"I dunno," Fedorson shook his head, turning to Ender. "If she's not everything Dr. Crile thinks she is,
then we could be just running around in circles while
the killer keeps on doing what he pleases."

"He's doing that anyway, even with all our bulletins
and searches and modern analytical techniques," Ender
responded. "Rothstein hit it on the head that very first
day: when science fails us, we might be forced to call
upon a sorcerer for aid. Perhaps Elizabeth can be that
sorcerer for us. We've got no other leads at the moment and I certainly have been impressed by what
Elizabeth has shown us so far."

"Then it's settled," said Crile, rising from his seat.
"Take us to the site of the first murder, the place where
all of this began. Let Elizabeth examine the site with her
mind and see what she comes up with. It certainly can't
do any harm, and it may do quite a lot of good."

As if with one accord, they rose and started for the
door. Elizabeth was at Crile's side but Ender suddenly
touched her elbow and pulled her aside. Fedorson and
the others left the office and headed for a waiting squad
car.

"Yes, Mr. Ender?" asked Elizabeth.

"I . . . I just wanted to tell you that . . . I believe . . . I believe you can do all that Dr. Crile says you can do." He had great difficulty in keeping his large, moist eyes focussed on her face so he turned his head from her, desperately searching the office for some spot where his awkward gaze could linger.

Elizabeth smiled. "I know that you believe," she said. "It's difficult to see all the things you've seen and experience a premonitory dream yourself and not believe."

"Myself?" exclaimed Ender, startled. "What do you know about my dreams?"

"I know nothing of your dreams, in general. But there was one in particular which you just surveyed in your mind while Dr. Crile was talking. Even you recognize that it was a dream different from all the others you've had. It sort of . . . felt different, didn't it?"

Ender absentmindedly rubbed his thinning hair and perched on the edge of the desk. "Yes, you're right. It felt different. Somehow more real than any other dream. And it's clung to me tenaciously, the colors growing ever brighter, the images sharper and more . . . more malevolent. Are dreams such as that something that you've had to learn to live with?"

"Until a few months ago," she replied, "my dreams were never terrifying. No more terrifying than reading a newspaper or listening to a friend tell you about a bad date. If my dreams could be used to help someone out of trouble, I've always done my best. But then I was more like an oracle: in control, in full command of my powers and my will and completely free to take whatever action was required. Those are the dreams I'd come to accept as part of my life. But my latest dreams, the horrible nightmares involving that boy and the . . . the other images . . . well, I'm no more on top of them than you are with your dream. I feel weak and threatened, like a child who inadvertently stumbles onto some secrets of the adult world which he was never meant to see."

She turned to Ender and raised his face to hers with a gentle hand. "Some . . . force has already almost killed me by overwhelming my mind with its power. I didn't ask to be a telepath any more than I asked to be born. But I am and I've always tried to make the most of my abilities. Now I'm frightened, just like you. I've seen your dream and I've felt the horror that it's brought into your life. I can sense how very real and malevolent are the events it foretells. Just like the nightmares that have tortured me for so long. But there's no escaping it. As much as I'd like to run and hide and pray for it all to pass away, it can't be done. There are tendrils reaching out for all of us from some unknown point and drawing us all together to participate in what is about to happen. My nightmares, the fact that I happened to be on the pier at just the right moment to see the boy pass by, the fact that the newspapers in their sketchy way printed just enough for me to know to go to Dr. Crile and tell him. And your dream. About the monster with the unicorn's horn. You, who've never had a premonitory dream in your life. We're being guided, Mr. Ender, by a hidden fate that uses us like puppets. We've got to flow with the energies. If we resist, then I'm convinced that whatever's manipulating our strings will reach further and further out for us and hunt us down like stray dogs until the destiny is fulfilled, whether we will or no.

"Perhaps when I'm brought to the scene of that first murder, I'll be able to see where the next steps are destined to take us. But I must warn you, Mr. Ender: I've got a feeling that these murders will draw us ever deeper into a destiny that's ready to fall upon us. All I can say is that we're simply doing what we must."

And Ender followed Elizabeth's retreating figure as she went out into the hall along the maze of corridors.

Jade awoke in the morning astounded by his vigor. There wasn't a stiff or sore muscle in his body and the contusions and abrasions of the night before had vanished completely from his flesh. He sat bolt upright on his mattress and quickly ran his hands along the contours of his limbs and torso, prodding and squeezing to see if any trace of his battle with the giants remained. There was none.

He turned quickly and saw Daniel sitting lotus-legged by the side of the mattress merely gazing down on him with distant, indifferent eyes.

"Daniel!" Jade exclaimed. "Have you been sitting there all night?"

Daniel nodded. "There were swarms around you all night. I had to fight them off so that you could heal."

Jade stared with raised eyebrows at Daniel. The old man's face seemed old and flaccid and haggard with fatigue. "What do you mean there were swarms around me?"

"Hostile energies. Bits of force sent here specifically to drain you of your energy and your life. I've had to keep them at bay all night while you slept." Daniel lightly tapped both knees with his hand and rose to his feet. "Heinreich Mercadante doesn't like having his plans thwarted. He tried to make up for his servants' ineptness with some psychic energies of his own. Fortunately for both of us, he had no better luck. Now get up and don't worry. The swarms have gone. Mercadante must be busy with some other aspect of his plan."

As Daniel started to move toward the kitchen to see about breakfast, his knees buckled and he started to collapse onto the floor. In a flash Jade had one strong arm around his shoulders which sustained him on his feet.

"Are you all right, Daniel?" Jade asked, frowning with concern.

"I'm . . . I'm just a bit weak, my son. I'll be all right shortly. Hand me my staff, will you?"

Jade's free hand closed upon the carved staff which leaned against the wall near the mattress. A strange, irritating tingling pulsed through the palm of his hand from the staff. He quickly passed it to Daniel, who clasped it lovingly and leaned with his full weight upon it. A weak smile crossed his lips.

"I'll be fine, Jade. A little walk in the park, some fresh air . . . I'll be fine."

Jade walked next to him as they entered the living room. "How about taking some of your own tea?" he said to Daniel. "Last night I was sure I'd be sore as hell for a month. Yet today I feel great. Better than before the fight. And I was feeling pretty good then. How did you fix me up?"

Daniel smiled again. "It's within your power to do as much and more, if you want to. If you'd only believe me long enough to let me train you to use the powers now latent within you."

"Well, that's what you say. It's still a skillful dodge from my question. But I must say that for a man who can fix me up the way you did, you sure as hell should devote a little magic to yourself. You look like shit, if you don't mind my saying so."

"A passing weakness. Perhaps someday you'll understand about such weakness. I didn't pass an easy night. Mercadante's quite desperate to have you out of the way."

Daniel went into the kitchen while Jade hung back staring after him, his mouth pursed strangely in an expression of both sarcasm and bedevilment. Then he passed with a shake of his head into the bathroom.

When he came out, Daniel had a folding table set with toast and coffee. Jade started to gently scold him. "What kind of host do you think I am? I didn't expect you to make breakfast for me. You shouldn't have bothered."

"In the first place, it's not for you, it's for us. You may indulge if you wish, but you needn't force yourself. Secondly, a pleasant little breakfast gives me the opportunity to talk with you a little more about my plans for the day."

"Really, Daniel, I don't think that any more talk will do either of us any good. You told me last night that today you'd prove to me that I possessed extraordinary powers of some kind. Fine. Enough weirdness has gone on so that I feel I owe you an opportunity to prove what you've been telling me. I can't for the life of me guess how you're going to do that, but I stayed away from the cops to give you that chance. Now more talk . . . !"

Daniel leaned forward in his seat, his eyes intense. "Then I'll be brief. I'm taking you this morning to the site of the first manifestation of that other spirit, the counterpart to the one lodged within you."

"You mean the one that took over the boy?"

"Yes. I will show you how to marshall some of the

vibratory energies that you now possess and you will then be able to witness that manifestation for yourself."

"But you said it occurred days ago!"

"It did. But you shall witness it anyway. Perhaps then you'll begin to respect the power that is lodged within you. But I mainly wanted to tell you this morning a few words of harsh truth and caution. I presented my case to you last night as if you had a concrete choice between believing me and disbelieving me. Perhaps I made it seem as if, should you have chosen to disbelieve me outright, you could then walk away from the whole affair, whistling. Perhaps you'd try and rescue Adrienne, perhaps not. You might simply turn the case over to the police and let it go at that. I'm not saying that I think you're that kind of person. It's just an option that one might expect you to consider. But, unfortunately, it's not that easy. O sure, if you tell me to go to hell, I'd leave you alone and never bother you again. You've nothing to fear from me on that score.

"But I must make it clear to you, Jade, that the entity within you is irrevocably linked with the entity that has taken over the boy. They are both halves of the same whole and neither half will rest until there is some sort of unification or resolution of their separateness." Daniel's azure eyes began to smolder with a cunning fire. "If you choose not to pursue that other force with me, it will pursue you, sooner or later, and unwittingly precipitate that final end of all things. You can't escape that reality through indifference. And as that other force shall evolve under Mercadante's tutelage, so shall you, almost by osmosis, imperceptibly, begin to come under that evil man's sway. Mercadante seeks to create a monster. Unless you learn to fight that man's mental energies with energies of your own, you can't hope to resist him. You'll begin to see yourself becoming something that disgusts you, and there'll be nothing you can do about it. The force that overwhelms one entity, shall without resistance be able to overwhelm the other. I ask you only to consider that before making a final decision."

Daniel sipped his coffee in silence. Jade watched the

old man's haggard face, his fingers negligently playing with a crust of toast. A profound terror seemed to shiver itself beneath his skin.

Although the heat and humidity of the day were oppressive, the glorious brightness of the sun and the colors it scattered through Central Park redeemed Jade's spirits. He and Daniel entered the park across from the natural history museum and passed a playground filled with the happy shouts of children. Then they crossed the park drive and plunged through the bushes that lined the riding path. Daniel was leading the way, his staff swinging jauntily at his side. He stared around him at the gnarled tree limbs and the scattered patches of gold that danced between the shadows of the leaves. He seemed to search the air for some sort of invisible clues, like a prowling cat. Then he suddenly stopped short.

"We're coming near to the spot," he said to Jade. "It's time for you to take over."

"Me?" cried Jade, startled.

"Take my staff in both your hands," Daniel commanded, not waiting for Jade's protest. Jade looked at him queerly, then followed his instructions. The staff tingled electrically between his palms and Jade had to force himself to hold onto it. "You must first learn to focus the power of your consciousness through the lines of force that surround my staff. Now close your eyes and hold the staff at arm's length upright in front of you." Jade did as he was told and his lower lip suddenly went limp as he felt a stunning beam of force pass from the knob of the staff into the center of his forehead. "Don't speak," cautioned Daniel. "You're feeling it now, that beam of power which links you with the potency of my staff. Don't resist it. I know it can be scary but you must learn to accept the force so it can enter deeper within your mind. Now, very slowly, focus your thoughts on the exact point of entry through which the energy from my staff is flowing into you. That point in the center of your forehead, in triangulation with your eyes, is the seat of all your psychic energies. You may have come upon it in your readings as the mystical third eye. Focus on that point; relax your rational faculties and feel the power of my staff flow into you; let all doubts and mental blocks dissolve themselves within the stream of force. My staff can burn its way through to your third eye, but only if you help clear the way from within."

It was a pleasant feeling, really, that tingling in the center of his forehead. Gentle pulsations spread throughout the interior of Jade's skull, massaging neurons and dilating the infinity of blood vessels at the primitive core of his brain, arousing tissues that had lain dormant since infancy. Jade began to feel light-headed and giddy. The tingling on his forehead seemed to spread and dissolve into the bony plates of his skull, rapidly sinking into his brain, becoming one with his consciousness and no longer an alien presence.

"You've almost completed the link, my son," Daniel whispered excitedly. "Concentrate on your third eye, open yourself up a little more to the force, yield yourself to the pleasure of the connection. It's a beautiful sensation, Jade. Let it flow into you, submit your will to the loveliness of the pleasure."

Daniel's words came to Jade as if they were little whispers from the center of his mind and not from outside himself. It was as if he were hearing the strange old man with his entire brain and not just through his ears. The pleasure of the pulsations became intense and Jade centered his will upon his third eye until he felt the core of his consciousness begin to dissolve. Suddenly Jade gasped: although his eyes remained tightly shut, a vision of the park foliage around him unfolded itself. It was as if his entire skull and facial flesh had been transformed into the clearest crystal. But the park vista he now saw was not that of the summer day; it was the park in the cool of a summer evening, the foliage burnished with the silver of a full moon. Jade could feel night breezes caress his flesh and he seemed to smell the night dew on the grass. And that moon: Jade gasped again in recognition; it was that moon he and Adrienne had admired that night, that moon with the oddly brilliant star poised beneath it like a jewel.

And then Jade heard voices some distance ahead in the darkened foliage: high-pitched voices, the voices of children.

Without a word to Daniel, Jade walked slowly forward, the staff upraised before him. The night shadows of leaves and branches parted before him. The voices of the children grew closer; he made out little bursts of laughter and shy endearments. Further into the bushes Jade plunged, into the darkness, into the sweet shelter of fragrant bushes and soft moss.

And then he saw them.

The boy lay on his back on the soft moss and the girl leaned over him, hugging him close to her. They chattered and kissed, her tiny hands stroking his soft cheek, his hands entwined in strands of her fine golden hair, made spun silver by the filtered moonglow.

Her thin blouse was open in the front, fluttering lightly in the gentle winds. The boy's hands trailed gently all over her naked flesh. She gasped with sudden pleasure when his thumbs brushed her immature nipples. Then he stretched luxuriantly on the grass while the girl buried her face in his soft neck. He moaned, hugging her tightly, his eyes open to the moon and the beautiful star.

The boy suddenly stiffened. He pulled the girl more closely to him, squeezing her tightly. His eyes glowed like silver mirrors. And then his body began to writhe and twitch, elongating, broadening, patches of thick, coarse hair mottling his smooth young flesh. His tender sighs and words of love became hoarse, lustful growls, deep and throaty, his mouth stretching into a wide, leering grin. Ever larger the boy grew, ever more bestial and powerful, his torso rippling with broad muscles, his arms bulging with thick knots of strength. His face became thick and bony, framed in long shaggy curls of coarse hair, while his mouth swelled and filled with broad equine teeth.

A nob of bone on his forehead suddenly lengthened into a gleaming, sharp spiral of ivory, a unicorn's horn.

The girl's eyes widened in terror; she was paralyzed with fright. The beast encircling her with its brawny arms rose to its full height. Its legs were covered with thick curls of dark hair and its feet had become cloven hoofs: the legs of a satyr.

The young girl stared speechless as from between the beast's furry legs a stiff horsecock bobbed up obscenely. The beast stared down at the girl in its arms, its head rolling madly, its eyes bright with lust.

And then the beast ravaged the girl: tearing her clothes off her body, forcing her legs widely apart, lunging its enormous cock deep within her, straining its immensity with smears of blood. As the beast lunged and humped, a ludicrous, frightening figure in the throes of its mad lust, the girl screamed a horrible, alien scream, a scream of abject terror, a scream of orgasmic ecstasy. And then the child was silent and the beast, in the frenzy of its triumph, tore the still body into pieces, ramming its deadly horn again and again through the limp torso.

The boy's metamorphosis and the murder of the girl occurred within seconds. Yet, as Jade surmised the child's danger, he plunged wildly through the bushes, shouting his terror at the beast, instinctively running to intervene as if his presence could, in fact, alter the outcome of the child's ordeal. He dashed through the underbrush, his eyes still tightly shut, his arms outstretched bearing Daniel's staff, crying "No! No! No!" in desperation.

"Stop, Jade!" cried Daniel after him, "Stop! You can't do anything! It's all a shade of what was! An illusion! You can't do anything!" And he plunged into the bushes after him, clutching at Jade's shoulders, pulling him back with all his might, being dragged by the charging, outraged man deep within the copse of trees. And Jade saw the beast finish with the child. It cast her bloody corpse thoughtlessly to the ground and passed out from beneath the shelter of the foliage.

Far in the background an old man watched the creature lurch from the bushes for an instant and then plunge into the shadows of the night.

At last Daniel dragged Jade to the ground, their two bodies a tangle of thrashing arms and legs. With a quick heave the old man broke Jade's grip on his staff and pulled it from him.

"Awake!" commanded Daniel, the staff raised high in the air. "Awake! The vision is no more!"

Jade's eyes glowed like flaming emeralds.

Suddenly all was sun and silence and the gentle caress of summer air. The glow in Jade's eyes dimmed and he cast his arms about him like a man deranged. Daniel held him tightly around his shoulders, soothing him with gentle words. And then, at last, Jade realized where he was.

"My God, Daniel!" Jade gasped. "My dear God, what I've seen, the horror, my God, the horror!"

"You've tasted of the force, my son," Daniel said softly, cradling Jade like a child. "You've seen it manifest itself here on earth. You've felt the power within you, a mere shadow of its totality. You've seen much this morning. Perhaps only now can you comprehend the magnitude of our mission. Perhaps only now you can understand why I've traveled the world to seek you out."

"That . . . that devil is inside me?" Jade weeped.

"The power is inside you. Not in itself a devil. Not in itself an object of fear and terror. Just the power. Limitless power. What you've seen is the counterpart to what is within you. That is what is destined to seek you out, to pounce on you cowering even in the blackest pit of hell. There's no escape. Nowhere to run." Daniel brushed Jade's blond hair from in front of his eyes, feeling him pant and heave beneath his sheltering arm. "All you can do is arm yourself against it with the power that is your own. That's the only hope any of us have, if the universe is to survive."

"I believe . . . I've seen the power, I've felt it inside me, so limitless, so irresistible." Jade clung to the old man's arm in silence, then pulled himself up to his feet. "You've done what you said you would. You've proven your case." Daniel looked into Jade's eyes with the profound sorrow of a father who knows that his son will leave him soon to die. "Just tell me what I must do, Daniel. From now on you're my guide and my only hope."

A sudden shout broke upon their conclave: "You! It's you!"

Jade turned and saw a young blond woman standing a few yards away, her breath coming in heaves as if she had just run a great distance. In spite of his agitation, he turned to her with a tender, quizzical smile. She approached him slowly, her eyes wide with wonder.

"You're the man in my dream," she said, staring into his eyes.

Jade looked beyond her and saw four men and a woman running toward them. His street sense told him that the largest of the men was a cop. He looked down upon the girl in silence, returning her wordless gaze.

Daniel simply smiled, tender and wise.

24

STULLY had the air about him of an unsuccessful
boxer. He was a large brawny man with calloused,
ham-hock paws, a broken nose, two twisted ears, and a
broad, bony jaw. His eyes shifted rapidly from the vacant lusterlessness of unconcern to a sudden darting
wariness as if he were poised to duck a blow. Yet there
was no blow. No enemy. Just phantom whispers and
vague figures flashing past the corner of his eye. Stully's
sudden stares and twitches made it difficult for other
people to be around him, so Mercadante assigned him
the task of keeping watch from the stone bell tower of
the Chateau. Stully felt a kinship with the tower; he
liked its lonely elevation, the coolness of the stone against
his skin, the eternal silence in which it was shrouded,
broken only by vagrant lashings of the wind and faint
bursts of revelry from the castle complex below.

And Stully loved the new iron bell which he had done
the major work of installing. He'd stare at it for hours,
his fingers stroking the pull-cord, trying to comprehend
the raised figures and inscriptions that covered its surface. Geometrics: pentagons and circles circumscribed,
triangles radiating from a common point, folding in
upon themselves like paper origami figures. And inscriptions: in bold letters across the top of the bell,
"TERRAS ET ASTRA REVISI MERCADANTE"; demonic

names—Phaleg, Ophiel, Aratron, Bethor, Hagith, and Phuel—scattered about the surface of the bell in alignment with the major divisions of the compass; and planetary symbols, like the mirror of Venus and the spear and shield of Mars, equally spaced around the lower lip of the bell. It was whispered by some that the demon Biscornet had been conjured by Mercadante to forge the bell from the raw ore of the Brocken Mountain itself, just as he had supplied the arabesque ironwork for the doors of Notre Dame Cathedral. But Stully discounted such rumors. He knew the powers of his master to be such that he had no need for demons. The bell had been weeks in the making under conditions of strict secrecy and solitude. One thing Stully knew for certain was that the two artisans brought in by Mercadante for assistance never emerged again from the makeshift foundry in a Brocken cavern. Stully ran his fingertips along the smooth curve of the bell, studying the waxy sheen of its polished surface in the light of the lantern he held in his left hand. It looked to him like the sheen of human tallow and blood.

Stully left the bell and sat by the window, looking out upon the dark Brocken evening. The moon hadn't yet risen and the inky sky was sprinkled with ice-crystal stars. To the north was thick darkness, the towering cliffs and ridges of the Brocken waiting to be washed in silver by the moonlight. He sniffed the mountain air, inhaling the fragrance of the gnarled, ancient pines that draped the mountain.

And then he noticed the tiny flash of green light rise out of the shadows and grow steadily larger.

Stully tensed, not daring to breathe, his ears alert for the slightest sound. A faint hum at first and then a purling, rhythmic throb. The green light grew steadily nearer and then it began to blink. It was the master's private cargo helicopter from the Munich airport.

Stully's lips opened into a wild, twisted grin. He bounded out of his seat, sending the stool sprawling along the floor, and flung himself upon the bell cord, pulling with all his might.

The Great Hall of the medieval castle had been converted by Mercadante into a necromancer's ritual chamber. Stone walls towered precipitously over the High Altar, fringed near their juncture with the ceiling by a series of narrow windows which, during daylight, permitted spears of pale light to mottle the stone flagging of the floor. At the rear of the Great Hall and facing the High Altar was an ornate balustrade some thirty feet above the floor from which Mercadante and select cohorts could look down upon the various satanic festivities that were held throughout the year. The balustrade railings were filigreed with silver arabesques and florations while grotesque gargoyles leered lasciviously down upon the celebrants below with distended eyes of stone. A dancing fire blazed vigorously in the huge basalt fireplace, transforming the orgiasts who coupled and mingled before the High Altar into elongated shadows that lurched and twitched in frenzy upon the massive stone walls. Smoking torches rested in sconces placed all around the chamber, filling it with the scent of pine resin and pitch. Other torches were borne stiffly in the hands of naked slaves bearing Mercadante's brand and shackled in heavy iron cuffs and chains. They watched in resigned agony as the celebrants indulged their lusts while awaiting the announcement of the great event.

For in preparation, Mercadante had gathered hundreds of satanists from all around the world to witness the Incarnation of Satan. There were men and women of vast wealth and prestige who worshipped Satan as their benefactor and protector and thought nothing incongruous about leaving the boardrooms of major corporations and institutions to return to their mansions and don the robes of satanic priests and priestesses. They brought with them their retinues of favorites and slaves. There were diviners and necromancers among the noisy throng, snaggle-toothed old men and hideous crones who held out to initiates and devotees the promise of wealth and power and eternal youth. There were mass media evangelists who, because of their intimate knowledge of the mystical, satanic mind, could speak with eloquent rhetoric and hypocrisy to a stupefied audience of an even greater master. There were common people whose raucous devotion to evil had brought them to the attention of the satanic community and who had been welcomed into the fold with eagerness and lust.

And of course the slaves: men, women, and children bought or stolen from their homes to be offered up as playthings to satiate the perverse lusts of Mercadante's guests. They were chosen mostly for their beauty, the men for their robust musculature and genital endowment, the women for their firm seductive flesh, and the children for the look of outraged innocence in their eyes. But there were a few freaks as well, culled from the impoverished countrysides of a hundred nations: diminutive men and women, smaller than midgets, clasped naked to their masters on elegant chains of gold, like dogs or trained monkeys; hermaphrodites and others with genital deformities, distended scrotums and multiple nipples, half-formed Siamese twins with extra pairs of withered legs and genitals who could be made to cry out their torment in two voices; and freaks whose abysmal ugliness and bestial lineaments were in and of themselves sufficient to provoke the ardor of their masters. One poor woman stolen from an outcast's cave in southern India had multiple, withered arms which hung from her shoulders and beneath her breasts manacled with a profusion of bronze and gold shackles in a cruel travesty of the goddess Kali. Another man was much enjoyed by the celebrants because he possessed two anuses.

The ritual chamber had been cleared of its wonted ceremonial tables and kneeling benches. In their place Mercadante had provided implements of torture and restraint gathered from his own dungeon: racks, wheels, whipping posts, bastinados, thumbscrews, testicle-crushers, spiked cradles, and even an iron maiden which had seen frequent use in the hands of the Catholic Church during the Inquisition. The victims caught in the embrace of these devices howled their agony to the empty, vaulted ceilings, their misery mingling its resonance with groans and growls of orgasm, and staccato bursts of phlegmy laughter.

An old man with filmy red eyes finished sodomizing a

young girl who was shackled over a leather vaulting-box. In the brief minutes of the lecher's satiety, he licked his lips listening to the girl beneath him weeping with rage and pain and humiliation. Suddenly he looked up toward the high, narrow windows.

He thought he heard a bell.

He listened again more intently, dragging himself off the girl's body, his sagging neck stretched taut like a turtle's in his concentration. He heard the second peal of the bell more distinctly now, struggling to isolate it from the raucous frenzy all around him.

—Be quiet! he shouted to the crowd, straining his weak voice to be heard. Be quiet so you can hear! I think I hear the bell! I think I hear the bell!

The somber ringing of the iron grew louder until scattered pockets of celebrants stopped what they were doing and listened. Gradually silence grew among them as the funereal peals of the bell became majestic in intensity, trembling the stone walls with its triumphant resonance.

—He's here! the old man shrieked hoarsely. Almighty Satan, the Holiest of Holies! He's here! He's here!

A subterranean cavern linked the heliport to the inner sanctum of the Chateau. It was down this cavern that Mercadante, shrouded from the cold in a thick cloak, led the half-formed beast and his attendants. The limestone walls sweated a greasy muck and the air was thick and stale. In his left hand Mercadante held a smoking torch; his right arm was wrapped around Marco's shoulders.

Marco stared about him at the dank walls and the billowing blackness of the torchsmoke. His pupils were slivered like a cat's.

—What You must first grow to understand and accept, whispered Mercadante to the boy, is that all life owes its beginning and its end to You. The creatures of this world are but flecks of Your magnificence, scattered from Your great power like raindrops off a cloak. All life tends toward one end and that end is Your pleasure and dominion. Life, in and of itself, is without meaning. Like sprouts of wheat or the beasts of the field or the mindless scaly creatures of the sea, we have been given the breath of life for the sole purpose of satisfying Your desires, of filling the needs of Your majestic spirit. Behold! Two maidens have been born and shall die solely to light Your way through the portals of the palace I've prepared for You.

Far ahead in the darkness was a misty golden glow. As they drew closer, two marble slabs could be seen flanking a heavy iron door. On each slab a naked woman was shackled, her arms stretched far above her head. Their breasts were slit and thick tallow candles were insterted in the bloody mounds, which were then restitched to hold them in place. Hot wax dripping from the candles seared their torn flesh. Their skin was numb and pale with the cold of the marble and the moist limestone and they could no longer cry out with the agony of their pain but merely mumbled incoherently to each other, arching their spines at intervals with each drop of fresh hot wax. As Marco was led closer to them, rats scurried off their enchained limbs.

—All is for You, said Mercadante as he unlocked the iron door and pulled it open. It is done in reverence, fear, and love.

Adrienne was in total darkness. Her knees were shackled to the floor and her hands were chained far above her head, placing her in perpetual salaam to the dark powers.

She tried to blot out the memories of her recent torments as she had tried to close her mind a thousand times before against the impinging cadence of the lash and the panting frenzy of her nameless, faceless tormentors. But even the forced memories of her father and family, the blissful times she had had with Jade, were of no avail. Her father's face, a ghostly haze, swirled like a mandala, impotent yet reproachful, upon the surface of her visions. Her body ached with a thousand wounds, stripes and florets of scabs stiffening her flesh, and she couldn't forget, she couldn't transform the agony of the present into the illusion of the past or even into the black emptiness of death. She wasn't yet blessed with madness, though she looked to it for her salvation as she looked to the skeletal face of death to bend down upon her and take her for his lover.

And then, without warning, she thought of Jade's eyes in the moonlight . . .

A voice outside her dungeon door, raised in display, the voice of her husband:

—Within lies one who would have been Your bride but for her faithlessness. She pays daily for her sin. In the new mythology of Your reign, it is she who will personify all that is weak and despicable and worthy of torment. Her name shall be chanted for eons among the conclaves of the faithful, amidst curses and spittle.

The voice paused so that the ghosts of its words could sink into the tortured woman's soul.

—You will have her yet, Great One. Though now it will be amidst pain and derision rather than sublime ecstasy. Soon, Great One. When our first work is finished.

Faint footsteps growing fainter, then silence. Impenetrable silence.

Adrienne looked about her in the darkness.

—Jade? she whispered. Jade?

She thrashed against her chains.

—Jade! Jade! Jade!

Her body was racked with sobs and her chin fell heavily down upon her breast.

An aged crone with slack, wrinkled flesh, pale as limestone, spoke feverishly to a knot of eager listeners.

—As sure as I stand before you now, I saw 'im with the fledgling on the castle wall last night, showin' 'im the black and starry sky after the setting of the moon. Like shadows they was, dark against dark, and 'e was talkin' to 'im softly. I couldn't catch the words.

—Better that you couldn't, returned another old hag.

A third old crone, cupping her deaf ear to the speaker, queried:

305

—What? Fledgling? She cackled obscenely. Heinreich's lover, for sure. She licked her toothless gums with a pasty tongue. Was he a pretty piece?

The first crone cuffed the deaf one viciously on the side of her head.

—You brainless fool! It was the Great One, 'imself. Not a fleshy joy. And Heinreich was teachin' 'im. Makin' 'im strong so 'e'll be fit to be worshipped.

The beaten hag pressed her bony hand against her head, wincing with pain, her long tongue darting from between her shrivelled lips in serpentine contempt.

—Pig! shrilled the first crone. Mock me, will ye? I'll see ye dead first.

And she with the others who had gathered to listen to her began to pummel the deaf one with fleshless, bony arms until she sank in a dizzy heap upon the stone floor.

The first crone looked down upon the other in triumph, her hands fisted on her hips.

—I don't for the life of me understand 'ow Heinreich can surround 'imself wi' such people.

A tiny secret chamber with room for just the two of them and a marble slab. A smoking torch provided light. On the slab a bound lamb squirmed.

—The ancients understood the ways of the universe, Heinreich began. They knew that the murmurs of greatness were mirrored in the whimpering of the weak. That the magnets of stars and the twisting ways of destiny eat into the very flesh of creatures that crawl and wail here upon the earth.

The old man curled his fingers among the knots of lamb's fleece, turning the trembling head so that one wide, frightened eye flashed in the torchlight.

—I speak of portents, the knowledge of the future. You will learn to know Your enemies, to seek them out no matter how far from You they flee, to beat them to their knees and make of their hot blood the stuff of Your greatness. Watch and learn.

Heinreich draw a silver sacrificial blade from beneath

his cloak. Marco's pale cat's eyes widened, as Heinreich chanted:

—It is Truth, unmixed with the false.
What is higher is that which is lower;
What is lower is that which is higher.
From this are miracles accomplished.
As All finds its birth in the One,
So does the One take All to its breast.
The father is the Sun, the mother the Moon.
It has been carried in the belly of the wind
And the Earth has nourished it.
It completes the universe.
Its power is boundless once linked to the Earth.
Separate the earth from the fire,
The fine from the coarse,
With great skill.

He raised the blade high over his head and plunged it into the lamb's breast. The beast lurched and squealed. Hot blood sprayed the slab and the floor and the warlock's cloak. Slowly, he slit the beast's belly, spilling the tripes upon the marble.

—Feel of it. Drink in its wetness, its smell, its living heat. Take the soft and sticky curves of flesh into Your hands and open Your inner eye to read therein the mysteries.

The boy-beast stepped slowly toward the fuming mess of guts, sniffing. Then he plunged his hands in the living slime, the dark blood seeping slowly upward among the coarse strands of hair that blanketed his arms. His eyes closed and his thick, equine lips twisted in a grotesque smile. His fingers squeezed and stretched amidst the entrails and from his throat emerged a throaty growl.

—Read therein the mysteries, whispered Mercadante, his eyes on fire. Open Your mind to the power within You.

Marco was caught up in an ecstasy. As his fingers worked ever more deeply among the steaming organs, his heavy head rolled forward and back, nodding in phase with mystic planetary rhythms known only to his secret consciousness. Intense joy was mirrored on the boy-beast's face.

—You've but whetted your taste, my Lord, said Mercadante, restraining Marco with a hand on his elbow. Surfeit Yourself on a greater wisdom.

The old man pulled a bell cord and a muscular slave presented himself at the door of the chamber bearing a velvet-shrouded bundle on a silver platter. Heinreich placed the platter on the end of the marble slab and pulled off the velvet. A human infant wriggled and cooed on the platter.

—He's grown, said the man over a brimming goblet of purple wine. Or so I've been told. Haven't had the good luck to see Him myself, though I've taken to prowling the courtyard after dark. After midnight's the best time, they say.

The man who spoke had his cheeks chalked with lime powder. The wrinkles in his skin seemed gouged with knives. His lips were painted a glossy red.

—Be careful, another cautioned. If you're seen . . .

—You needn't think me a fool. Besides, my eagerness to view the Master is nothing more than an act of homage.

—You always were a daring one, simpered a third man.

—He has grown, another man interjected after downing a large draught of wine. Having captured his listeners' attention, he slowly, carefully patted his lips clean with some frilly linen.

—Damn it, man! said the first, have you seen Him?

—Quite by accident, I assure you. I walked upon the eastern parapet last night to clear my head of the fumes of our celebration. The night was clear as crystal. I was admiring the stars and the shadows of the foothills when I heard an . . . an intonation coming to me on the wind.

—An intonation?

—A chant, if you will. Rhythmic, soft, intense. A deadly serious chant, I could tell that, though I couldn't make out any of the words. I looked over my shoulder into the wind and saw upon the southern wall two figures.

One I'm certain was Heinreich. I could tell by his billowing cloak.

—And . . . and the other?

—No longer a boy, I'll say that, if ever a boy it was. You know how foolish rumors can be. O it was lithe and slender enough, yet fully as tall as Heinreich and furred like a beast in broad patches spread over Him from top to toe. I knew immediately it had to be Him.

—I'd have perished at the sight!

The others nodded in unison.

—So I thought would be my fate, as well. I turned my face away, yet, I blush to confess it, my eagerness to view the Master with my own eyes overcame my better judgment. Besides, they were so far from me I couldn't really make out any but the broadest features. I thought surely I wouldn't be punished for looking at Him from such a great distance. But, admittedly, I was lucky.

—And what did you see? one of the other men cried out, leaning forward on the table in his eagerness to hear.

—Yes, yes, tell us! demanded the others.

The narrator lowered his voice confidentially.

—Heinreich intoned a chant with arms upraised to the stars. The Master, at his side, stepped forward after the chant was ended and raised His arms to the stars as well. He paused, as if waiting for the right moment, and then He clenched His upraised fists. All of a sudden a great flash of light shattered the darkness, consuming the whole night sky. And there was a terrible roar of thunder . . .

—I remember that, late last night it was, we all heard it from the Great Hall! We all fell silent, terrorized. Even our slaves paused in their groaning. We thought it was just a sudden summer storm.

—No summer storm ever rained lightning and thunder like that, the narrator continued. I fell to my knees thinking I was surely a dead man. But then I saw a great rosy glow far in the southern sky, a glow as of a terrible fire.

—Did you discover what it was? one of the men asked eagerly, his face a mask of awe.

The narrator nodded but didn't say a word. Instead he took a folded newspaper from his waistband. He unfolded it upon the table:

CHURCH DESTROYED BY LIGHTNING FROM CLEAR SKY
138 KILLED, 40 INJURED
METEOROLOGISTS BEWILDERED

After permitting his listeners to absorb the headlines, the narrator took another hefty draught of wine and then leaned back in his chair.

—It kind of makes you shiver, he said quietly.

Beneath the Chateau was a jewelled grotto. Its arched vaults were surfaced with bubbles of obsidian and mica, amethyst and jasper. The stones sparkled and the shadows of stalactites writhed and danced because at the very center of the grotto was a fountain of gold-glowing molten rock. A geological oddity, the grotto opened onto a seam of magma through which the stuff of the very core of the earth could rise and froth and bubble, and then be returned through natural convective processes to the depths from which it originated. Months before Mercadante had turned this grotto into the foundry in which the iron bell had been formed and cast. Now it would serve a different purpose.

—You fear dissolution because of what You were, Mercadante began. You have become Another. The ancient fears and vulnerabilities are in Your past now. Look upon Your own limbs, feel with Your fingers the burgeoning iron of Your flesh, understand once and for all that omnipotence which flows through Your veins.

Marco no longer looked up at Mercadante but faced him squarely in the eye. His torso and shoulders had broadened with rock-like muscles and locks of beast hair tumbled onto his shoulders. A six-inch spear of spiralled bone protruded from the center of his forehead, shimmering with the spurting flares of the molten fires. His slivered cat's eyes stared into the eyes of his mentor, betraying neither wisdom nor confusion nor wonder; simply a supreme readiness.

—Wrest from the bowels of the Great Earth Mother the manifesto of Your greatness. From within those fires

You shall bring me a sign, a testament to the absoluteness of Your power. Concentrate upon my prayers as You descend into the flames. Feed upon my words, suckle upon the milk of my lips, and You shall feel the majesty of galaxies pulse within You.

Mercadante clasped his hands together and raised them high above his head. He shut his eyes tightly and pursed his brow in intense concentration.

—O great power of the night,
The flames of the universal mother beckon.
She waits to be ravished . . .

The beast left Mercadante's side and slowly trudged down the steps and shelves of rock toward the fountain of lava. The heat from the fires bathed Mercadante's face in beads of shining sweat, and his face shone like naked bronze in the glare of the fountain.

—Enter the fiery depths of her womb;
Combat her fury with Your limitless strength.

Steady, unhurried progress to the fountain: sharp shards of rock crumbled beneath the beast's cloven feet: ever nearer, the floor of the grotto throbbing with the jets of magma, the beast's eyes glowing in the corrosive light, its bony mouth curled in a vacuous smile:

A mind link between master and pupil: incantations spilled in torrents from Mercadante's lips, feverish words, tripping one upon the other, rash and defiant, his arms upraised against the enmity of the heavens. His words gushed like a fountain of water, cooling his heat-ravaged body as the beast drew ever closer to the spumes of molten rock:

—Though she squirms to be rid of You,
Though she burns You with her embrace,
You shall not weaken, You shall not fall prey
to her wiles . . .

The rock beneath its hooves glowed red as blood; still the beast kept stalking the liquid fires, eager lust in its

glowing eyes. Closer still, and the gold droplets fell upon
its shoulders, blushing furiously to deep blood red, cooling
into hard nubs of stone which clung tenaciously to its thick
hairs. Closer still, until it breathed fire, until the very air
of the grotto seared its lungs in outrage, its smile undaunted, its steady pace unabated.

The beast's horn reflected the carnelian of the grotto
floor, shining, beginning to dwarf the fire of the fountain
with its own savage light.

It paused at the rim of the fountain amidst the comet-
spray of molten rock, impervious, defiant, its chest rumbling with deep growls.

Mercadante fell to his knees on the rocks, tearing his
flesh, his fists clenched in desperate agony against his
temples.

—The Mother! The Mother! Defy her sanctions! She
is Yours! Her legs spread wide for Your strength, Your
immensity!

The beast plunged, grinning, into the magma fountain.
Its torrent of golden heat sprayed high up toward the roof
of the grotto, turning blood red like a solar prominence
on some ancient, giant sun.

With a hideous shriek, a howl of triumph and agony,
Mercadante fell heavily to the grotto floor.

The beast sank through the lake of fire, transparent to
the flames. It fell, swirling, out of time, out of space,
falling, thrilled by licking tongues of hot metal as it
splashed through, swirling, endlessly swirling, in the
harshest embrace of orgasmic ecstasy. And the beast
howled its triumph as it fell, unconsumed by the burning
flood, its great body freed of its dross, lurching in wave
after wave of orgasm.

Mercadante was awakened on the floor of the grotto
by the gentle press of a heavy hand. The beast knelt beside him, its eyes glowing like twin silver beacons. Avert-
ing his sight from the glow of its eyes, Mercadante could
still make out the enlarged bulk of the creature, grown
even more powerful after its purgation in the flames. The
beast's left hand had caressed its mentor into consciousness.

In its right hand it held out to Mercadante a perfect

sphere of diamond, clearer than the finest crystal, larger
and heavier than a cannonball.

In the darkness of her cell, Adrienne heard the scurrying of rats.

—I've had dreams, she said to herself softly. Things
I've wanted to be and to do.

She laughed in the darkness. Then she smelled the
torches as they approached. Mercadante had again given
leave to some of his guests to toy with her.

The scent made her mind swirl blackly as her gorge
rose in terror. She wanted to pull against her chains but
she had no feeling left in her arms. Her lips pursed into
an angry pout. She addressed the darkness:

—They'll have to leave me my dreams. Dreams have
that kind of reality. Hard, like jewels.

A song crossed her mind from years back. A child's
words of wonder and despair:

—Mommy, mommy, come and see such things
    I've never seen;
There are happy faces all around and all the
    grass is green . . .

Her voice was cracked and weak as a whisper. She
chuckled at her ineptitude.

Footsteps and laughing voices drew closer.

Her head sagged on her neck.

—They've taken me away from you, she sighed, her
own voice unfamiliar, hoarse and throaty. No sooner did
I taste love than I was punished for my joy.

Another rat scurried noisily in the darkness.

—Have they taken you, too? Have they hurt you, like
me?

She paused, her eyes brimming with tears.

—You were so beautiful. Your voice so gentle. In your
arms I was consumed in hot fires.

The laughter and footsteps drew even closer. Suddenly
she tried to throw herself in rage against her chains, her

eyes wide with terror. But outwardly there was no movement.

—Your eyes! Have they taken the beauty from your eyes, jade eyes, eyes like soft jewels? No, no, no, NO! I won't let them. They may try to burn your eyes with fire, crisp them like scorched marbles, but I won't let them! No, not your beautiful eyes!

The door to her cell sprang open, flooding the total darkness with the light of the torch. A rat scrambled for shelter between two cold stones set in the dungeon wall.

Another rat jumped off Adrienne's shoulder where it had been nibbling her arm.

As Mercadante's cohorts laid impious hands on her, she tried to scream at them, but her voice emerged only as a mournful groan:

—Why didn't God permit me to love? Why didn't God permit me to love?

The evening revelry in the Great Hall was about to recommence. An immense fat man, his pendulous breasts and midriff criss-crossed with leather bandoleros decorated with silver studs and his pudgy hands garbed in spiked leather gloves was just finishing the shackling of a frail woman to a whipping post. He had spent his life camouflaging his gross, slovenly weakness behind leather trappings to convey the illusion of strength. He hated fine-boned women especially, because their acceptance of their frail forms, indeed, their reliance on strengths other than physical, was a bitter reproach to him. He deliberately picked such women first out of packs of slaves for whipping. And always the final pull on the leather bonds of his victims drew from them a whimper of agony.

Yet his fat, flaccid face and dull eyes betrayed his weakness.

He stood back from the whipping post and admired his handiwork. The wrist and ankle bonds cut into the victim's flesh. She was not quite out of puberty and was infinitely beautiful in her helplessness.

A friend of the fat man's, tall, skinny, and with shoulder-length hair, came running up to him excitedly.

—He's done it! he shouted, pulling at the fat man's arm. Heinreich said he could, and he's proven it!

—What are you babbling about? asked the fat man.

—The great power of the Master! Heinreich said that even in His fledgling form it could span oceans! And He's done it!

—He's not such a fledgling anymore, according to what I've heard.

—Maybe not as much as He was. But you know as well as I that there's still much left for Heinreich to do before the Day of Ascension. But wait'll I tell you what the Master has done already, inspired by Heinreich. I've just gotten word from some of my operatives in New York.

The skinny man's face sparkled gleefully.

—The city's in an uproar. It's in all the papers.

—Well, are you gonna tell me what happened or not?

—Remember Heinreich told us that during the Master's early transformations, He murdered the father of His corporeal host?

—I remember somethin' like that.

—Well, because it was a case of murder, there was a big bureaucratic delay before the funeral could be held. When the cops finally realized that nothing could be gained by keeping the body in the freezer of the funeral home, they gave the okay to have him buried. Now catch this: the funeral was held yesterday with all of the old guy's family and rich friends in attendance. And the Master, the Great One, using the pure power of His will, reanimated the corpse, disfigured as it was, right in the middle of the service! From here, mind you, right here in the Chateau, thousands of miles away. The casket was closed and then all of a sudden it springs open and the old guy's body, pulling all its pieces together, jumps out and onto the floor and starts to chase everybody out of the parlor.

The skinny man had tears of laughter rolling down his cheeks.

—Can't you just see it? Everybody running around hysterical, killing each other just to get to the door, screaming, jumping out of windows. I'm told that the old guy's wife literally shit all over herself and passed out.

There were at least two heart attacks among the mourners that I've heard of. Isn't it a scream?

The skinny man collapsed in raucous hilarity.

—Then how'd they stop it? asked the fat man.

—They didn't. The Master simply let go of it, let it drop. Let those morons try and figure out what happened. It's good to give them a hint of the things that are to come.

The fat man's mouth twisted into a weak smile. Then he returned his attention to his victim on the whipping post.

—There are no energies greater than those of terror, agony, and despair, said Mercadante to the Master.

They stood in the catacombs beneath the Chateau, Mercadante dwarfed by his pupil. The Master's shaggy presence filled the dark, rat-infested tunnels with a hideous stench and his guttural breathing echoed in a thousand reverberations. But to Mercadante the sound of this breathing was the cadence of freedom, and the stench the fragrance of dominion and power.

He filled his lungs unrestrainedly with the tainted air as he spoke.

—This castle has known innumerable victims to the lusts of its owners in the hundreds of years since it was built. Their corpses have all been brought down here for disposal. You see lining the stone walls of these catacombs the skulls and bones of these victims: row upon row of grinning death's heads, their vacant eyes now inhabited by rats and other vermin.

Mercadante paused while they both listened to the scratches and scrapes emitted by the rows of countless skulls, an intensity of living sound which had abrogated the wonted silence of the tomb.

—The blood of generations has soaked into this soil. Generations of people in pain and torment. The red fingers of blood which reach down into the earth from here bear with them psychic energies equal to a thousand flaming suns. And I have brought with me casks of earth of even greater potency.

A large iron trunk rested beside a wall of skulls. Mercadante unlocked it and withdrew a small silver casket. The casket was filled with earth.

—The soil of Auschwitz, he said, sprinkling the earth on the ground at the Master's feet.

The Master quivered with a sudden influx of energy.

—The soil of Belsen, the soil of Dachau, the soil of Treblinka . . .

Mercadante continued opening casket after casket, pouring the earth at his pupil's feet. The soil from great battlefields, from sites of particularly heinous murders: the soils of Hiroshima and Nagasaki and My Lai. Again and again the raw earth settled in clumps at the Master's feet and with each addition the creature moaned orgasmically, its eyes blazing ever brighter, sucking into itself the megaton energies, quivering with the delight of power, growing larger, heavier, more massive and forbidding.

—Open Yourself more fully to these energies, said Mercadante as he began to rapidly chant the litany of infamous names. To all this blazing energy You are heir and successor. Feed on these bloody and stained soils. Take from the earth that which she strives to keep hidden, that which she strives to mourn in silence and secrecy. You have ravished her and all that is hers is now Yours. Feed, O Great One, upon these my offerings of mankind's heritage.

The beast writhed deliciously with the waves of energy that quivered through it. And then, as the clumps of soil mounted at his feet in rhythm with its mentor's dark chant, its mind blossomed with fearsome force and its skull opened like a glass dome to the torchlight and the scuffling vermin and the walls of skulls.

It was then that the wondering beast witnessed the rising of the ghosts.

Vague, billowing transparencies at first, like the shadows of chimney smoke on a wall. Then the slender forms and faces, rising up from the mound of earth at the beast's feet, wailing, agonized faces howling their misfortunes to the stars. Some held forth their severed limbs and heads in macabre bundles, some were content to recite the atrocities that had claimed them, some weeped more for loved ones risen in horror by their side than for themselves. A million voices murmuring, weeping, howling at once as wraith upon wraith rose like vapors into the light of the Master's mind.

At last the beast grew dizzy with the horror, dizzy with the maddening influx of human misery that it sucked from the bloody clumps of earth into the very essence of its being and energy. It howled its triumph and exultation in a massive, trumpeting wail that sprawled Mercadante flat upon the ground, his hands tightly pressed against his ears, his face contorted in pain.

Far above the catacombs, in the Great Hall, the celebrants grew silent and trembled, fearing the rumbling in the earth.

—It won't be long now, the old crone announced to her friends.

—A matter o' days, I'm told, said another.

She leaned secretively toward her companions, drawing their close attention.

—I've already 'eard 'im walkin' around down below, she whispered. 'E's grown to be a big feller now.

—Have you seen Him? Have you seen Him? another asked eagerly.

—I didn't quite see 'im, no.

—Then how do you know he's big?

—I 'eard 'im breathin'.

—What?

—I 'eard 'im breathin'. I was passin' through one o' those tunnels down below and I 'appened to stand next to a door that led into another tunnel . . .

—That Heinreich, he's got tunnels up the ass down there.

—Will you let her finish? Go on.

The narrator paused majestically for complete silence.

—Well, anyway, she continued, I was standin' by this door and I 'eard 'Einreich pass by on the other side, talkin' to someone. So I listens but I don't have to listen very 'ard. I 'ears the sound o' breathin' comin' from the other side, big growly kind o' breathin', like a dragon in a barrel. I says t'meself, That must be 'im, girl! That must be 'im! And I knew 'ow much 'e must be growed 'cause anythin' that breathes like that must be big as an oliphant . . .

—Ssh! one of the hags cautioned. Be quiet!

The ladies were silent while a short black man with a goatee and a shaved skull passed by on his way to one of the racks.

—See that little nigger?

—I wonder if they wax their heads to make 'em shine like that . . .

—He's an American . . .

—Aren't they all?

—New York, I think.

She drew her companions' heads close to hers with the twitch of a forefinger:

—He only does white women.

—What!

—He only does white women. Walks around with 'em two at a time on his arm, just like a showy pimp.

—Basically insecure, I suppose. Never grew tall enough to play basketball like the rest of his friends.

—Not only that, he makes his money off what he does with 'em.

—How d'you mean? *Is* he a pimp?

—Nah. But he takes photos, though.

—And what's wrong with bein' a photographer, may I ask?

—Bondage, S&M, whips, chains . . . all o' that.

—A pornographer!

—Y'mean 'e makes money off o' what we does for fun? Then what the 'ell's 'e doin' 'ere? 'E's no better than a common shopkeeper. And a nigger, at that. Don't 'e know we're a religious institootion?

—Those Americans. A strange lot.

Mercadante summoned Bennett to his private quarters in a castle tower. The servant stood in front of the large carved mahogany desk, facing his master. Mercadante looked more haggard and paler than usual, his face and forehead creased with more and deeper lines. Yet a great fire smoldered behind his eyes. Bennett stood before him as straight and stiff as he could in his twisted condition.

—Have preparations been completed for the Ritual of Ascension? asked Mercadante, his voice soft, tired, yet tinged with excitement.

—Yes, Master. Everything's in readiness. We've only been waiting for word from you.

—Yes, yes, I know you've seen very little of me these past few days. There was much that had to be done and very little time to do it in. But the work's almost completed, now. Some ghosts remain that must be laid to rest but, after that, the Master shall be ready to enter upon His lordship.

Bennett flashed a twisted smile.

—I'm very gratified to hear that, Master. I know how long you've worked for that moment.

—Thank you, Bennett. Yes, it has cost me the dedication of my life and my fortune. But that's little enough when you consider the infinite rewards of bringing to fruition that which I have accomplished. A new world, Bennett, a new universe, even. I tell you, He possesses powers that make me feel like an infant in swaddling. Such things I've seen, such things He's done! And you should see Him now, Bennett. Not the faun we found in the mountains any longer. He's a hulking, massive brute with eyes of silver flames and furred like a satyr. And He's grown a horn, Bennett, a beautiful spiral of ivory fully a foot and a half long, sticking right out from the center of His forehead. A magnificent creature He is, really.

Mercadante's eyes drifted in a pleasant revery like the eyes of a father thinking of the son he adores. Bennett, again, expressed his happiness.

—And the new bride? questioned Mercadante suddenly. Nothing has gone awry on that score, has it?

—Rest easy about that, Master, answered Bennett, smiling. She's already been acquired and is down below under heavy guard.

—I rested easy about that once before, said Mercadante bitterly. You know what it cost me. I've lost my taste for resting at all. You're certain that my guests have been kept away from her?

—Absolutely certain, Master, though it's been no easy task. She's a real beauty.

—And my guests can be an unruly lot at times, Bennett. I know that. But my faith in you has been restored. I'm sure you've been doubly careful that there will be no mishaps on the Day of Ascension.

Bennett bowed his head shyly.

—I have been careful, Master. I've tried hard to restore myself to your good graces.

—And you have, my friend, said Mercadante smiling. Which brings me to another matter that I'm sure is of the utmost concern to you. Since the Great One's progress has been so rapid and admirable, I've been in a rather effervescent and munificent state of mind. I've decided to restore your body to its former shape, such as it was.

—O Master, exclaimed Bennett, his eyes wide with wonder. This is beyond hope, beyond the poor power of my words . . .

—Yes, yes, I know that it's all quite beyond any of your poor powers. But I'm feeling too joyous to leave any conflict with my personal servant unresolved.

With a sudden twist of his head, Mercadante stared harshly into Bennett's eyes, his own eyes glowing like fiery red coals. Bennett lurched backward against the door, gasping in sudden pain, pinned and immobilized by the force of his master's mind. His humpback began to level out amidst a great crackling and snapping of gristle. His teeth clenched from the desperate agony, and his face broke out in a cold sweat.

—You will remember . . . only this . . . that there will never again be . . . a second chance . . . Offend me again . . .

Bennett squirmed against the door, his bones and joints snapping, gasping for air.

— . . . and you will surely die!

Mercadante released his servant, who collapsed on the floor in an unconscious heap. He pushed the body away from the door with his foot and made to leave.

—I'll take away your pain as well, he said, addressing

the collapsed form on the floor. I'll have no sad faces on the Day of Ascension.

And then he passed out into the corridor.

—The enemy within is most treacherous, Mercadante cautioned. It's easy to defend ourselves against others. It's natural to look first to the impregnability of our outer walls. We think of the enemy within only after it is too late.

Mercadante and the beast faced each other across a small circular wall of stones which resembled a well. The top of the well was covered with an iron circular plate in the center of which a thick iron hook was attached.

—Draw the cover off these stones, Mercadante commanded, and confront Your enemy.

Mercadante stepped back, all the while staring into the beast's eyes. It approached the iron plate slowly, grinning its odd, mindless grin, its cat's eyes shimmering with power. Linking its massive fingers through the iron hook, the beast began pulling upward. Mercadante then quickly stared down at the iron plate and it wouldn't rise. The beast, still grinning like a cretin, its eyes fiery but expressionless, kept pulling upward. Mercadante's forehead broke out in a furious, cold sweat. His breathing became tense and rapid, and he began to massage his temples with his fingertips, concentrating all the while on the iron plate. The beast remained unhurried, still smiling, seemingly amused by its mentor's efforts to test its strength. Suddenly, with a sharp metallic squeal, the iron plate bowed outward toward the beast's fist. Then, with a lurch, the beast effortlessly ripped the cover off the stones while Mercadante fell to the floor, exhausted.

It looked like the deepest of wells, its origin somewhere amidst the blackest pit of Hell. A sound rose from within, a rushing sound, a sound of furious vapors rising to the surface. Suddenly, billows of dark purple smoke spilled out of the opening and instantly filled the room with a swirling, thick fog. Startled, the beast stepped back a pace, flinging the iron plate harshly to the floor.

In the midst of the dark vapors an image began to

slowly coalesce, illuminated by its own mysterious inner light. It was the image of a handsome fifteen-year-old boy with soft pale blue eyes and long dark hair.

The beast stared into the image that floated before it, seemingly confused.

A soft resonant voice emerged from the image, filling the small chamber:

—You killed Jenny, it said, its lips motionless. She loved us and you killed her. And you killed Father as well. He meant us no harm. Why did you kill them?

The beast just stared into the image, its eyes wide, barely breathing.

—Jenny loved us so much. She did everything in her power to make us happy. She let us be the first to make love to her. And she so young. Remember how we'd sing to her that poem of Byron's, making up a tune as we went along?

> She walks in beauty like the night
> Of cloudless climes and starry skies;
> And all that's best of dark and bright
> Meet in her aspect and her eyes:
> Thus mellow'd to that tender light
> Which heaven to gaudy day denies.

The vapor-filled chamber blossomed with soft music as the boy's tender voice rose and fell, so gentle, so soft. Then the music trailed off into silence.

—And the way you killed her . . . a horrible way to die. It was your horrible face she last saw before she died. She knew it was you, not me. And our father. And the others. Why them? Tell me that at least if you can't justify Jenny's death and Father's.

The beast stared at the image in stony silence.

—Innocent people dead because of us. Because of you. All our dreams, all the tender sentiments we loved so much in our poetry, what happened to all those ideals we held so holy? You betrayed them. You are a horrible creature. You're bound by all that's honorable and decent to make restitution. To do that you must die. You must die so that I may live again. And you must make whole all those poor souls you brutalized and tore apart.

You've got the power. You can make the dead live, as well as the living die. Now do for once what is right and good. Undo what you've done and then obliterate your name and face and memory. Be scattered again amongst the nothingness of the stars.

The beast stared silently at the vision, its slivered pupils narrow and malevolent. Then its equine mouth began to curl into a grin and the creature started to laugh, a bestial, alien laugh akin to a howl and a dying man's death rattle. The voice of the vision began to plead NO NO NO NO until the beast's eyes suddenly flared silver, illuminating the darkness of the purple cloud with its own irresistible radiance. The beast laughed and howled and kept laughing as the vision slowly blurred and dissipated, forming a new image in the blinding glare of the beast's eyes.

The new image was the duplicate of the beast itself.

As the beast and its image united in a howling, triumphant frenzy, the purple clouds swirled and faded, sucked back again into the dark pit from which they had emerged.

Mercadante rose from the floor rubbing his temples, smiling. The beast watched the old man with his wonted cretin's grin.

—You've done it, Great One. You've laid to rest that spirit with admirable ease. Only one final test remains.

Mercadante bent over a small trunk that had been deposited in the chamber beside the entrance. He opened its lid and withdrew, with difficulty, the weighty diamond sphere that the beast had retrieved from the pit of fire. He placed the sphere in the creature's hands.

—Within this sphere will be revealed Your final enemy. Look closely into its depths, open Your eyes and Your mind to the mists that will unmask the single soul that threatens Your dominion. Look, look closely . . .

The core of the sphere began to fuse and darken, like frost cyrstals forming on glass. Then the crystals flashed like radiant jewels, rubies, sapphires, emeralds, glowing, fusing, swirling in kaleidoscopic profusion.

And then the colors dimmed, fading, revealing in their place the image of a man's head. The man was blond, bearded, and had jade-colored eyes. Around his neck a jade unicorn hung on a thin chain. The unicorn glowed like an emerald fire.

The beast stared for long, lingering moments into the diamond sphere. Then suddenly the creature howled in rage and squeezed the sphere brutally between its palms. It strained for but an instant and then the sphere shattered into a billion scintillating diamond chips, showering the small chamber with a galaxy of sparkling, rainbowed stars.

Mercadante emerged from a shadowy corner of the chamber, exultant joy lighting up his face.

—After uncounted ages, he said to the creature, after eons of impotent time, at last, my Lord, You are ready.

25

O N the road to the Mt. Marcy trail in the Adirondacks, Jade glimpsed through the car window the small sign that said "Chapel Pond." He smiled. Those girls that day years ago, swimming naked in the cold still water, laughing, shouting, splashing each other . . . He'd left his bike beneath some pines and had scurried down a short incline to the edge of the pond, wanting to swim, himself.

And the girls saw him and fell silent but didn't run to cover themselves. And he had smiled at them . . .

The car trembled with a harsh spray of gravel as they turned into the trail road marked with little arrows.

A different time that was, he thought, so very long ago.

The climb was a tough one and Jade marvelled at the old man's agility: arms and legs working rapidly in perfect unison, Daniel scurried up the last half mile to the cabin like a spider, his staff jostling up and down on top of his pack to which it was tied with a leather thong. Some yards behind him Elizabeth and Beverly puffed and grunted, looking back frequently at the heights they'd already covered and moaning with chagrin at the distance left to go. Jade brought up the rear in case of mishap, though he couldn't imagine what good he'd be in the event of a real emergency. For the success of this entire adventure, in all its aspects, he depended on the old man leaping to and fro upon the rocks so far ahead.

The beauty of the mountains, however, mitigated much of Jade's fatigue. The tree-shrouded slopes, the scent of pine resin and wild flowers, the vast panorama of stalwart mountains and soft green valleys spreading out as far as the eye could see filled him with a sense of wonder and exhilaration. He had often bewailed the few scraps of nature permitted in the concrete environs of the city: a glimpse of cottony cloud stolen from between two towering skyscrapers, a dirty river frothing with sea gulls feeding on the garbage, stray scents of flower blossoms culled with care in the parks amongst the predominant stench of putrid hot dogs and dog shit. Here, all around him, was the Real Thing—nature. When at last he crawled the final few yards to the cabin, Jade was grinning with pleasure.

"Daniel!" he cried out, his arms spread wide to embrace the entire sky. "What a great place to live!"

The two women, collapsed on the grass in front of the cabin, looked up at Jade wordlessly with very tired eyes. They couldn't speak for panting.

Daniel had already unloaded his gear in the tiny cabin. He emerged smiling.

"I'm glad you like it," he said. "I'm afraid we'll be cramped in there, the four of us. I built it only for myself, not expecting many visitors."

"I wonder why," panted Beverly sarcastically. "Not much traffic up here, huh?"

Daniel laughed. "No, not much. A stray hawk now and then. That's about it."

"You mean the bears don't come up this far?" Jade asked with a smile.

"Bears!" exclaimed Beverly, her eyes wide with fright. "You mean real bears?"

"O Bev, don't let them tease you," cautioned Elizabeth. "Jade's just as much a city slicker as the rest of us. He just wants to make you squirm. Isn't that right, Jade?"

He returned her smile. "Listen, Beverly, if I thought for one moment that we'd be fighting off bears in the night, I'd be miles from here right now. I'm no Daniel Boone."

Nice women, those. Good-looking, too. Nice view from below, watching them climb. Almost as impressive as the trees. Too bad it's strictly off limits. Couldn't ask for a more romantic setting.

They'd reached the cabin none too soon. The sky was already a bloody gold streaked with magenta. Another half hour and it would be too dark to crawl. Although they were far from the summit of Mt. Marcy, they were high enough to watch the sunset in all its glory. Elizabeth snapped some pictures while Beverly changed her sweaty socks. Suddenly Jade heard Elizabeth's camera clatter on the stony ground and he turned hastily to see her knees buckling beneath her. He darted forward and caught her shoulders before her head hit the ground.

"Elizabeth! What's the matter?" he asked, his voice filled with concern. Beverly came dashing out of the cabin, falling to her knees by Elizabeth's side.

"Beth! What happened?" she gasped.

It was a few moments before Elizabeth could answer. She just rested in Jade's arms staring out over the mountains, blinking against the sunset. Finally, a little color returned to her cheeks and her face became animated.

"I'm . . . I'm all right now," she said softly. "It must've been the climb . . . the thin air . . . something . . ."

Daniel bent over close to her, studying her lips and eyes.

"I think she could use some of your tea," Jade suggested.

"Good idea," said Daniel. "Help her inside with me and I'll brew some."

"No, no, really," Elizabeth protested as the men lifted her to her feet and started to lead her into the cabin. "I'm fine now. It was just the exertion, I suppose. Bev and I don't climb mountains everyday."

Daniel's eyes were filled with concern when he turned them to Jade, but to Elizabeth he was all smiles. "Of course," he soothed, "it's been an arduous trip. Most mountain climbers won't take a hike like this without a week or so of vigorous practice and training. I'm impressed that the three of you made it up without greater problems."

Beverly dropped back behind the three of them as Elizabeth was carried into the cabin. Her mind was filled with the image of her lover's face as it had been during the seizure that had almost killed her a few short days before. She fumed angrily that Elizabeth should have gotten herself involved in this whole bizarre affair.

"I'm going to leave you for a while," Daniel said after brewing Elizabeth a cup of his tea. "Settle yourselves. If you need me, just shout. Voices carry remarkable distances up here in the mountains."

But after he left, their spirits palled. Beverly's anger hovered over them like an invisible plague. Elizabeth sipped her tea in silence while Jade spread out his sleeping bag. Somehow he felt guilty about their being there, yet it had been Elizabeth's idea in the first place. She'd insisted on it, in fact; Daniel had merely acquiesced. But each time Jade chanced into Beverly's field of vision, he felt the bitterness of her gaze burn into his flesh.

Beverly squatted beside Elizabeth on the floor. "How are you feeling now?" she asked. Her voice was filled with concern.

"I'm fine now, Bev. Really. Daniel's tea seems to work wonders." Elizabeth laughed but Beverly simply scowled.

"You look exhausted and pale and . . . consumptive. You've got that feverish look in your eyes. You seem to forget what an ordeal you've just gone through, both mentally and physically. I told you you weren't well enough to get any further involved with this nonsense so soon after . . ."

"O for God's sake, Bev, of course I look exhausted. We just climbed a damn mountain! That's all you see in me. No consumption, no pleurisy, no lung cancer."

"Go ahead. Make jokes. I know what I see and I know what you've just been through. You still haven't recovered. I don't care what you say."

"Dr. Crile checked me over and he gave his okay for me to come up here . . ."

"Dr. Crile! Sure he gave his okay. He practically insisted you involve yourself further in this business. He doesn't give a shit about your health; all he's interested in is psychic phenomena and all that other crap. You're just an . . . an experiment to him. If you drop dead here on this mountain, what's it to him? He'll shake his head and then go off and find some other psychic to play with. But what about me?"

Beverly's voice had become agitated; she tried to draw back on the reins of her irritation, not wanting Jade to hear them arguing. Elizabeth attempted to soothe her but Beverly was brusque.

"Forget it, Beth. I'll make us some coffee. Real coffee. No . . . magic potion."

Jade remained silent on his sleeping bag. Beverly clattered among the cooking utensils in her backpack, heated water, and hunted for coffee. She brought out another cup.

Elizabeth looked uneasily at Jade. "Excuse me, but would you like a cup of coffee with us?"

"For Christ's sake, Beth, what is this? A restaurant?" Beverly barked angrily.

"Please, Bev, I don't know why you're being so—"

"Listen," Jade interrupted, "thanks for the offer but I'm not a coffee drinker. Don't hassle on my account."

Beverly turned to face him, her eyes flashing fire. Jade simply smiled pleasantly in return and then returned to his meditations with closed eyes. He heard a quick scuffling of shoes and then the cabin door opened and slammed shut. Some moments of stony silence followed and then Jade recognized Elizabeth's voice.

"I want to apologize, Jade, for Bev's behavior. She's really not like this at all."

Jade opened his eyes and smiled amicably at Elizabeth. "Don't apologize. She loves you very much and she's worried about you. That's not hard to understand." He looked closely into Elizabeth's face and eyes. "And I know your health is none of my business but I tend to agree with her. You do kind of look like shit, if you know what I mean. I remember what you told us about your psychic seizure. You almost died then, didn't you? Are you really sure that you're up for all this mountain climbing? It gets pretty cold up here at night and I'll bet the winds can really blow. I'd hate to see you get seriously ill so far away from a doctor."

Elizabeth sat on the floor facing Jade. "To be perfectly honest with you Jade, I'm not in very good health. I don't want Bev to know that, so let's just keep it between us. When I first came out of that seizure, I felt pretty good. Maybe it was the medication, I don't know. But as the days have passed I have become more and more aware of how much has been drained from me. I just don't let myself think about it, that's all."

"Did you tell all this to Dr. Crile?"

"Yes, I did."

"And he still gave you the okay to come with us?"

"It wasn't his okay to give. I simply know that this is where I must be. I don't know why or for how long or any significant details at all. It's just that ever since I saw you in my dream, I knew that our fates were linked. Dr. Crile understood. That's why I'm here."

"A hell of a reason," Jade said, shaking his head.

Elizabeth smiled. "Look who's talking. I'm at least a telepath who's spent years studying and understanding the miraculous potencies of the mind. To me, premonitions and visions are perfectly reasonable and valid. But you've had all this suddenly thrust upon you. A strange old man, a wild story . . ." Elizabeth paused, studying Jade's face closely. "Why did you believe him?"

Jade leaned back against the cabin wall, stretching his long legs. "I'm like a confirmed atheist who is confronted one day by a puff of smoke and, lo and behold, out of the smoke pops the devil, complete with pitchfork and horns. Once that so-called myth is shown to be real, then a lot of other fanciful and naive notions assume a reality by extension. The intelligent atheist reconsiders his past philosophy and turns into a believer. And suddenly he looks upon the herd of priests not as fools but as oracles."

"You mean you saw the devil?"

"A reasonable facsimile, I'll grant you. Though don't talk to Daniel about God and Satan. He's strictly a rationalist, not a moralizer. $E = mc^2$ is his gospel, though you'd never know it to look at him."

"And you? Do you vote for the God and Satan theory or Daniel's 'polarities'?"

"I'll be damned if I know! And besides, it doesn't much matter either way, does it? All I know is that Daniel saved my life, that he seems to know what he's talking about, and that he's demonstrated to me the powers neces-

332

sary to prove most of his points. Beyond that, there doesn't seem to be much worth worrying about."

"But why are we here on this mountain? What does Daniel hope to accomplish that he couldn't do back in the city?"

"Well, I don't know about you, but I'm here basically 'cause I'm scared shitless! Daniel says that the thing I saw is going to come looking for me sooner or later, whether I look for it or not. Confronting that thing in my normal, mortal state is not a scenario I relish. Daniel says I have latent powers within me that can even the score, if only I let him develop them. Damn—I never play poker when I know the dealer's stacked the deck, unless I've got a few aces tucked up my sleeve myself. So that's why I'm here. As for why this mountain, you've got me. I assume Daniel knows where he can do his thing best." Jade curled his legs into a half-lotus, regarding Elizabeth with concern. "I tend to agree with your friend, however; you shouldn't have come with us."

"Daniel doesn't seem to agree with you," Elizabeth retorted. "Besides, you've got to discount a lot of Bev's objections. She's upset . . . jealous, I think."

"Jealous? Of what?"

"Of you?"

"Me? That's crazy! If I understand the nature of your relationship correctly, I should think that she'd be above jealousy. I mean, I'm really not your type."

Elizabeth laughed. "You mean because we're gay? Bev's not sexually jealous—not really. It's just that here you are, an oracular figment of my dreams suddenly sprung to life. Naturally, I'm far more fascinated by you than under normal circumstances. Not sexually, you understand, but fascinated nonetheless. Bev's jealous of your aura of mystery and intrigue, an aura that she knows she can't project. Besides that, she envies your sudden and unsought possession of miraculous powers, whatever they may prove to be.

"You see, Beverly has always been kind of the head of our house. She cares for me like a child, sometimes, and I must admit that I enjoy it when she gets all cuddly and maternal with me. But at the same time she's had to accept the fact that I'm a psychic—that I possess mental powers most people consider extraordinary. She can't even approach me on that level, regardless of her leadership or dominance in the rest of our relationship. That's why she's basically down on psychic research in general, and Dr. Crile in particular. Now, all of a sudden, you show up in the picture as the unwitting recipient of all those powers —and more—that Bev has always craved. It's like when Superman and Wonder Woman are rapping: nothing much is left for Lois Lane to do but take notes."

Jade laughed. "I like your analogy. I was a real comic book freak when I was a kid."

"You were? Me too. Somehow it's lamentable that we have to leave that world behind us when we grow up."

"I don't know about that," Jade commented drily, looking about him at the four walls of the little cabin. "I've got the strangest feeling that that world has caught up with me and is steadily sucking me back in."

"Wake up, Jade," Daniel whispered, gently prodding Jade's shoulder. "It's time for us to begin our work."

"Huh?" Jade forced open his heavy-lidded eyes, yawning and stretching. "What time is it?"

"Just after midnight."

"Midnight? Don't you believe in sleeping? I'm bushed from this afternoon's climb and you've been going steadily for two days. Why don't you get some sleep before you kill yourself?"

"I appreciate your concern and will take it under advisement," Daniel said. "Now get up and follow me."

Jade shook the vapors out of his head and rose quietly to his feet.

"Take this cloak," Daniel commanded, handing him a heavy woolen bundle. "It's quite cold and windy outside, in spite of the season."

"Mountain country," said Jade crankily. "How I love it."

But once out in the swirling, chill air beneath the canopy of stars, Jade forgot all about his fatigue. Darkness shrouded the landscape and, as Jade stared around him, he had the exhilarating sensation of somehow floating in the black void between planets with nothing there but shadow and stars. He looked up into the diamond-dusted heavens and sighed.

"Christ, Daniel, it's so beautiful."

Daniel stood at Jade's side and paused to admire the sky with him. He placed a paternal arm around Jade's shoulders.

"James Joyce once described the night sky as a 'heaventree of stars hung with humid nightblue fruit,' " he said softly to Jade. "I've not yet heard it put better."

They watched the sky in silence until Jade suddenly gasped "Look!" his finger raised to the southern sky. A fireball streaked majestically across the firmament, golden and furred with sparks. And then, as suddenly as it had appeared, it vanished.

"Did you see it?" Jade asked eagerly. "Did you see it? I've never seen such a sight in the heavens before. It was so beautiful and fiery." Suddenly Jade's voice was tinged with concern. "Was it some sort of portent, Daniel?"

"I've found in the heavens and upon the earth things that inspire awe, things of great beauty, things that exemplify the imposition of order upon chaos. But never portents," replied Daniel. "Our minds extract knowledge from the universe dynamically. To wait upon the season of a comet or the special rising of a star for wisdom is a falsely alluring path." The old man turned from the vista of stars and started up a rock-strewn slope deeper into the mountain shadows, the silhouette of his staff thrusting in and out of the starry backdrop. Jade followed behind him, feeling for handholds. Daniel's voice rose out of the shadows, vaporous yet threaded with perplexity: "But tonight we'll both begin to see the ways of the universe with freshly opened eyes. There may be more to fireballs than even I imagine."

The climb upward was treacherous, especially in the dark. More than once Jade felt a stony foothold give way beneath him and heard rocks clatter and thump their way off the edge of the cliff. Yet Daniel's alacrity and encouragement kept Jade from fear. The old man climbed steadily up, pressed close to the mountain, unerring as a suckling hungry for a nipple. At last they pulled themselves onto a rock ledge and sat down facing each other, their legs lotused beneath them. Between them was a wooden bowl of water.

"To understand the force within you," said Daniel, "to learn the wisdom of its control, requires that you become aware of the matrix and texture of the universe in its mirrored and faceted forms. An act of submission, really. Like a fisherman with a net, you must cast your mind out to the far reaches of the macrocosm and deep within you to the microcosm and then be pliant and observe. Your thoughts must be silent, your will must be empty, your eyes must be focussed and clear. Never look to the power itself, for then you will be overwhelmed and its use will be lost to you forever. Now, take my staff."

Daniel placed his staff across Jade's knees. Jade gripped it with one hand at either end, feeling again that electric tingle pulsing across the surface of his palms. He squeezed the staff more tightly and the tingling became more intense.

"Look into the surface of the water," Daniel commanded. "Tell me what you see."

Jade stared down into the bowl. "I see the stars reflected in the water."

"Triangulate your vision. Look with your right eye, your left eye, and with that mystic third eye I've shown you how to use. Concentrate and look deeply within the surface of the water. Tell me what you see."

Jade stared more intensely. His breathing slowed, fading to dove's breath. The energy from Daniel's staff began to rise from his fingertips to his brain. "I see . . . the stars . . . still . . . the stars . . ."

Slowly the surface of the water began to swell. The reflection of the stars grew larger and larger, the stars themselves swelling, drawing farther apart from each other, engulfing his field of vision, the bowl of water becoming like unto a lake, the heavens sparkling beneath him.

Jade spoke to Daniel, yet he knew his voice was silent.

[the stars . . . i'm sinking into the stars . . . sucking me to them . . . a comet . . . like a comet . . .]

"Tell me what you see."

As the pulsations from the staff swirled through his brain, Jade felt as if he were floating face down on the surface of the water, staring at the swelling vision of the heavens. Jade's mind reeled dizzily. Then, a sudden downward plunge among the stars, the plastic press of an invisible membrane upon his cheeks and hands, a bursting plunge into cool darkness.

"Tell me what you see."

[into the water . . . flying past the stars . . . vast distances, vast seas of nothingness . . . gentle press of dust across my skin . . . winds . . . gentle winds from the suns . . .]

Jade plummeted through the galaxy, eyes impossibly wide, his skin chill with the void. Star upon star rushed past him, some ringed with dark planets, some in eternal *pas de deux* with a flaming companion, some casting sterile fires upon vacant emptiness . . .

[nothing moves . . . too fast . . . frightened . . . too fast to see movement . . . balls of colored fire . . . immobile . . . drawing me faster . . . starflames frozen in their outward thrust and curl . . . too fast . . . too fast . . .]

"Tell me what you see."

Jade plummeted through clouds of magenta gas and black dust, thick and fiery against his cheeks. Star clusters rose before him, burst like skyrockets into a canopy of a million flaming suns, then disappeared into the dark vastness far behind him.

As the multitude of stars rose up before him and parted from his path, Jade saw a single point of reddish light shimmering directly before him.

[my god a giant sun . . . falling into a giant sun . . . not swerving . . . not swerving . . . closer . . . red glare like hot metal . . . smell of ions like seared blood . . . falling . . .]

The ether around the star churned in hot waves of energy. Jade flushed in the glare and heat, expanding like heady cosmic fumes, fading, dissipating into the inferno of the star.

"Tell me what you see."

[pillars of flame a million miles high . . . pulling me . . . faster . . . much too fast . . . they dance on the oil-slick surface of the internal fires . . . help me . . . help me . . .]

"Tell me what you see."

Jade's swollen and ghostly shade plunged into the body

of the star. It emerged unabated on the other side, trailing scintillas of starglow.

And then his spirit froze in terror. A jet black stain in space, a sinister blotch in the fabric of the universe, loomed before him, blotting out the distant light of galaxies.

A black hole.

[dizzy . . . spinning . . . furious blurs of light surrounding me . . . catching up to sundust and stray planets caught eons ago . . . faster . . . tumbling . . . faster than light yet unmoved . . . a bend in space and time . . . coming apart . . . i'm coming apart . . .]

"Tell me what you see. What do you see at the center?"

[spinning . . . darkness . . . coming apart . . . coming apart . . . coming apart . . .]

"Focus on the center. Tell me what you see."

[trying . . . trying . . . hard . . . a glimmer of light . . . reflection . . . light skimming upon water . . . a pool of water shrouded in night . . .]

Jade focussed on the central shine of light and was hurled into its midst. An instant of blaze and glare and he burst through an invisible membrane, a cacophony of exploding atoms shrill in protest . . .

Jade's eyes blinked, staring down into a bowl of water in which the night sky was reflected. His face was ashen and his heart pounded in his chest. His limbs were trembling uncontrollably. On one bent knee Daniel was stroking his hair and his pale cheeks. "You've come through it," he soothed, "it's over for now, all over."

Jade looked up into Daniel's face like a pleading child. The old man was smiling.

When Elizabeth awoke, the interior of the cabin was awash with sunlight. It was the rigors of the climb up the mountain that had kept her asleep so late but it wasn't the sunlight that had awakened her. She quickly turned to Jade's sleeping bag from which sounds of thrashing and groaning emerged, as if Jade were in the throes of a nightmare.

She crawled quickly to his side and found him flat on

his stomach clutching the fabric of the sleeping bag tightly in both fists, his legs shifting and squirming violently, his forehead drenched with sweat. He was mumbling in his sleep, groaning softly and gasping in desperation. Suddenly he started to thrash about even more wildly until Elizabeth grabbed him by the shoulders to shake him awake.

"Jade! Jade!" she cried out. "Wake up! You're dreaming!"

In response to her vigorous shaking, Jade's head turtled upward in bewilderment. His eyes snapped open, staring wildly around the room. Elizabeth gasped as his face turned toward her; she fell backward with a violent start upon Beverly's sleeping bag.

"Elizabeth!" Beverly shouted, awakened by her lover's fall. "What's the matter?"

"Look! Look quickly at Jade!"

Beverly stared through sleepy eyes, straining to focus. "O my God!" she exclaimed, grabbing tightly onto Elizabeth's arm.

Jade's eyes were glowing like floodlit emeralds.

"What in God's name has happened to him?" Beverly whispered.

"I don't know. It must be some sort of reaction from whatever went on last night between him and Daniel."

The two women stared in wide-eyed silence. Then Jade's eyes began to blink and the glow faded very slowly.

"He's waking up now," said Elizabeth. "His eyes seem to be returning to normal." She waited for the glow to fade completely, then she crept a little closer to Jade, eyeing his face cautiously. He rubbed his tired eyes with his hands.

"Are . . . are you okay, Jade?" she asked, her voice urgent.

"Yeah . . . yeah, I'm okay." He sounded completely wasted. "What's the matter? What happened?"

"You were having a . . . a nightmare. I tried to wake you . . ." Her voice trailed off to a whisper as she kept staring at him.

"Yeah . . . a nightmare. I suppose you could call it a review of last night's lesson." Jade shook his head wearily, dabbing his forehead with a bit of his T-shirt, swallowing drily. "I hope to God that every night isn't going to be the same."

"What exactly happened last night?" asked Elizabeth, her eyes bright with curiosity and concern.

"Let me save the story for later. Right now I'm too dizzy to think straight."

Suddenly two hands were thrust in front of Jade bearing a cup of cold water. Jade looked up in surprise.

"Thank you, Beverly," he said, his tired voice edged with surprise. "Thank you very much." He sucked the cold water greedily down his throat.

"Shall we tell him about his eyes?" Beverly whispered to Elizabeth.

There was a lengthy pause before Elizabeth answered. "No," she said, "don't say anything about it. We should speak to Daniel first. I don't think Jade could explain it anyway. He'd only be more confused."

Jade placed his empty cup next to him on the floor.

"More?" asked Beverly.

"No, no, thank you," he said, a feeble smile crossing his face. "I'm okay now. I'm starting to mellow out. Whew." He leaned against the wall, tousling his hair with his hand. "Tell me, Elizabeth, do you think you could read my mind about last night? It would certainly save me a lot of trouble trying to figure out how to put it all into words."

"Don't think I haven't tried," she answered. "Ever since I met you I've been trying to probe your thoughts. But I can't do it. O, I get a lot of vibrations about you, but nothing directly from you. Some . . . some energy from within you is shielding you like armor plate."

"Did you . . . learn anything last night?" asked Beverly.

"I hope so. I'd hate to have to repeat that same lesson over again. It was all so . . . so very bizarre, so real. I felt like my mind was being taken from me and flung out to the end of the galaxy. I had to learn to hang on to my mind, not let it fly away from me completely." Jade shut his eyes tightly in concentration. "That's something, I suppose. But . . . but there was something else. It was like I was learning to focus . . . yeah, I learned to focus my mind, to pinpoint where I was travelling. It was kind of like gymnastics: you can study all the charts showing you how to do a certain move, but until your muscles have felt you doing that move properly, you've learned nothing. Last night I was forced to direct my mind like it was some sort of radio-operated toy plane. I had to strain and focus until I got it right."

Jade leaned forward to his rapt listeners, trying to share with them the fruits of his experience as completely as he could. "I can't really sort out all the details right now. Only in time . . . well, anyway, let me just say that in order to get back from wherever the hell I was, I had to sort of nose-dive into this shining light. I know it sounds ridiculous, but let me tell you that last night it was the most important thing in this world to me to be able to dive into that light and get the hell back home. I suppose the closest analogy I can make is when you try to focus on an object or an idea in order to keep yourself from flipping out on acid. Slowly you wean yourself from the colors and the textures and the molasses-like grip of distorted time and float back down to earth gradually. Well anyway, as far as I know, I saw the light, I focussed, and I plunged right in. When I came out of my . . . my trance, I felt like the whole experience had taken only a few minutes, in spite of my heavy breathing and physical agitation."

Jade's eyes drifted dreamily as he tried to piece together the scattered fragments of the experience. "But we were up there for hours. Daniel tells me I kept trying to hit that light and that I kept missing. I had to keep trying, over and over again. Finally, I scored. I felt what it was like to . . . to aim correctly, to force my will on my disembodied, floating consciousness. No mean feat, believe me. I suppose if I'm called upon to do the same thing a second time, it'll be a lot easier. So I guess I learned something."

"But what if you hadn't been able to hit that light?" asked Beverly. "No matter how hard you tried."

Jade leaned back against the wall, his eyes shut, an ironic smile playing upon his lips.

"I suppose I'd still be up there," he replied.

26

THE sun was high in the clear sky and Mt. Marcy sparkled. The pine trees glowed with a deep green luster, flecks of mica in the rocks blazed and shifted with each step Jade took, and the mountain birds soared over the rills and valleys far below them, their feathers gleaming richly in the sun.

The last tremors of terror had just begun to fade from Jade's memory of his nightmare. The fragrant air and the sun were dissipating the somber vapors that clouded his mind. But a new, more real terror began to swell within him, a daylight terror that he couldn't dismiss as the by-product of a dreamy illusion. He needed desperately to escape.

He raced a few hundred yards down the slope to a forest grotto ringed by tall pines. He burst through the scrub brush, past saplings and tall ferns, and threw himself at length upon a bed of cool moss. His heart was racing and his lungs heaved. His cheeks were wet with tears.

Blades of golden sunlight filtered through the leaves, swarming with tiny flies and spider webs. Once he'd brushed his eyes clear with the back of his hand, Jade watched the motes of life whirligig throughout the grotto. A great bitterness swelled within him.

"O God," he moaned, tears springing anew to his

cheeks, "why the fuck was I made to be a man?" He slammed a heavy fist into the soft moss beneath him. "Goddamn bugs float around like they don't have a care in the fucking world. They don't worry about how death'll creep up on them. They don't even know what a bird is until they're down its goddamn throat!" He suddenly rose to his knees and raised both fists high above his head, shaking them at the sky. "Why me, man?" he shouted, his angry voice muffled by the leaves and moss. "WHY THE FUCK ME?"

He fell limply backward on the moss, his eyes shut. "I don't want to die . . ." he moaned softly, his head rolling from side to side, "I don't want to die . . ." From the depths of the forest a warbler shrilled throatily, its liquid cry risen above all the other voices of the mountain. "And I don't want to lose my mind . . . not my mind . . ."

Jade rose up on his elbows and looked around, somewhat calmed by his flood of tears. "He's got me flipping out like some goddamn acid freak," he muttered. "My mind flying outside of my skull like that . . . like a fucking cue ball bouncing off planets. That's my mind he's playing with, man! Shit!" He kicked a small rock with his heel and watched it tumble down the slight incline into the midst of a patch of scrub. "It's that tea of his, I bet. Makes you go crazy . . . Ah, shit, it's not the goddamn tea! I wish I knew just what the fuck it is but it's not the tea. It's not his fault. The cops, those bodies, Adrienne's damn old man . . . Fucking psychopath!" He rolled onto his stomach twisting blades of grass around his fingers. "A fine mess this is . . . a monster on one side of me and lunacy on the other. Scylla and Charybdis."

Jade stood up and strolled negligently through the underbrush, watching the insects and the wild flowers and the leaves bending in the wind. "Nobody gives a good goddamn, either," he said to himself. "So what if the fucking universe falls apart? I should put my balls under the cleaver so that five days after I'm a hero some asshole'll start a nuclear war and blow this planet to smithereens anyway!" He stooped suddenly, staring down at a large green praying mantis. It stared back at Jade with stony, faceted eyes, its antennae wiggling furiously. "O, so you don't think I'm altruistic enough," he said to the bug. "I've got a selfish, limited outlook, you say? Well, fuck you then!" He wandered away from the mantis, its slender feelers still wiggling. "I don't mind being a nice guy . . . put myself out once in a while . . . for my friends. But why should I be the one . . . I mean, all this, monsters, head trips . . . Shit!"

He came upon a thick branch that had recently fallen to the forest floor. He picked it up, hefting it, estimating its greenness, then leaned one end of it upon a rock. Holding the other end in his left hand, he raised his right high above his head and then snapped it down swiftly upon the center of the thick branch, splitting it with a piercing crack. "That's more like it! Get together with a few of those cops and bust into that chateau place or whatever the hell it is and drag her out with us. Not fuck around here on top of a mountain. That I can handle."

Suddenly a flash of bright orange flew past Jade's face and landed on the bark of an immense, aged pine. He jumped, following its path with startled eyes. "Shit!" he exclaimed. "Will you look at that!"

He recognized it as an immature form of salamander called a red eft. It was already its adult size and shape but its skin was one soft mass of dayglow orange. Pressed against the full bark of the tall tree, it stuck out like a sore thumb. "You can jump like a sonofabitch, can't you!" Jade said to it, walking up to the tree. The eft froze where it landed, feeling Jade's vibrations travel up the tree trunk as he walked closer. It didn't move.

"Pretty little thing," he said smiling. He leaned over the eft, placing one hand on either side of it against the bark of the tree. All of a sudden an irresistible dizziness swept over him, buckling his knees and making his vision swim. Tingling pulses flowed from the great tree into his hands, swirling his brain with energy as he kneeled upon a loop of root at the tree's base.

Jade gazed upward with wonder. Filaments of spider-silk, barely visible, blossomed from the tree and rose into the heavens. Strand upon strand, weaving, curling, drawing the height of the great tree upward, far into the sky, past the clouds, the nascent moon, the spinning planets. And Jade felt a counterthrust of growth digging deep into the earth, winding ghostly roots through tables of rock, through hidden underground springs, deep, deep into the fiery bowels of the earth. The heavens seemed to darken and the stars shone like silver balls in what should have been the afternoon sky. Jade stared upward, captivated by the immense phantom tree that brushed its upper branches upon nebulae and wheeling galaxies, his brain wrenched and tickled by the pulse of energy.

"Ygdrasil!" said a voice from behind Jade.

"What!" gasped Jade, startled, his hands flying off the tree trunk. As suddenly as the vision appeared, it ceased. The phantom limbs, the ghostly roots, the celestial spheres and suns . . . all faded into ordinary sunshine and moist, fragrant earth. "It's you!"

Daniel smiled. "I'm sorry I frightened you. I thought you heard me coming."

"I . . . I was distracted." Jade bent a wary eye to Daniel. "Did you . . ."

"I saw. It was Ygdrasil, the Tree of Life. At least that's what the Norse called it. It's been known by a variety of names."

"Then . . . then it was real?"

"Let's simply say you now have the power to see it. Whenever you wish. As for whether or not it's real . . . well, it's as real as any of the other illusory forms in which matter is perceived by us."

Daniel stepped closer to Jade and wiped the wetness from his eyes with a gentle finger. "Come, walk with me a bit." He placed his arm around Jade's shoulders. They stepped gingerly away from the tree and wandered around the grotto.

"Where'd you come from?" Jade asked in bewilderment.

"I've been here all along. You spoke to me but you didn't know me."

"What's that supposed to mean?"

Daniel smiled. "Never mind, Jade, it's not important. What is important is that you understand what you've just seen. I know how confused and frightened you are. If the working of the universe were left in my hands, I never would've involved you in this . . . this undertaking, nor anyone else. But it's ordained that I not handle it alone. I can't. And it hurts me more deeply than you'll ever know to see you suffer like this."

They came upon a log fallen near some slender saplings. Butterflies fluttered among the foliage, bright yellow and white and black streaked with red. They sat down on the log, Daniel resting his hands upon the head of his staff, his white hair and beard mottled with sunlight.

"You've just discovered for yourself one aspect of your powers," he began. "The ability to see beyond illusion, beyond what we've been trained by our culture to recognize as truth. When you seek them again, the visions will come to you as symbols or metaphors of a concept, and that concept is Truth. It's so difficult to put into words, my son. It's important that you feel truth, that you become aware of reality deep inside you, and not just remain a poor interpreter of truth through poetic strings of words." Daniel drew his fingers through his long white hair, frowning. "How shall I tell you? When I've finished guiding you through to the fullness of your powers, we'll then be able to communicate with each other in the most ideal manner, without words, without gestures. You'll simply understand me, and I shall understand you. Like when you touched that tree. Suddenly you saw that that ordinary tree was, in reality, a manifestation of the entire universe. That it was linked by root and branch to the depths of the earth and the outermost fringes of the universe. And so are all things: the tiniest creatures that crawl upon the earth and the most majestic stars spinning stately in the heavens. I could have told you the same thing in words, like a thousand philosophers and mystics before me, but you possess the power to see reality without words, without interpreters.

"Last night on the mountain I wanted you to see two things: I wanted you to experience the essence of the universe, what it really is way out there in the night sky, so that you'd understand just what it is that's facing destruction; secondly, I wanted you to learn to use the power of vision you now possess, learn to control it and to be able to return at will from the grip of Truth to the world of illusion, which is your cultural heritage and within which you must function. It was a struggle last night. I almost lost you. But your will triumphed in the end, as I hope it will continue to do."

"And if my will hadn't been strong enough?"

"Like Phaeton in the chariot of the sun, you would've been lost, destroyed by the sheer magnitude of your own power and vision. But you weren't. And you won't be, not if you understand just what it is that you are seeing."

"But why did that . . . that tree suddenly spring up like that out of nowhere? I wasn't willing anything to happen. I was just looking at a goddamn lizard."

"That's all you were aware of at the moment," said Daniel, amused. "But you know what was really troubling you. Helplessness. Isolation. The fact that you've been told to put your life on the line for a cause nobody else but me believes in or understands. You are facing a death that seems to you without purpose. That's what was really inside of you when you touched that tree and that's the dilemma our vision resolved. You saw with your own eyes how inextricably linked all of creation is, from top to bottom and side to side. If you and that . . . that beast unite, then all is lost. In that one great vision, the universe was pleading with you to save it."

Jade cupped his head between his palms, fuming with frustration. "You keep saying that!" he shouted. "You keep telling me how important it is that I risk my life by encountering and somehow defeating that other . . . thing! But you don't say how, Daniel. You don't say how! If I don't go after it, it'll come and get me. If I do go after it, it'll . . . it'll 'unite' with me and the whole blasted deal's shot to hell anyway! What am I supposed to do?"

Daniel's face looked somberly into Jade's pleading eyes. "I can't tell you what you're supposed to do. It's not in my power. What I can tell you is that 'doing' isn't as important as 'knowing' or 'being aware' or 'understanding.' Sure, we could grab some guns and storm Mercadante's chateau with police or commandos at our side and try to rescue your friend. That would be 'doing' something. That's the way Mercadante's mind works, certainly: violence, bloodshed, destruction. But it would be pointless. Futile." The old man gently stroked Jade's cheek, his aged eyes, azure as the sky, brimming with tears. "My last hope is to teach you, to show you, to make you understand, my son. And then, when the time is ripe, you'll know what to do. The 'understanding' must come first."

Daniel sat lotus-legged on the ledge facing Jade. "Tonight there is no bowl of water to propel your vision outward. Tonight you will learn to look within yourself. You will close your eyes, yet there will be vision. You will see what few men have ever seen before, and none in precisely the same way. Close your eyes and triangulate your vision; focus on your third eye."

Jade took a deep breath and closed his eyes. He felt Daniel place the staff on his lap and Jade grasped each end eagerly, smiling at the tingling that agitated his palms.

"Focus on your third eye in that inner darkness. Turn your vision into a beacon that will illuminate the vistas of your mind. There is one within you who would help. Only after you've seen and spoken to him may you return."

Jade's breathing became ever more slow and shallow and he felt himself descending into darkness. He floated slowly downward, jostled like a leaf, rocked to and fro in his descent. He strained to focus on that inner, third eye, yet the intensity of concentration needed for the task was achieved far more easily than the night before. It seemed that only moments after his concerted efforts began, a light did, indeed, appear within his mind, illuminating a surreal landscape.

"Tell me what you see."

[a flat, featureless plain striped in lines of latitude . . . the sky is black, blacker than a thunderhead . . . yet a glow, light without a source . . . i concentrate and the glow intensifies . . . i relax and the glow diminishes . . . i control the glow . . . i control the glow . . .]

"Center the glow on your third eye. Concentrate." A sudden summer squall wafted billowy black clouds in front of the stars. Daniel's white wizard's hair and beard swirled in the rising wind. "Tell me what you see."

[the glow spins . . . trapped . . . a cold sun . . . spinning . . . blurred . . .]

"Stop the spinning of the sun. Steady it. Slowly. Tell me what you see."

The spinning glow stopped before Jade's inner gaze, a vacant triangle of cold light. It was poised like the apex of an invisible pyramid above the vacant plain. Far in the distance were shadowy mountains, darker shadows beneath a dark and ominous sky.

Jade brought his inner vision in direct line with the floating triangle and he was smitten by a great spinning dizziness. The triangle was sucking him into itself, spinning forward, base over point. Jade's hands tightened upon the staff and his palms became cold and sweaty.

[a light within . . . spinning . . . bright . . . brighter than the heavy sky . . . brighter than the dull glow of the plain . . . a desert . . . mountains far away . . . spinning . . . sucked into the center of the triangle . . . the light . . .]

In an instant the landscape was obliterated by the magnitude of the triangle and Jade felt himself fall into the spinning brightness. He felt dizzy, nauseous, and terrified. And then, in a flash, he realized what the spinning light had become.

[memory . . . i'm watching my mind search for memories . . . closer to the spinning light it slows . . . images . . . flipping past impossibly fast . . . one after another . . . searching . . . a train of thought i dive in . . . bright images . . . suck me until the right one . . . so bright . . . so quick . . . then i withdraw . . .]

The wind rose, hurling stones precipitously off the rock ledge. Daniel stared into Jade's face: "Tell me what you see."

The flipping images of Jade's searching memory were akin to a child's cartoon book made by flipping the pages of a pad of paper. Each image led into rolling drums of newer images, classified, organized, chains upon chains of related images, brightly glowing, dizzying, hypnotic.

[fascinated . . . thoughts upon thought . . . fall in, keep falling . . . keep falling . . . the way memory works . . . circles and chains . . . spinning . . . easy to let go . . . not escape . . . follow my thoughts upon thoughts to the end . . . all the way . . . no, mustn't . . . all the way . . . no, mustn't . . . too fascinating . . . no, mustn't . . .]

"Withdraw, Jade. Tell me what you see."

[no, mustn't . . . all the way . . . no, mustn't . . . fascinating . . . all the way . . .]

"Withdraw, Jade. Tell me what you see."

With a stupendous effort of will, Jade hurled himself from the spinning center of the triangle. The bright lights dimmed with distance, the succession of images blurred into one continuous dull glow, and the triangle returned to where it had been poised above the dark, surreal desert.

In the distance, as if walking slowly from the far mountains and buttes, a black shade approached.

[a creature . . . drawing closer . . . black as the sky . . . tall . . . lanky . . . creature of smoke . . . vapor . . . its eyes . . . its eyes . . . drawing closer . . . eyes of mirrors . . .]

The shade approached, its hands clasped together.

YOU CALL UPON ME. AGAIN. AT LAST YOU DARE TO LOOK UPON MY ESSENCE. WHAT DO YOU WISH?

[my god . . . don't know what . . . don't know . . .]

A TASK FIRST. THEN YOU WILL KNOW.

The shade unclasped its hands and presented them, palms upward, to Jade's vision. On the right palm a square was inscribed. On the left palm, a circle.

THESE FORMS MUST BE UNITED, ONLY YOU CAN DO SO. HELP ME.

[impossible . . . a circle . . . a square . . . don't know . . . makes no sense . . . don't know . . .]

ONLY YOU CAN DO SO. HELP ME. YOURS IS THE POWER. HELP ME.

Wild winds whipped the ledge of rock. Billows of black cloud shuttered the risen moon, a liquid shimmer of silver intruding around their upper edges. Daniel stared into the face of the man before him, his fists pressed harshly into the surface of the ledge to hold himself steady against the wind. Jade's eyes were tormented flames, tightly closed, his hands fiercely gripping the old man's staff, his forehead bathed in sweat despite the frigid winds.

Within the dark landscape of his mind, Jade saw his

own hands emerge and cup within them the hands of the shrouded figure with mirror eyes. The figure's long, thin fingers were cold as the sparkle of stars in the winter. Jade pressed the figure's cold palms together, the circle tightly against the square, and endowed them with the warmth of his own living substance. Then his hands withdrew.

IT IS DONE.

The shrouded figure opened its palms. In place of the circle and the square an apple-like sphere floated delicately above the figure's palms, glowing a soft, lustrous blue. The figure's eyes sparkled resplendently.

NIGHTBLUE FRUIT. IT IS DONE. WHAT DO YOU WISH?

Jade felt his thoughts go lank with the query. Then suddenly:

[the power . . . i want to know . . .]

THE POWER IS NOW YOURS. BY WILL. BY DEED. YOU WILL BE SHOWN.

The shrouded figure brought its mirrored eyes close to Jade's inner vision. Jade saw reflected within them his own eyes, greenish purple, glinting with a harsh metallic cast in the cold light of the surreal landscape. Suddenly, the image of his eyes flared like burning emeralds, swirling with colors, specters of green and yellow and amethyst, his own eyes, aflame like those of a demon.

And Jade knew. A tingle of electric warmth shivered his spine.

His eyes snapped open. Daniel was staring with furious intensity into Jade's face, his long white hair and beard whipped by wild winds. Then his stony face relaxed.

"Come, my son. It's time that we returned to the cabin."

27

"I suppose that the best analogy I can come up with," Jade explained to Elizabeth and Beverly the next morning as they sat together on the slope, "is the training of a Zen monk. Unlike Western students of metaphysics, they aren't lectured to or dogmatized. They're taught to apprehend the truths that lie beyond all ritual and philosophy. It's that apprehension he's trying to teach me to master."

The women were silent, letting the import of Jade's words sink in. At last, Beverly said, "We saw your eyes like that the other morning. When you were having your nightmare."

Jade smiled. "I can imagine how shocked you must've been. When I saw them myself, I almost flipped out."

"But . . . but then you understood?" asked Elizabeth.

"Some, I suppose. I don't know how much is left for me to apprehend. But at least I'm not frightened like I was."

"Do you feel any . . . wiser?" asked Beverly, worried that her question sounded stupid.

"I feel as if I'm looking at the world through different eyes, that's for sure. I respect the mechanism of the universe far more than before. I find it both eminently simple and illuminating, as well as extraordinarily fascinating and complex. A contradiction, I know, but that's how it is nonetheless. Wiser, though?" His eyes drifted off to some distant cloud. "Let's just say I'm far more confident now that, when the time comes, I'll know what I must do."

"And what does Daniel do while you're in the trance?" asked Elizabeth.

"He's a foxy one, that Daniel," Jade answered, smiling. "Slippery as an eel. He takes on more forms than Proteus." He leaned closer to both women, lowering his voice confidentially. "When I had that vision in the forest, the vision of the tree, Daniel was there before me. He said I spoke to him but I didn't know it. As God is my witness, I spoke to only three things in that grotto: a praying mantis, a salamander, and myself. Of those three, I can account for only one with assurance: myself. That means one of the other two . . ."

"Jesus!" breathed Beverly.

"Maybe he was both of them," offered Elizabeth.

"That could well be," Jade said, reflecting. "But beyond that, I've got a feeling that the dark figure which appeared before me last night was also Daniel. Yet it was as much a part of myself as my intestines, as well as an aspect of the power that's caught inside me. All three entities merged into one."

"Daniel—the figure you saw in your mind," mused Elizabeth. "What an idea . . ."

That night, Daniel and Jade fought their way up to the rock ledge against mighty winds which were still rising. Both men were wrapped tightly in their cloaks, lotused on the ledge, facing each other; yet they could barely see each other in the darkness of the descending thunderheads. From far in the west the clouds cascaded like ink through the clear mountain air. No stars, no moonglow, no portentous meteors: just black heavy clouds and the distant rumbling of thunder.

"Daniel!" Jade called out, raising his voice above the wind. "The storm . . . shouldn't we come back . . ."

"Not enough time!" Daniel retorted. "We must finish tonight. Mercadante's almost ready with the . . . creature!"

He looked out to the west at the shimmer of sheet lightning that was silhouetting the distant mountains, his hair twining and slithering in the wind like Medusa's deadly locks. For an instant Jade's blood chilled, terrified by the man sitting before him, grown a sinister stranger in the darkness of the approaching storm. Daniel sensed his terror and leaned forward to gently press Jade's knee with a comforting hand.

"Don't be afraid, my son," he soothed. "Tonight your training will be over. You've seen the macrocosm of the heavens and the microcosm of your mind. There's but death left to conquer. Tonight."

"Death! I don't understand . . ."

"Tonight you'll go to a realm I've never had the power to survey. Tonight the student shall become the master . . ." A blast of wind howled like a mournful dog, sucking them dangerously by their cloaks, teasing them toward the edge of the cliff. They leaned against the pull of the wind, silent and straining until the gust passed. Jade gripped the rock beneath him, his knuckles white.

"I must warn you," Daniel continued in the sudden silence after the wind, "I must warn you about the lure of death. It has its beauty and its season. But you must return! There is the mission . . ."

Jade looked upward at the clouds. A network of cumulus shadows formed a web-like skeletal hand that pointed down at them. Another gust of wind and the jade unicorn around his neck blew up into the air, spinning at the end of its chain.

"Learn, Jade," Daniel called out, "learn, become aware, but remember the mission! Now close your eyes tightly and concentrate . . ."

Jade shut his eyes and suddenly everything was silent. His mind's eye saw no clouds or sheets of lightning: just clear mountain skies and masses of sparkling stars. No wind, no whipping, frigid air, no rumbling thunder. The tranquility of his vision made Jade relax, the tension draining from his muscles. His breathing slowed, he felt his thoughts begin to float upward against the inside of his skull, and his mouth bowed into a serene smile.

Daniel deliberately withheld from Jade his staff.

Suddenly a strange chant, a throaty, rumbling chant

pervaded Jade's consciousness. Its cadence was hypnotic, a mantra throbbing throughout the sea of stars, elongated, rhythmic, somehow joyous. An amorphous core detached itself from the center of Jade's being and rose like a vapor to float upon the surface of his mind. It sprayed trailing plume-jets outward upon the rising rhythm of the chant, curling around it tenaciously, rising, meteoric, yet unhastened and unmoved.

Without warning, the stars with one accord blinked out.

"Tell me what you see!"

Jade floated, serene, wondering, staring about the blackness, awaiting something marvellous, eager, without fear. And seemingly far, ever farther in the blackness, the undulating serpent of the chant faded.

An endless moment of darkness and thick silence, a moment lodged like a worm between the fleshy pulses of time, poised:

A burst and splash of impossible swirling colors and a pulsating electric hum:

"Tell me what you see!"

[the glory of it . . . spinning . . . the mass of stars . . . again . . . circling . . . circling . . . daniel . . . daniel . . . the beauty . . .]

Glee! parabolas of color, twisting and squirming, a ballet, purple, red, orange, perfect colors, swaying, nodding with the throb and electric hum, strangely pleasant, a perfection of sound and color and swaying form:

[bend for me . . . genii risen from lamps and bottles . . . dancing . . . nodding . . . quivering . . . perfect energies . . . perfect unison . . . such bliss . . .]

Jade marvelled at the vision, the dancing forms, the bright and perfect colors, wondering, smiling, nodding like a slave to an opium ecstasy.

Forms, parabolas splitting, vibrating, shimmering into thousands, mutating into squares, cubes, triangles, an infinity of forms and perfect angles, blending, quivering, dancing, slowly, lingering:

[slow . . . flowing on the hum . . . the forms and shapes spinning . . . i'm floating . . . spinning in the middle of the universe . . . the universe . . . not like the other . . . the stars . . . the darkness . . . the clouds of dust . . . no . . . not that . . . a river of jewels . . . spinning . . .

no sense of motion yet spinning . . . the stars swirl . . . rotate . . . i'm floating in space with the forms . . . staring at the forms . . . an infant bounced and spun by invisible hands . . .]

Jade blinked his eyes against new colors, indescribable, the invisible spectrum made visible, burning purples, reds, and ochres that bloated and popped with the husky throb of the electric sound, new forms arising in unison with the hum, the hum that bound it all together, orchestrating, transforming.

"Tell me what you see!"

[fascinated . . . can't turn away my eyes . . . floating . . . my brain floats disembodied . . . see all . . . all directions . . . up and down . . . behind and ahead . . . see all simultaneously . . . fascinated . . . can't turn my eyes from it . . . so beautiful . . .]

Slowing, the sharp lines faded into slow-swelling rainbow clouds, drifting spectra wrenched into diffusion, pastel ghosts floating between the galaxies, slowing, the electric music weaving amidst the drifting colors, blending them:

[i anticipate the changes . . . it's my will . . . no more of your world . . . no more of your world . . . what was sharp and linear becomes a rainbow . . . ghostly . . . drifting . . . my mind sucks it in . . . greedy . . . hungry . . . i will the beauty . . . i will it daniel . . . i will it and it's so beautiful . . .]

Daniel's lips still worked with his now silent chant, his eyes heavy-lidded yet intent upon Jade's eyes. Storm winds whipped viciously against the narrow rock ledge, dousing the two men with needle shreds of rain. Jade's eyes snapped open, glowing like fiery emeralds. The smile never left his face.

"I'm losing him," thought Daniel bitterly. "It's too soon . . . too sudden . . . damn the haste!"

Great hexagons and beehives and spinning mandalas, collapsing, swelling, throbbing with the music, shimmering, holograms floating in the velvet black of space, shivering into multiple images as they turn, round and round, perfect colors, floating and spinning with the electric music, the crackling hum:

[death then . . . so this is the great terror . . . con-

357

template this for all eternity . . . if i'd only known . . .
all the terrors gone . . . the colors teach . . . the forms
teach . . . Harmony . . . Virtue . . . i see . . . i know
the ideals . . . plato's ideals spinning . . . weaving before
my eyes . . . such is death . . . no longer of your
world . . . a better world before me . . . a better
world . . .]

"Focus, Jade! Direct your will to me! To me, Jade! To
me!"

Jade stared in rapture at a square of golden light that
rotated around its center leaving a trail of residual images
until the perimeter of the spinning figure was a perfect
circle. The spinning vision splashed and danced with the
ethereal music.

[the color of gravity . . . the vision of light as particle
and wave . . . a rainbow of cosmic rays . . . i see daniel
. . . i see so much . . . the way it was before time and
movement . . . before the polarities . . . i see . . .
i learn . . . i crave these visions . . . i crave . . . these
visions . . .]

Daniel stared intently at Jade's glowing eyes, his lips
still mouthing the chant, his thick-veined hands reaching
out from under his cloak and caressing the bizarre carved
forms of his staff.

"He'd been toughened but not enough," thought Daniel. "Perhaps it's impossible to possess that strength. No
one mind can resist . . . Damn! It's over then. I'll lose
him and it's all over. He's strong . . . impossibly strong
now that he's seen . . . yet he still couldn't resist enough."
His old, thick fingers traveled nervously up and down
his staff, concentrating his mental powers with the feel of
the wooden faces and forms, a tactile koan to his desperate, aged hands. "What sublime joy he's experiencing
. . . what I wouldn't give for just a glimpse of the marvels
he's enraptured by . . . just a glimpse. But he's not strong
enough . . . not enough . . ."

[what wisdom in this disembodied state . . . the freedom of consciousness after death . . . a feast for the
intellect . . . freedom . . . an orgasm of analogy and
vision . . . how foolish we are to fear death . . .]

A million points of light, like iridescent opals, bursts
and fragments of colors, floating in hypnotic immensity,

spinning, slowly at first, then faster with the hastening hum, a thrusting hum, deepening, throbbing, a thousand facets of a vast mandala that filled the universe with its beauty and its motion:

"Tell me what you see, Jade! For God's sake, send me your thoughts! Send them to me!"

[daniel . . . daniel . . . i'm learning death . . . these secrets open to us all when we die . . . no matter how stupid or confused we were before . . . no matter our rages and torments . . . so sweet is death . . . daniel . . . daniel . . . my love for you fades into laughter . . . I know you shall join me at the end . . . and i'll be like a jewel then . . . a swirling color . . . to please you . . .]

"No! No! It's not the time! There's the mission, Jade! Don't renounce the mission!"

[as i contemplate the universe . . . the colors . . . the shapes . . . the ideals . . . i contemplate myself . . . i am absolute form and color and harmony . . . i am what i see . . . i can forget now . . . the wisdom floods through me . . . i can forget all else . . .]

Daniel's eyes streamed tears from the frigid wind. He shut them tightly, his cheeks bitter with frost, his lips pale with fatigue. "Come back . . . come back . . . renounce your joy and come back . . . please, Jade, remember . . . only you can stop the disintegration . . . come back, Jade . . . don't abandon us . . . force yourself . . . you must . . . Jade . . . you must . . . come back!"

Far below the two men a solitary figure climbed the face of the mountain, defying the torturing winds and the freezing rain, clutching with thin white fingers the brutal shards of rock that were the only handholds. In spite of her weakened condition, Elizabeth pulled herself slowly, toehold by toehold, along the fragile path that led to the rock ledge on which the two men struggled against death. Daniel's desperate thoughts resounded like clarions in her mind. She was pressed up against the slick wet rock of the mountain-face, fearing to look behind her at the airy darkness. She feared that irrational leap, that plunge into the abyss which beckons when such immense heights are confronted. The winds beat against her legs and shoulders, drenching her with rain, trying to pull her from her precarious hold upon the face of the mountain. Her chest heaved with bloody coughs. But still she kept creeping upward, slowly, flaying her knees, her fingers and cheeks upon the sharp edges of the rocks.

The jade unicorn, hanging around Jade's neck, glowed suddenly with malice and mockery in its fiery eyes, deriding Daniel's impotence.

The old man rose to his feet, stumbling dangerously against the wind, and raised his staff high over his head. His long white hair and beard swirled violently in the savage wind, stinging his flesh and blinding his eyes. He stood stiff-legged and defiant against the raging backdrop of the storm. His head bent forward toward the mute, unseeing body of his disciple.

"You will return! . . . come back! Let my strength lead you . . . come back! pull yourself from its grip . . . come back! You will return!"

An immense bolt of lightning shattered the black storm with its brilliance like the skeletal hand of death. The mountain trembled with the roar of thunder. Daniel's upraised staff sparked and flashed like the eyes of its owner, furious in the midst of the swirling storm.

But suddenly Daniel shivered and was startled by the pull of a mind working in unison with his own. He turned behind him quickly and saw the death-pale face of Elizabeth as she struggled past the final few feet of crumbled rock, her eyes wide with terror and determination, her face and arms torn and bleeding. He moved to help her but she quickly waved him off.

"Don't stop pulling him back!" she shouted, trying to be heard above the fury of the storm. "I felt you calling him back! I felt him lost to you! Perhaps both of us . . ."

With a final mighty effort she heaved herself onto the ledge of rock. She looked up at the powerful old man with his swirling hair and his staff upraised in his arms and the agony written in his eyes, which shone with a pale, unearthly glow. Then she looked at Jade, still huddled beneath his cloak, his eyes on fire. The serene, peaceful smile never left his lips.

Then Daniel bellowed his throaty chant to the wind. Elizabeth joined her voice to Daniel's and the two focussed the power of both their minds upon Jade's inert body.

"He can't be made to return!" Daniel shouted to her. "We haven't the strength to bring him back against his will. No power in the universe can do that!"

"Then we've got to make him want to come back!" Elizabeth shouted in return. "We've got to make him remember what he is and where he comes from and what it is that he must do!"

She knelt on all fours, staring at Jade's passive form, her forehead creased with the agony of her concentration. Daniel continued his chant, growing ever more desperate and urgent, his staff glowing brighter, more intense, making of Jade's form a solid lump bathed in light and sharp shadow. The power of both their minds was united in a single profound beam of recall.

Solar flares and dancing cubes, tongues of sensuous flames flicking the rotating backdrop of stars, ghostforms of rainbowed angels nodding, the pulsating, electric hum grown to a roar, an ecstasy of contemplative form and harmony:

And then .. .

[darkness . . . no . . . the visions . . . growing dark . . . no . . . fading . . . a blindness . . . sudden . . . overwhelming . . . the visions . . . no . . . the music is still . . . silence . . . total darkness . . . where are the visions . . . where is the music . . . no . . . bring them back . . . come back . . . you can't take them from me . . . no . . . no . . . wait . . . wait . . . i remember now . . . now that the visions are gone . . . now in the silence . . . i remember . . . another time for the visions . . . i'll return . . . later . . . later . . . i'll return . . . at the proper time . . . yes . . . yes . . . i remember . . .]

Slowly Jade released his mind from its concentration. Once freed from the hypnotic rapture of the visions and the celestial music, the emerald glow faded from his eyes and his shoulders began to shiver with the cold. Suddenly his lungs heaved with the sharp mountain air and he began to tremble and shake the dizziness from his head.

Daniel fell forward, weeping, clutching Jade tightly to him, stroking his face and hair with gentle hands.

"She brought you back, my son! She risked her life to join us on the ledge because she knew you were lost and that I alone didn't have the power. She brought you back! You're back with us now, really back, I was so afraid, so very frightened. But thanks to Elizabeth . . ."

A sudden shriek startled both men. They turned to face the collapsed body of Elizabeth as it sprawled face forward in all its wretched pallor upon the cold gray stone.

28

THE door of the cabin burst inward with a rush of wind and a spray of rain. Jade hurried inside, bending beneath the low doorway, Elizabeth's limp body clutched in his arms. Daniel followed after; he hastened to light a lantern. After placing Elizabeth down gently on his sleeping bag, Jade felt for her pulse and raised her eyelids with a delicate thumb.

"Daniel! I don't think . . ."

Beverly sat bolt upright in her sleeping bag, aroused by the light and the commotion. "Wha . . . what's going on?" she asked sleepily, her eyes squinting in the propane glare.

"It's Elizabeth," said Daniel. "She followed us up the mountain. She collapsed . . ."

"O my God," gasped Beverly. She jumped up and raced to Elizabeth's side. Her lover's face was cut and bruised and her flesh was chill and death pale. "O my God," she began weeping, "can't we do something? Did she fall? Do something, please, please, do something! Please, please . . ." She hugged Elizabeth's body, chanting her pain, weeping.

Daniel gently prodded Beverly off Elizabeth's body. Elizabeth's pale face, framed by the blankets beneath her, appeared to be in sweet repose. Daniel examined her rain-drenched flesh with swift fingers and a canny eye but he could find no breathing and no pulse. The old man rose up on his knees, dropping his hands to his sides, helpless.

"There's nothing I can do," he sighed. "She's dead."

There was a stunned silence while the import of Daniel's pronouncement sank in. Then Beverly collapsed in a weeping heap on Elizabeth's corpse.

"No! No! NO!!" she shouted, sobbing. "I told her not to get involved! I told her she was still too sick! Did any of you listen to me? Did you? Did any of you care that you might kill her? Now look at what you've done. Just look at her." Beverly gently caressed Elizabeth's cheek. "She was so wonderful. So beautiful . . ." She collapsed in sobs. "Look what you've done to her, all cut and bloody and wet with the rain . . . O Beth, how could you let them take you from me? How could you listen to them and not to me? Beth . . . Beth . . . O Beth . . ."

Daniel bent over Beverly, gently hugging her shoulders. "Beverly, please . . ." he began.

She shook him off violently. "Get the hell away from me, old man!" she shouted. "I hope you're damned to hell for what you've done!"

"Please, I . . ."

"Leave me alone! You're murderers, both of you! Now leave me alone!"

Daniel backed away from the weeping woman, his eyes brooding and penitent. Jade joined him in the shadow as the cabin filled with the sound of Beverly's wretched sobbing.

"You can't blame yourself, Daniel," he said softly. "You didn't mean for her to die. She involved herself in all this fully aware of her poor health and the potential risk."

"But I let her come with us, don't you see? I knew what she'd been through and still I let her come along with us." The old man pressed his forehead with a weary palm. "I'll always bear with sorrow the memory of her face tonight . . ."

Jade's firm hand caressed the sorrowful old man's neck. "You're being too harsh on yourself. You let her come with us because she convinced you that her psychic intuition dictated that she come. Unfortunately, both you and I learned too late just exactly what her role in all this was to be. It was my life she saved tonight and that's a debt that only I can repay. Your remorse is meaningless."

"But, my son, you can't burden yourself with such an insurmountable obligation. There's much left for you to do. Your involvement is only beginning. Who knows—before this is all over, you may have given up your life as well. You can't—"

"And will you then blame yourself because I was killed? I know what's at stake. I know the risks. And I know that if you'd had any choice in the matter, neither she nor I nor anyone else would've become involved. But it just didn't work out that way. It's not your fault. Now there's a debt to be paid and I'm the one who's going to pay it."

"And just how do you expect to pay such a debt?" Daniel asked, his voice just a tinge derisive. Jade didn't reply but merely looked into Daniel's inquiring face with eyes of stone. Then he turned to join Beverly as she mourned Elizabeth's death on the cabin floor. But Daniel's eyes went suddenly wide with realization. "No!" he said harshly, calling Jade back. "No! It's not possible. Not even you . . ."

"Daniel, you yourself said that the pupil will become the master and the master the pupil." He smiled down on the old man, gently brushing his long white hair with his hand. "Let me try."

He approached Beverly, who cradled Elizabeth's body in her arms. Beverly's eyes flashed fire when she saw him coming closer. "Get away from me, damn you! There's nothing that can be done to help her and there's nothing you can say that'll pacify me. So get the hell away from both of us!"

"I can help," Jade said simply.

"You and that old man have helped her enough already. Don't you understand that I loved Elizabeth? That all I've got left now are these few minutes with her dead body in my arms? And after that? Nothing, damn it! Not a goddamn thing."

"Then why waste your time in useless mourning?"

Jade's eyes grew tender, thwarting her rage with gentleness. "Let me bring her back for you."

Beverly stared up at Jade for long, silent moments, aghast at his words. "What kind of cruel joke . . ."

"It's neither cruel nor a joke. I owe her my life and now I'll repay my debt."

Without waiting for a response, Jade took Elizabeth's pale head from Beverly's arms and laid her flat out on the sleeping bag. He placed both his hands on her temples and closed his eyes.

Beverly looked wildly at Daniel. "He's mad! You've got to stop him . . ."

Daniel motioned her to silence with a finger raised to his lips.

Darkness once again, yet far in the distance Jade saw a shimmering cocoon of rainbow light flitting like a butterfly in a far-flung meadow undecided as to which blossom was most fitting for rest and nectar. Jade concentrated intently, drawing the light ever closer to his mind's eye.

"Elizabeth . . . Elizabeth . . . Elizabeth . . ." The name resounded throughout the darkness of his vision. "Come closer to me, Elizabeth."

A few light swirls of random spinning, an arabesque, a wobbly nod, and the rainbow cocoon rested gently like a spinning top awaiting further words. Within the translucent shimmer Jade saw a shadow.

[That name . . . said a light voice from within the shimmer, that name . . . it seems so very long ago . . .]

[It's marvellous here, isn't it? the floating, the colors . . . you look so lovely draped in lights.]

[The cocoon sparkled. I remember now . . . as a child . . . the strange dreams . . . like . . . like . . .]

[Memories? Of what had been before. Yes, and now it's no longer frightening or even unfamiliar. A beauty all its own.]

[When I was a child I remember . . .]

[When you were a child you bore within you a gift that few children shared. You nursed it like a flower, tended it with such gentle care, made it grow strong and pliant to your will. You've used that gift to help people many times. And you've used that gift tonight. To help me. I am grateful]

[Tonight? rose the disembodied voice from the swirl of colors. Was it tonight?]

[Yes, just tonight. Only a few short minutes ago.]

[It seems so very long ago . . .]

[Just minutes. I was here earlier. A different place, in a way, a bit deeper perhaps, a bit further from that other world. Yet I was here just before.],

[And you've returned? asked the voice gleefully.]

[For a moment. I've not come to stay. I've come to bring you back with me. It's not your time. There are those of us who love you, who need you back . . .]

[The swirling colors dimmed, grew somber. There are laws . . . some things are irrevocable . . .]

[There were laws. That was before you pulled me back. I would've remained here but for you and all that's left for me to do would've been lost. You made me remember. I'm asking you to do the same.]

[I . . . I remember. My work is done. You've been saved.]

[There's more for you. Come closer. That's it, closer.]

Like a shy woodland creature, the cocoon of colors nodded, spinning forward, tentative, drawing backward, nodding, hesitating, drawing ever closer.

[Touch me, Elizabeth.]

The cocoon swelled, the colors flaring like beacons. Jade willed himself within the cocoon, his shade blending with hers.

In the cabin, Jade's body began to nod and rock back and forth, slowly, sensuously, his fingers pressed lightly against Elizabeth's temples. Daniel and Beverly stared down at him, watching his lips purse themselves into half-kisses and gentle sighs. Suddenly the jade unicorn around his neck burst into glowing splendor, trembling at the end of the chain in emerald fury. From the dead woman's lips a passionate moan emerged.

[Touch me, Elizabeth.]

The shadows swirled within the cocoon of light, bending around each other, twining, weaving a braided rhythm that sent sensuous pulses of color out into the far darkness.

[There's another gift that you must bear, Elizabeth. It too must be nurtured and cared for.]

Again, the supine woman moaned on the cabin floor.

[It is a gift of joy and life. For its sake I've stolen you from the dead. The laws that were are no more. The new laws bring with them new duties. Touch me, Elizabeth.]

For a third time, Elizabeth moaned: orgasmic, intense, and suddenly her arms rose from her sides and over her head, clutching with tigress claws at the fabric beneath her head, tearing at it in her ecstasy. Beverly fell to her knees on the floor, terrified, astounded. Daniel clutched his staff with white knuckles.

The jade unicorn lurched like a trapped boar at the end of its chain, its angry eyes glowing like rubies. Then Jade's eyes opened quickly, twin beacons of emerald. With his hands still gently touching her temples, Elizabeth stretched and moaned one final time. Then her eyes, too, opened.

Beverly gasped in horror. Daniel stared down at Elizabeth, his staff shining.

Elizabeth's face flooded with pink color. Her limbs lost their rigid chill and a warm smile crossed her lips.

"Daniel," said Jade softly, his eyes still afire. "It is done."

29

ABE Ender hastened down the long airport terminal corridor searching for the right gate. Sweat beaded on his balding brow because of the oppressive August heat and because Manhattan traffic had detained his cab long enough so that there were only scant minutes before the flight to Germany was due to board. But before he spotted the gate marker, he saw Daniel and Jade standing quietly off to one side of a passenger departure area watching the large, slouch-hatted figure of Lt. Fedorson being harangued by a flush-cheeked John Brock. The lieutenant endured Brock's angry words in smug silence, chewing negligently on his stogie, his lips half curled in a disdainful smirk.

"But you've got no business getting involved in the internal affairs of a foreign country," berated Brock, pounding his fist into his hand for emphasis. "Your place is here with the goddamn NYPD chasing muggers, not flying halfway around the world to harass one of the wealthiest and most respected financiers. Do you realize what you're doing with your career? Flushing it down the fucking toilet, that's what! All those years you put in on the force are gonna go straight down the tubes. Your pension, your benefits, all shot to hell! And for what? You'll get to Germany, stand around with your thumb up your ass, and then come crawling back with your tail between your legs 'cause you'll never be able to pin anything on Mercadante. Never. Even assuming that that bullshit story that old weirdo sold you and Ender is true, which it isn't, there isn't a tribunal in the fucking world that won't laugh you out of court. You can't fight a man like Mercadante with crap about sorcerers and magic. Fraud, tax evasion, business shenanigans, maybe. But that's way the hell out of your league, Fedorson. Now why don't you listen to reason and get back to the precinct to do the job the taxpayers are paying you to do?"

Fedorson was silent for a moment, surveying Brock's dapper face and form. "Tell me, Brock," he said slowly, "are you advising me on behalf of the mayor's office or are you moonlighting?"

"Well, well, well," said Ender, slightly out of breath, "I see that the money men have gotten to you already."

Brock spun on his heel and looked down at Ender, fuming.

"I'm really impressed," Ender continued. "That Mercadante's got feelers everywhere, it seems. Little eyes and ears scampering around the world doing his dirty work for him."

"Listen, Ender, you little sonofabitch, you better be damn careful about any accusations you make about me . . ."

"And you listen to me! Th-that 'wealthy, respected financier' of yours is a sadistic pervert and murderer. He's been personally responsible for scores of kidnapings and murders and we can positively link him to the disappearance, and G-God knows what else, of his own wife." Ender paused to cool his mounting rage and tame his unruly tongue. "I know you're not here officially because both the mayor and the DA have personally arranged for leaves of absence for the lieutenant and myself. After what happened at the McConnelly funeral, it seems they both decided to look upon this whole affair in a new light . . . a b-broader perspective, you might say."

"But, damn it, you've got no proof!"

"And that's what we're heading to Germany to get!" Ender spat back. "Through a connection at the British Foreign Office, the lieutenant and I, along with those two," he said indicating Daniel and Jade, "have been put on loan to Interpol. It seems that they've been keeping an eye on your respected financier for a long time. There were just strange rumors in the beginning, nothing substantial. But the hard evidence's been mounting. And now we're going to get the final proof we need to put Daddy Warbucks away for a long time." At these last words Daniel looked at Jade and shook his head in pity over the illusions of omnipotence characteristic of bureaucracies. "So now why don't you go back to your rich friends and tell them that you delivered their message and . . . and we're taking it under advisement."

Brock purpled with rage and clenched his fists, glaring down at Ender. Fedorson stepped between them.

"I suggest you get the hell out of here, Brock," warned the lieutenant in a low, gravelly voice, "before you do something that you're gonna regret."

Panting with frustration and hatred and unwilling to defy Fedorson's meaty fists, Brock turned away abruptly and strode rapidly down the terminal corridor. Ender and Fedorson watched in silence as Brock disappeared into the airport throng.

"I hate that guy," said the lieutenant decidedly.

Ender merely laughed.

The sultry voice of the flight attendant came over the loudspeaker announcing that their flight was now ready for boarding. Ender looked around nervously. "Have you seen Inspector Washburn?" he asked Fedorson.

"No. Why? Is he supposed to be here?"

"He told me he'd see us off. He's got some papers that we'll need when we get to Germany."

"Well, he better get his ass over here soon," the lieutenant said as he watched the long line of passengers crowding into the boarding gate, "or he's gonna have to do a lot of swimming to catch up with us."

"I'm here, gentlemen, I'm here," said a voice hastily behind them. They turned and saw Washburn hurrying over to them, pulling a thick envelope from his jacket pocket.

"Right under the wire," smiled Ender. "I was getting worried."

"Please, Mr. Ender," returned Washburn, "you don't

think I'd let a chance to round up Mercadante and his cohorts slip through my fingers, do you? I was just finalizing the paperwork with airport security for the transport of our weapons." He handed two folded documents each to Ender and Fedorson. "These are your temporary Interpol IDs," he said. "And here are the security forms for the guns. Airport security in Munich will handle the weapons on their end. We've just got to present them with these." Two more documents passed from Washburn to Fedorson and Ender. Fedorson's eyes widened.

"Counsellor!" the lieutenant exclaimed in mock horror. "You? A gun?"

Ender dropped his eyes, a shy, embarrassed grin on his face. "Well, I've got to have something," he explained. "I've been told that Mercadante surrounds himself with some pretty rough types."

Jade nodded in silent agreement.

"Tsk, tsk, tsk," clicked the lieutenant, shaking his head. "Whatever will your mother say? For myself, I ask only one thing."

"What's that?" asked Ender.

"Don't aim it anywhere in my direction. If I've gotta cash in my chips, I'd like it to be at the hands of an enemy."

"Excuse me, inspector," Jade interjected. "Are there any papers for Daniel and myself?"

"No, I had to handle the two of you differently. You'll be going with us under a special status arrangement. Sort of as 'essential nonpersons.' A purely bureaucratic maneuver to cut through the red tape." Washburn's heavy mustache arched in an amiable grin. "Don't worry. Just stick with us and you'll be passed through without difficulty. On the way to Brocken Mountain we'll dole out the weapons."

"I don't think that will be necessary for the two of us," said Daniel.

Washburn looked at the old man curiously. "Suit yourselves, gentlemen," he said. "You've got plenty of time to reconsider."

"You keep saying 'we' and 'us,' inspector," said Ender. "Can I safely assume that you're coming with us?"

Washburn smiled broadly. "Of course, Mr. Ender!

Without me your papers are useless. Besides, you wouldn't deprive me of the thrill of the hunt, would you?"

Ender smiled in return. "Not at all. I'll feel better having you with us."

All documents sorted and tucked safely away, the five men headed for the airliner. As they passed along the enclosed ramp leading to the plane, Fedorson tapped Ender on the shoulder.

"What is it?" Ender asked.

Fedorson made a gun with his fingers. "Bang, bang!" he said sharply, jerking his thumb like the hammer of a gun. Ender smiled, reddening, and hurried onto the plane. The sound of the lieutenant's deep laughter drifted all the way back to the boarding gate.

The Great Hall of the Chateau was being prepared for the Ritual of Ascension. Mercadante stood upon the high balustrade robed in black velvet, looking down upon the progress of his workers.

All traces of the preceding weeks' orgies had been removed. The unfortunate victims still left alive had been herded into large subterranean holding cells. The racks and whipping posts and other implements of restraint were returned to the dungeon, replaced by long rows of polished mahogany pews set facing the High Altar, which rested upon the raised stone steps at the front of the Great Hall. Some of Mercadante's burly servants were grunting and staggering under the weight of huge ornate silver floor candelabra, which were being placed along the broad center aisle between the rows of pews that led up to the altar. As the candelabra were hoisted carefully into place, other servants followed with bundles of black tapers, filling the many silver sconces. Still other servants were busy hanging a black velvet curtain behind the altar; it loomed in soft folds more than thirty feet high against the cold stone walls. Painstaking embroidery worked in silver thread glittered from the curtain in the flickering light of torches. An immense silver ram's head filled most of the central portion of the curtain, representing the Incarnation of Satan. This, in turn, was surrounded by silver symbols of the zodiac, signifying Satan's dominion over the heavens.

Mercadante looked down upon the bustling activity with a smile of intense satisfaction curling his thin lips.

The High Altar itself was a marvel of woodcraft, carved from a single ebony bole. The wood gleamed with a rich black luster, as yet uncovered by altarcloths and ceremonial objects. Across the front of the altar was a magnificent array of relief carvings: gargoyles and death's heads and a scattering of Satan's minions, black wooden faces twisted in grimaces of lust and violent frenzy.

Suddenly a voice from beneath the balustrade shouted, "Make way! Make way!" Servants scattered out of the aisles between the pews and stared at the entrance of the Great Hall. A slow scraping of heavy boots and intermittent grunts rose from beneath the balustrade to Mercadante's ears. He leaned slightly over the stone railing to watch what was happening below him. All the servants stopped their work and stared in silence as the heavy scraping and nasal grunts inched down the left aisle toward the High Altar.

Two of the giant brothers, Pimm and Brud, bore between them an immense statue of Cerberus, the three-headed guardian hound of the gates of Hell. The statue was wrought of pure silver, the serpentine necks of the beast seeming to twist and writhe in the flickering torchlight. The six angry eyes were made of rubies the size of robins' eggs, expertly faceted to flash wrathfully with the reflected fires of the myriad candles. The statue was bolted onto a broad, heavy base of shining black obsidian, and the two brothers lurched slowly, painfully, one leaden step at a time, their huge arms clutching the smooth obsidian. There wasn't a sound in the entire hall; all the servants waited with baited breath while the two giants slowly eased the massive sculpture into place to the left of the altar. First Pimm lowered his end to the stone floor, groaning, his forehead dripping with sweat. The obsidian touched the stone slowly, silently, finally at rest. And then Brud eased his end into place, straining, sweating.

Once the magnificent statue was in place, the two giants disappeared ponderously back down the aisle and out of the Great Hall.

Mercadante looked with sublime joy upon the enormous silver beast with flashing ruby eyes. It represented the invulnerability of Satan's dominions to attack from without. The three hideous heads appeared to snap and snarl in defiance above the ebony altar, their silver jaws vicious with sharp, silver teeth.

The servants started to return to their various tasks but were again interrupted by a herald shouting, "Make way! Make way!" Again they scattered, suspenseful, staring back at the entrance to the hall. More heavy scraping of boots this time, yet only the sounds of two boots instead of four, and the grunting of only one man. Mercadante leaned forward again, listening, smiling to himself.

The sounds approached the altar from the right aisle this time. All the servants, with one breath, gasped at the sight of a prodigious spectacle: Porfex, the largest of the three giant brothers, bore all alone upon one shoulder a giant inverted crucifix, cast, like its fellow Cerberus, out of a mass of pure silver. Once the inverted statue of the crucified Jesus was in its place on the right side of the altar, the flowing silver hair of the tortured Son of God would rest upon the floor, awaiting defilement by the urine and feces of the satanists. Porfex worked his slow, ponderous way up the steps to the right side of the altar and with a single intense hefting of his right arm, lowered the statue to the stone floor. He waited a moment to assure himself that it was steady upon its obsidian base and then turned and left the Great Hall as well.

Mercadante smiled down from the balustrade, well pleased. The inverted crucifix symbolized the contempt he and the other satanists felt for all religious and ethical philosophies that were opposed to their own, all that dared deny the omnipotence of their dark and fearsome Lord.

The two statues flanking the High Altar were dazzling in their bizarre beauty. It was long minutes before the awestruck servants could take their eyes from them and return to their tasks.

To the right of the right aisle was a section of floor space roped off with silver braid. A number of heavy iron chairs were placed in that section, a pair of iron shackles bolted to the legs of each. A sudden sharp wailing and groaning and the snapping of whips interrupted the work of the servants a third time while a group of naked captives, shackled hand and foot and carrying musical instruments, were brutally cudgelled and shoved past the silver braid, each to his own chair. They were utterly bewildered, screaming out their rage and pain and terror with every vicious slash of the whip. Once each captive was seated a few of their tormentors hopped up and down between the rows of chairs beating the pathetic prisoners upon their heads and shoulders, making them howl with pain. The rest of the guards hastily shackled each prisoner to his chair.

Mercadante watched from the balustrade until the last musician was imprisoned. He then turned and left the balustrade and descended to the floor of the Great Hall. By the time he joined the enslaved musicians, he was accompanied by a servant who bore a large sheaf of parchments in his arms.

"Gentlemen," barked Mercadante in his resonant and commanding voice, silencing their groans and curses, "and lady," he nodded, acknowledging a blond flutist weeping in her chair, "my servant is distributing among you some music of my own composition. Tonight, at midnight, in celebration of a ritual that will be celebrated here, you will perform this music. And you will perform my music to the very best of your abilities because, indeed, your very lives depend upon the artistry and sensuousness with which you interpret my composition. You have until midnight, therefore, to study the music and perfect the synchronization of your playing. You will remain as you are until then after which, depending upon the success or failure of your performance, you will be released. You are each among the best in your discipline, and I expect you will have little difficulty in delivering a performance that lives up to my needs and expectations."

"Now just a goddamn minute!" shouted a bearded french horn player, clutching his horn to his lap to cover himself. "Who the fuck do you think you are to shanghai us like this and think that you can make us perform for you? I'm not gonna . . ."

Before he could finish his tirade, two of Mercadante's servants beat him about the head and ears with rattan clubs, silencing him in agony. Stray drops of blood spilled upon his gleaming silver horn.

Mercadante glowered down upon the french horn player, his angry mouth drawn tensely into a thin, rigid line. "For the benefit of those of you who share this man's rebelliousness, I will say to you only once that you are in no position to defy me. Do as I tell you, and you will go free without further harm. Defy me, and you will suffer horrible tortures." He approached the bleeding horn player more closely, jerking his head backward suddenly with a painful yank of his curly, blood-matted hair. The old man bent closely to the horn player's face. "Think, my defiant friend," he snarled acidly, "how difficult it would be to pursue your musical career without lips. Or you," he said loudly, facing another musician, "a cellist without fingers. All of you, beware my anger! To provoke me is to condemn yourselves to horrible suffering and death!" He scornfully snapped the horn player's chin to his chest, releasing his hair. "I haven't the time to bother myself with any of you any further. You know what you must do," he sneered, "now do it."

Mercadante strode haughtily away from the musicians toward the High Altar. He watched silently as the altar-cloths were laid and the thick black candles were screwed into the heavy silver candle holders placed on each end of the altar. His servants scurried about their tasks desperately, terrified beneath the gaze of their master.

At the end of the central aisle, just beneath the steps leading to the front of the altar, stood two large sacrificial slabs. Iron shackles were embedded in the four corners of each. Mercadante approached the one on the right side facing the altar and ran his tendonous fingers delicately across the cool marble. Then he approached the one on the left, his brow darkening.

With a grimace of disgust, Mercadante spat upon that second slab of marble, then strode quickly out of the Great Hall.

The dark sedan bearing Ender and the others sped swiftly through the night along a winding ribbon of mountain road silvered by the cold light of the high quarter moon. Washburn was at the wheel, his eyes intent upon the sharp curves that rocked the passengers from side to side, his face alight with the metallic blue glare from the instrument panel. Outside the car was nothing but the black shadows of woods and mountains. The last lights of farmhouses and country inns had been left far behind and Ender kept his face pressed to the window, marvelling at their speed along the hairpin twisting cliff road, searching for signs of human habitation. Jade, on the other side of the car, stared out of the window as well, keeping his eyes trained upward toward the high peaks, searching for the distant lights of an isolated castle.

"We have two advantages in approaching the Chateau tonight," Daniel explained to the group. "Mercadante, himself, will be too occupied with the Ritual of Ascension to personally keep the environs of Mt. Brocken under his psychic surveillance. But don't think that he's let down his guard. He's aware, though somewhat obscurely, that Jade's a potent threat to him. And I'm sure he realizes that tonight he must depend on his lackeys to guard against any outside interference, so he'll have them swarming all over the mountain."

"So what's the advantage?" asked Fedorson.

Daniel smiled. "It may not seem like much of an advantage once we start our climb, but we're far better off dealing just with Mercadante's servants than having to contend personally with the master."

Washburn swerved into a wild series of sharp curves, forcing the passengers to hang on to the seats and the padded handles of the doors. Fedorson, seated up front, blanched as pale as the sullen moon.

"Jesus Christ!" he exclaimed. "Can't you slow down a little around those curves?"

Washburn grinned. "I can see that you're not used to our European roads. Don't worry, my friend, I'm quite accustomed to this kind of night driving."

"Listen," the lieutenant retorted, "I may not know anything about these European roads but we must be doing ninety!"

Washburn looked at the speedometer. "Ninety-three to

378

be exact. But we are in a hurry, don't forget. We've got a way to go yet, and it's already past eleven."

"Shit," muttered Fedorson, and fell back into his accustomed silence.

"The second advantage we have," continued Daniel, "is that I don't think Mercadante is aware of my involvement in all this. And I'm rather familiar with the Chateau and its environs. I've had some run-ins with Mercadante before, many years ago in my youth. At that time I was biting off more than I could chew, but I did learn about a difficult but passable footpath leading up the Brocken to the base of the Chateau. Mercadante will have most of his henchmen spread near the main roads leading up the mountain. We'll be able to avoid a lot of them."

"You hope," said Fedorson.

"We'll just have to do what we can and prepare for the worst," said Daniel. "But I warn you that Mercadante has surrounded himself with a pretty bizarre crew. They're well trained, intensely loyal, and each one is deadlier than the next."

"And they're ugly as hell," Jade commented, thinking back upon that night in the alley. "Don't get psyched out by them if they should pop out at you in the dark. Just keep your guns ready."

At the mention of guns Ender's mouth went dry. He kept silent, staring out the window.

"Speaking of guns," said the lieutenant, "what kind of stuff did you get for us?"

"Two handguns apiece," said Washburn, "Walthers, equipped with silencers. Should we need them on the way up, we don't want to alert everybody in the damn castle that we're here. Then, once we're in the place we've each got a small automatic. In case the going gets tough."

The talk about guns aroused painful memories in Jade. Fetid jungle swamps, the cold finger of Death disguised as a tiny fly or pretty striped beetle. He rubbed his eyes with his palm.

"I don't know about those Walthers," pondered Fedorson out loud. "They're pretty small and with the silencers not very accurate past pretty close range. Still, they're quiet and in the dark in a forest we'll have to keep close. I just don't know . . ."

379

The discussion of small arms that ensued between the lieutenant and the inspector excluded the passengers in the back seat. They kept quiet, watching carefully out the windows for the first signs of the Chateau. Some minutes passed and then Daniel suddenly told Washburn to slow down. The car carefully braked, gliding smoothly through a couple of final curves and then halted at Daniel's command, pulling off the road amidst a low spray of gravel. They climbed quickly out of the car and stared up at the mountain looming before them.

The moon was at first obscured by clouds, making the outline of the Brocken difficult to discern. But as Washburn passed the arms from the trunk out to Ender and the lieutenant, the clouds cleared. The ridges and outcroppings of the Brocken glowed a dull pewter in the moonlight.

The entire mountain seemed to be nothing more than a massive shambles of boulders.

"What a goddamn ugly mountain!" Jade breathed softly to Daniel as they both stared upward. "Not at all like Marcy or any of the Adirondacks."

"It's not like anything else in the world," explained Daniel. "It was entirely built up from glacial rubble many thousands of years ago. That's why it looks so sparse and alien. Its name is derived from the German verb 'to crumble': the crumbling or broken mountain."

Jade and Daniel stared upward silently while the other three harnessed themselves into their gun belts.

"It's ghastly," Jade concluded. "I can see why it attracts witches and devil worshippers from around the world for their sabbaths."

"Yes," Daniel agreed, "this mountain had quite an occult history long before Mercadante ever established himself here. You see, legends claim that when Satan was expelled from Heaven by the Archangels, it was at this very spot that he and his infernal legions fell through the earth into Hell. Mt. Brocken is supposed to have been built up by the Archangels when they piled boulder upon boulder to seal off the entrance to Hell forever, keeping the demons and sinners trapped within."

Jade stared upward at gray, spectral shadows of the

mountain, his senses pulsing with alert energy. "It's unfortunate that the Archangels left so many gaps."

Daniel was somber. "It's unfortunate that evil doesn't need any gaps in order for it to permeate the world," he retorted.

"But I don't see the Chateau, Daniel. Can you point it out to me?"

"You can't see it from here. We have to follow a path that curves up and around that far slope over there," Daniel answered, pointing. "From that point it's a rather straightforward climb upward at a tolerable incline." Daniel's jaw was set with remorseful determination. "You'll see the Chateau all too soon, I'm afraid. It's high up but not all the way up the peak. It's not a difficult climb, really, if you know this path like I do. Although in the dark it won't be any picnic. What will mainly concern us is avoiding the guards."

Washburn walked up to the two of them bearing weapon belts in his arms. "Last chance, gentlemen," he said smiling, offering them the guns.

"No, inspector," said Daniel. "Divide them up among you three. Jade and I have other . . . alternatives."

Washburn looked at both of them quizzically, then shrugged his shoulders. "Suit yourselves," he said and returned to the lieutenant and Ender to give them more weapons.

Suddenly from far away among the mountain peaks, the despondent peal of a bell drifted down to them faintly on the night winds. Daniel stiffened, listening intently. A second peal, then a third followed in obsequious procession.

"We must hurry!" Daniel called out. "They're beginning to assemble for the ritual! Follow me!"

The old man plunged hastily into the underbrush, his cloak wrapped sleekly around him as protection against stinging nettles. Jade followed quickly, then Fedorson and Washburn. Ender, burdened comically by bandoleros of weapons like a Mexican bandit, brought up the rear.

The climb at first was steep and the footing difficult in the dark. But Daniel's agile swiftness was an inspiration for the others. He weaved and danced between outcroppings of rocks, dodging the jagged overhangs of trees and vines, wielding his heavy staff like a light shepherd's crook. At times all vestiges of the moonlight were lost beneath the interlocking branches of oak and elm, and the men stumbled as clods of stony earth crumbled beneath their feet. But they hastened forward following the old man, silent, swift, prodded to exceptional steadfast skills by the urgency of their mission.

And then they disappeared from the moonlight altogether as they climbed forward into the night shadow of a Brocken peak. Daniel worked his staff like a blind man's cane, refreshing his memories of years past when he'd last followed this path to the Chateau searching for dangerous points of erosion that might have accumulated over the years. Ender marvelled at the old man's sense of the invisible path which didn't become apparent to him until he found himself standing right on it. But suddenly Jade called a halt.

They froze in the darkness.

"What's the matter?" whispered Daniel.

Jade crept forward to his side, studying the configuration of the underbrush. "Something's not right," he mumbled softly to himself. "Too symmetric, these leaves here . . ." He bent over about a yard in front of Daniel. "Look!" he called out. "I thought so."

He pointed down in front of him amongst some scrub bushes. Washburn came forward and flashed a dim red light down among the leaves. A thin strand of metal glinted in the light, stretching across the path.

"Evidently Mercadante knows about this path as well," said Jade. "He's got it wired."

Ender heaved a sigh of relief. "Damn," he gasped, "that was close! What would've happened if we tripped it?"

Washburn examined the wire closely. "It's difficult to say," he answered. "It seems a bit too thin to set off any kind of projectile booby trap. A mine, perhaps."

"Or a silent alarm," Jade offered. "It might even be part of some kind of infrared system, in which case we might've already tripped an alarm without being aware of it."

Fedorson looked at Jade with a new respect. "Where

the hell did you learn so much about booby traps and alarms?" he asked.

Jade laughed. "Lieutenant, I've been in some spots in my time where if you just nudged a wire like that with the edge of your shin, the next thing you knew your balls were hanging by a spear off a tree ten yards away."

"You must've been in Nam, then!" said Fedorson. "The Marines, I bet."

"It doesn't matter," Jade concluded. "And there's no sense worrying about the infrared either. Assume the worst and let's just move our asses."

They stepped carefully over the wire and plunged headlong into the darkness. Daniel knew now what to watch for and his staff quivered before him like a divining rod. The five men moved swiftly, like predatory cats stalking an elusive prey in the inky shadows.

"I feel strange, Daniel," Jade whispered to the old man as they hastened upward among the rocks and scrubby bushes. "Kind of sick . . . nauseous . . . nothing physical, really. Just a . . . a feeling . . ."

"You'll feel it worse as we get closer to the Chateau," Daniel whispered over his shoulder.

"It's the evil, isn't it?"

Daniel nodded. "The others will feel nothing but you and I can feel the rocky sinews of these mountains cry out with the abominations they've been made to witness. So much innocent blood has been spilled on these peaks. Sacrificial rites, blood worship, all sorts of superstitious cruelty. For hundreds of years. It gets worse the higher up we go. If you made your way to the very pinnacle of the Brocken where most of the sabbaths have been held, you'd be able to feel the mountain quiver beneath your fingertips."

They'd gone quite high up the Brocken when Daniel called a sudden halt. Stray shafts of moonlight revealed the precipitous cliffs looming below them. The rubbled mountain fell down steeply into shaded gashes of valleys, ornamented at sparse intervals by stubborn, gnarled trees clinging to the rocks.

"What's the matter?" asked Washburn.

"Listen!" Daniel commanded and the men fell silent.

From far up among the wooded slopes came the faint barking of dogs.

"I hear them!" Ender exclaimed. "That's dogs, right?"

"Yeah," said Fedorson, "dogs. With armed guards right behind 'em, no doubt."

"Do you think they know we're here," asked Ender, "or is it just a routine patrol?"

"We can't be sure," Jade answered. "Let's go up a little further and then we've gotta scatter for cover. We'll wait and see what happens."

"But Jade," cautioned Daniel, "we haven't much time!"

"Don't worry," Jade laughed. "We'll find out sooner than we care to."

They scampered up the mountain path at a trot, the sound of dogs growing closer with each passing second. Then, at Jade's command, they dove into a copse of saplings and thorny scrub, rolling for cover behind the low bushes. They were silent and breathless as they heard the dogs barking very loudly, tearing down the mountain at a frantic pace, heading straight for their place of concealment.

Suddenly Ender gasped. Two vicious German shepherds burst through the underbrush, their jowls frothing and their deadly fangs bared to kill. They paused just an instant to sniff out the hiding places of the humans and then poised to attack.

Fedorson rose on his knees to fire his gun but Jade slapped his gun arm down. The dogs, seeing the movement, leaped toward them, but Jade rose to his feet, his eyes blazing like emeralds.

The dogs tried to scurry out of the momentum of their leap, startled. They fell to the ground, barking savagely, threatening Jade with their upraised hackles and fangs. But they didn't approach any closer.

"Ssh!" Jade commanded the dogs. Their barking ceased and they looked at each other as if puzzled. Then they began to quietly whine.

Jade approached them slowly, his eyes shining, staring down at them. The dogs squirmed beneath his gaze and then the larger of the two suddenly rolled upon its back playfully. Jade walked forward, bent down, and tickled its belly.

The other dog ran to Jade, pawing his shoulders playfully, licking his face. Jade laughed. "Good boys," he said to the dogs who were now frolicking around him. "Good boys, good dogs, such good dogs." Jade's eyes dimmed back to normal.

"I don't fuckin' believe it!" Fedorson exclaimed to himself as he rose cautiously to his feet, his pistol in his hand.

When he could free his face from the dogs' enthusiastic tongues, Jade simply said, "I prefer making friends to making corpses."

The sudden crashing of boots through the underbrush interrupted the merriment. Then there were two clicks from rifle bolts. But before any shots were fired, Jade heard two gentle pops like bursting bubbles.

Both Fedorson and Washburn had their pistols leveled at the shadows.

Two of Mercadante's guards collapsed among the underbrush, their rifles clattering upon the stony ground.

Jade stood over the bodies. "I guess some creatures weren't born to be friendly," he said half to himself. Then he turned to Washburn and Fedorson. "That was some fine night shooting, gentlemen," he told them. "I'm impressed."

Fedorson pushed his hat far back on his head in a bewildered gesture. "Not half as impressed as we are, pal. Not half!"

Jade laughed and hastened after Daniel who had already started back up the path. The two guard dogs scampered at his heels like playful puppies.

30

SOLEMN, stately: the pealing of the iron bell.
  Once.

Funereal strains of music and chanting mounted thick and slow, swirling like a heavy vapor above the flickering fires of a thousand black candles, phrases swollen with anguish, terror, and reverence. The Great Hall glowed with the golden warmth of the flames and sparkled with the dancing shine of silver.

Twice.

Mercadante, robed and cowled in black linen and astride a shaggy he-goat, its horns filigreed with silver, entered the central aisle of the Great Hall and rode slowly toward the High Altar. He bowed to the east and to the west as he rode, his voice deep and resonant, echoing throughout the Great Hall, chanting:

Nonne Salomon dominatus daemonum est?
Nonne Mercadante dominatus daemonum est?

At the conclusion of each line he took a small wooden cross from an embroidered bag in his lap and dropped it gently behind the goat, like tiny turds.

Three times.

The celebrants, robed and cowled in black as well,

filed into the Great Hall behind Mercadante bearing black tapers. They stepped slowly, two by two, intoning the refrain of Mercadante's chant:

> Il fuoco viene addosso a noi!
> And the fire is coming upon us!

As the celebrants stepped forward, they ground the wooden crosses beneath their heels.

The last reverberation of the bell's pealing died away while the music of the winds and strings luxuriated among the buttresses of the ceiling.

At the foot of the steps leading up to the High Altar, Mercadante descended lightly off the goat's back. An acolyte approached from the left and took the goat from him, leading the beast out of the Great Hall. Mercadante approached the steps but before setting foot upon them, he raised his arms, chanting:

> Veni, diabole, discalcea me!

He then stepped out of his soft velvet slippers and walked barefoot up the steps to the altar from between the two sacrificial slabs of marble. The celebrants, still chanting, divided toward the right and to the left, filing in somber procession one by one into the rows of pews, each bearing his candle. When the last celebrant reached his allotted place among the pews and they all stood facing the altar, the music and chanting ceased.

Mercadante stepped behind the altar, throwing back his cowl. The flickering candlelight carved his face into sharp lines and harsh planes of shadow. Flanking the altar on each side was a candelabrum aflame with many thick black candles. In front of Mercadante upon the black silk altarcloth rested a small silver cauldron, etched with mystical figures and swollen with gargoyles. To the left of the cauldron was a heavy silver chalice; to the right, a slender sacrificial blade with a jeweled handle and scabbard. Mercadante stood facing the celebrants from behind the cauldron, his arms bent at the elbow with his palms raised to the level of his shoulders, facing outward. The two middle fingers of each hand were bent down toward the wrists, leaving the first and last fingers, the horns of Satan, upright.

—By the virtues of the ten Decans, he announced in a stentorian voice, by the powers of the fires above and the fires below, by the love we bear for Thee, Satan, and by the hatred we bear for Thy execrable brother, we most humbly welcome Thee to our midst!

—Xilca! Xilca! Besa! Besa! the celebrants intoned.

—I call upon the fearless Asiccan! I call upon the vaporous Viroaso! I call upon the grasping Sith! I call upon the mighty Thuimis I call upon the violent Aphruimis!

—Xilca! Xilca! Besa! Besa!

—I call upon the tyrannical Sithacer! I call upon the sensual Arpien! I call upon the ever-besieged Thepiseuth! I call upon the wrathful Senciner! I call upon the evil Chenen!

—Xilca! Xilca! Besa! Besa!

—Protect us, O dark Powers! Let not the Great Lord rise against us in His omnipotent wrath! Let Him accept our servile and humble submission to His most sovereign Will!

—We bow our heads to Thee, O Satan, the celebrants chanted, and offer unto Thee our flesh, our blood, and our souls!

Mercadante dropped his hands and took from behind the altar a silver bowl with two handles. He placed the bowl on the altar and removed its lid. It was brimming with dark brown turds.

—O mighty Satan! Mercadante shouted to the ceiling with upraised arms, we do hold Thy greatest foe in most vile contempt and do not fear his vengeance! We spit upon his eyes and smear his countenance with our offal!

Mercadante wound a black cloth around his left hand, then dipped it amidst the turds. He grasped the bowl with his right hand and carried it over to the inverted crucifix. He placed the bowl on the cold stone beside the agonized head of Jesus. Kneeling beside the bowl, Mercadante shut his eyes and raised his arms to the heavens:

—We do renounce thee and thy cold minions! We cast thee in thy turn into eternal fires and damnation! We do spit upon thee, now that thou art cast down from the heights and contemptible!

—Sathanus adjutor meus! shouted the celebrants Sathanus adjutor meus!

Mercadante spat upon the silver face of Jesus. Then he made the sign of the cross upon the statue's brow with the black cloth, staining the silver with a brown smear. He rose to his feet, leaving both bowl and cloth beside the statue and returned to the High Altar.

The musicians, seeing Mercadante's nod, once again burst forth with the eerie, phantasmal music. Flute tones quivered defiantly above the dismal moaning of the deep horns. The bass strings throbbed lustfully, impatient, while the woodwinds phrased a processional melody that seemed to rise from the bowels of the earth. One by one the celebrants rose from their places among the pews and, handing their candles to an acolyte, knelt beside the crucifix. Each, in turn, wrapped his left hand in the black cloth and, dipping the cloth into the bowl, made a mark upon the statue's face, spitting onto its beard. One by one they approached, their faces bright and eager, their eyes flashing fire. The music cradled them like swaddling, thick, profound, seeping into the darkest recesses of their souls.

It took a long time for each celebrant to defile the crucifix and return to his place among the pews. The music played all the while.

When the last celebrant had returned to his place, Mercadante stood behind the silver cauldron, his arms raised again in satanic homage, and delivered the invocation:

—Most mighty Lord of Darkness!
  We most heartily welcome Thee to our coven
  And pray that we find acceptance
  In Thine eyes!
—Sathanus adjutor meus! intoned the worshippers.
—For long hast Thou languished in darkness,
  Stolen from those who love Thee,
  Deprived of the richness of our incense,
  And the thick, steaming blood of our sacrifices!
—Sathanus adjutor meus!

—But this day hast Thou burst Thy bonds
   With Thy might,
   And made of the heavenly sepulchre
   A Foot-stool!
—Sathanus adjutor meus!
—The bull is turned loose upon the cows,
   And bellows his frenzy!
   The shaggy ram tups the mountain ewe,
   Bleating its triumph to the four winds!
—Sathanus adjutor meus!

Mercadante took the silver cauldron in both hands
and raised it high above his head.

—We acknowledge Thee as Most Worshipful Overlord,
   And beg Thee to renew Thy covenant
   With Thy cringing and dutiful servants
   For all time!
—Sathanus adjutor meus!
—We anoint ourselves afresh
   In sacrificial blood
   To proclaim our homage to Thee
   For all time!

Mercadante returned the cauldron to its place upon the
altar while an acolyte entered the Great Hall from the
right, bearing upon a silver platter a bundle in soft black
velvet. The acolyte set the platter upon the altar in front
of the cauldron and unfolded the velvet.

A living human infant lay naked upon the platter,
silent, drugged.

The acolyte knelt before the altar, his eyes averted to
the floor. Mercadante took the sacrificial dagger in his
right hand and raised it above his head, reciting the
demonic invocation of the ancient conjuror Salatin:

—Bagabi laca bachabé
   Lamac cahi achababé
      Karrelyos!
   Lamac Iamec Bachalyas
   Cabahagy sabalyos
      Baryolos!

Lagoz atha cabyolas
Samahac et famyolas
   Harrahya!

—Sathanus adjutor meus! responded the eager celebrants.

With a sharp hiss of metal, Mercadante jerked the
dagger from its jeweled scabbard. He set the scabbard
down on the altar and, with his free right hand, raised
the infant in the air by one tiny foot, holding it over the
silver cauldron. The child didn't utter a sound.

—Look upon us, O Satan,
   With the mercy of Thy countenance,
   And accept from us, as freely given,
   Our flesh, and our blood, and our souls!

Swiftly, the dagger descended upon the infant, slitting
it open. A torrent of blood spilled into the cauldron.

Mercadante nodded for the musicians to begin playing
again but most of them were unable to bring their instruments to their lips or work the strings with their trembling hands. They wept, they moaned, they vomited in
their laps at the horrid spectacle. The celebrants began
grumbling and cursing, and Mercadante widened his
eyes in fury. A cadre of servants hurriedly leaped among
the musicians and set upon them brutally with rattan
clubs. They shortly began to play, but the music was
tremulous with their terror, anguish, and revulsion.

Falling in with the ghastly processional music, the
celebrants once again approached the altar in single
file, awaiting baptismal anointment at the hands of
Mercadante. The kneeling acolyte had risen and removed the pale corpse of the infant from the Great Hall.
Mercadante drew forth from the cauldron a fine silver
ladle with which he filled the silver chalice with the infant's blood. He raised the chalice over his head and
closed his eyes in silent prayer.

Then he drank.

The satanists could barely restrain their eagerness
enough to remain in single file. Each one climbed the
steps to the High Altar, kneeled at Mercadante's feet, and

pronounced a personal vow of obedience to Satan. Then each sipped ecstatically from the bloody chalice. After the portion of blood was swallowed, each satanist stepped down from the altar and disrobed, handing a waiting acolyte his black garment and receiving, in return, his candle. Other acolytes would take the robes and dispose of them outside the Great Hall while the celebrant, bearing his black candle, returned naked to the pews.

The stone walls of the Chateau trembled with the resounding triumph of the great iron bell.

Daniel paused before a narrow wall of stone which brought to an end the precarious rocky path they'd been following. Vague steps had been hollowed out of the wall which Daniel felt for in the darkness. Jade and the others were gathered right behind him, single file.

"Hold my staff, Jade," Daniel said, passing it to him. Then the old man groped briefly with both hands and began pulling himself upward into deeper shadow. Soon, even his feet disappeared.

"It's only about ten feet high," Daniel whispered back down to the others. "The handholds are pretty secure. Not crumbly or eroded. But be careful."

Jade handed Daniel's staff up to him and then started climbing after him. Washburn was next in line, watching tensely in case Jade should start to slip. Ender had his back pressed up against the side of the mountain, breathing a silent prayer. It was only a couple of feet to the edge of the precipice and he could imagine the taunting abyss in the thick darkness below him covered with jagged boulders and distant, gaunt trees. Nightwinds brushed Ender's cheeks, and his knuckles whitened as he pressed his bare palms behind him upon the cold stone.

Jade made it to the top and leaned over to assist Washburn. But suddenly the crack of a rifle shattered the night silence. Washburn lurched, gasping, and plunged off the narrow wall with a shriek, falling headlong into the black shadows.

"Sonofabitch!" cursed Fedorson, pressing himself more

tightly against the ledge. Jade and Daniel pulled back away from the wall, deeper into the darkness. "Lousy bush-whackin' bastards!" The lieutenant's hands trembled with rage.

Ender was nauseous and terrified. Pressed up against that mountain he felt like a sitting duck.

Suddenly an intense volley of rifle shots picked away at the hollowed wall. The noise was deafening as the blasts reverberated from peak to peak, while the scream-ing bullets sent shards of stone spraying dangerously all over the rock ledge.

"Get back down there!" Fedorson shouted at Ender, indicating the path along which they'd come. Ender scrambled sideways pressed tightly against the moun-tain, his eyes shut against the tiny chips of stone that were flying all around him. By the time the rifles fell silent, he and Fedorson had backed down the path about ten meters.

"They're not too sure where we are," Fedorson whis-pered. "That's why they sprayed the wall like that. A fuckin' fluke they got Washburn," he concluded bitterly.

They remained silent and motionless, hidden in the darkness, uncertain as to what they should do. Soon a scraping sound from the ledge above told them that one of the hunters was coming closer to see if he had bagged his prey.

Listening intently, Federson heard the barrel of a rifle scraping along the ledge of rock above the path, evi-dently trained downward. The rifleman could see and hear no movement and Fedorson heard him curse with disappointment. Then the rifleman clung to an overhang of rock and descended swiftly to the footpath below, right in front of the narrow wall.

Squinting in the sparse moonlight, the lieutenant could just barely make out that the rifleman had hung his weapon over his shoulder.

With a startling forward sprint, Fedorson tore along the path in the darkness until he slammed against the be-wildered rifleman, pinning him against the rocks and began pounding his heavy fist into his face.

"You cocksucker!" he shouted as he beat the man

mercilessly, "you crummy sonofabitch cocksucker, I'm gonna bust your ass with my bare hands!"

The rifleman was Stully, Mercadante's reclusive servant in the bell tower. His nose and upper lip opened up with a spray of blood with the lieutenant's first punch, and the rest of his beefy boxer's body grew increasingly limp beneath Fedorson's furious blows. He tried to hold the lieutenant off with a groping stranglehold but Fedorson dodged, weaved, and pounded with such lightning fury that Stully's grasping fingers couldn't hold on to his neck.

"You rat bastard!" Federson shouted as the two of them tangled precariously close to the edge of the cliff. "You fuckin' asshole! Take this! And this! And this, you crummy bastard!" The lieutanant's voice quivered with tears of rage.

Ender was frozen with terror, fearful that Fedorson would toss himself and Stully from the ledge in his uncontrollable rage. The two men clung to each other, lurching, their boots kicking sprays of pebbles off the footpath and far out into the empty darkness. Suddenly Ender thought he saw the slender shadow of a rifle barrel in the dim moonlight pointing down upon Fedorson from above.

Then he heard the click of the bolt.

Fedorson turned swiftly around on his heels looking upward, his eyes staring wildly down the barrel of the gun. But before the rifle fired, he heard a succession of pops coming from down the path. The rifle was poised delicately for a moment on the edge of the precipice and then tumbled forward, bouncing off the footpath and rebounding out over the cliff. It was followed by the upper torso of Karl, which hung lifeless over the footpath, its dead arms widespread.

Ender scraped along the path, coming out into the moonlight. He was pale and trembling and his forehead was beaded with sweat. In his trembling right hand was his pistol.

"Damn!" breathed Fedorson, amazed. "Of all the fuckin' miracles!"

He turned his attention to Stully who was still pressed up against the narrow stone wall, bloody, limp, and almost lifeless. With a contemptuous push, Fedorson shoved him off the cliff.

Stully wasn't even conscious enough to scream.

Fedorson reached out for Ender's arm because the little lawyer seemed to be dazed. "I don't believe it, counsellor!" the lieutenant said as he pulled Ender close to him. "And there I was raggin' your ass at the airport about you and guns. You saved my fuckin' life!"

Ender could muster only a weak smile.

Jade's head peeked over the top of the narrow wall and he called down, "Hey! Is it all over down there?"

"Yeah," Fedorson answered, his arm wrapped tightly around Ender's shoulders. "We got 'em. Gimme a hand with the counsellor, here."

Fedorson practically lifted Ender up the wall bodily, while Jade reached over and pulled him up the rest of the way. Then the lieutenant followed suit.

"We'd better move quickly," came Daniel's voice out of the darkness. "Those rifle shots will bring any of the other guards patrolling these slopes right to us."

"You ready to go on?" the lieutenant asked solicitously of Ender. " 'Cause if you're not, they can go on ahead while I wait here with you until you're ready."

"No, no, lieutenant," Ender answered slowly, snapping out of it. "I'm okay. Let's keep going."

"You follow Jade, then, counsellor," Fedorson smiled. "From now on I'm gonna keep my eye on you."

Suddenly out of the darkness they heard the frantic tolling of the iron bell.

"Damn!" Daniel exclaimed, "That means they've already started the blood sacrifice! We must hurry!"

The three men followed Daniel as he raced through the darkness. Jade heard far below them, on the slopes where they'd had to leave the two dogs, a piteous howling.

Mercadante waited in rigid silence for the last peal of the bell to fade slowly into nothingness. The last celebrant had received his blood baptism and was making his way naked to his seat. Surveying the naked host with a stern visage, Mercadante at last stepped in front of the High Altar and raised both his arms.

—There is one, he began, who but for her wanton sinfulness, would this night have been made Queen of the Dark Minions!

—Foul! Foul! Most foul deed! the celebrants responded in unison, their fists upraised in anger.

—There is one who, in her ignorance and rutting lust, betrayed our Most High Lord and Master!

—Foul! Foul! Most foul deed!

—There is one who, as a mark of Satan's vengeance, has been made to suffer. But her full retribution to our Lord has yet to be made!

—Foul! Foul! Most foul deed!

Mercadante fairly shrieked with anger, dark veins swelling on his forehead:

—This night, before us all, she will surely be made to pay! This night you all will see the fate awaiting those who defy our Master, the Lord of the Universe!

—Make her pay! shouted a naked crone, make her pay with her blood!

Other voices were raised in anger, cursing the defiant one, calling for a lingering, painful death. The scattered imprecations soon resolved themselves into a wrathful chant:

—Make the sow pay! Make the sow pay! Make the sow pay!

Mercadante looked down upon the frenzied, gesturing celebrants, smiling. Then he motioned for silence.

—Be seated, all of you, he commanded, that her entrance among us be not greeted with respect!

The celebrants seated themselves, gaping eagerly behind them at the entrance to the Great Hall. Mercadante made a sign to the musicians and slow, funeral music wailed throughout the room. The large bronze doors were opened and Bennett entered, robed like his master. Behind him, borne on a leash and burdened with shackles and chains, was naked Adrienne.

She looked neither to the right nor the left. As she was led slowly up the central aisle, her eyes were glazed with inner visions and her lips worked themselves in mad whispers. Her flesh was torn and swollen, stained black with bruises, and her nipples still bore within them the lancets of nipple rings which had been used as a part of her torment. The satanists reviled her from their seats as she passed, cursing her foully, reaching out into the aisle to pinch and cuff at her, spitting on her flesh. But her mind was gone. Her lips would suddenly smile brightly and she'd mumble nonsensical phrases to herself but then in a moment the delusion would pass and she'd be biting her lower lip, her eyes wet with tears.

Bennett led her slowly up the aisle to the marble slab on the left. He was joined by an acolyte who helped him lay Adrienne, unprotesting, on top of the slab where she was spread-eagled and shackled.

Her lips kept churning with smiles and scowls.

The shouts and imprecations of the celebrants crescendoed almost to hysteria. Mercadante raised his arms again, demanding silence.

—There is yet another, he cried out, destined to be the most blessed of all women! She, too, will be presented this evening to our Great Lord in order that He may take her and make her His bride. Rise, you worshippers of Satan, that you may welcome her and honor her and prostrate yourselves before her!

The celebrants rose quickly to their feet, craning their necks to see the bronze entrance doors to the Great Hall. They chattered among themselves excitedly, eager to view the bride of Satan. Solemn yet joyous music wafted upward from the musicians.

The bronze doors opened inward, revealing a massive, bulky shadow. Slowly the bride of Satan entered the Great Hall astride a huge ram, its horns curled and massive, its body cascading with thick fleece. The celebrants gasped with awe at the girl's naked beauty: she was very young with taut, smooth flesh and full breasts that jostled delicately as she rode up the central aisle. Her hair was long and chestnut brown and woven within her delicate tresses were sprigs of baby's breath and bright daisies. Her eyes were glazed like Adrienne's because she'd been heavily dosed with Pago Pala, a virulent aphrodisiac. Her wide brown eyes stared sightless before her while her pubis thrust lustfully into the thick fleece of the ram's back, as the beast swayed with each step forward. At intervals the bride would suck in her breath and bite her lower lip with pleasure as her body trembled with waves of near-orgasmic arousal. She twined her slender fingers among the stiff curls of the fleece, caressing the beast's sides with soft palms.

When the ram drew near to the marble altars, Bennett and the acolyte helped the girl off the beast and led her yielding to the sacrificial altar on the right. When she was laid out gently on the cold stone, her eyes seemed to glimmer for a brief moment with conscious memory. She stared about her at the thousand candles and the gleaming silver statues and the throngs of naked people admiring her with lascivious lips. As her wrists and ankles were fitted into the shackles embedded in the marble, she began to struggle weakly against the iron. But her efforts only caused more of the drug to seep in fresh waves into her brain, relaxing her, inflaming her, making her sink languidly down onto the cold stone.

The acolyte guided the ram out of the Great Hall. Bennett joined his master upon the altar.

Taking his place behind the cauldron, Mercadante stretched his arms out toward the celebrants, his fingers widespread.

—Take heed, all ye who would worship the Dark Master! Take heed, all ye who desire to spend eternity in the throes of unspeakable pleasure! Take heed, all ye who would feel the power of the Master course through your veins! I display before ye the blessed and the cursed. Think ye neither that the Master will be deceived nor that the Master will withhold reward from ye who are deserving of it.

Mercadante plunged both his hands into the bloody cauldron, smearing them to the wrists. Then he stepped from behind the altar and descended to the sacrificial slabs. He held his bloody left hand over Satan's bride.

—I summon thee, O Baal! I summon thee, O Astarte! I summon thee, O Ashtoreth! Look with favor upon this woman, the bride of Thy Master! Bring unto her all blessings, all manner of glory, and eternal contentment!

He placed his bloody hand on the woman's left breast, squeezing it gently. She gasped, writhing with

399

pleasure in her bonds. He withdrew his hand, leaving a bloody print on her soft flesh.

—Make, O demons, of this woman offered up unto Thee, a worthy consort for her Lord!

He placed the same hand upon her right breast, likewise caressing it. She moaned with pleasure, stretching her legs against her bonds, arching her back high in her ecstasy. He then withdrew his hand, leaving the bloody imprint on her breast.

—And make, O demons, the womb of this woman to yield unto the Master's flock, fruitfully and with largesse, a multitude of princes and princesses, lords and ladies of the Infernal Kingdom! And make of this woman our intercessor, that we who are of the faith may enjoy the protection and guidance of the omnipotent dark forces!

He pressed his bloody hand onto the lips of her genitals, staining the brown public curls deep auburn. Her pelvis thrust upward beneath his hand, and the firm muscles of her inner thighs squeezed the fingers tightly into her flesh. She panted, moaning, her features writhing in orgasm. Then slowly, reluctantly, her pelvis dropped back onto the marble slab.

The Great Hall was completely silent as the celebrants stared forward at the woman, their tongues sliding wetly between their lips, their hands straying to their genitals.

Mercadante then crossed the central aisle to the altar upon which Adrienne lay bound. He held his bloody right hand over her.

—I summon thee, O Amduscias! I summon thee, O Eurynome! I summon thee, Belphegor! Look upon this creature with hatred and contempt, the betrayer of our Master! Bring unto her all torments, all manner of suffering, and eternal misery!

His bloody hand hovered over Adrienne's left breast. Her lips kept working in deluded and oblivious whispers. Then his hand descended. The blood upon his hand burned like acid into her flesh, tainting the air with foul vapors, causing her pale skin to sear and curdle. Roused from her insane stupor, Adrienne shrieked piteously.

Mercadante leered down on her while she writhed and twisted beneath his palm, grinning.

—Make, O demons, of this woman offered unto Thee, an example of Satan's wrath and Satan's justice!

—Justice! Justice! Justice! the celebrants began to chant.

His bloody hand descended upon her left breast and again the dark fumes of scorched flesh rose into the air while Adrienne howled her agony to the heedless stone walls.

He took his hand from the blistered, swollen breast. Adrienne was weeping uncontrollably.

—And make, O demons, the womb of this creature to be a pit of vipers, a sewer in which the faithless may prick and tease their insatiable, tormenting lusts.

His hand descended on her genitals and the moist flesh hissed. She shrieked and lurched to pull herself away from him, screaming for him to stop, screaming so lustily that even the most hardened satanists almost cringed. Mercadante grinned down on her, working his fingers more deeply into her flesh, savoring her relentless agony. Then at last, fearing that she'd pass out from her torment, he took away his hand.

Her body went limp on the slab.

With a flourish of his black robe, Mercadante ascended the steps to the High Altar. He withdrew from behind the altar a large silver ring which bore upon its face in heavy gold a jutting replica of a cock's fighting claw. Standing with legs widespread behind the altar, he raised his hands over his head, the ring poised to slip onto the middle finger of his left hand.

All at once the candles in the Great Hall dimmed with an eerie blue flame. Sulphurous vapors floated thickly to the high ceiling. The satanists babbled nervously among themselves, their eyes darting around the hall, marvelling at the unearthly flames and the foul stench.

The growl of thunder could be heard from outside the chateau's walls.

—Rise, you miserable wretches! Mercadante shouted, the ring still poised above him. Rise, that you may pay homage to the power of the Master!

The naked celebrants rose hastily to their feet, their candles clutched tightly in their hands. Mercadante thrust the ring onto his finger and sudden bolts of lightning shattered the stillness of mountain night, cracking again and again with electric fury. The walls trembled with the savage blasts and the celebrants cowered where they stood in the flashing glare of the lightning, which flashed over and over, white and hot and exultant. They stood hiding their faces from the blasts, shielding their skulls with their arms, falling to their knees on the stone floor to cringe behind the pews. Mercadante was majestic in the midst of the swirling maelstrom, his hands clasped high over his head, the cock's claw pointing upward, his face averted to the floor. It seemed an eternity to the celebrants before the savage lightning ceased, but at last the bolts became spaced farther and farther apart and the explosive thunder faded into the distance.

The hardier souls among the celebrants rose from the floor and looked up at Mercadante. He was still standing steadfast behind the altar, his hands clasped over his head. But in the sullen blue light of the candles, he was a surreal and alien specter.

And the jutting cock's claw glowed like a flaming sapphire.

Daniel slipped carefully into the fracture of a tremendous boulder. Pressed tightly against the two jagged surfaces of rock, he shimmied himself along the fracture until he finally came out on the other side. He heard the others behind him grunting and straining their way through.

They emerged one at a time and paused to catch their breath.

"It's dark enough . . . out here . . ." Ender panted. "But in that rock . . . I really felt . . . claustrophobic . . ."

All around them on the mountain they could hear the savage barking of dogs and the ominous shouts of men.

"Those rifle shots," Fedorson snarled. "Now all those bartards know where we are."

"Not exactly," Daniel corrected, "but they're closing in. Luckily we're almost there."

Jade looked ahead of them. He could distinguish nothing in the depths of the night shadows except a single yellow glow about two miles away.

"That's the glow of candles from the Great Hall," Daniel explained. "Mercadante uses that as his ritual chamber. They're all in there now."

"Then it's not very far, now," Jade concluded. "And the trail seems to level off." When confirmation wasn't forthcoming from Daniel, Jade looked for his shadow.

"Daniel," he asked, "are you okay?"

The old man was silent.

"Daniel," Jade repeated, "what's the matter?" He gently placed his hand on Daniel's shoulder. At his touch, the old man seemed to startle into awareness.

"No . . . no . . . nothing's the matter . . ." Daniel covered his eyes with his hand, rubbing his temples. "Just a . . . a strange feeling . . ."

"Are you sick?" Jade asked.

"No . . . no, my son, I'm not sick. It's just that I feel sort of . . . fatigued. Fatigued and distracted . . ." Then Daniel forced a cheery note into his voice. "Don't be concerned, my son. All this climbing . . . the pressure . . . at my age, now . . . really . . ."

Jade faced Daniel in the dark, studying him. He caressed the old man's soft, bearded cheek with his hand.

"No, it's not your age," Jade said. "You're like no other man. It's this mountain . . . this land. We've come too close to the Chateau and Mercadante's cursed the very ground. Like those . . . those swarms you told me about. The very stones beneath us are draining you of your strength."

Daniel was silent for a long moment. Then he finally said soberly, "I'm not accustomed to other people being more perceptive than I." He ran his slender fingers through his fine white hair. "It's not affecting you, I suppose."

"I'm beyond that," Jade laughed. "But you're still a sly one. You'd have me think that that's all that's troubling you. You know more than you're telling me."

"That's not true!" Daniel protested.

"Okay then," Jade corrected himself, "maybe you don't *know* . . . But you've got some very strong feelings."

Daniel sighed. "And feelings of that sort aren't substantial enough to burden another person with." He turned and faced out over the Harz mountains, sweeping the sudden accumulation of black clouds with his eyes. "It's just that I feel that I'm . . . I'm failing you. The dangers to you are grievous from now on. Though my powers aren't like yours, I know that much. And I'm weakening . . . I've been able to come so far, so many months searching . . . and at the most . . . the most inopportune moment . . . I'm dying out."

Jade gently turned Daniel's face to his. He smiled.

"I know what you must be feeling, Daniel, and I understand. But there's a destiny beyond us both that forces us to play a game that has rules. It has to be. No matter how apparently invisible they are or how malleable . . . ya can't have a game without rules, as they say." Jade laughed. "So we gotta do what we gotta do. As long as we can. I've been more and more reconciled to that, the last day or so. And I'm even starting to feel kind of good about it. I'll get a chance to try my wings, see what it feels like to really stretch them. Whatever happens after that, whether good or bad, has gotta be anticlimactic. That's when it'll be my turn to pass out of the picture." Jade thought he saw a humid sapphire sparkle in the old man's eye. "It would be best, I suppose, to go at the pinnacle, before the decline ever starts to hit . . . but that's too much to ask of one lifetime."

Jade looked ahead at the light from the Chateau. "There's something else, too. That . . . that man, Mercadante. I've fed on the vibrations of these mountains . . . the rocks, the grasses, the very air around the place have shown me its secrets. Such things . . ." Jade turned his face from the old man, looking out at the clouds. "He and that creature . . . my counterpart . . . no, Daniel, they've gotta be destroyed." Jade turned back to the old man. "I could use a little more help from you on that account, that's for certain," he said smiling.

Daniel shook his head. "I've shown you all I can. Remember this carefully: it will cling to you like your shadow and when it gets within you, then all is over. Everything. You are of its nature and it is of yours. Its lungs will breathe with yours, its heart will beat with yours, its thoughts will follow yours however cunningly you think you hide them." The old man's long white hair swirled and flapped in the risen wind, as he stroked Jade's cheek. "Remember this as well, my son: there's always a price that must be paid. I wish there weren't, but that's just not to be."

Jade smiled upon the old man in return and grasped his hand. "I understand, my dearest friend."

"Uh, excuse me, gentlemen, for interrupting your heavy conversation," Fedorson broke in, "but there are men running around these mountains looking to kill us and, judging by the barking of the dogs, they're getting closer . . . So do you think we could reconvene at another time? Please?"

"Of course. You're right, licutenant," Daniel said and, without another word, hastened toward the yellow light with renewed energy. The others followed.

The path widened comfortably for almost a mile, a good portion of it being a downward slope. They passed through, in the dark, without incident.

"We're gonna pay for this good luck, I can feel it," Fedorson muttered aloud to himself as he jogged along the path. And shortly, Daniel brought them to a halt.

"You can't see from where you are in the dark," he said, pointing ahead of them and to the right, "but the path narrows considerably at this point. This is complicated by the fact that, for about one hundred feet, the path becomes nothing more than a narrow ledge running across the sheer face of a cliff. We must all keep ourselves close to the face of the rock the entire time we're crossing that ledge. Keep in mind also how vulnerable we'll be to attack: that's why this is one of Mercadante's most cunning defenses. We'd never bc able to make it in the daylight: we'd just be target practice. Now, I'll go first; follow after me slowly . . . and be careful."

Daniel stepped next to the ink black shadow of the mountainface and pressed himself against it. Jade followed suit, then Ender, then Fedorson, slowly, barely breathing. "I knew it," Fedorson grumbled beneath his breath, clinging to the face of the cliff. "I fuckin' knew it."

The sheer stone was cold against their cheeks and, from far over the mountain peaks, thunder growled ominously. They inched their way along the ledge, their outspread palms pressed against the face of the cliff level with their heads, sidestepping carefully to the left. Ender was grateful that it was too dark to look down and see the great heights they were defying on that narrow ledge, so he shut his eyes in keeping with the darkness and mumbled a little prayer to the ancient gods.

Jade suddenly called a halt. "Ssh!" he whispered. "Listen!"

The four men clung to the face of the cliff in deathly silence. From above them, emerging from the fading thunder, they heard a throaty burst of laughter.

"There's somebody up there!" Ender whispered desperately.

"Shit!" Fedorson cursed, "I knew it . . ."

All at once the cliff face trembled violently, sending the four men scrambling for a tighter grip on the rocks to keep from plummeting. Something pounded above them in the darkness, falling swiftly toward them, scattering splinters of rock in its path.

"Scatter!" Jade shouted, and he and Daniel sidestepped hastily forward while Fedorson and Ender backed off. A thundering black shadow caromed off the ledge between them with a great crash and continued falling into the black abyss below.

"Somebody's dumpin' boulders on us!" exclaimed Fedorson. "Tryin' to knock us off the cliff!"

"And I got a good idea who's doing it," Jade called out. "You guys get the hell back off the ledge. Daniel and I'll try and make it to the far side."

But before any of them could move, they heard more laughter, louder this time, more bold. The cliff face trembled again, this time more violently, and a second boulder slammed past them, fortuitously striking a slight outcropping of rock that sent it bounding outward and away from the ledge on which they were trapped. But the quaking of the cliff was as dangerous as the falling rock. Ender's left foot was jolted off the ledge, causing his whole leg to swing out over nothingness. He clawed at the cliff with his fingernails, desperately balancing on his toes, struggling not to fall backward. He finally drew his foot back onto the ledge, striking it against loose pebbles, and swayed himself back into equilibrium against the cliff. His lungs heaved with terror.

"The bastard's got us pinned," Fedorson whispered. The laughter from the darkness above grew even louder, more contemptuous. "And he knows it!"

They could hear another boulder being rolled into place.

Fedorson reached for his pistol, leaning precariously against the mountain. "I'll see if I can keep him pinned long enough for you guys to get the hell out of here," he called out. He aimed blindly upward into the darkness, his pistol kicking with a series of quiet pops. There was a pause in the activity above them and the men began to shimmy in opposite directions off the ledge.

But suddenly the laughter returned, followed by a third bounding boulder.

The boulder was larger than the others and fell even closer to the lieutenant. Fedorson gripped the surface of the cliff with his one free hand while the boulder jolted past him, clutching at him with the fingers of its downsweeping wind.

"Damn!" Fedorson growled when the boulder passed. "I'm probably not even reaching that sonofabitch with this fuckin' pistol." He listened above and heard the slow scraping of a fourth boulder being rolled into place. Very slowly and carefully, Fedorson slipped his pistol back into its holster and moved his left shoulder out slightly away from the cliff. With a free hand he carefully worked the automatic machine gun by its strap and slipped it off his shoulder and into his hand.

"What the hell are you trying to do?" Ender called out to him harshly. "You want to kill yourself?"

"Don't worry about me, counsellor. You just keep heading back off the ledge. I'll take care of the rest."

"B-but he'll be behind the boulder . . . you can't . . ."

"Just keep movin', damn it! I'm doing what I can!"

Ender shut his mouth and backed off. He watched what happened next as if in a dream.

As the fourth boulder tumbled down toward the ledge,

the sky was shattered by incredibly savage lightning, bolt upon bolt in a continuous barrage. The lightning flashed with such frequency that, for a few brief instants, everything appeared to Ender in stroboscopic sluggishness. The boulder plunged close to Fedorson, who was holding the center of the ledge. It struck his shoulder and Ender watched with wide eyes as the lieutenant fell backwards off the ledge, in tandem with the spinning rock.

Silhouetted against the wild glare of the lightning was the immense bulk of Pimm, one of the giant brothers, staring down from the top of the cliff, not more than fifty feet above them.

Fedorson seemed to float for an instant, free-falling over the abyss, staring upward. And then his weapon belched sudden flame. He fell like a comet, leaving a diminishing trail of flickering light.

Pimm's massive body fell after him, smashing at intervals against the mountainface.

"Hurry!" Jade shouted. "Let's get across before the lightning does us in!"

Ender hastened along the ledge, pressed tightly against the cliff. His big eyes were swollen with tears. He didn't dare look behind him.

When they finally came to the widening of the path, they raced for cover behind some bushes, shielding their heads with their hands against the unnatural onslaught of lightning. The Chateau could be seen now in the stark chiaroscuro of the lightning's glare: turreted, ancient, forbidding.

Ender could well believe it was the end of the world.

Then just as suddenly as the lightning began, it stopped. The sudden stillness of the air around the Chateau was almost as frightening as the storm. The three men raised their heads like inquisitive turtles from the underbrush in which they'd plunged. All was silent and black as a tomb.

Then the jade unicorn around Jade's neck burst into emerald fire.

When the lightning ceased and the blue glow of the candles returned to normal gold, Mercadante held his glowing ring aloft over the congregation. They gasped with wonder.

—By this mark of Satan shalt thou be known! Mercadante cried out. Let thy blood and thy flesh be witness to the infernal covenant that is in thy heart! Renew thy fealty to thy Lord and Master and thou shalt know the joys and riches of this world!

The naked celebrants presented themselves to Mercadante in single file, kneeling upon the steps of the High Altar, kissing the proffered ring. Each made a personal pledge of adoration and loyalty to Satan and then was bidden by Mercadante to rise. Then Mercadante forced the celebrant's cheek to one side with his hand, laying bare his throat. With the sharp, glowing barb of the ring, the old man scored the pale, soft flesh, watching the blood gather, swell, and drip in a fine line down the neck. As the ring plucked through their flesh, the celebrants winced with both pain and pleasure, feeling their fellowship with Satan speeding through their blood as if it were something tangible: embryonic and joyously pervasive.

The celebrants returned to their pews, renewed and expectant.

—O mighty Satan! Mercadante thundered after all vows and pacts were sealed, O mighty Lord of the universe! Thy children cry out to Thee in their wanderings. Long and bitter has been our exile. We face into the wind and weep with the stinging sands. We probe for Thee in our hearts and discover only emptiness. Now, mighty Satan, Thou hast come upon us in the fullness of Thy strength and majesty! Let this night see our wounds healed and our souls assuaged! Let us rejoice that Thou, O shepherd of our souls, hast returned to the bosom of Thy loving tribes and canst once more assume Thy rightful place in the forefront of Thy legions!

Mercadante stared down upon the congregation, his eyes wild with triumph, his stony face rigid with exultation.

—Thou piteous mortals! he cried out, flinging wide his fists. Bend thy knees to thy Master!

The celebrants hastily fell to their knees on the cold stone floor.

—Behold the Great God Satan!!

The bronze doors to the Great Hall flew open. A massive, black shadow extended along the central aisle, darkening the High Altar.

31

"CAN'T you turn that damn thing off?" Ender shouted, distraught. "The darkness was our only cover!"

Jade squinted against the glare of the unicorn that blazed upon his breast. "I can't turn it off," he said simply. "I didn't turn it on."

"Then get rid of it!" Ender yelled, grabbing the glowing jade and tugging on the chain.

It wouldn't break.

Suddenly, Ender dropped the unicorn, grimacing, shaking his hand desperately in the chill mountain air.

"It burned me!" he hollered, startled, angry, almost offended. "It burned the shit out of my hand!"

Jade stared down into the figure's malevolent eyes. "Intractable little bastard, isn't it?" he said ironically. "I think it's out to get me."

"If you don't stop it from shining, somehow," Ender retorted, nursing his hand, "it's going to get all three of us. This place is swarming with Mercadante's men!" He looked around distractedly and listened for the sound of boots scraping on rocks or the clicking of rifle bolts. He heard nothing. He rubbed his hand. "Doesn't that thing burn you, hanging on your chest like that?" he asked bitterly.

"No. I suppose I'm immune to it." Jade faced Ender,

smiling, his skin green with the glare. "Just lucky, I guess."

Ender considered the glowing unicorn with antiquarian curiosity. "Amazing!" he breathed. "Can't you unhook it or something and put it in your pocket?"

"That's not the way," Daniel intervened, "even if Jade could do it. It means something . . . I'm sure of that." The old man studied the puzzling phenomenon, stroking his beard.

"It means that Mercadante's men know where to shoot," Jade countered.

"Being around me isn't safe . . . you both stay here and protect yourselves. I'll continue alone."

"No, Jade!" Daniel objected. "There's a better way . . ."

Suddenly they heard a sharp hiss from out of the darkness. Something black and massive flashed past them, striking Ender full in the chest. With a painful grunt he collapsed onto the ground.

"What the fuck . . . ?" Jade exclaimed stooping beside Ender. "Somebody's hit him with a log!"

He rose up on one knee and faced the darkness from which the missile emerged. The jade unicorn cast an eerie glow on the foliage and the jumbled rocks.

The second giant from the alley, the one called Brud, grinned back at them.

"O Christ!" Jade spat out angrily. "Not you again, you cocksucker!"

The grinning giant lumbered forward like a rampaging elephant. But without warning Daniel leaped through the air at him, his staff raised high above his head. Brud halted in his tracks, recalling the strength of the old man and the damage he could wreak with his strangely carved stick, so he hastily shielded his face with his arm. The blow landed flush on his forearm but there wasn't nearly the force behind it that Brud had remembered. Daniel backed off for another lunge and Brud stared down at him, suddenly contemptuous. With surprising alacrity the giant hurled himself at Daniel, sweeping the old man up in his bear-like arms.

The staff fell with a hollow clatter upon the rocks.

The intense pressure on his ribs prevented Daniel from calling out but Jade saw the agony all over his face. He hadn't time to hunt for Ender's gun so he just leaped like a green meteor at the man-mountain, side-kicking his head. The toe of his boot caught the giant full in the temple and the creature howled with pain. He threw Daniel brutally to the ground and charged Jade.

When he looked up from where the giant had thrown him to the ground, Daniel thought he was suffering the effects of his injuries. It was only after some moments that he realized he was witnessing something wondrous.

Hundreds of glaring emerald lights swirled all around Brud, a kaleidoscope of images of Jade, taunting the bewildered creature, confusing him: "Here, shithead, right behind you"; "No, fool, here I am!"; "Hey, you fat asshole, over here, over here!" The irate giant jostled his bulk backward and forward, swiping at Jade's grinning face but always ending up with a fistful of air. Jade's laughter echoed over the mountains as the lights swarmed and swelled, forcing the giant to his knees in sheer confusion.

Suddenly the false images disappeared. The real Jade stood behind the kneeling giant. There was a quick blur of motion and the side of Jade's hand landed full on the back of the giant's skull. The creature's eyes widened momentarily and then he fell forward on the stone, motionless.

Jade walked over to where Daniel was sitting on the ground, staring. "How are you?" he asked.

"I've never seen such a sight!" Daniel breathed in amazement. "What . . . what cunning!"

"You saw? I thought you were out cold."

"I saw." With Jade's assistance Daniel rose unsteadily to his feet. "I'm fine now, really . . ."

"Yeah," Jade said sarcastically, "you look just great."

"It's . . . that weakness. Nothing more. I'll be over it in a few moments." He pressed his temples with his palms, shaking the vapors out of his head. "Come, my son. We must help Mr. Ender."

Ender was still unconscious, lying next to the small log that had laid him low. Daniel opened his shirt, running his deft fingers over his chest.

"He's still alive," Daniel announced hopefully. "That's something, at least. But he's pretty broken up inside. He could puncture a lung."

"Let me take a look," Jade offered. He kneeled over Ender, placing both of his hands on his chest. He was perfectly silent and motionless and then his eyes began to glow, dimly at first then more fiercely, rivaling the shine of the unicorn.

Suddenly Ender stirred, coughing.

Jade's eyes went dark.

"Wha . . . ?" Ender looked about bewilderedly, squinting in the glare of the unicorn. "What happened?"

"I think you must've been mistaken, Daniel," Jade said, smiling. "Mr. Ender here's gonna feel just fine."

The beast strode stately up the central aisle toward the High Altar, mantled in its own magnificence. The celebrants quailed before it, stupefied by its glowing eyes, its towering frame, its glinting, spiral horn. Its slow, even breathing could be heard echoing savagely throughout the hall and its furred and curling flanks glistened with a beautiful softness in the flickering flames of the candles.

Mercadante, himself, was rendered speechless by the creature's aura of strength and by its sublime dignity. Then he fell to his knees beside the altar, his arms outstretched in supplication, his cheeks wet with tears.

—O most noble Form, he cried out, O Thou beauteous and omnipotent Master, we beseech Thee to look upon us, Thy worthless and wayward servants, with mercy and with love! We prostrate ourselves before Thee and tremble before Thy Greatness!

The beast looked down on Mercadante kneeling, then smiled as the old man touched his forehead to the floor.

—Sathanus adjutor meus! the celebrants shouted with one voice. Sathanus adjutor meus!

The beast stepped slowly up to the altar, its hoofs clicking against the stones. It looked down upon the inverted crucifix and ran its rough hand along the smooth, silver flanks of the Savior. Then it stepped to the statue of Cerberus, taunting one vicious silver head with a long, calcine claw, smiling.

Mercadante rose up on one knee, quizzically, watching the beast. It approached the High Altar and looked down into the cauldron. It sniffed, studying the sticky red liquid then reached in with its hand. It withdrew bloodstained fingers, drawing them up to its mouth.

The creature licked its fur clean and then stared out over the sea of naked worshippers, grinning.

The satanists went wild with joy.

Amidst the cheers and the weeping, amidst the frenzied dancing and hugging, amidst the howls of hysterical pleasure, Mercadante rose to his feet and pranced around the beast, kissing its malodorous fur and welcoming it on behalf of his flock with gestures and glowing words.

The beast gazed upon the frenzy in silence. Its bizarre equine face was expressionless.

Then it saw the shackled women.

The beast stepped in front of Mercadante, thrusting the adoring disciple rudely to the floor. Mercadante stared up at the retreating hindquarters of the beast, his face pale. The celebrants, gradually becoming aware of the affront to their priest, fell silent. Its eyes shimmering with green fire, the beast stepped down from the altar to the sacrificial slabs, surveying the two women.

Mercadante hastened to its side.

—Most potent Lord, Mercadante began, these are the two women about whom I spoke.

The beast didn't acknowledge his words. Mercadante scurried in front of Adrienne's slab, pointing to her bruised body.

—This, O Great One, is she who betrayed You. Her body has been twisted and broken and violated that she may learn the heavy price to be paid for defying Your sole majesty. Her mind has been driven to madness so that the very germ of her rebelliousness is crushed out of her.

The beast regarded Adrienne without expression.

—But You must show her, Yourself, the fullness of Your holy wrath!

Mercadante beckoned the beast forward to Adrienne's side. It stepped forward, sniffing.

—You must demonstrate to Your gathered worshippers the depth of Your rage and the remorselessness of Your vengeance!

The beast studied Mercadante's intense eyes and then

stepped nearer to Adrienne, looking down upon her face. Her lips churned in a hushed, mad dialogue with her shattered soul. The beast carefully ran one claw along the bruised flesh of her thigh and her glazed eyes suddenly became lucid. She stared up at it, seeing it for the first time, staring at the point of its terrible horn glinting in the candlelight, staring into its fiery emerald eyes.

Her face became a mask of horror.

—Jade! Jade! she cried out, straining at her shackles. My God, Jade . . . !

Mercadante seethed with rage that the name of that man should be spat in Satan's teeth. He stepped forward and slapped Adrienne hard across the face.

—Slut! Mercadante shouted. My Lord, she must be shown . . .

The beast had been startled by her sudden cries. Its eyes suddenly blazed, bathing her in green light. Mercadante backed away from the slab. Not a sound could be heard throughout the Great Hall.

In the midst of her struggles, Adrienne's eyes suddenly widened and her body stiffened with pain. Her mouth trembled, struggling to form words to voice her agony but the pain was too intense. She fell stiffly back upon the marble, her limbs straining against her bonds.

A lump appeared beneath the flesh of her abdomen slightly below her ribcage. The lump grew larger and more taut until the skin suddenly split open, spewing blood.

A small viper emerged from the hole and slithered onto her thigh. It began to bite its way back into her flesh.

Other lumps sprang up all over her body.

She could neither scream nor weep. Her body was simply rigid with pain.

—How exquisite is Thy vengeance! Mercadante exclaimed, his eyes wide and sparkling. How potent is Thy wrath!

And Ender did feel fine, except for his bewilderment over his unconscious lapse and the throbbing headache he was getting behind his eyes from the glare of the unicorn. He was stretched out on the rocky path, leaning on his elbows and squinting at the two men who spoke in hurried whispers.

Coming closer in the darkness were the sounds of shouting men and the barking of dogs.

"It's the only way," Daniel was saying. "I'd do you both more harm than good if I stayed with you: I can feel myself weakening by the second. At least this way I can do some good."

"You can also get killed playing decoy," Jade retorted.

"And you can get killed going into the Chateau. That's not stopping you."

Jade was silent.

"I've no intention of arguing with you about this, my son," Daniel concluded finally. "Another few seconds and the others will be swooping right down on us. I'm going." He rose quickly to his feet, wrapping his cloak tightly around himself. "Cover the unicorn as much as you can with your hands and continue along the path. It's easy from here, if I can keep the guards distracted. Once you're in the Chateau, head straight for the Great Hall." Daniel pointed toward the window with the yellow glow. "There won't be any guards to stop you; they're all out here hunting us on the slopes."

Jade made as if to speak but Daniel silenced him with a finger raised to his lips. Their eyes met and lingered and then the old man fell upon Jade, hugging him. Jade returned the embrace vigorously, his eyes wet with sudden tears.

"Here," Daniel said softly, gently freeing himself from Jade, "take my staff with you. It's yours now." He forced it into Jade's hands.

"No!" Jade protested. "I couldn't . . ."

"Take it!" the old man commanded. "It's of no use to me now. Only you can work its power on this mountain. Take it with you now, quickly, and put it to good use."

Jade hefted the staff in his hands, feeling its power tingle through his palms and fingers. "All right," he answered, "I'll take it then. But only as a loan. Until after . . ."

The old man nodded with a somber half-smile. "As

you wish," he said and, without another word, turned and scampered up some boulders piled up at the side of the path, disappearing into a large black fissure.

From the other end of the fissure a bright green glow emerged.

Jade covered the unicorn with his left hand, returning himself and Ender to darkness. They watched as the green glow danced like a fairy sprite away from them up the hill. The guards could be heard shouting to one another and shots rang out.

"C'mon," Jade said bitterly to Ender. "Let's get going."

They ran swiftly along the last mile of the path, Jade feeling for his footing with energetic sweeps of the staff. They heard raucous shouting and volleys of gunfire behind them and Jade knew that as long as the guns kept firing, Daniel hadn't been hit. As the old man had predicted, they encountered no further guards.

The path ended at a small clearing at the base of the Chateau. Set into the granite foundation was a large iron door with an iron ring for a handle. Ender ran eagerly up to the door and, grabbing the ring with both hands, pulled with all his might. It wouldn't budge.

"I think it's locked," Ender said sorrowfully. "What'll we do now?"

"It figures it'd be locked," Jade answered sullenly. "Well I don't have the time to fuck with it."

Jade took his hand off the unicorn and grasped Daniel's staff with both hands. He raised it high over his head and brought it crashing down into the center of the door. With a resounding crack of shattering metal the door fell backward off its hinges, flat onto the interior paving stones.

"Hurry!" Jade cried out and they passed quickly into the nether passages of the Chateau.

The glow from the unicorn lit the grim tunnels brilliantly as they ran searching for a pathway upward into the Great Hall. Jade knew the general direction from having seen the window, and he tried to compute its spatial alignment with the iron door. But for the most part they could do little but follow the winding passages.

Suddenly, Jade stopped dead in his tracks. They'd burst upon a wide stone hallway on one side of which was set another smaller iron door. There were bars in the top of the door and one limp hand hung between them.

"Look!" Ender cried out, pointing. "Somebody's in there!"

They approached the door more closely. The hand remained motionless. Jade brought his face closer to the iron bars, trying to peek within. All at once the hand twitched and grabbed for Jade's face.

He jumped back, startled. The hand pulled back into the darkness, then returned clutching one of the iron bars, joined by a second hand. Between both hands a wild man's face was pressed up against the bars. The man babbled incoherently at Jade, desperation and terror filling its strange, gobbling speech.

It was then that Jade and Ender saw that the man's tongue was cut out.

Jade stepped forward again, lifting the glowing unicorn on its chain so that he could see into the darkness behind the door. The tongueless man squinted painfully in the glare and drew back.

"No . . . no . . ." Jade groaned, peering inside. "O my God!"

They'd found the holding cell for the Chateau's helpless victims.

Jade staggered backward, sickened by the stench of offal and decay. He kept Ender from the door with his staff.

"Stand back!" he told Ender. "We've got to get them outta there."

He stood in front of the door, grasping the staff in both hands and raising it over his head. It began glowing with rusty fires, then Jade shut his eyes in concentration and the staff blazed blue-white, flooding the dungeon with light. A sharp click and the door flew open. The mutilated, half-crazed prisoners cringed uneasily before the sudden flood of light, their shackles rattling. Jade stood motionless in the open doorway, the staff glowing ever brighter. Suddenly a volley of clicking metallic sounds echoed throughout the subterranean chamber as the prisoners' shackles fell to the floor.

Then the staff dimmed.

In the light of the jade unicorn, Jade and Ender walked

among the victims, raising them to their feet, soothing their panic. They had no idea what was happening to them or whether the glowing lights were one more torment concocted by the infernal Mercadante. Jade's eyes, not yet dry from his parting with Daniel, were freshly flooded in compassion for the plight of these poor tormented creatures. He walked among them, trying to soothe them briefly with soft words, wishing he could heal their scarred minds and their broken bodies. But there wasn't time.

"This way! . . . This way! . . ." Jade said to them as they staggered out of the dungeon, staring about vaguely, like cattle. He pointed anxiously down the corridor from which he and Ender had come. "Run from here, all of you!" he shouted to them. "Follow that corridor, keeping always to the right, and you'll get outside. Hurry, please, for God's sake!" Gradually the prisoners realized they were being liberated and they began to pour out of the door and scramble down the corridor, guided by the light of the unicorn to the first turning. "Get off this cursed mountain!" Jade cried out after them. "As quickly as you can, flee this God-forsaken place!"

They spilled out of the dungeon, clinging to one another, the able helping the cracked and crippled. Some wore shreds of rags while most were naked, urine-soaked straw and offal clinging to their pale, bruised flesh. Jade and Ender stayed and watched until the last of them was carried out of the green light by his fellows. Adrienne wasn't among them.

"A wealthy and respected financier!" Jade snarled, spitting on the floor. He looked at Ender. "C'mon, let's get him!"

The corridors passed like a blur in Ender's mind, as he followed panting at Jade's heels. He prayed that Jade knew where he was going because he, himself, was totally confused. Finally, they came upon a short, transverse passage which was blocked by a door on each end.

Jade was stymied.

"Shit!" he swore. "We've got to get to some stairs or something heading upward. Through one of these doors . . ."

Before he could finish speaking, Ender ran up to the

door on the left, kneeling beside it. He moistened his finger with his tongue and felt the opening beneath the door. Then he ran to the right-hand door and did the same.

"This is the one," he called to Jade. "A lot more fresh air coming through here." The door opened outward at Ender's touch.

As they dashed along the corridor, Jade said, "That was pretty quick thinking. Where'd you learn that trick?"

"A trip I once took," Ender gasped, running. "An archeological dig in Egypt . . . during college vacation . . . a summer fling . . ." He was silent a few moments that he might regain the wind to speak. "A trick I was shown . . . in case I got trapped . . . in a tomb . . ."

"Appropriate," Jade nodded, running. "Very appropriate . . ."

They followed the corridor until it began to slope discernibly upward. Jade followed the slope with his eyes and then pointed.

"Over there!" he said. "Look!"

They ran to where a flight of stone steps rose out of a niche of shadows. Jade bounded up the steps two at a time, Ender stumbling behind. It was a very long flight of stairs and at the top landing a door was lighted by a smoking torch. Jade cautiously opened the door.

He wrapped his fist around the unicorn. With one eye, he saw a huge reception hall that towered upward into grim shadows. One flickering torch rested in its sconce, leaving much of the hall dark. At the center of the hall two massive bronze doors glinted like armor in the light of the torch. A couple of armed guards stood rigidly in front of the doors, while a number of acolytes lounged carelessly off to one side, awaiting their summons. Off to the left, however, and much closer to the door from which he peered, was a stone arch beneath which was a flight of steps rising into dark shadow.

He withdrew his head and turned to Ender. "There are guards and a bunch of other people hanging around two huge doors," he whispered. "I think they're having their ceremony behind those doors. Let me just think a minute . . ." he said, rubbing his forehead with his free hand. "I just gotta think . . ."

Suddenly a swelling chant echoed throughout the reception hall from the far side of the bronze doors: "VIR-ESCIT, SATHANUS!! VIRESCIT, SATHANUS!!" The acolytes jumped to their feet, crowding around the doors with their ears pressed to the metal.

"Now's our chance!" Jade exclaimed to Ender. "Follow me and keep real close to the wall on the left so we won't be seen."

He rose and slipped like a shadow out the door and up against the wall, the unicorn still in his fist. He shimmied his back along the stone wall, his eyes staring from the shadows into the faces of the rigid guards, watching for signs of movement or awareness. Then he dashed beneath the arch and stormed up the stairs.

Ender followed breathlessly behind him, "VIRESCIT, SATHANUS!! VIRESCIT, SATHANUS!!" ringing horribly in his ears.

At the top of the stairs was a rich velvet curtain from behind which Jade peered. With a grimace of rage and horror he leaped forward, planting himself firmly on the balustrade overlooking the Ritual of Ascension, the staff gripped tightly in his hand.

The beast stepped back from Adrienne's corpse, which now swarmed with vipers. It turned its attention to the naked girl whose hair was bedecked with flowers. Mercadante hastened to her side.

—O most mighty Satan, Thou most omnipotent Lord! he called out. Accept from us, Your worshippers and the ministers of Your will, this gift of a most noble and beautiful bride!

Even the massive dose of aphrodisiac couldn't keep the terror from rising within the heart of the bleary-eyed girl. In spite of the burning, physical lust that spread from her genitals to her outermost limbs, she focussed her swimming vision on the face of the beast that grinned down on her and she started striving weakly against her bonds.

—No! No! she tried to scream, but her words spilled heavily from her numb lips like marbles.

The beast stood before her outspread legs and ran his claws slowly along her smooth inner thigh down to her ankles, leaving thin tracks of blood. It stood back from the marble slab, grinning, its eyes beginning to blaze. Slowly, very slowly swelling, its pendulous horsecock began to rise . . .

The celebrants gasped in lewd admiration at the impossible size of their god's member.

—Virescit, Sathanus! Mercadante shouted, grinning wildly, his arms flung far above his head in homage and exultation. It grows, O mighty Satan! Our offering is received and found worthy!

—VIRESCIT, SATHANUS!! VIRESCIT, SATHANUS!! the naked minions shouted, taking up the chant from Mercadante. VIRESCIT, SATHANUS!!

The terrified girl squirmed against the shackles, her red-rimmed eyes filled with the vision of the beast lowering itself upon her. And then she screamed the scream of ecstasy and horror.

The beast plunged mercilessly inside her, spewing blood all over the marble slab between her fighting legs. It bucked and thrust against the marble, inching the heavy stone altar of sacrifice slowly backward along the floor. Mercadante, flushed with the passion of the rape, suddenly threw off his black robe, revealing his own nakedness.

Between his legs he had neither penis nor scrotum: a flopping lip of scarred flesh only, the remnant of an act of self-mutilation done in the satanic religious fervor of his youth.

—VIRESCIT, SATHANUS!! the satanists chanted, fingering their own genitals. VIRESCIT, SATHANUS!!

Growling its ecstasy with its shaggy head thrown back and its ivory horn quivering in the candlelight, the beast surged one final time against the marble, its cat-like eyes blazing.

Then it backed off the girl's still body.

—VIRESCIT, SATHANUS!! the celebrants shrieked in frenzy.

—VIRESCIT, SATHANUS!! Mercadante howled to the rafters.

Suddenly:

"NO! NO! NO!!!"

The beast spun its face to the balustrade, its features

twisted in an angry, deadly grimace. The satanists gasped into silence. Mercadante stared upward, his eyes wide with awe.

Jade stood upon the balustrade, his eyes aflame. He had seen Adrienne's bloody and crumbled corpse. He had heard the young girl's terrified scream. The staff in his upraised hand glowed brilliant as a meteor, and, like a meteor, he flung it blazing at the heart of the beast.

With a speed unknown to mortals, the beast grabbed Mercadante by the arm and heaved his naked body high up in the air to intercept the glowing staff. The old man chortled as the staff transfixed his heart, spewing streamers of blood out behind him.

The staff fell upright into the floor, Mercadante's corpse still pierced upon it, fissuring the stone.

And then the miraculous occurred: the fissure widended and lengthened and the Great Hall began to crumble, great masses of hewn stone falling upon the satanists from the buttressed ceiling. The very mountain began to quake and tremble.

The satanists howled and shrieked in terror. They tried to flee the Great Hall but couldn't stay upon their feet for the quaking of the mountain and the shivering of the Chateau's stones. They screamed, clutching madly at each other for balance and leverage, falling helplessly upon the heaving floor, crushed and bloodied by the catapulting debris.

The musicians, suddenly aware that their shackles had fallen from their ankles, rose and fled. They made it out the bronze doors.

Jade stood above the fuming beast in shining magnificence. His heart was mad with hatred. He poised to leap upon the beast and feel its monstrous neck yield to his powerful fingers but he stirred himself before he sprang with the sudden recollection of Daniel's words.

NO GOOD, YOU BASTARD! NOT THAT WAY!

He grinned down into the monster's flaming eyes.

WE'LL FIGHT. BUT ON MY TERMS.

And then Jade leaped off the balustrade, diving toward a point in empty space. He cast a mocking eye at the beast as he seemingly floated, bit by tremulous bit, into nothingness.

He was gone.

The beast stared up at the point in space through which Jade disappeared, confused. As more of the Great Hall crumbled, the beast warded off the falling blocks of stone with powerful forearms, still staring at that point.

Then suddenly it grinned.

Before Ender's frightened and amazed eyes, it, too, leaped toward that point in space, floating ever more slowly until it disappeared as well.

Ender gripped the trembling balustrade amidst a rain of heavy stones. It shattered and began to lurch downward, inch by inch, as the destruction of the Chateau proceeded with ever-increasing momentum.

Ender's eyes were wide with panic. There was nowhere he could flee to, nor anything he could do to save himself. Far below him the dying satanists writhed like a pit of snakes.

He looked down upon the beast's bride, helpless in her shackles. She was dying slowly from her bloody wounds and her eyes looked up to Ender in silent prayer.

Too slowly.

He took his pistol from his belt and tried to hold it steady on the sinking balustrade. Central stones from the ceiling began falling all around the girl, shattering into dust and sharp shards as they impacted near her flesh. There was a sudden, soft pop and a black hole appeared in the center of the girl's forehead, releasing her from her misery.

A tumble of stones fell upon Ender's shoulders and the balustrade swayed beneath him. His body burned with pain, yet, before he lost consciousness, he remembered the gruesome scene in the morgue. He aimed the pistol at the dead girl's womb and fired.

Everything went black as the balustrade crashed to the floor.

Daniel was sprawled face down on a ledge of rock, a few feet from the precipice. Only by clinging to the rugged roots of some mountain scrub had he kept himself from rolling over the edge.

He'd been shot in the chest and the leg but he'd been able to keep fleeing long enough to draw the guards away from Jade and Ender. The ledge of rock beneath him was slick with his blood.

"No more . . ." he thought to himself. "Dizzy . . . too weak . . ."

The shouts of men and dogs came closer.

"The pain!" he gasped aloud this time. "The pain . . . !"

And then a great dark shadow moved nearby. He heard sneering laughter.

"You!" the old man exclaimed, craning his neck toward the shadow. "You . . . !"

Porfex, the third giant brother. The man-mountain lumbered closer to the dying old man.

Suddenly Daniel laughed weakly. "You'll be the one then," he gasped up at the giant. "You'll send me to . . . to where he's already been . . . The lights! . . . The beauty! . . . O to have been with him then . . ."

Porfex came closer, suspicious. Daniel smiled up at him.

"Do it, you ignorant freak, and I'll owe you. I'll owe you. Do it!"

But suddenly the smile disappeared from Daniel's face and he raised himself with great pain onto his elbows, staring malevolently into the black obscurity that was Porfex.

"I'll owe you nothing!" the old man raged. "Nothing, do you hear? Nothing!"

Daniel let go of the thick roots and heaved himself over the ledge. He plummeted silently through the darkness.

And then the miraculous occurred: the entire bulk of the Brocken heaved and quaked, spewing avalanches of boulders over the twisted peaks and cliffs, mingling the terrified shrieks of the guards with the splintering of great boulders.

Porfex stared about him, terrified. But before he could hasten his huge bulk to safety, the ledge collapsed beneath him.

The giant fell for a long time.

Jade floated, lotus-legged, in darkness. An interspatial realm, without time, without dimension.

The battlefield.

Jade's face was immobile and serene, his eyes glowing like emeralds. The jade unicorn around his neck sliced through the swirling, inky mists with its beacon light, far, far into the distance.

Afraid it won't find me? . . . soon . . . soon enough, little demon . . .

Jade recalled Daniel's warning and forced his thoughts down deep within him, shrouding them in opaque serenity.

In the distance, a glimmer of light: a flying, flashing beast with the glowing nighteyes of a cat.

A sparkle of sharp horn.

It was upon Jade swiftly, grinning, its horn leveled at his heart. Jade floated serenely, poised, then floated suddenly upward, unharmed, as the raging beast plummeted past.

Jade sensed the presence of the beast with the totality of his mind, ready for its second lunge. Again the beast flew at him, howling, and again Jade floated away, serene.

To kill me you must touch me. You'll never kill me . . .

The beast gazed upon Jade's floating form from a distance, hesitant yet grinning. The unicorn around Jade's throat throbbed with taunting light.

Touch me . . . to kill me . . .

The beast stared at the glowing jade unicorn, enraged. Then suddenly it grinned.

Touch me . . . must touch me . . . to kill me . . .

Flushed with the arrogance of his powers, the beast kept away from his serenely floating adversary. It treaded the currents of dark mist, staring intently at the glowing unicorn hanging from its chain.

It would prove it could win . . .

The jade unicorn flared like an exploding sun.

. . . without touching him.

The jade unicorn began spinning at the end of its chain. As it whirled faster and faster, it seemed to glare up into Jade's serene face, furious, triumphant.

And as the unicorn spun, the thin chain tightened around Jade's neck.

No . . . not that way . . . mustn't . . .

The beast stared at Jade as the spinning jade figure rose higher and higher up his chest, approaching his neck. Then the chain began to tighten around his throat.

The beast grinned.

The unicorn kept spinning and the chain wouldn't snap. It cut into the flesh of Jade's neck, drawing blood.

To know . . . to be aware . . . more than to do . . .

Jade rallied all the powers of his mind to still the agony. His throat constricted tightly and he felt his arteries throb against the cartilage of his windpipe. His temples pounded.

The pain . . .

He remained floating in the lotus position under the arrogant eye of the beast. The grinning creature savored his torment. It growled contentedly as the sweat poured down Jade's empurpled cheeks.

Can't breathe . . . Daniel . . . the pain . . . horror . . .

Suddenly startled, the beast clutched at its own throat. Its cat's eyes widened with the realization of its defeat.

Daniel's words . . . as I am . . . so too the beast . . .

It is done . . .

(the forms . . . the electric hum . . . swirling colors . . . forever this time . . . such joy . . . such infinite joy . . .)

Jade and the beast remained floating in that interspatial realm, their bodies caressed by the gentle wash of dark winds. Jade, lotus-legged, serenely smiling . . . the beast supine, its eyes wide with sudden terror, clutching forever at is own throat . . .

And as Jade revelled in the contemplation of the forms and colors, he glimpsed a rainbow-cloud drift past. Within the rainbow shimmer he saw the specter of a young boy smiling down at him.

Epilogue

First the dust tickled his nose, then he began to cough. He hacked away, springing awake, his chest convulsed. Sitting up quickly, he scattered the rubble that had half-buried him. Then his coughing fit eased, and he blinked uncomprehendingly in the glare of daylight.

Ender awoke to the sunlight and blue sky of the Harz Mountains, surrounded by the rubble of the Chateau and scattered boulders which had fallen from the upper slopes. The sun was high in the sky and the mountain breezes were gentle and refreshing.

Quite a contrast to the night before. Or was it the night before?

Ender hadn't the slightest idea how long he'd been unconscious.

He tried to stretch his upper body so as to peer over the mounds of rubble but a sudden, sharp pain in his side sent him flat on his back once again.

A hawk made slow circles far above him.

This time he lay back and inventoried his body before he tried to get up. Wiggling his toes, rotating his ankles, flexing his knees. When he first bent his knees, a rock spilled off his lap and onto his groin.

Ender cursed like a stevedore.

The weight on his groin brought the detailed survey to

an end. He shimmied hastily out from under the pile of rocks, and sat upon one of the square stones that had fallen from the Chateau's walls. He hurt like hell but nothing was broken. He was lucky.

From atop the stone he surveyed the damage. Nothing but rubble all the way to the edge of the cliffs. No, he wasn't just lucky. It was miraculous.

When he first looked around at the piles of rock and dust, he couldn't tell that any human being had ever been up on this mountain. He was willing to believe that the collapse of the Chateau and the deaths of the satanists was an incredible nightmare.

Until he looked more closely at the debris.

Hands reaching up through spaces between rocks, curled like hawk talons. Dried smears of blood. Naked feet sticking out from beneath immense boulders.

No, it had been too real.

Sticking out from among the rocks were some mirror-like surfaces reflecting the sun. Ender struggled over to them painfully, scooping away debris. The statue of Cerberus and the inverted crucifix: bright silver mounds crushed almost beyond recognition. One of the heads of Cerberus had been wrenched into a grimace of what looked like genuine pain.

Ender backed off.

Then he noticed a familiar phallic silhouette protruding from the rubble. He crawled, aching, over the rubble until he came close to it.

He was right: the head of Daniel's staff.

Then that meant . . .

He thought long and hard before digging out that staff but then he set to it as quickly as his bruises would allow. He lifted one rock after another from around the staff until he revealed the pale flesh of Mercadante's naked corpse from the waist up. Its ashen face was frozen in a horrible grimace.

The staff still stuck through its heart.

Ender nursed the hope that Daniel had survived the night on the mountain and had made it back to safety. The same with Jade. He also knew they'd both appreciate the return of the strangely carved stick. So he gripped the head of the staff with both hands, placing his left boot on Mercadante's chest.

Then he thought of the vampire movies and paused.

If Mercadante's corpse so much as flinched when he withdrew the staff from its heart, it was getting shoved right back in.

Ender held his breath and pulled hard. The staff slid out easily, stained with gore. Mercadante's corpse didn't move.

"Yecch!" Ender groaned, scraping the staff against some rocks to clean it off. When he did as best he could, he studied the staff closely. To him it seemed like just plain wood, intriguingly carved. Faces, gargoyles, abstract forms. Then how did it . . . ?

He shook his head. If he were meant to know, then he'd know. Until then . . .

Suddenly a bit of shine flashed in the corner of his eye. He looked back down on Mercadante's corpse.

That ring on his finger. The cock's spur.

Ender reached hesitantly for the corpse's hand. He touched it, his hand trembling, then he drew back.

"Yecch."

One more time, holding his breath, and the ring was off. He held it up shining in the sun.

For his personal collection.

Leaning on the staff, Ender picked his way through the rubble, hoping to get away from the environs of the Chateau and find a path back down the Brocken. But as he worked his painful way across the rock shelf on which the Chateau had stood, his blood suddenly chilled.

Beneath a light sprinkling of small stones lay the bride of Satan, still shackled to the marble slab.

He scraped the stones off the unfortunate girl with the staff. Christ, she'd been beautiful . . . He remembered her horrified, imploring eyes. Now, at least, her face seemed to be in serene sleep. He felt glad about that. It mitigated the disgust and remorse he felt looking at the ugly hole he'd put into her forehead.

He'd done what he thought was best.

Then he recalled the horrible scene in the city morgue . . .

He hastily scattered the rocks off her abdomen. He swallowed hard.

There wasn't any second bullet hole. Her abdomen was split wide open . . .

Using the staff desperately, almost like a crutch, Ender hurried like hell to get off the damn mountain.

Elizabeth sat upon the bed with her legs crossed beneath her, her eyes focussed on the vacant air. Seemingly from some far-off place, a distant mountain peak or across a gently rippling lake, she heard the ringing of a telephone.

His eyes in that dream, smiling down on her, and then that last night, when he seemed to rise before her from the deep darkness like a bubble in thin jelly . . .

She heard Beverly shuffling some magazines in the living room, reaching for the phone. Beverly's voice seemed soft and muffled, fringed with cotton.

He'd smiled then, too, all shimmering and dreamy. A gift, he told her. Then his specter, cocooned in rainbows, seemed to fall upon her, mingling with her floating luxuriance, and their minds laughed together . . .

Suddenly, Elizabeth turned and stared out the bedroom window at the bright lights of downtown Manhattan and the few swollen stars that defied the city's glare to be seen floating coldly above the dark waters of the Hudson. She stared frightened yet intrigued, poised to witness the end of all things, the universe falling in upon itself, the streaking death of stars . . .

Beverly quietly opened the bedroom door and entered the darkness. For long moments she stood silently watching Elizabeth gaze out the window, and then she softly called her name.

Elizabeth turned and faced her.

"That was Abe Ender on the phone," Beverly announced. "He's coming here shortly from the airport."

Elizabeth's eyes widened excitedly, her lips arching in a quizzical half-smile.

"Then . . . they've come back?" she asked.

"He has, at least," Beverly answered. "He said he

couldn't talk and that he'd tell us everything when he got here."

Beverly stared coldly at Elizabeth's strange smile. "He didn't sound very happy. He just sounded worn out."

The smile vanished from Elizabeth's face and her eyes fell to her lap. "I don't wonder," she said dully. "They must've gone through a lot. It's only to be expected."

Beverly made a movement as if to say something to her lover's shadow in the darkened bedroom but she said nothing, just turned and left the room, shutting the door behind her. But later, as Elizabeth hastened down the hallway at the ringing of the doorbell, Beverly stared after her, her jaw rigid and tense.

The sight of Ender at her door conflicted with Elizabeth's memory of him. He seemed even slighter and more fragile and the large expanse of flesh upon his balding forehead seemed deathly pale. His large, sad eyes were red and swollen and his slender fingers were nervously playing with the string that was tied around a long slender package wrapped in brown paper. Although he managed to force a polite smile of greeting, he seemed very distracted and hesitant, like a lost child burdened with the memories of a horrible past being welcomed into a new and unfamiliar home.

"Mr. Ender," she said to him softly, reaching for his hand, "I can't tell you how glad I am that you've come back."

"Somewhat the worse for wear, I'm afraid," he answered, trying to smile. "But, yes, I'm glad to be back as well. Extremely glad."

Elizabeth ushered him into the living room where he was welcomed in turn by Beverly. A glass of ice tea rested on the coffee table, awaiting him. Ender sat on a couch facing the two women's silence, searching for the words that he'd rehearsed so often on the flight over from Germany but which now fell from his grasp, eluding him with their banal inconsequence.

"The others, Mr. Ender," Elizabeth suddenly queried. "Where are they?"

Ender looked down at his hands folded in his lap. "Washburn and F-Fedorson . . . are dead." His fingers squeezed together until the knuckles whitened.

433

"I'm sorry," Elizabeth offered gently. "I'm so sorry."

Ender just shook his head, an ironic half-smile playing upon his face. "Yeah, well, it's funny how quickly you can get attached to some people. I didn't know either of them for very long. Still, just when you start to feel comfortable with someone, when you begin to feel like you've known him all your life . . . It's really strange, this feeling."

"And what about Daniel and Jade?" asked Beverly.

"I don't know, really," Ender answered after a thoughtful pause. "All the way back from Germany I nursed the long-shot hope that you might be able to fill me in on them . . . that they somehow reached you before I did . . ."

"You mean you got separated?" Elizabeth betrayed a note of urgency in her voice. "We've heard nothing from either of them."

Ender sighed. "Well, so much for clutching at straws. The best I can do, then, is just tell everything that happened and maybe you, Ms. Wylie, with your . . . your powers . . . can take a shot at the answers."

And Ender began a long recitation of the events that night on the Brocken, choosing his words slowly and with care, forgetting nothing and mindful of the precise chronology. And the women sat like children around a campfire in the woods, listening in silent awe to a tale spun from the dark threads of night, eager that each word trip quickly upon the next.

And then, a long while later, the tale was done and Ender, for the first time, sipped his ice tea.

"So you see," he began once again, "the last I saw Daniel, he was luring the guards and dogs away from us. I didn't hold out much hope for him but, well, he's an incredible man. So who could say for sure? And as for Jade, it's like I said, he just . . . j-just disappeared . . ."

Elizabeth felt a sudden, ticklish chill deep within her womb. She rose and walked to the window in silence, staring out at the flickering city lights and the cold stars.

"It's still out there," she said at last. "The buildings, the stars, the people strolling under the streetlights . . ." Her voice trailed off into the thoughtful whisper.

"Yes," Beverly added, "what about all that stuff about

434

the end of the universe? What's to happen now? Everything still seems to be the same as it was."

"I did a lot of thinking about that on the plane as well," Ender continued. "Perhaps Jade's beaten the beast and nothing will change . . ."

"Then where is he?" asked Elizabeth as she turned from the window, her voice suddenly sharp.

Ender looked up at her with quizzical eyes. "Perhaps he can't return . . . at least, not as easily as he disappeared."

Beverly averted her eyes. "Maybe, for some reason, he's chosen not to return."

"Perhaps," continued Ender, "and perhaps they're still battling . . . there's no outcome as of yet. I wouldn't doubt that the two of them could play a pretty lengthy and impressive game of cat and mouse between them." He looked out the window from his seat. "We may yet have to watch the skies to see what suddenly starts to fall." Ender then turned from the window. "But we sure as hell can't live like that, every day watching the skies . . . waiting to see . . ." Ender's shoulders visibly shivered. "No . . . no, that's not my idea of living."

The three were linked in a heavy silence until Ender reached for the package wrapped in brown paper and held it up to Elizabeth.

"I hoped to return this to Daniel," he explained, "but, under the circumstances, that's not possible. I think you, Ms. Wylie, are the logical person to keep this, then."

He handed her the package and, once its weight rested fully in her hands, her eyes narrowed with the realization of what it was. She carefully tore the paper on one end of the package and slowly withdrew Daniel's carved staff.

Her eyes closed as she ran her fingers lightly over the raised symbols and faces that comprised the staff's surface and her hands thrilled with a pleasant tingling.

"Such power in this staff," she marvelled almost to herself. "Such strange dancing energies . . ."

"You mean you . . . y-you can feel something?" Ender asked. "I guess you *are* the right one to keep it, now. It just felt like an ordinary piece of carved wood to me."

Elizabeth nodded soberly and laid the staff gently on the table. Ender rose to leave.

"I apologize for keeping you both up so late," he began. "I thought you'd want to know as soon as possible . . ."

"Please don't apologize, Mr. Ender," said Elizabeth. "We appreciate your taking the time to tell us. Thank you. Thank you very much, Mr. Ender. Now go home and get some rest. You look . . . exhausted."

Ender smiled wanly. "Some rest . . . I've spent hours on a plane all tucked in and comfortable, trying to sleep . . . and I couldn't. I couldn't shake all that I'd seen and felt from out of my mind long enough to fall out. Maybe now that I've been here, now that I've told you both the story, sort of unburdened myself to you, maybe now . . ."

Ender turned and walked toward the door followed by Elizabeth. Once out in the hall, he quickly turned and faced Elizabeth.

"If you should learn anything," he began, his eyes darting and shy, "about them, I mean . . . if you should f-feel anything in your mind . . ."

Elizabeth smiled kindly at Ender. "I'll let you know immediately when I do, Mr. Ender. Immediately."

Ender looked down at his feet, nodding his head. "Yeah, well then, good night, Ms. Wylie."

"Good night, Mr. Ender."

And he disappeared into the elevator.

Elizabeth walked back silently through the apartment and stood in front of the window, looking out. Beverly sat on the couch stroking Daniel's staff, wondering what Elizabeth felt that she couldn't. In a minute or so, Elizabeth saw the slight figure of Ender emerge from the building and travel east along the street.

"That was some incredible story he had to tell," Beverly commented, breaking the heavy silence in the room.

Elizabeth said nothing. She just stared out the window at the city lights and the few bright stars, her hands linked serenely, pressed gently against her womb.

AN EXPERIENCE IN HORROR
YOU MAY TRY TO FORGET . . .
AND TRY . . . AND TRY . . .

COLD MOON OVER BABYLON

BY MICHAEL McDOWELL
AUTHOR OF *THE AMULET*

Terror grows in Babylon, a typical sleepy Southern town
with its throbbing sun and fog-shrouded swamps.

Margaret Larkin has been robbed of her innocence—
and her life. Her killer is rich and powerful,
beyond the grasp of earthly law.

Now, in the murky depths of the local river,
a shifting, almost human shape slowly takes form.
Night after night it will pursue the murderer.
It will watch him from the trees.
And in the chill waters of the river,
it will claim him in the ultimate embrace.

 AVON 48660/$2.50

CMO 2-80

AVON ◆ THE BEST IN
BESTSELLING ENTERTAINMENT

☐ Fires of Winter Johanna Lindsey	75747	$2.50
☐ The Jade Unicorn Jay Hulpern	50708	$2.50
☐ Chance the Winds of Fortune		
Laurie McBain	75796	$2.95
☐ The Heirs of Love Barbara Ferry Johnson	75739	$2.95
☐ Golden Opportunity Edith Begner	75085	$2.50
☐ Sally Hemings Barbara Chase-Riboud	48686	$2.75
☐ A Woman of Substance		
Barbara Taylor Bradford	49163	$2.95
☐ Sacajawea Anna Lee Waldo	75606	$3.95
☐ Passage West Henry Dallas Miller	50278	$2.75
☐ The Firecloud Kenneth McKenney	50054	$2.50
☐ Pulling Your Own Strings		
Dr. Wayne W. Dyer	44388	$2.75
☐ The Helper Catherine Marshall	45583	$2.25
☐ Bethany's Sin Robert McCammon	47712	$2.50
☐ Summer Lightning Judith Richards	42960	$2.50
☐ Cold Moon Over Babylon		
Michael McDowell	48660	$2.50
☐ Keeper of the Children		
William H. Hallahan	45203	$2.50
☐ The Moonchild Kenneth McKenney	41483	$2.50
☐ Homeward Winds the River		
Barbara Ferry Johnson	42952	$2.50
☐ Tears of Gold Laurie McBain	41475	$2.50
☐ Monty: A Biography of Montgomery Clift		
Robert LaGuardia	49528	$2.50
☐ Sweet Savage Love Rosemary Rogers	47324	$2.50
☐ ALIVE: The Story of the Andes Survivors		
Piers Paul Read	39164	$2.25
☐ The Flame and the Flower		
Kathleen E. Woodiwiss	46276	$2.50
☐ I'm OK—You're OK		
Thomas A. Harris, M.D.	46268	$2.50

Available at better bookstores everywhere, or order direct from the publisher.

AVON BOOKS, Mail Order Dept., 224 W. 57th St., New York, N.Y. 10019

Please send me the books checked above. I enclose $_____ (please include 50¢ per copy for postage and handling. Please use check or money order—sorry, no cash or C.O.D.'s. Allow 4-6 weeks for delivery.

Mr/Mrs/Miss _____

Address _____

City _____ State/Zip _____

BBBB 9-80

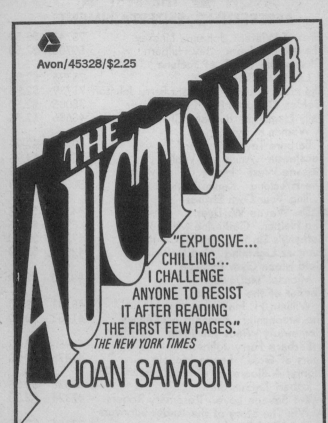

Avon/45328/$2.25

THE AUCTIONEER

"EXPLOSIVE...
CHILLING...
I CHALLENGE
ANYONE TO RESIST
IT AFTER READING
THE FIRST FEW PAGES."
THE NEW YORK TIMES

JOAN SAMSON

At first no one feared the smooth-talking outsider who ran the weekly auction. The slick, magnetic stranger was irresistible. The people of rural Harlowe, New Hampshire, willingly donated their antique junk for his auctions.

Then his quiet demands increased. Horrifying calamaties befell those who refused him. What was behind his ever-growing power? After the heirlooms were gone, what would be next? The farm . . .? The children . . .?

SELECTED BY THE BOOK-OF-THE-MONTH CLUB

EER 2-80